BIG JACK, COWBOY AVIATOR

A NOVEL BASED ON A TRUE STORY

CINDY WEIGAND

For Mom

Here's to you, Jack. You're not forgotten. Your family is proud of you.

To those aviators whose names are lost to history.

*I guess we were a strange lot, those of us who flew those old traps
every Sunday at the field. Maybe we were a sort of mixture of the
cowhand of the Old West, the hot-rod driver of today, and the
real gypsy. We thought we were as free as the birds, just the way
the oldtime cowhand thought he was as free as a coyote. We
deliberately missed death by inches, just like the hot-rod driver of
today. And we played the suckers wherever we could find them,
which meant roaming the face of the earth like a gypsy.*

Slats Rodgers, from
Old Sloggy No. 1: The Uninhibited Story of Slats Rodgers,
Hart Stilwell

PROLOGUE

Early December 1924
1,500 Feet in the Skies near Shreveport, Louisiana

Jack Ashcraft squirmed to get his six-foot, four-inch frame comfortable in the cockpit of his JN-4, Jenny, airplane. With clouds moving out in the north and anxious to get back to Shreveport, he eased the throttle forward to get more speed out of the OX-5 engine. Grudgingly the old plane obliged, a little. His partner, Buck Steele, would be waiting for him. As mechanics, they operated a business fixing just about any engine that broke down, as well as cramming whatever they could fit into the front cockpit of one of their two airplanes and delivering it to neighboring towns.

Every Friday afternoon, they had a ballyhoo of stunting to drum up business for the weekend when townspeople would turn out to pay for a ride. This supplemented their business income, which had been dwindling lately. Jack was returning from a last-minute delivery to Shreveport. He listened to the wind in the wires, humming a song that he titled "Jenny's

Song." Only he knew the tune. He tried to think of a stunt or move that Buck wouldn't be expecting, but they had done this for so long they instinctively knew what the other was thinking. Their showing off usually ended with the two coming straight at one another, wondering who would chicken out first.

Jack was still musing when his eye caught objects above and below his plane. He ducked. The two overhead rocked his aircraft as they passed, traveling to his right. The one underneath merely flew on. *What the hell?* He looked to see what had scared the crap out of him. Three Standards were banking to make another pass at him. He searched his brain for a maneuver he had learned in the army to avoid further harassment. As a mechanic, he repaired airplane engines and insisted on checking his work. The pilots who went up with him had taught him to fly, including simple evasive maneuvers. Only then, he'd flown Spads and Nieuports that had horsepower and speed, not junk surplus Jennies used for training and giving people rides.

Before he could put together a plan, they were upon him again—one above, two below. The instant they passed, Jack pulled the stick to his gut and rose straight up into a loop, up, over, and down so that the sun was to his back. The three airplanes banked this time to fly next to him, two on his left, one on his right. The pilot on his left grinned and gave him a thumbs-up. Jack nodded. The one on his right grinned and saluted. Jack acknowledged the salute. He noticed an inverted triangle with words and wings spanning the insignia on the tail, but couldn't make out the words. With one last wave, the three headed southeast and were soon out of sight.

On the ground, Buck ran up to meet him. Bill Wunderlich, their mechanic, followed and took charge of Jack's plane.

"Where you been?"

"The damnedest thing happened to me," Jack said. "I was on my way back, minding my own business, when three guys jumped me."

"What do you mean jumped you?" Buck said.

"They appeared out of nowhere and flew all around me," Jack said, walking toward his motorcycle. He explained what had happened.

"Dang, you get all the fun," Buck said.

Wunderlich caught snippets of the conversation and tagged along.

"They sure scared the crap out of me the first time, though. You don't see many planes flying out this way. Their planes had a triangle with wings logo, but I couldn't read the words." Jack shrugged, straddling his motorcycle. "See you at Gil's."

Jack roared off.

At the café, the picture of airplanes on the newspaper in the rack caught Jack's eye, and he pulled one out. "Well, I'll be damned," he said, walking to a booth. He tossed his flight helmet on the bench and slid in while reading the newspaper.

"What?" Buck asked.

"Look," Jack said, pointing to the headline that read: *GATES FLYING CIRCUS SETS UP HEADQUARTERS IN NEW ORLEANS.*

"These are the guys I saw!" Jack said.

"I've heard of 'em," Buck said. "Good outfit. I heard that Gates can be kind of a jerk, though."

"Says here that they're going to overhaul their planes and equipment, then fly the south and head up the East Coast next spring," Jack said. "Damn, that would be fun."

"I guess, if you like being on the go all the time," Buck said.

Like Jack, Buck was in his mid-twenties, but he was seasoned for his young age. He had been in the Indiana

National Guard, chased Pancho Villa and his bandits into Mexico, then harassed them in airplanes. He'd joined up again when World War I started.

Jack had been a mechanic in the Army Motor Corps based in France and learned to fly as well. He'd returned home to Protection, Kansas, for a time, but soon got bored. He had bought a plane and flown around the western United States before returning to Shreveport, where he had worked before he went into the army. That's where he'd met Buck, Bill Wunderlich, and Gardner Nagle, who taught him more about flying. Now Jack was teaching Wunderlich how to fly. Jack and Wunderlich also raced cars on dirt tracks at county fairs in the region; Jack in his Hudson and Wunderlich in cars he built himself. Nagle had moved on.

With two somewhat flyable airplanes, they'd set up shop as mechanics. They expanded into Texarkana, flying between the two towns, taking up passengers, and accepting any paying job that involved flying.

"Hey, you're not thinking of joining them, are you?" Buck asked.

"Sure am," Jack mumbled without looking up.

"Damn," Buck said. "Don't do anything on impulse. Think about it over the weekend, okay?"

"Not much thinking to do," Jack said without looking up.

That night, Jack read and reread the article and considered his options. The circus was owned by Ivan Gates and Clyde Pangborn. Gates was the business manager; Pangborn was the lead pilot, and a great one. Jack had heard of him. Gates was quoted as saying that they had traveled from the West Coast, where they had performed at numerous air shows before thousands of spectators. They would headquarter in New Orleans, then head out in the spring to put on air shows throughout the South, heading north along the East Coast and Mid-Atlantic states as the weather got warmer.

As he slept, Jack dreamed of performing daring feats for thousands of spectators packed in grandstands in towns and cities like New York, Baltimore, and Philadelphia. On the ground, he stepped from the cockpit and waved to adoring fans who swarmed his plane. He signed autographs and flirted with pretty girls.

Jack loved working with Buck and Wunderlich. They were like brothers, but he couldn't see a future for the business. Most of all, he couldn't see growing old in Shreveport or Texarkana. Selling hardware in Protection like his father wanted him to do would be worse. He wanted to fly. He wanted to perform for thousands like the newspaper article described. He wanted people to know his name, to be famous one day. He knew what he had to do.

The next morning, Jack stuffed his belongings into his duffel, left a note and some money for his landlady saying that he was leaving, and walked out.

At their headquarters, he tossed the bag in the front seat of his plane and was getting ready to put his motorcycle on the wing when Buck walked up. "So, you're really going to do this, huh?"

Wunderlich strolled over to see what was going on. He looked at Buck quizzically.

"Jack's going to join up with Gates," Buck said.

"That true?" Wunderlich said.

"Yep. Help me with this, will you?" Jack said.

The two guys helped Jack secure the cycle next to the fuselage. Jack talked while he worked. "You ever heard of Cal Rodgers?"

"Yeah."

"I saw him in Kansas City when I was a kid," Jack said. "I thought he was alright, flying that flimsy old Vin Fiz from coast to coast. Even though there wasn't much left of the original plane by the time he got there, people remember him. I want to do something people remember like Rodgers. I want people to know my name and what I did. At least, I want to try."

Jack looked at his friends for encouragement.

"Good luck, then," Buck said and Wunderlich nodded.

"Who knows, maybe I'll join you sometime," Buck said.

Jack nodded. "You do that. So long, guys."

Jack shook hands with the two and climbed into the cockpit of his plane.

"What do you want me to do with the Hudson?" Wunderlich asked.

"You race it. Then you won't have to keep building those jalopies you race in," Jack said with a grin.

Wunderlich pulled the propeller, Buck jerked the chocks, and Jack was off.

PART ONE

CHAPTER 1
JACK JOINS THE CIRCUS

Jack Ashcraft, circa 1925. *Courtesy of Allen Keller.*

December 1924
Skies over Texarkana

Jack eased back in the cockpit for the flight to New Orleans. He hadn't had time to say goodbye to his fellow Masons, but thought they would understand. With a couple of stops to refuel, Jack calculated that he would arrive around four o'clock. He hummed "Jenny's Song." The cool winter air and brilliant blue sky exhilarated his soul. God, he loved to fly.

Following the Mississippi River, he saw planes in a park outside of New Orleans and knew they had to be the Gates outfit. He buzzed the area to get a better look and hedgehopped out. Circling back, he grabbed his bugle and prepared to land. He turned off the engine and glided in. On the way down, he blasted out a little tune to signal that he was making a dead stick landing and to make a memorable first impression.

He'd just alighted from the cockpit when a guy Jack recognized as Pangborn from the picture in the paper hurried over. "What the hell was that about? Who are you?"

"The name's Ashcraft—Jack Ashcraft. I've been flying out of Texarkana way. Maybe you've heard of me."

"Can't say that I have," the man replied. "What do you want?"

"I want to fly with the group of fine airmen known as the Gates Flying Circus. Can you tell me where I can find Clyde Pangborn?"

Pangborn sized Jack up. He had seen guys like him before. During World War I, Pangborn had been stationed at Ellington Field in Houston as a flight instructor flying Jennies. Since he'd connected with Ivan Gates to form the flying circus, he had seen plenty of young men chock full of themselves, but their flying proficiencies didn't match their verbal skills describing them. However, Pang had to admit that Jack had nailed his dead stick landing. There was something about him that Pang liked. Jack had swagger and confidence but not arrogance.

Announcing his landing with a bugle blast, a gimmick he hadn't seen before, amused Pang.

"I'm Pangborn. Want to fly for Gates, huh?" he said. "You've got to be a good mechanic and be able to fix things if you want to fly for us. Can you splice an aileron cable? See that plane over there? Fix it all right, and we'll go up for a test flight." With that, he turned on his heel and walked away.

The plane was a Standard J-1. As the proprietor of a mechanical company, Jack had become a jack-of-all-trades. He rummaged through the parts and tools on the workbench to find what he needed and went to work and got it fixed in no time. He was jawing with some of the guys when Pangborn returned.

"Thought I told you to fix that control cable."

"I did. See for yourself," Jack replied, gesturing toward the plane, inviting Pangborn to examine his work. It was a damn good job, and Jack knew it. One could hardly tell where the cable had been spliced.

While Pangborn was examining the cable, two pilots walked by, then retraced their steps.

"Wait a minute, are you that guy we gave a hard time outside of Shreveport?" one asked.

"I believe I am," Jack said. "You startled the livin' daylights out of me."

"You've got be on the alert at all times," the second pilot said loudly.

"How'd he do?" Pangborn asked, looking at all three men with steady, piercing gray eyes.

"He held his own," the first pilot said. "If he wants to fly with us, I think you should give him a chance."

"I'll be the judge of that," Pangborn said. "See that plane out there? Climb in. Let's take her up."

Jack climbed into the back cockpit, and Pangborn got in the

front. A stockily built guy with black hair named Joe propped for him. Although Jack hadn't flown a Standard much, he found it basic. The instrument panel was a lot like his Jenny's. He would never admit it to anyone, but he was a little nervous flying with a pilot with Pangborn's reputation.

Once in the air, Jack moved the stick slightly to the right and then to the left to get the feel of the plane. He went into a shallow dive, pulling out of it and going up to about 3,000 feet. Feeling more comfortable with the ship, he did an Immelmann and a wingover that wasn't his best effort, but what was done was done. Feeling particularly confident, he performed a loop.

After about fifteen minutes, Pangborn looked back at Jack and pointed to the ground. Jack nodded, understanding that Pangborn wanted him to land. He sideslipped into a perfect landing. He cut the engine, and they rolled to a stop. A sturdily built man with sandy hair and a thin mustache waited for them. A woman stood beside the man, along with the two pilots and handsome German shepherd.

"Name's Ivan Gates," the man said, extending his hand. "This is my wife, Hazel. She does our bookkeeping for us."

The dog ran over to Pangborn. "And this is Judge," Pangborn said, petting the dog. "Hazel helps me take care of him."

"Nice to meet you, Mr. Gates," Jack said, shaking his hand. "Nice to meet you, ma'am." Then he knelt to scratch Judge behind the ears.

"Call me Van or Gates. Doesn't matter to me," Gates said.

"How are you, boy?" Judge licked Jack's face, and he laughed.

"So, you're the guy Pangborn says wants to join up with us?" Gates said.

"Yes, sir. Name's Jack Ashcraft, and I'd sure like to fly with your fine organization."

"Why is that?" Gates asked. "There are other outfits out there."

"Because I think yours will be the best. I'll do all I can to make it the best," Jack said.

Gates turned to Pangborn. "How'd he do in the cockpit?"

"A little uneven, but the basic skills are there," Pangborn said. "With more experience, he'll be good. He's a mechanic and did a good job on that broken control cable."

Then Pangborn turned to Jack. "You've got to learn more stunting and learn fast to fly with us."

"I'm up to the task," Jack said.

"But I don't have the last word. What do you think, Judge?" Pangborn said to his pet.

Judge trotted over to Jack and put his paw on Jack's leg, and Jack patted him on the head.

"That's all we need. Welcome to our organization," Gates said.

"This is Ive McKinney and Bill Brooks," Gates said. "Know any other pilots who would like to fly for us?"

"I might know of one. And a mechanic," Jack said.

"Tell them about us. Brooks. McKinney. Show Jack around," Gates said and walked off.

"Welcome to Gates Flying Circus," Brooks said loudly as he pounded Jack on the back.

"Never mind Bill," Ive said. "He's a great guy. Just been around too many loud engines. We call him 'Whispering Bill.'" They both laughed.

Then Ive looked around to make sure no one was following them. "Gates is the high potentate. We call him the Pope, but he's no saint."

"What can you tell me about Pangborn?" Jack asked.

"He'll watch you like a hawk for a while, but he's okay."

January–March 1925
New Orleans, Louisiana

Jack was now a full-fledged member of the Gates Flying Circus, the premier flying group in the country, and on his way to making his mark in aviation. He called his mother and dad to give them the news. While not overjoyed, they did seem proud in their own way. They had learned long ago that Jack had to make his own destiny, which included flying. They both told him that they would pray for him. What else would good Methodists do, especially when one was named after John Wesley? He also called Buck to let him know and told him what Gates had said. Buck was glad for Jack, but still wasn't interested in joining him yet. Wunderlich showed up in New Orleans in the Hudson a couple of days later.

The next week, Jack was in the air every minute possible and learned a lot from Pang and the other fliers. He got to know other ships, because his had seen better days and wasn't great for stunting. Bill Brock had joined the circus about the same time Jack did. He'd been flying with Mabel Cody and other outfits. Jack had heard of Cody and her flying circus, and there was something he was dying to know. "Was Buffalo Bill really her uncle?" he asked.

"Yep, and her name could be Wild Mabel Cody. She'd do anything to get a crowd, just like Bill. She's every bit the showman her uncle was."

Another crucial member of the team was Diavolo, the stuntman and wing walker. His real name was Aron Krantz, but everyone called him Duke. He was Swedish and the latest "Diavolo" for the organization. His time in the army with parachute training gave him a confidence and professionalism others didn't have, with less devil-may-care attitude. Scuttlebutt had it that the circus had lost several stuntmen, so Gates had to throw away a lot of posters with their names on them. Gates had even received a telegram that said, *WHEN PRESENT STUNTMAN DIES, CONTACT ME.* Gates had gotten tired of reprinting posters and losing money, so he gave all stuntmen the name "Diavolo."

Right away, Jack went about making himself a part of the team, doing whatever he could to help. The group welcomed his skills as a mechanic and learned from him. Aloft, he learned teamwork from the other pilots. Pang had all the pilots take Duke up to see how they handled the plane with him wandering around on the wings and below on the landing gear. Jack found that he was able to manage just fine. He attributed his ability to control the plane to his size and strength, and his experience with flying cargo that shifted.

With each passing day, Jack's confidence grew, and he expressed this to the other pilots. He and Pang developed a friendly rivalry. Pang would watch Jack fly and say something like, "That was a pretty good loop. . . for a rookie."

While impressed with Pang's signature stunt, flying upside down for extended distances, Jack thought his other flying was okay, but nothing spectacular. Each caught wind of what the other was saying. One Wednesday afternoon, Jack and the guys were standing around hangar flying when Pang approached Jack.

"Hey, Jack. You've been with us a couple of weeks now," he said, "and I've heard that you've been doing some bragging and not altogether impressed with some of my flying."

Jack grinned. "Well, I wouldn't put it that way, exactly."

"Whatever way you put it, it's time for you to put up or shut up, wouldn't you say?" Pang said. "Why don't you and me have a little race?"

"You bet," Jack said enthusiastically.

The other guys chuckled knowingly, making smart remarks and jostling one another.

"We'll make it our Sunday afternoon show," Pang said. "Three o'clock. We'll start at Audubon Park, then head to the east bank of the Mississippi, around Loyola University, and over the park again to where we started."

"Sounds good," Jack said, and set out to find a map and to put together a strategy.

Gates sent the local paper a press release, and they responded:

Pangborn and Ashcraft, Gates Pilots, to Race High Over City

Boast of Flyer Over Speed of His Plane to End In Speed Contest Sunday Furnishing Thrills For Thousands of Citizens,

Jack Ashcraft, who hails from out in Texarkana, Texas, where men are men and also big and tough, believes mightily in the worth of small things.

On the other hand, Clyde Pangborn, although not diminutive, is considerably smaller than Ashcraft, who lightly packs 195 pounds of bone and sinew. Pangborn believes mightily in the worth of large things.

And because of all this, New Orleans is to have its first airplane race at 3 p.m. Sunday over the flying field at Audubon Park.

When Ashcraft "checked in" a few days ago he looked over the four airplanes which the Gates Flying circus has here in New Orleans, its winter headquarters. He chose one of the Standards, with a 180-horsepower Hispano motor. He flew it a few times then he started boasting.

Meanwhile, Pangborn had appropriated for his use the biggest plane of the quartet, a husky Martin, of the bomber type, equipped with a powerful 220-horsepower Liberty motor.

. . .

. . .Years ago men boasted of their fast horses, later of their automobiles, so most naturally, Pangborn and Ashcraft entered into acrimonious debate regarding the power and speed of their airplanes.. . .

. . .The test will be at 3 p.m. Sunday over the flying field in Audubon Park, and Ivan Gates, manager of the circus, consented to let the pilots settle their dispute and at the same time make the race a feature event of the weekly "show", which is staged every Sunday. . .

The 10-mile course which will be followed is from the flying field, thence to the east bank of the Mississippi River, back around the tower of Loyola University and to the field again.

The finish will be spectacular, the planes swooping low over the field so the spectators can get a good view of them. They will leave the field 30 seconds apart.. . .

. . .Passengers will be carried at the Audubon Park before and after the race. There will be no admission fee at the field.

At 2:45 on Sunday afternoon, Pang and Jack thoroughly checked their planes one last time. The plane Pang flew had an engine with more horsepower, but Jack figured what he lacked in horsepower, he would make up for in agility.

Jack had been so intent on his plane and strategy that he hadn't noticed what was going on around him. Finished with his task, he looked around him while he wiped his hands on the rag Wunderlich handed him.

"Will you look at that?" he said.

The bleachers were packed. Additional spectators jockeyed for a position near the front behind the rope that separated the additional viewing area and the flying field. Police held them back and kept them orderly.

Pang strolled by. "Looks like 'Big Jack, Cowboy Aviator' can attract a crowd."

Jack grinned and waved to the onlookers. They clapped and waved back, shouting greetings.

Gates walked out in front of the bleachers with a megaphone. "Good afternoon ladies and gentlemen," he said loudly. "Welcome to the Gates Flying Circus Sunday afternoon extravaganza!" The spectators cheered and applauded.

"We promise a sensational race between Clyde 'Upside-Down' Pangborn and newcomer 'Big Jack, Cowboy Aviator' who hails from Texas!

"Howdy everyone!" Jack yelled and waved, grinning broadly. The crowd went wild with applause and cheering.

The men got into their airplanes.

Brooks stood at the starting line with a flag raised to start the race. Jack ran up his motor for a fast takeoff. When Bill dropped the flag, a roustabout pulled the chocks and Jack was off. His ship rose to two hundred feet, where he leveled off. Before he knew it, Pang was off his right wing. Pushing the throttle forward, Jack got a little more out of his ship, but couldn't shake Pang.

Clearing the river, Jack jerked hard left on the stick, beating Pang around the first turn, but Pang quickly caught up with him on the straight stretch. Jack glanced over and could have sworn that he saw a smirk on Pang's face.

He's playing with me. I'll show him, Jack thought.

Jack peered over the side of the cockpit to see if people were watching and felt a rush of adrenaline. When he looked up, Pang was nowhere in sight. In an instant, he had vanished. Then, as suddenly as he had disappeared, Pang rose ahead of and slightly below Jack's plane on his left wing. Jack couldn't bank as sharply as he wanted to, so Pang maintained the lead.

The instant he was around the tower of the university, Jack rammed the throttle as far forward as it would go, so hard the motor protested with a shudder, but it obeyed. As promised, they flew low in front of the grandstands for all to see the finish. The spectators were on their feet, applauding. Brock brought down the flag with Pang from propeller to cockpit ahead of Jack.

Before they landed, Pang caught Jack's eye and made a loop with his index finger and held up three fingers indicating that he wanted them to do three loops. They did side-by-side loops and then performed some stunts on their own.

Pang's finale was flying upside-down as usual. He flipped his plane over and flew in front of the crowd less than a hundred fifty feet above the ground. He flew that way for half a mile or more. It was the most remarkable flying Jack had ever seen. The crowd applauded and cheered when he landed.

For his finish, Jack did a spin, pulling out at about two hundred feet above the ground. Bystanders scattered. Spectators ducked. After a climb and barrel roll, Jack circled back. He blew on his trusty bugle, turned off his engine, and made a dead stick landing.

Jack flipped his goggles back. Waving and smiling, he clambered from of the cockpit. Before his feet hit the ground, spectators broke through the rope and streamed down from the bleachers on to the airfield. They swarmed around the pilots and the airplanes. The policemen guarded the planes to keep the mob from damaging them to get a souvenir.

The scene was like he had dreamed about, but more chaotic than he imagined. Guys slapped him on the back. Pretty girls flirted when they asked for his autograph, and he winked at others.

Later, Brooks broke the news to Jack. "Sorry to tell you, Jack, but Pang beat you by three seconds."

"Damn! Three measly seconds!"

Pang wandered by. "Keep your mind and eye on your task, Jack."

Jack had to admit to himself that he'd gotten a bit cocky reading what they said about him in the newspapers. What the heck? There would be other races and it was a hell of a lot of fun, but he took heed of what Pang said about taking his eye off his task. Looking down at the crowd had cost him the race. Jack didn't want to lose any more races, or worse.

Now it was time to kick back and relax. Sabbath or not, it was time for more than a snort of hooch.

This was in the time of the Volstead Act and so-called Prohibition, but there was no way the federal government was going to "prohibit" anyone from getting liquor if he, or she, so desired. Jack loved his parents dearly, but this was one area where they parted ways. They were strict Prohibitionists, teetotalers all the way, and had gotten in on the act early.

The notorious prohibitionist Carrie Nation, called the "Hatchet Lady," was from Medicine Lodge, east of Protection. While growing up, he and his brothers and sisters had heard stories about her going into saloons with a Bible in one hand and a hatchet in the other, smashing things up. Then she showed up at the house.

His mother and dad knew her well, and she came by the home often in Kansas and Oklahoma. She was nearly six feet tall and used her height to full advantage to intimidate people. Jack remembered her hovering over him and his brothers to put the fear of the Almighty in them if they consumed alcohol. Some described her as having a "stern countenance." Even as a cocky teenager, Jack had thought she was just plain scary. He remembered her looking down at him over her glasses. "Now, young man, you have your whole life ahead of you. Don't you succumb to the evils of alcohol, hear?"

Jack always gave her the answer she wanted—"Yes, ma'am" —to get away from her. He couldn't say that he had followed her advice much since then, especially after being in the army and such. To him, it just wasn't realistic not to drink with the guys in a war zone, knowing you could be blown up the next minute. Jack had enjoyed his share of hooch since leaving home.

CHAPTER 2
OFF TO A BAD START

April–May 1925
Working Louisiana

The circus geared up to leave for Alabama as a group, but their launch was less than stellar. It was as if someone had cast a voodoo spell on them. Pilots drifted in and out of the circus. In addition to Pang, there was Jack, Bill Brock, Bill Brooks, and Ive McKinney, plus Duke. Wunderlich had stayed on as a mechanic, or maintenance engineer as he preferred to be called, along with a couple of others. One day, Brock was flying in the countryside, looking for prospects to take up for rides. He found what he thought was a perfect situation, but when he got down, the people told him that he'd landed in the United States Leprosarium at Carville, Louisiana. The current belief was that leprosy was not contagious through casual contact, but Brock didn't want to take any chances and skedaddled out of there.

Then there was this kid who was trying to make a name for himself as a stuntman. He would hang from the spreader bar by his teeth. There was a ball on the end of a cable, which was tied to the spreader bar, that he put in his mouth. With a harness under his armpits attached to the spreader by a wire that was invisible to people on the ground, there was an element of safety, but it was still a dangerous stunt.

One day, during Mardi Gras celebrations, Brock took him up, but the guy couldn't get back on the wing, so Brock had to dump him in the Mississippi River, where he thought someone who could fish him out. Some guys went after him in a rowboat. One even dove into the water to rescue him, but no one ever found his body. Jack liked to think the kid drifted downstream and swam to shore, but more than likely he didn't. The circus posted a $1,000 reward. Later, it was learned that the young fellow was not using the safety wire and simply didn't have the strength to hold on. Being the lightest guy in the group, Wunderlich was promoted to stuntman.

Bad luck followed Jack too. In Baton Rouge, he took a couple of paying customers up for a stunt flight. Usually, the circus didn't do any stunting with passengers, but the two young men insisted on it. The Standard was a relatively new plane, and they had given the plane a thorough going-over that morning. The boys offered to pay a little extra, so Jack ran it by Pang, who gave his okay. Jack did a few loops and a simple roll with no problems. What he intended to do next was a voluntary spin and then pull out, something he had done many times before.

The spin was to the left, and he counted, "One quarter, half, one and a quarter . . ." After one and a quarter, he started his recovery. "Center stick, right rudder, close throttle." Right rudder was supposed to stop the spin but didn't. He released all controls to see if the plane would right itself. Nothing happened. "Sit tight!" he yelled back at the boys, and they crashed into the ground nose first.

"I believe I've killed them," Jack remembered saying when they pulled him from the wreckage and before he passed out. He was taken to the hospital. One kid, Albert Gladney, was killed and the other severely injured. Jack would never forget Albert's name, the accident forever etched in his psyche. This was the first passenger ever killed in a circus airplane. Jack had a broken arm and some cuts on his face, but the worst thing he had was a bad case of the nerves afterwards. The mother of the young man who was killed sued, so they called an inquiry. Wunderlich and Ive picked Jack up at the sanitarium and drove him to the courthouse.

The whole thing was reported in the newspaper, which Jack read later in his room. He winced at the headline:

Bad Air Blamed for the Crash Costing Life of One and Injury of Two
Jack Ashcroft, Pilot, Tells His Story of the Flight

Jack Ashcroft[sic], the pilot, is at the Lady of the Lake sanitarium, badly bruised and shaken up, but apparently not seriously hurt. His face and head were severely cut, so was his right arm, one ligament in his leg was strained. When seen by the State-Times representative, he was in a somewhat nervous condition.

"As nearly as I can tell, the accident was due to bad air," said Ashcroft [sic]. . . . Nothing was attempted that I have not gone through with thousands of times before.

"Just before we went into the spin, I looked at my altimeter and it showed we were 2000 feet high. I have made spins at 1000 feet and considered it perfectly safe. We dropped into the spin, at 1000 ft we struck the bad air. The machine began to get out of control. I don't think there was anything the matter with the controls themselves or with the machinery, for it

seemed to be working all right, but I couldn't bring the machinery into running shape. As we dropped. . .I realized nothing could be done, we were due for a crash. Then I tried to make the landing as safely as possible, although I knew there was little hope of doing much. I could not change the course of the machine. I called to the boys to sit tight. Maybe they heard me and maybe not, above the roar of the motor. Then came the crash.

At this point, Jack had to stop to regain his composure before continuing, just as he had to in the courtroom.

Jack told those who had assembled that in addition to his army experience, he had about 2000 flying hours in exhibitions and carrying passengers on short flights. His conservative estimated was that he had made 15,000 flights or more. *"This is the first time I ever had a scratch, or any one with me,"* he told them.

He continued reading the article.

It was plain that the mishap had come with such suddenness and Ashcroft[sic], had been so intent on trying to right the plane that he had not been able to study the cause. All he could explain was that in his belief it was due to bad air.

Ashcroft [sic] Tuesday was recovering from the affects of the smashup, but was advised by physicians at the hospital to remain there longer until entirely recuperated.

Scene at the Field

"The plane lay crumpled on the ground in the northeast corner of the flying field, a broken silver thing that shone in the pleasant late afternoon sun. On the road outside, cars were lined up, just within the field entrance, and many people stood in groups of a dozen or more talking excitedly of the tragedy

they had just witnessed, or gazing somber-eyed across the field at a white something spread on the ground just beyond the crushed plane and almost hidden by it and guarded by khaki-clad officers of the law.

It came down like a "wounded butterfly," according to one spectator, who said she was standing very close to the place where the plane fell.

It was ruled that there was inherent danger in flying and passengers understood this when they took a flight in an airplane, so they didn't find Jack at fault. Jack was relieved, but his nerves were shot. They were so bad afterwards the doctors advised him to stay in the sanitarium for a couple more weeks.

Wunderlich would have none of it. "That place is no good for you. It's for sick people. My dad is a doctor and lives in the country in New Orleans. He says you can stay there until you're ready to come back," he said.

Jack took a lot of walks and sat on the porch staring, often into the night watching lightning bugs. He did a lot of thinking about his future during that time. Not being a pilot himself, Gates just called it "tough luck. We'll get you another plane," he said.

You can replace a plane, Jack thought, *but you can't replace a person, a son.*

Pang paid him a visit and was sympathetic to a point. He told Jack about an incident that happened early after the organization had formed. "I had this guy, Jones, who flew this guy named Marsh for a parachute jump. One time they were over water, and Marsh yelled to Jones not to get him wet. Well, Jones didn't get him wet, because Marsh landed in a tree, the branch broke, and he was killed. There was this other guy named Johnson who was killed too."

Pang paused a few thoughtful moments and took a breath before continuing. "Their deaths were inexcusable in one way, but they wanted to earn their money the way they did and knew full well that they courted death. I was fond of them both. After the accidents, I resolved never to let crashes get the best of me or get stirred up over them.

"As a consequence," he continued, "I developed a philosophy that some view as hard-hearted. I have friends and I'm devoted to them, but I'm prepared to lose them as long as they indulge in foolhardy stunts. I don't particularly like it, but I've got to be practical to survive. The way I see it, the public is as responsible for the loss of their lives as anyone. Spectators, and obviously passengers, aren't interested in straight flying, so we have to give them what they want in order to survive."

Before he left, Pang said, "We're leaving for Alabama on Monday. You're a good pilot, Jack. I hope you can shake this off and join us."

Jack had less than a week to decide his future. Wunderlich, Ive, and Brooks checked on him as well to lift his spirits, which helped. During his time of recovery, he vowed to take every precaution he could to avoid crashes. He developed a healthy respect of fear so that he could remain alive to do what he loved. He needed an attitude of self-preservation to make sure nobody else ended up dead like Albert. Dr. Wunderlich saw to it that Jack got the care he needed to get back into the air. The home environment and homecooked meals restored his soul.

Early Monday morning, Jack folded the article about the accident and put it in the envelope addressed to his parents with the one about the race in New Orleans. Enclosed was a short letter saying that he'd been depressed right after the accident but was doing better and they were headed for Alabama.

Dr. Wunderlich drove Jack to the circus headquarters where the group was making final preparations to leave. Jack thanked the doctor and got out of the car. He retrieved his belongings.

"Hey, you're not going anywhere without me, are you," he yelled.

The guys gathered around him with delight, welcoming him back. Judge jumped up and down, barking excitedly.

"There's your plane," Pang said, pointing to a new Standard. "Monty will fly you until your arm is better. He's new, so you'll have to navigate for him."

Jack and the others headed toward their vehicles, but Wunderlich remained in the hangar.

Jack shouted to him. "You're going with us, aren't you?"

"I'm not so sure about this," Wunderlich said.

"Come with us. You're a good mechanic. You're a good friend," Jack said.

Wunderlich relented. "But no stunting. I want to fly."

Jack smiled and nodded.

Logtown, Mississippi

Gates and Pang decided they had better get out of Louisiana quickly before someone else tried to take legal action. Bad luck followed, but they tried to stay upbeat. With Jack's arm broken, Pang trained a kid named Monty to fly, and they headed east. Pang gave him directions.

"Okay, Monty, you've learned to fly pretty well. With Jack out of commission, you need to learn to follow a map," Pang said, spreading a map out on the hood of a truck.

"You're here," he continued, and Monty nodded. "Just fly slightly northeast till you get to here. Don't take the line across the lake. Watch your compass carefully. Jack will help you."

"Sure, as much as I can," Jack said, "but my arm hurts something awful, so I'm going to sleep for an hour or so. You'll be okay till then, won't you, Monty?"

"Yeah, I think so," Monty answered.

"Sure you will," Jack said, climbing into the front cockpit. He took a snort and was fast asleep soon after Monty took off.

After an hour, Monty wasn't sure he was where he should be, so he yelled, "Hey, Jack, are we in the right place? I'm seeing a lot of water."

No response from Jack.

"Hey, Jack, were we supposed to fly over a lake?" Monty yelled.

A half hour later, almost out of fuel, Monty punched Jack in the back. "Jack, we're out of gas. Where are we?"

Still no response from Jack.

"I'm going to land," Monty yelled.

The roughness of the landing jostled Jack and woke him. "Where the hell are we?" he said when the plane had stopped. "Why didn't you wake me up?"

"I tried," Monty said, looking frantic, "but you were dead to the world."

"Okay," Jack said, "let's check things out. I'm sure I've been in worse situations."

They got out, and Jack looked around. A worse situation didn't immediately come to mind. Monty had set down near a marsh full of stumps with not a house or town in sight. Water was already up to the ankles of his tall boots. Gnats and mosquitoes swarmed and buzzed around them. They swatted them when they landed on their faces and necks and tried to brush them away.

Jack looked around. "Well, Monty, this is a bona fide predicament. I haven't been in much worse."

Monty's face reddened, and he hung his head.

"Now, now. Don't you fret none. We'll get through it. First, let's check out the plane," Jack said. He sloshed around the airplane, his boots making sucking sounds in the mud, as he examined it. "First impression is that you did a heck of a job of landing the plane without completely tearing up the bottom. And you landed without flipping it. That's danged impressive. Or lucky."

Monty looked relieved.

"Second impression is, we're still stuck in a swamp," Jack said.

Jack continued to look around for any sign of civilization as he splashed around the plane. To the south, east, and west, all he saw was water and stumps. He didn't see much to the north, but then he noticed a faint trail of dust stirred up by a vehicle.

"There! You see that?" he said to Monty. "You take the gas can and follow that dust trail—see if there's a town close by and find out where we are. Check around and get somebody to help us get this plane out of here. Take a canteen of water."

Monty took off. Jack had done all the assessing that he could and was tired of swatting mosquitos, so he got back into the plane before his boots soaked through. He hunkered down hoping the insects wouldn't find him. He dozed, looking for Monty when he awoke to adjust in the cramped cockpit.

Two hours later, he thought he heard singing and laughing, so he leaned up and looked out. Sure enough, there was Monty on a logging truck with other fellas singing loudly, "Don't cut timber on a windy day . . ." and laughing hysterically.

"That sounds like good advice," Jack yelled from the cockpit. "Who are you fellas?"

Monty jumped off the truck, looking pleased with himself. "These are loggers who I got to help us."

As luck would have it, they had come down near Logtown, Mississippi, and Monty had found seven guys willing to help a young aviator in distress. They even brought Jack something to eat and drink.

In no time, those strong logging men had the plane lifted, carried, and secured on the logging truck for the ride into what was left of the town. The guys rode on the truck at select locations to make sure that the plane didn't shift while being transported.

Neither he nor Monty had sustained injuries in the landing, but it took Jack several days to fix the plane since he had to do it with a broken arm. Monty helped when he could, and other guys helped when more than three hands were needed. Jack enjoyed the bantering and singing. Before they left, Jack and Monty offered rides to those who wanted one as thanks for their help. Then, like any good cowboy, Jack made Monty get back in the saddle and fly them on to their destination. However, he stayed awake.

One day, Brock ground looped badly after landing when he took two girls for a ride. One broke her arm, the other was bruised something terrible, and Brock was lucky he didn't get his eye poked out when his head hit the panel. In Montgomery, Alabama, Jack had to start Brock's engine even though his arm was still in a sling. He lost his balance, and the prop smacked his leg. So for a time, Jack's arm was in a sling, and he limped around with a sore leg using a broken strut for a cane.

That wasn't the end of it. Gates had made a deal with Texaco to be their sponsor, and they'd agreed to supply all the circus's gas as a way to advertise the company. One day some guys delivered several barrels of gas and left them in the middle of a field. No one knew where his head was, but Brooks landed right on top of them and busted up the plane. It was a wonder there wasn't an explosion.

Pangborn was usually a cool-headed guy, but when Brooks did that, he had had enough. "Half of the state to land in, and you pick the place with barrels in the field," he said. "We can't have anybody making mistakes like that. You could have killed someone." Wherever they went, there were always kids and other folks that came out of nowhere to look at the planes.

"You've flown your last flight with us," Pangborn said, and fired Brooks. Brooks sued Pang, saying that the barrels shouldn't have been left in the middle of the field, and he won, but there were no hard feelings. Brooks went to Nicaragua to help fight in the revolution. Somehow, Jack knew that their flight paths would cross again.

CHAPTER 3
WORLD'S GREATEST EXHIBITION AVIATORS

Clyde Pangborn (center, standing) with a group of Standard J-1 aircraft (and pilots) of the Gates Flying Circus, Birmingham, Alabama, circa 1925. The Texaco logo is painted on the planes' fuselages. *The Clyde Pangborn Collection/The Museum of Flight, Seattle, Washington.*

Clyde Pangborn (right) and Ivan R. Gates (left), circa 1922.
*The Clyde Pangborn Collection/The Museum of Flight,
Seattle, Washington.*

Photograph of Clyde Pangborn (left) and Aron
F. "Duke" Krantz, standing in front of
Pangborn's Standard J-1 aircraft in Audubon
Park, New Orleans, Louisiana, circa 1920s. *The
Clyde Pangborn Collection/The Museum of
Flight, Seattle, Washington.*

Early April 1925
Birmingham, Alabama

Gates hired some non-flying people, and their luck began to change. The MacClatchie brothers, Al and Jim, came on board to do advance work and run a concession stand for the circus, among other things. The pilots and mechanics wouldn't have to take the time to go into town to eat. Plus, they could bring in cash by selling food and drinks to spectators at the airfield so they would hang around for rides. Another guy Gates hired on salary was George Daws, who was a well-connected newspaperman, and was quite taken with the circus. He became their publicity man. Daws put together a twenty-four-page color brochure about the circus, their stunts, and the cost to perform them.

The rest of the group would get a cut from gate receipts and the number of people taken for rides. Gates hired Red Murphy as the barker with Al and Jim helping him. At last, there was an atmosphere of being an honest-to-goodness show.

Other additions were a supply truck and tent to fix the planes under when the weather was bad, a truck to carry the tent, and a fuel truck. Gates bought a touring car to drive the pilots from the hotel to the airfields and back. The planes were outfitted to hold four passengers in the front cockpit. The engines were overhauled once more, and then Gates had every vehicle and plane painted fire-engine red, with the Gates Flying Circus green triangular insignia on the vertical fin of each plane and on the sides of the ground vehicles. "Texaco" and the star were painted on the fuselage of the airplanes and under the bottom wing so people on the ground could read it when they looked up. The Texaco star was also painted on the ends of the top wing.

The crowning touch was that Gates had "WORLD'S

GREATEST EXHIBITION AVIATORS, GATES FLYING CIRCUS" painted on the sides of the truck. They were ready for business.

It was hard for Jack to believe that he had been with the circus for three months. He felt as if this was where he belonged. Eventually, he would make his way back to Protection and possibly take over the hardware store when he had to give up flying, but for now, while he was young, the cockpit was his home. He was a vagabond of the sky. At twenty-eight years old, he sensed that he was embarking on the adventure of a lifetime.

Everything came together in April in Birmingham, Alabama. Daws did his job and got them connected with *The Birmingham News*, as well as the 106th Observation Squadron of the Alabama National Guard for a show at Roberts Field. Daws arranged for the use of the field for free if Gates agreed to give a part of the proceeds to them for maintenance. Dozens of posters were nailed to rural electricity and other poles around town, and on barns in the country. Nearly every barn and every electric pole on every road leading to town had a poster on it announcing the circus was coming to town. Roustabouts arrived before the circus and painted the field with lime for visibility.

There were three pilots—Pang, Billy Brock, and Jack—with Duke as stuntman. Jack learned that the group didn't travel all together and that not all personnel were available for every show. Pilots drifted in and out. One day, Freddie Lund appeared in his own Standard, so they had four pilots. Lund flew with the circus on a seasonal basis.

Daws made sure there were articles in *The Birmingham News* to build up interest. One was titled *Daredevil Aviators And Aerial Acrobats To Give Free Flying Circus in Birmingham and Bessemer; Rides To Be Given*. Right before the show, one read, *Crowds Thrilled as Flying Circus of News Starts.* To help promote the air show, the newspaper advertised that tickets for five free rides would be randomly pasted in fifty papers that the pilots would drop from the air. For those who didn't get a ticket, the circus would give rides for a nominal fee.

Pang had gone to Fort Worth, Texas, to pick up a plane but couldn't get back in time for the show. Brooks hadn't reappeared, so that left Jack and Freddie as pilots with a new guy named Eddie Bond and Krantz as stuntmen, but that was enough.

Sunday morning, before church services, they got together and divided up the newspapers. Jack decided that Krantz would fly with him, and Freddie and Eddie would fly together. They would do a short ballyhoo and then drop papers. Jack would fly over Woodrow Wilson Park and drop his. Freddie would drop his at Capital Square.

Even though they were going to do stunts they had done before, Jack got excited and nervous. His heart started pounding, and the palms of his hands got sweaty. This was his first big show and chance to prove himself. It was also the first big outing since his crash, and Pang was trusting him to get the job done. He wanted everything to be perfect. He pulled out a cigarette to calm down and concentrate on the task at hand.

You've done these dozens of times since Baton Rouge, he told himself. It wasn't so different than the fake dogfights and stunts he and Buck had done in the Texas sky back in Texarkana. He smiled, remembering that time, and wondered what Buck was up to.

While he waited until it was time to get in his plane, Jack decided what he would do in the way of stunts. He and Freddie had decided to start out with three side by side loops, then they would do their own stunting. He grabbed a stick and made diagrams in the dirt, then walked his way through the maneuvers, working his stick and rudders in the air. After the loops, he decided to go into some rolls, then a one-and-a half turn spin, followed by a hammerhead. This would be a bit tricky, but he thought he could pull it off. He'd then do a reverse Cuban eight, followed by a half loop and slow roll toward downtown. That should put him in position to fly over Woodrow Wilson Square and drop newspapers.

"Ready, Jack?" Duke asked, interrupting his thoughts.

"Yeah, let's do it," Jack said, climbing in and pulling the straps tight. Duke jumped into the front cockpit.

A greaseball turned the propeller to clear the lines, then yelled, "Contact."

Jack flipped the switch. "Contact," Jack yelled back, and the guy pulled the propeller.

The engine roared to life, and he headed down the airfield, Freddie slightly behind him. They hadn't flown together for very long, but they were really coming together as team, each sensing what the other guy was going to do. Heading southeast toward downtown Birmingham, spotting a line feature, Jack pushed his stick down to start a dive and talked himself through the maneuver.

He nosed his aircraft down, then pulled back on the stick. To maintain his direction and check yaw, back and forth motion, he adjusted using foot pedals to move the rudders. When the plane slowed, he increased back stick to keep enough speed to complete the loop. At the top of the loop, he used the stick to move the ailerons to keep the wings parallel with the horizon.

Jack looked over at Freddie. They were in sync, so he started a second dive.

After the last loop, Jack yelled "Yahoo!" into the wind and peeled off once he knew

Freddie was clear. Jack relaxed a bit after that first maneuver. Now he could strut his stuff. He prepared for some rolls.

Jack pulled the stick back to gain altitude and leveled off. He moved the stick to full right aileron to begin the roll, applying left rudder to control yaw. Then he moved the stick forward to maintain altitude and keep the plane level during the roll. After three rolls, he released the aileron and rudder to return to level flight. Jack continued stunting, talking himself through a few less taxing maneuvers and not those he had planned. He was having such a good time and considered a hammerhead but decided that he had probably done enough for a ballyhoo.

Instead, he dove into a loop, but stopped back pressure and rolled upright to complete an Immelmann turn, then headed to Wilson Square. He descended so Duke could drop the papers. Throttling back momentarily, he blasted his bugle to give people a heads-up. Duke dropped the bundle of rolled newspapers. As he headed back to the airport, he glanced down and saw people scrambling for them. "See you later, folks." Full throttle to airfield.

They landed back at the airport, and Jack jumped out of his plane, energized to do more. His heart was racing. "Wahoo, that was great!" Jack yelled, adrenaline flowing.

"Hell of a lot of fun. Hell of a lot of fun," Duke said, slapping Jack on the back.

"Kind of enjoyed it myself. Hey guys," Jack said as the others joined them for an after-flight briefing.

"Good job, Jack," Freddie said, "but lay off it a bit next time. Remember, we're just trying to get people interested so they'll come to the show, not give the whole damn show."

Jack grinned at him and the other guys. "Just trying to drum up business, that's all. Let's go get some chow. We may not have much time to eat this afternoon."

. . .

Later, back at Roberts Field, Jack couldn't believe his eyes. All the up-front work of Daws and the newspaper articles had paid off. A huge tent with a flag on the center pole had been set up, and flags flew from the top of the pole. People and their vehicles surrounded the field, overflowing to the hillsides. There were people as far as the eye could see.

So many people came out they had to get extra police officers and members of the National Guard to handle the traffic and huge number of people. The area outside the grandstand was packed with spectators waiting to get in. The grandstand was filling fast. The line of cars and trucks stretched for a couple of miles. People were honking their horns and yelling at one another, shaking their fists. Guys on motorcycles went around them and rode right up to the fence that had been put up around the field.

As they inched their way past the crowd, someone recognized them and yelled, "Look, it's the pilots! Let 'em through!" People started cheering and pulled back to let them through. Jack and Freddie felt like they were hot stuff, shaking hands and waving to everyone. Young boys chased after them, and wave after wave of people came up to shake their hands. Some asked for autographs. Jack had expected a few hundred, maybe a thousand people to show up, but there were thousands that day.

Jack relished the attention, shaking as many hands as he could and winking at as many girls as he could.

"This is great!" he yelled to Freddie.

At the airfield, their airplanes were roped off and guarded by National Guardsmen. Spectators were now crammed into the bleachers. Others stood behind the rope on the sidelines and had to be held back.

"I've never seen anything like this," Jack said to Freddie.

"Me neither, and I've been doing this awhile," Freddie replied.

"Let's give 'em a show," Jack said to Freddie. "We'll do some loops and play it by ear. After about fifteen minutes, I'll come back and get Duke for some wing walking. The wind's gotten kind of nasty out here, so let's nix the plane change. We can't take the chance of the planes smashing into one another. Same for the parachute jump." Lund nodded agreement.

Roustabouts propped their planes, and they took off. Their side-by-side loops went off like clockwork. Jack hadn't done very many right hammerheads because he found them more difficult, but he pulled it off. After an Immelmann and a chandelle followed by a barrel roll, he headed back toward the airfield. He motioned to Freddie that he was going to go on down to get Duke.

As usual, at about one thousand feet, he cut his engine, blasted on his bugle, and glided in. The crowd loved it, once they got over the initial shock and concluded that he wasn't going to crash. Duke climbed into the front cockpit of Jack's plane. The announcer explained what was happening.

To be a wing walker, one had to have nerves of steel, and Duke had them. Jack had walked the wings himself. All barnstormers do at one time or another, but Duke took it to unimaginable realms. Duke wore white coveralls so spectators could see him against the sky. He and Jack took off, and when Jack got to about 1,500 feet, Duke climbed out of the front cockpit and proceeded to do his tricks.

First, he stood on his head on the top of the plane. Then he went under the plane and hung from the landing gear by his knees and then by one hand from a skid under a wing. Jack could always tell where he was because he had to adjust for the shift in weight. The wind was crazy that day, so Jack had to concentrate intensely, constantly correcting for wind and weight shifts with his stick and working the rudders to keep it straight. Duke knew he couldn't pull any surprises on Jack; they had a routine worked out, and Duke motioned to Jack what he was going to do next, but they could almost read one another's minds.

After Duke hung from his knees and hands from the spreader bar, he came back on top and walked the length of the plane, then across the wings left and right. He stunted for about twenty minutes, then walked to the cockpit and motioned to Jack that he was ready for the loop, what Jack thought was the grand finale. Duke climbed up on the top wing, and Jack calculated the time it would take him to slip to make spectators look away while Duke hooked himself to the plane with a strap wrapped around his waist and got into position.

Centrifugal force would keep Duke on the plane in the loop, but he needed something to keep him from being swept off by the wind. The strap was one of the safety devices he used. Those old-timers would have laughed at him if they were still alive, but they weren't, and Duke was.

Confident that he was set, Jack moved his stick forward to go into a shallow dive to pick up speed, then pulled it back quickly to his gut. They zoomed up until they were upside down for a few seconds, and then they started down. Jack took a quick look back at the horizon to check his position and then down to make sure he hadn't lost Duke. He didn't see anybody falling, so he knew Duke was still on top of the wing.

With the loop completed, Duke did something they hadn't discussed. Holding onto the struts, he straddled the fuselage closer to the cowling than Jack would have preferred. Once in place, he looked back at Jack and pointed down. The crazy galoot wanted Jack to land with him up there. Jack shook his head and yelled, "No way, you're crazy!" and motioned for

Duke to get back into the cockpit. Jack knew Duke couldn't hear him, but he knew from his expression that Jack wasn't for it. Duke smiled back at Jack and pointed down again.

Jack knew there was no way he was going to get Duke back in the cockpit once he'd made up his mind, so he prepared to land and hoped for the best. No dead stick landing this time, because he needed the power with the extra weight on the front end of his plane. Duke rode all the way down, straddling the front end of the plane with his arms outstretched. Jack breathed a heavy sigh of relief when they touched down.

On the ground, the crowd was quiet at first, not knowing how to react. Everyone was relieved and surprised that they had made it down okay. Then suddenly the crowd started cheering and clapping. Duke bowed several times, then raised his hand for everyone to be quiet. Incredibly, he said, "I'm thirsty; anybody got some water?" After all that, all he had to say was, "I'm thirsty." Duke gestured toward Jack, who sat slumped on the edge of his cockpit, relieved they had made it down in one piece with the plane intact.

Jack came to life and took his cue. He jumped to the ground, bowed to the audience several times, and acknowledged their cheers. Then somebody brought Duke some water. Jack was ready for a different sort of drink.

Jack found out later that was typical of Duke. All that daredevil stuff was nothing to him, just another day's work.

"Good flying, Jack," Duke said, slapping Jack on the back as they walked back toward the tent.

Jack laughed and slapped him on the back hard. "You son of a gun." Jack grabbed a cigarette from his pocket to calm his nerves. "You damn near scared the hell out of me," he said, lighting up.

Duke looked at Jack and grinned. "Just trying to please the crowd. That's all."

Later, when he and the pilots were hangar flying after the show, Duke admitted, "You didn't land a moment too soon. I felt myself moving forward, and I've never been in any wind worse than it was today." And he'd seen a lot of days doing what he did.

Freddie landed, and they started taking up passengers. Red was reeling people in with his spiel. "We will take you high or low, fast or slow, any way you care to go. It's worth a ride to see whether you like it or don't like it. Like Castoria, children cry for it and old maids sigh for it. The thrill of a lifetime! We will bring you down so gently even the grass won't object. Our pilots land as softly as an old maid getting into a feather bed. Fly over your house. See who's visiting your wife. We have special rides for mothers-in-law. Come on up and fly high with the angels."

The pilots would get a cut of the proceeds from the number of paying passengers that they took up. That day, they charged two-fifty per person, so there was motivation to take up as many people as possible. They soon got their routine down to a science. First, the MacClatchies got people to an area called the "bullpen," where they waited to get into the plane. The Standards were rigged to take up four or five people at a time, with a ladder on each side for loading and unloading passengers.

As passengers were getting out on the left, more were loaded from the right. From landing to takeoff, they got the timing down to five minutes, and they got so good they timed their landings so that they rolled up to within a few feet of the plane ahead. They were already becoming a well-oiled machine.

Flights were short—two minutes, sometimes less—but people loved them. The expressions on their faces amused him. Some looked scared to death and vomited the instant they got off the plane. Others looked on with anticipation. Women climbed in, skirts billowing in the wind. People from other groups had told Gates that if they took up a couple hundred passengers in a week, they had a good week. Gates Flying Circus took up hundreds in that one day.

"You keep 'em coming," the pilots said to Al and Jim, and they would answer, "You keep 'em flying."

The next day, the newspapers reported on the performances. Jack grabbed a copy on the way to breakfast.

"Hey Jack, what did the paper have to say about us?" Freddie asked.

"Let's see here. They described the air as 'a little fickle.' Well, they didn't have to fly in it," he said. "But we put on a helluva show anyway."

"They had fun with Duke's antics," he continued. "Here's what the reporter said."

. . . and then he stood up right as the plane looped, only centrifugal force keeping him from plunging 2,000 feet. And then he came home riding the propeller shaft casing, his arms outflung, raising lusty shouts to the skies even as the ancient Vikings must have ridden home their booty laden ships over the North Seas.

Birmingham News, April 1925

"Those reporters are so full of it," Duke said.

Jack particularly got a kick out of the next part. He lowered his voice for effect. "*The plane was held steady by the mighty muscles of 'Big Jack.'*" He laughed.

This was mutually beneficial to the circus and the newspaper. They had to sell newspapers, and the circus needed people to come to the show.

Also, according to the paper, there was a certain Methodist

pastor in town who expressed displeasure from his pulpit at having a flying circus in town for a show on Sunday, even though the circus had made it a point not to fly while church services were going on. He attacked the "dare deviltry" in particular.

> To risk life on Sunday is the climax of great danger to our civilization," and for a great daily paper to become its sponsor greatly increases the danger.
>
> "Human life is entirely too cheap now, and everything that tends to put life in the balance of chances makes life still cheaper.

Birmingham News, April 1925

No doubt his mother and dad had heard something similar back in Protection after word got out that he had joined the circus. From the number of people at the air show, Jack didn't think very many agreed with the reverend. In fact, it might have even helped increase the numbers that attended the air show. What he did know was that one had to earn a living, and this was how he choose to earn his living. The great evangelist herself, Sister Aimee Semple McPherson, wouldn't have been able to convince him otherwise. God would have to understand.

The human pilots weren't the only ones who made the news. Pang flew in from Fort Worth, and sure enough, Judge was in the front cockpit. The canine made quite a splash with the press and the crowd. There was a picture of Judge with "JUDGE OF COSTILLA" written underneath, followed by an article:

Police Dog. With "Flying Circus,

Said To Enjoy Aviation "Stunts"

Most "champion dogs" are ornamental, nothing more.

But "Judge of Costilla," a husky police dog owned by Clyde Pangborn, of Gates Flying Circus, in Birmingham and in the supervision of The Birmingham News and the Alabama National Guard, is worth his weight in gold, they say, for services he has performed.

The "Judge" will occupy an important position in the Birmingham Kennel Show, which will be held at 2021 and 2023 Third Avenue, North, on April 28 and 29.

Often, when the circus is traveling and we're in a strange community, we leave the airplanes or the automobiles," said Mr. Gates. "But with them we leave Judge. We've yet to have a theft or damage to the property while under his guard.. . .

. . .Judge has traveled approximately 100,000 miles by airplane and automobile, believed to be a greater distance traveled by any other "non-professional" dog.

The dog, now thoroughly familiar with the intricate workings of the aviation business, takes frequent flights and has learned to brace himself safely while the "ship" is looping the loop and doing other trick stunts.

Clyde Pangborn and Judge in front of a Standard J-1 aircraft (tail number 12) of the Gates Flying Circus, circa 1920s. *The Clyde Pangborn Collection/The Museum of Flight, Seattle, Washington.*

CHAPTER 4
PARTY TIME

Early April 1925
Birmingham, Alabama

The circus had a good run in Birmingham those five days. Pang and Bill made it back early Monday morning and brought a paper with them. "Looks like you guys did all right yesterday," Pang said, and handed it to Jack.

10,000 People See Circus Fliers Act

Great Crowd Thrilled Sunday With Daredevil Acts of Stunt Performers.

If you should chance to meet a friend Monday and he would pass you by with head upturned and a look of wonder on his face, be not offended. He is only one of the 10,000 or so people who Sunday afternoon visited Roberts field, where a flying circus is being held daily under the auspices of the "Birmingham News" and the One Hundred and Sixth Obser-vation Squadron, Alabama National Guard.

"The article goes on to say what we'll do in the way of stunts and mentions Pang and Brock flying in," Jack said, then continued to read.

All highways leading to Roberts Field were jammed with automobiles and street cars were overloaded carrying thousands to the scene of the flying circus. Extra police officers were necessary to handle the crowd, which lined up all one side of the field many feet deep and found vantage points on hillsides for two blocks away.

Birmingham News, April 20, 1925

"This other one says,"

Plane-Changing Stunt on Card at Air Circus; Gates Fliers Promise to Outdo Breath-Taking Performance of Sunday Afternoon.

There were as many if not more spectators on Monday and Tuesday. Tuesday afternoon, the wind was calm enough for a plane change. They went up for the usual aerial stunting before Duke started his performance.

Jack flew up with a rope ladder dangling from the landing gear carriage. Pang followed with Duke, who got out of the cockpit and made his way out to the end of the top right wing. Once he was in place, Pang eased up under Jack's plane until Duke could reach the ladder. The trick was that when Jack felt his weight and was certain Duke had a firm grip, he had to pull up slightly and Pang had to drop down so that they didn't smash into one another, squashing Duke, if there was a gust of wind. This all went off without a hitch.

Once aboard Jack's plane, Duke prepared for the grand

finale—the parachute jump. When stuntmen and others had first started parachuting, they'd stood on a wing and held onto a strut, then pulled their chute and waited for the wind to grab it. This was traumatic for the men and caused a lot of whiplash. Duke did it differently.

Duke grabbed the chute from the front cockpit of the plane and put it on. Making sure the line that released the chute from the backpack was tied securely to the plane, he casually stepped off the plane, and the ripcord pulled automatically. Parachuting was okay once the stuntman got past the terror of the chute not opening, something Jack never got over. That was why Jack was a pilot. Jack looked down to see the mushroom shape of a fully open canopy and sighed with relief.

After the stunting, they took people up for rides. Over and over, Red gave his spiel, and Jim and Al helped load and unload passengers. Spectators got in lines a quarter of a mile long for a chance to fly. The routine was the same, and the pilots performed their jobs with precision time after time: load passengers, take off, fly a couple circuits around the field; land and roll up behind the plane getting ready to take off. Passengers unload on the left, load on the right. Repeat. Rides were short and low. Jack always did his dead stick landing, which didn't seem to bother folks once they saw that he made it down fine.

While they were on a run of shows and had to fly the next day, except for a short snort here and there, Gates wouldn't let them celebrate afterwards. They did get together to unwind, throw back a couple, and do some hangar flying. Jack learned more about the guys and about Gates. They said sometimes he could get a bit wonky and slug someone for no reason. Crazy thing is, the next instant, he'd stuff some bills in the guy's pocket and say he was sorry. These episodes usually followed some heavy drinking. Gates was a darn good businessman when he was sober, though.

Thursday night after the last show, Gates and his wife Hazel came by to talk to them. "You all put on some great shows this week. Go into town and have some fun." Then he gave each of them fifty bucks. "We've got to look at the totals before we divvy out the rest, but it looks good, boys. Looks real good."

The pilots did just as they were told. The stiffs in Washington had no idea what a joke so-called Prohibition was. There was nothing that could prohibit a man, or woman for that matter, from getting a drink if they wanted one and knew where to go. After the show, the guys loaded into the car, but Jack stopped a guy he caught sneaking a swig from a flask tucked in the inside of his jacket. Jack figured he'd know where to go for a good time.

"Come on Jack, let's go," someone yelled.

"I'll be there in a minute!"

Jack smiled and asked, "Hey, buddy, where can a hard-working aviator find a good time in this town?"

The guy noticed people watching them, so he grabbed Jack's hand and started pumping it like a pump handle, like the day when his mother had stuck Jack's head under the spigot to break him of playing in the water.

"Great show, great show!" the guy said. He pretended to be so excited he gave Jack a hug. "Third and Main, behind the bank," he whispered. "Knock three times and a tap. When someone answers, tell him 'Bernard' sent you." Then he stepped back and said loudly, "Keep up the good work. Can't wait till the show comes back to town." He walked off.

At the truck, Jack told the guys what the man had said. "I don't know about you, but I'm getting cleaned up and going out for a good time."

On the way to the hotel, still high from the enthusiastic crowds in Birmingham, they started singing at the top of their voices, "If you knew Susie, like I know Susie . . ." At the hotel, they jumped out of the car and ran inside.

"I'll be back down here in half an hour," Jack said, and took off to his room.

Half an hour later, Jack, Ive, and a few roustabouts walked out of the hotel looking for a fun time on the town. Jack found the place behind the bank and knocked like the man had said. Somebody inside slid back a little window built into the door and looked out.

"Bernard sent me," Jack said, hoping he sounded more confident than he felt. He glanced around to make sure there were no cops. The guy blinked and shut the little door. The guys waited for what seemed like forever, and nothing happened. They got uneasy and were about ready to hightail it out of there when they heard a bolt being pulled back and the big door opened just wide and long enough for them to slip through before it was quickly closed.

Inside, they squinted until their eyes adjusted to the dim light. Through the haze of the cigarette smoke, they could see men standing at the bar, one foot propped up on the brass footrests.

A few couples were on the dance floor. Pretty ladies were trying to teach some guys how to do that new dance called the Charleston. Moving folded arms up and down like chickens, it was no wonder people called them "flappers." Other girls sat with men at tables. As far as Jack could tell, all the ladies in the place were lookers. The whole place got quiet, and someone grabbed his arm.

"Hey everyone," a woman's voice said, "look who's here! These are the pilots from the Gates Flying Circus! They put on a good show for us the past few days, so let's show them a good time. Charlie," she said to the guy behind the bar, "the first round is on me." Everybody started clapping. Then she turned to Jack. "I'm Rosie, and I own this joint. You guys have a good time. But you get drunk and break up the place, I'll throw you out on your ear and Gates will get a bill for damages, ya' hear?"

On his way to the bar to get his free drink, Jack hooked elbows with two girls. Women swarmed around the other guys as well, clinging to them, telling them how handsome and brave they were. Guys slapped the pilots on the back and said things like, "One helluva show, men." Jack threw back the free drink, which tasted like rotgut, but he enjoyed the warm feeling it gave him. He'd started having a good time when he noticed Pang sitting in a dark corner, drinking what looked like root beer. Jack excused himself to go to the men's room. On the way, he stopped at Pang's table and straddled a chair opposite him.

"What's the matter, Pang? Aren't you going to celebrate with us?"

"Nah. Somebody has to make sure you guys don't get carried away and smash up the place. We have a reputation to maintain. Go have yourself a good time. You deserve it. I'm just fine with my soft suds."

"Have it your way," Jack said. He stood to leave.

"You did a damn good job of flying this week, Jack," Pang said. "You also did a good job taking charge without me there." Pang lifted his mug like he was making a toast. Jack acknowledged the compliment.

Back at the bar, Jack adored the attention, especially that of the ladies. There was one girl who was particularly to his liking, and he left with her at about two o'clock in the morning, when the music and dancing were slowing down. At her place, things got hot and heavy real fast.

· · ·

When he awakened the next morning, sunshine was streaming through the window, and he was in her bed with her snuggled up next to him. He wished he could remember what had happened in between but had a feeling it was good. "What time is it?" he asked sleepily.

"Don't worry about it," she mumbled. "It's still early. About nine, I guess."

"Damn," Jack said, wide awake, head throbbing. "Pang said to be back at ten. Where are my clothes?"

"On the chair."

He started pulling on his clothes.

She hurriedly got dressed as well. "I have a car. I'll get you back in plenty of time. Don't worry."

"I just started flying with the outfit, and I don't want to make Gates mad," Jack said. He remembered the guys saying that Gates had been known to throw punches for no reason, and Jack didn't want to give him a reason. He could take the punches, but he wanted to keep his job.

The girl pulled up at the hotel, put her arms around Jack's neck, and gave him a long, seductive kiss. He was tempted to stay in the car but pulled her arms away. "Sorry, I've got to go."

"My name's Emma. Look me up next time you're in town, sugar," she said.

Jack kissed back and was tempted again but quickly came to his senses. "Next time, babe," he said as he got out of the car. With a wave, she roared off.

Jack rubbed his temples to ease the throbbing in his head as he walked through the lobby of the hotel. The morning was already warm and muggy. He walked quietly to his room, then decided that if he was awake, the others needed to be as well. As he passed each room, he checked their doors to see if they were locked. If they weren't, he snuck in, pulled one of their big toes, and said, "Hey, short snorters, rise and shine," then rushed out.

Invariably, he was met with a loud response—"Leave me alone, damn it"—which didn't help his headache much.

At breakfast, they gave Jack a hard time about leaving with the girl.

"So, where'd you go with that dame?"

"It sure looked like you were having fun and going to have more."

To each he answered with a smirk on his face, "Wouldn't you like to know?"

As he had in New Orleans, Jack cut out newspaper articles to send home to his parents. He thought in their own way, they were proud of their son. Getting to fly for Gates was big stuff for a pilot. Of course, Jack didn't tell them how he'd celebrated because they wouldn't approve, but he suspected that they had figured that out anyway.

From Birmingham, they headed for Montgomery before going to Decatur and Atlanta. Daws and the MacClatchies headed out on Wednesday morning, the last day of the show, to get everything arranged for their next stop.

Jack considered himself a vagabond but wouldn't have it any other way. Pang was an avowed bachelor, and Jack decided that it was best he stay one as well. However, he decided playing the field was in his best interest. Who was he to deny fate if the right woman came along?

CHAPTER 5
FLYING THE SOUTH

Back row left: Jack Ashcraft, circa 1925.
Courtesy of Allen Keller.

May 1925
Richmond, Virginia

The circus continued its flight through the South. Their appearances in Montgomery, Decatur, and Atlanta were as successful as they'd been in Birmingham. Daws, taken by the circus since he first caught sight of them, knew his job and did it well. Ten percent of the gate receipts was an added incentive.

The *Atlanta Constitution* headlines read: GREAT THRONGS HELD SPELLBOUND BY AVIATION THRILLS; *New Sensations Offered today by Constitution Show*. As usual, they dropped copies of the newspapers with five tickets for free rides to draw people in.

In Atlanta, they literally had a captive audience. It was arranged for them to fly over the federal prison nearby. Jack and Pang received the honor of performing for the jailbirds. Duke would stunt from Jack's plane; a photographer with the *Atlanta Constitution* flew with Pang.

Aviators Thrill Prisoners
CONSTITUTION SPONSORS UNIQUE PROGRAM
With Daring Feats in Air

Dare-devil aviators flying under the auspices of "The Constitution" Tuesday brought brief surcease from the deadly monotony of prison grind to more than 3,000 men who are paying for past misdeeds in the great federal penitentiary whose grim walls forever frown down upon Atlanta....

As the daring aviators circled low and did breathtaking stunts on the wings and tails of the planes, the despairing silence of the prison cell was replaced with boyish shouts of approval, and for a short time the great penal institution was flooded with gladness, just as a shaded woodland pool may be turned into gold by a single dancing sunbeam.

Thrills "Old-Timers,"

But among the longlines of prisoners, a few white-faced men looked on with something of awe and terror in their eyes. And for good reason—for they were "old-timers," and this was their first sight of the marvelous machines they had read of in the gloom of their little steel-bound worlds. Men who lived bay a warden's watch year after year until all track of time was lost and only the deadly monotony of prison routine loomed ahead, they followed the darting, swooping ships of the air as a little child might gaze if the characters of a fairy tale suddenly sprang into life before its amazed eyes. . . .

Appreciative Crowd

. . . Diavolo Krantz then offered his program of feats in the machine piloted by Ashcraft. First Krantz stood upright on a wing of the plane while it described a complete loop. Next he hung head-down from both the top and bottom wings and crowned his feat program when he hung head-down from the landing gear while Ashcraft did a nose dive [sic] directly downward toward the heart of the prison grounds.

Barely Missed Wall.

Just before reaching the ground, Ashcraft swerved his machine to a horizontal position and swept barely across the prison wall. Krantz'[sic] head missing the wall by only a few feet. . . .

Atlanta Constitution, 1925.

Back on the ground, even Duke was rattled by the incident. "Dang, Jack. Did you have to cut it so close? When I saw how close that wall was, my life flashed before my eyes."

"Sorry about that," Jack said. "I wanted to give the fellas one last thrill. I guess I miscalculated some."

"I'll say," Duke snapped and walked off.

The Gaffney Ledger, South Carolina, publicized the circus's upcoming appearance:

GATES' FLYING CIRCUS COMING HERE NEXT TUESDAY; Drops tickets. FAMOUS CORPS OF DARING AERONAUTS WILL GIVE THRILLING EXHIBITION OF DAREDEVILTRY IN CLOUDS OVER CITY; free of charge, give away 5 free tickets for rides.

The Gaffney Ledger, May 23, 1925

Their appearance was under the "auspices of a chain of newspapers to present to citizens modern achievement in the air." The newspaper also reported that the American championship of consecutive loops would be flown.

Jack obliged by performing as many loops as he could, but it didn't matter how many he performed, it was always the number to win the American championship. Afterwards, he sat on the edge of the cockpit and waved to the crowd as they applauded and cheered.

Afterwards, Ive gave him a hard time. "How is it that you just keep breaking all of these records?"

"Hey, I'm just good, I guess," Jack laughed.

At Winston-Salem, North Carolina, headlines in the June 27, 1925, issue of *The Winston-Salem Journal* read: *JOURNAL AIR CIRCUS ATTRACTS HUGE CROWDS AT MAYNARD FIELD.*

It was here that Jack had the pleasure of meeting professional boxer Jack Dempsey. *That would never have happened in Protection,* he thought.

With each stop, Jack's confidence and popularity grew. He

soaked in the adoration of the fans. Still, at times, something would happen. A simple incident, word, or random thought would inflame the memory of the boy who was killed in his plane. Most of the time, he could shake it from his mind. Most of the time. Sometimes a snort helped.

They arrived in Richmond with much hullabaloo. After a successful weekend over the Fourth of July, they repeated the show the next weekend. As usual, they dropped newspapers to announce the show. For some reason, the newspaper decided they needed a disclaimer.

> *The Richmond News Leader is giving publicity to the Gates Flying Circus, which will give free exhibitions and stunt flying over Richmond and in the state fair grounds.*
>
> *The News Leader gives notice to all concerned that it is not responsible for any injury resulting from said exhibitions of the Gates Flying Circus. Nor is the News Leader responsible in any way or under any circumstances for obligations of the Gates Flying Circus.*
>
> *Any person, therefore, witnessing this free exhibition of the Gates Flying Circus in the fairgrounds or elsewhere in and around Richmond does so at his or her own risk.*
>
> *The Richmond News Leader, July 1, 1925*

They had never had any real problems, but Daws said that some people had complained of getting sick after a ride or claimed to have sprained an ankle getting out of the plane and other such nonsense and tried to sue the paper, so they'd decided to take the precaution. If anybody really wanted to sue the paper, or the circus, they could, but everyone concerned decided this was probably a good move.

Starting at precisely 2:30 p.m., one of the pilots performed spectacular stunting every forty minutes. The pilots that day were Jack, Pang, Eddie Brooks, and Freddie Lund. Krantz did his stunts from Jack's plane. For his part, Jack did an Immelmann and some barrel rolls before his dead stick landing. Pang did his usual inverted flight but flew longer than Jack had ever seen him. The crowd went wild.

Flying upside down was a difficult maneuver to sustain. First, Pang had to make sure to buckle his harness and fasten his seatbelt, then accelerate fast enough to not stall, and raise the nose to altitude. Then he would check his pitch rate and apply full aileron with a little rudder to balance. As the wings passed vertical, forward pressure until inverted. At this point, it was important to maintain aileron deflection and keep the stick almost full forward.

Nobody could fly upside down better than Clyde Pangborn. He could maintain this position for a mile or more and at incredibly low altitudes, almost eye level with people in the higher row of tall grandstands. He could stay inverted longer than seemed possible. The trick demanded perfect timing and maintaining a precise angle of glide. Since a Jenny's engine was fed fuel by gravity, it would barely idle when it was inverted.

Sunday afternoon, they did something they had never done before. A few minutes before 4:00, the four of them went aloft and circled the field. At precisely 4:00, roustabouts and people with *The News Leader* released a flock of helium-filled balloons, and they had a strafing contest to see who could bust the most balloons. When the inflatables got high enough, all the pilots spiraled straight up. Jack worked his stick and rudders to move right and left to get as many balloons as possible, constantly looking around to see where the other guys were.

Jack saw Freddie heading for a bunch of balloons, so to give the spectators a thrill, he turned toward them as well, but did a wingover to turn away to make it look like a close call from the ground. Pang did the same thing to Jack. They aimed for the balloons and dodged each other until there were no more balloons or they had floated out of sight.

On the ground, they jumped out of their planes and slapped each other on the back.

"That was fun for a change," Jack said.

"Dang, Jack, you about made my heart stop until I figured out what you were up to," Freddie said.

"You gotta give folks a good show," Jack laughed. "Daws said the crowd loved it."

Of course, the papers reported it all. Jack read their account to the guys the next morning.

The stars of the circus which consists of fourteen pilots, mechanics and helpers are Clyde Pangborn of upside-down fame, Big Jack Ashcraft, former motorcycle racer; Eddie Brooks, cross-country expert, who carried The News Leader to Williamsburg yesterday, and Freddie Lund, former wing-walker, and now the midget pilot of the squadron.

Richmond The News Leader, July 10, 1925

"Damn, Freddie, they called you a midget. Why the hell did they call you that?" Jack said.

"Hell if I know," Freddie said. "Does Daws give them this stuff? I'm not as big as you are, but I'm dang sure not a midget."

Jack continued reading. "*All are ex-army fliers of promi-nence. The planes are modern Standards, powered by Hispano-Suiza motors.*"

Of course, Jack had taken Duke up to do some wing walking for the show. As usual, the paper had a unique way of reporting this. "Hey Duke, here's what they say about you and me."

Diavalo Duke, the acrobat of the circus is one of the heaviest wing-walkers in the profession, it was learned today. Duke weighs about a 185 pounds and Big Jack Ashcraft, a 220-pound Texan, is the only pilot who can 'hold him on a wing' with safety. The technique of holding a wing walker on the wing consists of being able to keep the machine in control while air resistance pushes against an acrobat's body and the acrobat's weight is throwing it off balance. The wing walking stunt therefore is doubly spectacular.

"Well, they got that about right. The reporter came and asked me about that," Jack said. He went on reading the article.

In addition to promenading all over the top and bottom wing of the ship in flight, Duke does the 'standing loop' and the aerial bronco ride . . .

"There you go, Duke, you 'promenade' on the wing," Jack teased, strutting like he was walking with a cane.

"The hell I do," Duke said, throwing a grease rag at Jack.

Earlier, a reporter for another newspaper had been more thoughtful in an interview with Duke:

One of the features of the circus will be the daring stunts of Diavalo, which will include standing on his head on the airplane wings, swinging from the sides and the bottom by his hands and his toes, and standing on the top wing while "the ship" loops the loop.

Diavalo's attitude is one of keen interest in evry [sic] phase and pleasure of life, but towards death he holds an almost supreme contempt and indifference. He is a quiet and self-effacing youth. Scarcely ever does he laugh; rarely does he smile.

I know I face death constantly,' he says. 'I realize the danger of my work. But I have had enough of monotonous existence. Years that I have spent have seemed as decades, only dull routine, unending monotony.

In danger I find pleasure. In the minutes that I work, I breathe deep of life. Up there is the roar of the motor in my ears. Above it rises the whining wail of the wind rushing through the bracing wires. Beneath my feet as I stand on the wing lift of the airplane I can feel the lift and tilt of the delicate 'ship' answering each caprice of the air.

Below me in the crowd—men and women like ink spots against the green and gold of the dull earth. Up where I am, life is fast, and pleasant.

I wouldn't trade for all the insurance in the world against death. I know that there will be a 'some day' for me, that I'll slip and miss on that 'some day', but when it comes I'll have 'drunk deep of the cup.' I'll have had my fill of life.'

Diavalo, by work and exercise has toughened his muscles until they are as bands of steel. He comes to grips with death daily; his hands, his muscles, his judgment, flashing from a snap-trigger brain—these are the only guardians against destruction.

CHAPTER 6
GATES GETS DRUNK

Jack with unidentified women circa 1925. *Courtesy of Allen Keller.*

May 1925
Washington, DC, Bolling Field

The engagement in Washington, DC, was to prove the most interesting to date. Jack had the occasion to meet Major Henry Arnold, "Hap" to his friends. Gates and Pang knew him from back at Crissy Field in San Francisco. One who usually sought attention, Jack was content to sit and listen to these guys talk about the good ole days and the future of aviation. He soon determined that Major Arnold was a savvy guy and a good leader. He sensed Arnold would rise through the ranks to prominence, but that night, he was just one of them. He seemed a little tired and maybe a little down.

"Those were great days at Crissy Field," Pang said. "And the Marina. Golly, it was fun."

"They were quiet days," Arnold said.

"What do you mean 'quiet'?" Pang asked.

"Washington's a madhouse. Everybody's giving General Billy Mitchell all sorts of flack. They're threatening to court-martial him for insubordination and who knows what. All he's saying is we need a separate air force and the means to pay for it. He may not have gone about it in the right way, but he's right. I can feel trouble brewing. At this point, I don't know where it's all going to end, but I'm going to support him any way I can."

"Damn," Pang said, shaking his head.

"You think they'll go through with the court-martial?" Gates asked.

"At this point, I don't see any way out of it. They'll do it to finish what they started to save face," Arnold said. "Then the thing is that they'll adopt his ideas like they were their own. Seems a hell of a way to do things." They all nodded.

"Enough of what I think," Arnold said. "I've been reading about you guys. You're doing a heck of a job making sure everyone knows about aviation. It's our future, and it's time people accepted that. You've shown people that we need an air force. We need to be more than a stepchild of the army. Those fossils are probably still trying to buy horses for the cavalry."

When they all recovered from laughing, Arnold continued. "The Army Air Service has shown Americans that we can cross the continent in a day."

Gates laughed loudly. "Hell, Hap, it took Pang and me five years."

Daws and Gates outdid themselves organizing the show. According to arrangement, the show would benefit the Soldiers, Sailors, and Marines Club. This really got the guys excited about helping. The Army Air Service and the circus were to work together, and reserve squadrons were going to fly in to lend a hand. They even arranged for a military band to play. Except for some fly-bys and formation flying, Gates Flying Circus was to stage the whole show.

The Bolling Field show became one instance when all the publicity misfired. Gates and Judge called a meeting with circus personnel.

"Bad news, guys," Gates said. "In short, the brass has caught wind of the show. Oh, we'll put on the show all right, but the commanding general says that funds will go to the corps area hospital instead of the Soldiers, Sailors, and Marines Club." Everybody moaned.

"Yeah," Gates said. "Needless to say, the military guys have kind of lost their enthusiasm to help out. The brass has limited what they can do anyway. As always, the show will go on. You'll go up and do your stuff as usual and take up passengers afterwards. The military won't be participating much, but the band will play."

As was the routine before a show, Pang got them together before the morning bally. "We got a big show ahead of us, so take it easy this morning. As far as this afternoon goes, we've only got four planes, so we need to make it look like we have a dozen. Take off and land often. Change out pilots to take a rest. Okay, let's go."

They looped and rolled over the heart of DC to get people excited about coming to the show. In addition to the bally and the publicity in the newspapers, Pang dropped two hundred thousand circulars over the city advertising the show. He couldn't believe what he saw. There was a "sea of white," as he called it. He told the guys about it when he landed.

"I saw all these people in white hoods," Pang said, his voice shaking slightly. "It was quite a sight."

"How many do you reckon were there?" Jack asked.

"Must've been tens of thousands. Thank goodness they were peaceful. A crowd that big could cause lots of trouble," Pang said.

There was an article about it in the Saturday, August 8, 1925, issue of *The Washington Times*.

KLAN THRONGS READY
Kluxers Are Active All Over D.C.
City Filled with Klansmen Here for Big Parade.
DOWNTOWN CROWDED BY GOOD-NATURED HUMANITY
(partial article)

Washington, inured to crowds and conventions of all kinds, confessed itself somewhat awed and mystified today upon seeing the most picturesque and interesting throng in the city's eventful history.

The crowded streets, the swarm of traffic, the general commotion throughout the Capital was evidence that the coming of the Ku Klux Klan for its parade and demonstration today has given the old town the first real thrill it has experienced in a long time.

The streets are thronged with uniformed klansmen and their decorated automobiles. The ordinary uniforms of white are colorfully supplemented by the costumes, the kavaliers [sic], the drill teams, and the guards, whose spotless garb is set out with distinctive trimmings of black, red, gold and purple.

That afternoon, a great number of people came out to the field, but not many people were in the stands. Jack went up for a few stunts and immediately realized they had a problem. He landed right away and tracked down Pang.

"Pang, we've got to do something. People aren't coming through the gate," he said.

"Yeah, I noticed that. We can't make any money on rides if they don't. What's the problem?" Pang asked.

"The problem is, they don't need to come in—they can see everything from the outside—so why pay for it? You see what I mean?" Jack said.

Pang looked around. "You're right. Well, I'll do something about that." He strode off.

Pang talked to the commander of the field. About an hour later, three Martin bombers from Langley Field appeared and laid down a smoke screen between the paying customers and the ones outside the wire. Since they couldn't see the show, people were forced to go inside. Once people were inside, the show was tremendously successful. Jack took extra care in his stunts to make sure there were no slip-ups, though he did have one small one, courtesy of Duke. It concerned his parachute jump, particularly his chute, which Jack thought was getting pretty beat up, but Duke said it was safe and insisted on using it. The officer of the day had different ideas.

"You can't use that chute," he said.

"The hell I can't," Duke said. "It's my life."

Finally, the officer agreed as long as Duke wore a military breast pack that the army would provide.

Pang jumped Duke that day wearing the military pack. He landed in the Potomac River, which adjoined the airfield, soaking the military pack. It would take hours for it to dry out and be repacked.

"Damn it, Duke," Pang said after they fished him out of the water, "you went in the water on purpose."

"You know I wouldn't get the army's little ole chute wet," Duke said with a grin on his face. "I went in the river because it was softer than the field."

"Since when did you ever choose a water landing over one on solid ground?"

"Since an hour ago," Duke answered, and sauntered away.

Between the four of them, they took up nearly two thousand people for rides that day, and it felt like it to Jack. After he took the last passenger up, he was completely exhausted, even too tired to party. He turned his airplane over to the mechanics and roustabouts to check over and get ready for the next day. He was headed back to his room for some rest when he heard a girl's voice.

"Hey, Jack," she said, "you've worked pretty hard today and deserve some fun, don't you think?"

He turned to see who was speaking, and there stood not one, but two of the prettiest girls he had seen on the tour.

"How do you know my name?" he asked.

"It's on your plane, silly," the other girl said.

"Oh, yeah, I forget," he said. "I don't know. I'm filthy and kind of tired."

"We'll wait for you to clean up," the second girl said.

"You'll feel better after a shower," the first one said. "Then we'll escort you around town."

"I've got to be back by ten tomorrow."

"No problem," they said. So, he cleaned up, and off he went with two pretty girls to party in the nation's capital. Out on the town, they crossed paths with Pang.

"Hey, Pang," Jack said. "Meet Eleanor and Mary. What's going on?"

Pang nodded to the girls and pulled Jack aside. "Henderson called. You know, Arnold's aide. Van and Daws took Hap out to dinner, but Hap was called away, so Van and Daws went on a drunk. I've got to find Van and take him back to his hotel before he does something stupid. I can't let him ruin our reputation."

Jack nodded.

"Ladies, I've got to help Pang with something," Jack said. "You wait here, and I'll be back as soon as I can. If I don't make it back in an hour, well, that's just the way it is, and you can go on home." Jack walked off with Pang.

The two caught up with Gates on the roof garden of a hotel, of all places. They could hear him from the ground. By then, Daws had disappeared as well. Captain Henderson was sober and obviously frustrated with trying to get Gates to quiet down. He appeared embarrassed at Gates's foul mouth and looked relieved to see Jack and Pang.

"He's yours. I've had it with him," Henderson said, turning away.

"What's going on, Van?" Pang asked.

"Got to entertain the brass," Gates said, slurring his words.

"Hap's gone, and it looks to me like you've celebrated enough," Pang said.

"No, no. You know, got to be big stuff. Got entertainin' to do. Got to spend money on the brass. Newspaper guys too,"

Gates said with a laugh. "We're all a bunch of drunks, you know?"

Henderson looked at Jack and shook his head. Until then, Jack had only heard about Gates going on drunken benders, but this was the first time he had seen it.

"Come on, Van, let's get out of here," Pang said. "Me and Jack will get you back to your hotel."

For the first time, Gates noticed that Jack was with Pang.

"Hazel sent you, didn't she? That's it. You're spying on me," Gates growled.

"Hazel didn't send us, but I'm sure she's worried. Come on, we'll help you back to your hotel," Pang said more firmly, removing a bottle of liquor from the table.

"Damn you, Pang! Put that down!" Gates said.

"Easy," Pang said carefully, putting the bottle back on the table and holding his hands up. "I just want you to stop drinking, that's all."

"I'll stop when I damn well please," Gates said. "You pick up that bottle again and I'll throw you off the roof."

"Try it and you'll go with me," Pang said.

Gates rushed at Pang with his arm back, ready to slug him, but lost his balance and would have fallen off the roof if Pang and Jack hadn't caught him.

Pang straightened Gates's jacket and took his arm, motioning for Jack to take the other. "Come on, Van, let's go," Pang said. Knowing he was no match for the two of them, Gates allowed himself to be led to the stairway.

"Great partner you've got there," Henderson said, handing Pang Gates's hat.

Pang just shrugged his shoulders. "Isn't the first time, won't be the last. We'll take care of him from here. Thanks."

Henderson walked off, shaking his head.

. . .

Back at the hotel, Hazel, Judge at her side, opened the door the instant they knocked. There were dollar bills spread out on the bed. "Ivan, look at you. Thank you, Clyde," she said. She took her husband's arm to help him inside and quietly closed the door.

As they walked away, they heard Gates shout angrily at his wife. "Damn you, woman! You sent them after me, didn't you? Why, you! I don't know why I haven't thrown you out by now."

"Now, Ivan, calm down," Hazel cried, but Gates continued to berate and threaten her. Hazel started crying.

Jack turned to go back to help Hazel, but Pang grabbed his arm. "It's none of our business, Jack."

"He won't hurt her, will he?" Jack asked. "She didn't do a thing."

"I have my suspicions and asked Hazel about it one time," Pang said. "She says everything is verbal and begged me to not interfere, because it only makes things worse for her."

Jack shook his head in disbelief.

"Look, I'm just doing what Hazel asked. Believe me, it's hard," Pang continued. "I would never treat a woman the way he treats her, but this is how she wants it, okay?"

"Okay, I guess," Jack said.

"I expect him to slug me anytime, or worse," Pang said. "He goes crazy when he gets drunk and threatens me. Thank goodness it doesn't happen often."

Jack looked intently at Pang. "He would do that?"

Pang nodded and chuckled softly to lighten the mood. "But I have 'Big Jack' to protect me now."

Jack smiled ever so slightly.

"Hopefully he'll pass out soon," Pang said. "Let's go."

· · ·

In the lobby of the hotel, Pang told Jack that he was going to turn in and that Jack should do the same. Jack couldn't understand how Pang could calmly go back to his room and sleep as if nothing had happened. Jack worried about Hazel, even though he barely knew her. He decided to take a walk to clear his head. No matter what Pang said, it was hard to do nothing. He wondered if Hazel would be alive in the morning and what condition she'd be in if she was. Some of the other guys who had been with the organization longer whispered about the couple, but Jack had never witnessed anything. His confidence in the organization was a bit shaken.

"Why does Pang stay with him?" he wondered, then thought, *I can do this on my own.*

Jack walked by Gates's room on his way back to his and stopped to listen. He breathed a sigh of relief when all he heard was snoring.

The paper estimated that a hundred thousand people had come to the field to see the circus. Plans were to hit every big city in the East. Next stop was Baltimore.

The guys were assembling at the airport the next morning when Gates and Hazel stopped by. Jack tried to get a good look at Hazel without being obvious, but the brim of her hat was pulled low on her face. She avoided eye contact with anyone except Pang, and then it was only for an instant.

"Great showing here, men. Great showing," Gates bellowed. If he remembered seeing Jack the night before, Gates did a good job pretending nothing had happened, although Jack saw him cut his eyes in his direction one time. Jack couldn't help but feel a bit disgusted with everything and was having second thoughts about staying with the circus, but he had no other options at the present. He needed to save some money before he struck out on his own.

"Hazel and I are going to drive on to Baltimore. No hurry in getting down there," Gates said. "Al called this morning, and he's still putting some things together. When you arrive, get some rest. After Baltimore, we'll take a couple of days off, and then we have several engagements in Pennsylvania. I'll tell you more about that later." As he spoke, he looked at each one of them. Remembering the night before, Jack gave him a look of disgust, then stared ahead.

"Bye for now," Gates said. He took Hazel's arm, walked to their car, and drove off. Jack looked at Pang and shook his head.

CHAPTER 7
SAM AND MILLIE

Man, children, and location unidentified. *Courtesy of Allen Keller*

June–August 1925
Baltimore and Frederick, Maryland; Waynesborough, Harris-burg, and Philadelphia, Pennsylvania

In each city where they appeared, Daws came up with some gimmick to get people's interest. At Logan Field in Baltimore, he arranged for a wedding in Jack's airplane. This was the first time Jack had a wedding performed in his plane and the first wedding in a plane for the city of Baltimore. The *Baltimore American* duly reported the ceremony.

COUPLE WEDS IN AIRPLANE

While a crowd of spectators lined the edges of Logan Field, Miss Dorothy Salisbury, nineteen, of 1732 North Rutland avenue, was married in an airplane to William A. McC. Finnegan [sic], 2238 East Chase street, at 3 o'clock yesterday. It is the first airplane wedding in Baltimore.

The ceremony was performed by Captain John Logan of the Volunteers of America, who is also an ordained minister. The pilot of the plan was Jack Ashcraft, better known in flying circles as "Big Jack," After the wedding ceremony the newly-married [sic]couple were taken for a short honeymoon trip down the bay.. . .

. . .The most thrilling feature of the performance yesterday was a series of daring stunts, with Diavolo Krantz as the chief performer. He stood on the wing of the plane as it looped at an altitude of 1000 feet, stood on his head at an altitude of 700 feet, hung from the wing by one hand and crossed from one plane to another, walking on the wings.

An interesting chap who visited the airfield before the show. His name was Major Jack Savage, a British RFC pilot who was there showing people some skywriting with some S.E.5 planes. Pang and Jack thought it was something they might want to incorporate into their show someday. They were standing around talking about skywriting and doing some hangar flying in the afternoon before the fireworks show that evening, and mechanics were checking out Pang's plane. The plane was chocked, so Pang ran up his engine. The plane jumped a chock, spun around, and broke two longerons.

Pang cut his engine and checked out the damage. "Damn," he said. "I've got a show to do tonight. Well, guys, let's get to work."

"Are you saying you are going to fix the plane this afternoon and fly tonight?" Major Savage said in his proper English accent.

"That's exactly what I'm saying," Pang answered.

"That is not possible," Major Savage said.

"You just have a seat over there and we'll have this fixed in no time, you'll see," Pang said as he and the guys started getting the tools they needed to complete the repairs.

"That is the craziest thing I ever heard. Even if you get it fixed, there will be no time to test it properly," Major Savage insisted.

"Don't you worry about a thing, Major," Pang said. "Not a thing."

To Major Savage's disbelief, Pang and the guys had that thing fixed up in a couple of hours. The fireworks show went off without a hitch, and the plane didn't fall apart.

From Baltimore, they headed for Philadelphia via Frederick, Maryland, and Waynesboro and Harrisburg, Pennsylvania, for a Labor Day show, giving exhibitions in towns and cities along the way. The *Harrisburg Telegraph* reported: *THRILLING FLYING CIRCUS STUNTS TO AMUSE CROWDS.*

It was early August, so the afternoons were hot and the air was thick and heavy on the ground, but at higher altitudes, it was cooler and refreshing. Following roads and railroad tracks, they headed out in formation, breaking away for excursions, and flew in and around the green hills, swooping low in the valleys and over towns.

Jack raced a guy on a motorcycle, which reminded him of his board track racing days with Troy Putterbaugh. He flew alongside a train and waved to the engineer.

When he flew over a location, he got a hunch whether the people who came out would pay for a ride or not. On the way to Philadelphia from Baltimore, he decided to take an excursion over the countryside and stay away from the cities. Outside a small town, people came out of their houses and businesses when he flew over, so he headed toward the nearest field to land. They followed.

"Hello, folks. How's everyone today? How would you like a plane ride with Jack Ashcraft, the Cowboy Aviator, star pilot with the Gates Flying Circus?" Jack said, a little uncomfortable promoting himself. He would much rather let Al, Jim, or Red say the words and then bow afterwards.

Everyone nodded, and he heard a lot of *I do*s.

"Tell you what—since this is such a fine day, and you look like such a fine group of people, I have a special offer today. Three minutes for only three dollars. How does that sound?"

They started jockeying for a position in line.

A boy and girl stood to the side. The boy wore overalls with no shirt and only one strap clipped in, the other clip missing. His straw hat was too big for him, so Jack could barely see his eyes. The girl had blonde hair braided in pigtails and a worn calico dress that she had outgrown. Jack guessed them to be about eleven and eight. They didn't appear to have much. Jack got his gas can out of the plane.

"But I have a free ride for two special people," he said, walking over to them. "Hey, kids, what are your names?"

"I'm Sam, and this is Millie, my little sister," the boy said.

"She heard you and wanted to come see the plane, but Mom wouldn't let her come without me."

"I see," Jack said. "My best friend's name is Sam, but everybody calls him Buck. Sam, how would you and Millie like a free ride?"

"What do we have to do?" Sam asked suspiciously.

"You go into town and get me gas, and I'll give you and your sister a free ride after these folks," Jack said.

"Let's do it, Sam," Millie begged, tugging at Sam's shirt.

"Oh, okay," Sam said, taking the gas can and money from Jack.

Works every time, Jack said to himself. He proceeded to take up paying customers. There must have been fifteen to twenty. The kids came back with the gas. He filled the plane and sent them for more. He told them he would be finished taking up the others by the time they got back, but Jack sent them a third time. They returned, this time with the can in a wagon. Jack took the last guy up and was preparing to leave when he heard a voice.

"Aren't you forgetting something?" Millie said, her arms crossed.

Sam's arms were crossed as well. He didn't say anything, but his expression spoke for him: *Don't mess with us.*

"Sorry, kids, but I need to get on to Philadelphia. Hope you understand," Jack said. He really did feel bad about leaving without giving them a ride, but Pang was expecting him.

Millie, however, would have none of it.

She stamped her little foot. "You're going to take me and Sam for a ride, dadgummit," she said. "Our mama told us that if you acted like you weren't going to give us a ride, we were to tell you that she would send the law out after you or come take care of things herself."

"That's right," Sam said, jaw set, chin jutted out.

"She said that, huh?" Jack said, grinning. He thought to himself, *This little gal's got a lot of spunk to talk to a guy who is six-foot-four of packed bone and sinew.* Jack glanced across the field and saw a woman standing at the edge with her arms crossed. He waved, but she just stared.

"Well, I reckon I better give you a plane ride, then," Jack said. "I don't want your mama sending the law out after me, and I sure as heck don't want to get crosswise with her. Climb in."

Jack got the apple crate back out for them to step up on, buckled them and strapped them together, then handed them goggles. Millie barely had enough nose to keep them up and giggled. They laughed when Jack turned the propeller and the plane rolled away from him. They thought he was playing around, but Jack was tired and wasn't faking it. Out of breath, he caught up with the plane, and they applauded his victory.

Taking up those two kids and watching them laugh and carry on was one of the best flights of Jack's life. With them, he was taken back to his first ride in an airplane. Even as an eighteen-year-old, he had felt brief terror at takeoff as the earth receded below. Terror gave way to enchantment as breathtaking scenes scrolled beneath the wings and he saw trees as green fountains. Enchantment gave way to delight when Sam and Millie, holding their hands high against the wind, tried to catch and eat pieces of cotton candy clouds. Jack hadn't done that because it wouldn't have been frowned on back then, but as he flew with the children, he too grabbed pieces of clouds and ate them. He was so engrossed that he flew longer than he had intended. But all good things must come to an end, and he landed.

The children crawled out of the cockpit and jumped off the wing. Millie gave Jack a big hug and kiss. "Thanks, Mr. Jack. That was the best time I've *ever* had."

"Millie says she wants to be a pilot someday," Sam said, "but I told her girls don't become pilots."

Jack looked Millie straight in the eye. "Millie, your brother loves you and wants what is best for you, but don't listen to him. You can do anything you set your mind to," he said, "even fly airplanes." Then he turned to Sam.

"How about you, Sam?"

"I want to build the fastest plane in the world," he said.

"You do that and look me up," Jack said, "but I've *really* got to go now, kids. It's been fun."

"I hope you come back sometime," Millie said.

"I'll try to do that," Jack said. He started to get into his plane. "Wait, I owe you some change," he said, and gave each of them five dollars. Millie kissed Jack on the cheek again and ran off across the meadow, waving the money.

"Mom!" she yelled.

Their mother waved back.

As he gained altitude, Jack looked back at those kids running across the meadow with its green fountain trees. He looked until they were mere specks on the earth.

The circus performed in Waynesboro, Carlisle, Lebanon, and Harrisburg. In Harrisburg, they dropped rolled papers with free tickets inside some of them as usual, but Daws and the *Harrisburg Telegraph* added a twist. After they dropped the papers, they started circling. For those watching, the paper had a contest to guess what their altitude was. Any pilot could tell how high a plane was with a quick glance, but to those who'd never flown, it wasn't easy. Answers ranged from five hundred feet to a mile. They gave free rides to five people who came the closest. Gates also extended an invitation for a free ride to a special passenger. Here's what the paper had to say about her.

> *A feature of this afternoon's flying was the invitation of the Gates Flying Circus to Miss Kathryne Frick, daughter of Mr. and Mrs. William Frick, of this city and ward of the State, who has amazed doctors and educators by the manner in which she has overcome the handicaps which beset her. Deaf, dumb, and blind, Miss Frick learned to speak at the Mt. Airy Institute and by sheer strength of will and determination to succeed, is ready now to enter college. She is anxious to take her first airplane ride and expects to enjoy it tremendously. Accompanied by her parents, she anticipated 'taking off' at 5 o'clock this afternoon."*

If Miss Frick had learned to speak and was going to college, Jack thought, she might not be able to hear or see, but she wasn't dumb, that was for darn sure. This was one example of Gates's behavior that puzzled Jack. One night he threatened his wife, and the next day he showed extreme kindness to a blind girl. Sure, it was good publicity, but Jack was convinced that Gates was sincere in doing kind things like that. He guessed that was one reason Pang stayed with him.

They had to move on, but Harrisburg liked them so much that they asked them to return. From Harrisburg, they went to Coatesville. Doing so many shows in a row, one might have thought that flying would become routine, and it did at times, but that didn't mean the plane was going to fly itself. Before every show, Jack went through his ground routine of planning out the tricks he was going to perform. He also talked to the other guys to see what they were going to do after their simultaneous maneuvers.

At 2,000 feet, there was no room for mistakes. A pilot had to be aware of everyone and everything going on around him. While it was fun, it could be quite intense, and sometimes Jack still thought about that kid back in Louisiana.

CHAPTER 8
ZR-1 U.S.S. SHENANDOAH

Aerial view of the USS Shenandoah and biplane.
Photograph via NavSource.org

September 1925
The USS SHENANDOAH, Coatesville, Pennsylvania

The circus flew into Coatesville in early September, this time connecting with the Elks Lodge to sponsor shows. The local airport operator wouldn't let them use his field. Another pilot ran a business out of the airfield and he thought there would be a conflict, so they had to fly from the yard in front of the Elks Lodge. At their first show, the other guy flew into a field nearby and set up operations to take advantage of the crowds that came out to see the Gates Flying Circus. Pang watched him for a while and then called Jack over.

"Jack, I don't think this guy knows how to fly very well," Pang said.

Jack watched for a few moments. "I'd have to agree."

"He's chiseling in on our crowds," Pang said. "The next time he takes off with a load of our passengers, you keep him in the air."

It wasn't long before Jack and Pang saw some folks follow the pilot to his plane and get in. Someone turned his prop, and off they went. Pang looked over at Jack and nodded. Jack grinned and climbed into his plane. By the time he taxied and took off, the guy was circling to land. Jack didn't want to harm the guy or any of his passengers, but he wanted to send him a message that they didn't appreciate his tactics. Jack cut in front of the other pilot's plane, and he had to pull up and go for another approach.

For several minutes, Jack flew around, under and over the guy's plane. At one point, Jack was so close that he looked over at the other pilot and grinned. Jack expected the pilot to shake his fist at him or something, but what Jack saw was that the guy was getting flustered. His passengers looked frightened. Jack knew that he couldn't risk the safety of the passengers, so he let the guy land. Once on the ground, the pilot promptly called the sheriff, and the law came to pay Pang a visit.

"I got a complaint that one of your men engaged in some dangerous flying," the sheriff said to Pang.

"Nah. Jack here is one of my best pilots," Pang said. "He wouldn't put anyone in danger. But let me tell you what's happening here. They wouldn't let us use the local airfield because of this other pilot, and then the guy chisels in on our business."

"I see. I'll take care of it. Just make sure all passengers stay safe, okay?" The sheriff strode off to talk to the other pilot.

Their "competition" didn't take off again while they were in Coatesville.

Tuesday, September 1, 1925, in Coatesville was a day that everyone in the circus would never forget, especially Jack, Pang, and Freddie. They finished a string of shows, and it had been a very tiring day. Calling it quits about five thirty in the evening, they were tying down their airplanes when they heard a dull, continuous roar in the distance. The sound came from somewhere above them, but it didn't sound anything like an aircraft they had heard before.

"Would you get a load of that!" Pang said, pointing east. Emerging from a cloud and moving toward them was a dirigible, its silver coating glistened in the sunlight, flashing light when it caught a direct ray of the afternoon sun.

"Wahoo!" Jack yelled. His fatigue evaporated. "I'm going back up to get a better look." Pang and Freddie were right behind him.

Jerking the ropes loose, Jack scrambled into the cockpit and was airborne in record time. As the distance between them shortened, the cylindrical airship loomed larger and larger. Jack marveled at the sight. Its silver coating gleamed in the light of the setting sun. First he flew over it, then alongside. Letters on the side of the ship read ZR-*1*, *US NAVY*, and *Shenandoah*. Jack had seen airships in Europe, but this is the first he had seen one in the US, and he knew it could be the only time he would get the chance to fly alongside one. The ZR-*1* was the first inflated with helium.

Time went into slow motion as they floated past one another, his small plane and this silver wonder of aviation. From this point of view, it was hard to tell how long it was, but from the time it took to fly past it, he gauged the vessel to be six hundred feet long or more. He felt like a dragonfly buzzing around it. To Jack, she was beautiful and marvelous. Some crewmembers caught sight of the airplanes, so Jack and company gave them a free show.

They did loops, barrel rolls, and some short spins. It was getting late in the evening, the sunlight giving way to a haze and mist forming in the west. With gas running low, they settled into escorting the airship for a time on its journey west. Jack dropped down to the cabin below to wave goodbye to the crew and reluctantly turned back. Pang and Freddie soon followed. Pang was the last to land.

Back on the ground, they couldn't put into words what they had experienced, and they walked back to the hangar in silence, each man lost in his own thoughts. Jack didn't know what the other guys were thinking, but he felt calm, serene. It was a great way to end a busy day flying.

The *Coatesville Record* wrote about the incident the next day. Jack read it to the others, then saved the article to send home.

> *Capping the climax of the big show and more spectacular even than the wonderful exhibit which was staged Tuesday evening came the wonderful spectacle which greeted Coatesville resi-*

dents about 5:30 last evening when the big ship Shenandoah of the United States Navy passed over the city. The Shenandoah had been seen here previously, flying at a high altitude. Last evening, however, it flew low enough that details of its construction were plainly visible. And to give to the air ship's visit a real thrill, Aviators Pangborn, Ashcraft and Lund, of the Gates Flying Circus, traveled east of the city and escorted the gas balloon far to the northwest to speed it on its way.

It was a splendid sight as the airplanes circled high over the Shenandoah. For the benefit of passengers and crew on the airship the aviators put their planes through a series of stunts over, under and alongside the helium-filled bag. As the strange procession moved into the west the last rays of the slowly sinking sun were reflected upon the silver gray of the gas bag and the bright red of the planes, and as the colors were brightened the marked contrast, with its background of blue sky, stood out so that spectators gazed with awe upon the splendid sight they were witnessing. Coatesville never saw anything like it; few cities in the country have such a spectacle presented before their gaze.

Coatesville Record, Sept 2, 1925

As great as it appeared from the ground, nothing compared to flying and stunting next to the silver wonder. Back on the ground, the men slowly climbed out of the cockpits of their planes. There was no laughing or boisterous bantering. Just silence as they watched the dirigible disappear into the horizon.

Jack broke the silence. "I've never felt anything like I felt flying next to it. I felt a peacefulness that I've never experienced flying before. For me, the world went into slow motion."

. . .

The next morning, Pang came running in, out of breath, waving a newspaper. "Look at this!" he said, holding up the paper for all of them to see. The headline read:

14 DEAD IN SHENANDOAH CRASH.

The great bag fell in three masses of twisted and broken wreckage in a terrible storm near Ava, Ohio, killing 14 members of the crew including Lieutenant Commander Zachary Landsdowne. Officials suggested that the airship was caught in an updraft in the storm and the helium gas expanded faster than it could be vented out, breaking the vessel apart. According to the article, twenty-nine survivors rode three sections of the airship to earth. The largest group was eighteen men who made it out of the stern after it rolled into a valley. Four others survived a crash landing of the central section. The remaining seven were in the bow section that Commander Rosendahl navigated as a free balloon.

Mere hours after they had flown alongside the dirigible, it had crashed. The news socked the fliers in the gut as hard as Jack Dempsey's fist, so fresh were their memories of flying next to the airship, seeing the faces of the crew, and waving to them. Aviation was a fraternity no matter what your involvement was. Pang, Freddie, and Jack felt as if they had lost members of their own crew.

CHAPTER 9
GATES GOES BERSERK

September 1925
Labor Day

In Pennsylvania, they flew exhibitions in Carlisle, Phillipsburg, Berwick, and Somerset. Here and there, a program had to be delayed because of rain or wind, but always, the show went on. The newspapers played them up big time, and of course, they dropped newspapers over every town with free tickets inside. Back in Reading, the newspaper had a catchy way of talking about the circus. The headline read:

1925 Model Circus Hits Town Today: Aerial Thrills Will Supplant Elephants, Peanuts and Pink Pop.

The article didn't get much better from there.

A circus is coming to town today, a reg'lar [sic] circus bus without the customary elephants, peanuts, and pink pop, heretofore considered absolute essentials.

But this will be a 1925 model circus. The roar of mighty airplane motors will usher in the engagement of the Gates Flying Circus. An epidemic of stiff necks probably will be spread in its wake.

Over Labor Day weekend, the show was in Philadelphia on their way to the National Air Races at Mitchel Field in New York. Eddie had engine trouble in Pottstown and had to get a new engine but made it to Philly in good shape. In Philadelphia, Jack's picture appeared on the front page with the caption:

Cowboy Aviator is what they call this husky six-footer—'Big Jack' Ashcraft, who hails from Texas. He and other members of the daredevils of Gates Flying Circus will stage a flying carnival over Independence Square tomorrow at 12:30 noon, under the auspices of the Daily News.

Pang looked at the headlines and shook his head. "I'll say this about you, Jack. You keep us in the press."

Jack grinned. "Whatever I can do to promote the group."

As agreed, GFC collaborated with the *News* and roared over Independence Square. They looped, rolled, dove, and spun over Independence Hall where their forefathers had signed the Declaration of Independence. Jack wondered what they would have thought at such a sight. He flew so close to the statue of William Penn towering over City Hall that he could look him in the eye and gave him a quick salute. *The Daily News* estimated that two hundred thousand people watched from the streets below.

To live up to his moniker of "Cowboy Aviator," Duke and Jack added a "bucking bronco" routine to the show. Duke put on chaps and rode on a specially fitted saddle on the back end of the fuselage of Jack's plane while Jack made it "buck" by moving the stick back and forth like Buck had taught him as they flew in front of the grandstand. The Yankee crowd loved it.

Back on the ground, Jack and Duke grinned and bowed to the crowd. Jack thought they would never stop applauding.

Later, at the supply tent where the others had gathered to enjoy a snack of what else but a bag of peanuts courtesy of *The Daily News*, Jack arched his back to stretch it out. "Man, I enjoy appreciative spectators as much as the next guy, but enough is enough," he said. "I didn't think they would ever stop clapping."

"But you're the famous 'Cowboy Aviator,'" Ive said, and all the guys threw peanut shells at him.

Tens of thousands of people came out to see their entire show, and they took people up in droves afterwards. At the end of the day, Jack felt as if he'd taken up half of them himself. Red brought them in the gates; Al and Jim herded them in and out of the bullpens. The mechanics stood ready to assist in any way to keep the airplanes flying.

With each show, they got more and more efficient. To save time, they cut their engines and did a 180-degree sideslip to drop to the field. Since each field was different, they had to adapt to each one.

When the crowds got restless or the corrals started emptying, they pulled Duke out of the repair tent for some stunting. Mac would announce, "The Great Diavolo, the greatest stuntman in the world, will now make a surprise appearance." Then he'd go over to the tent and yell, "Duke, we need you out here." Duke would put down his wrenches and wipe his hands on a rag soaked with gasoline. After washing and drying his hands, he put on white coveralls and made his appearance.

Red or Mac hollered through a megaphone: "Ladies and gentlemen, we present to you the Great Diavolo, Master of the Air, King of the Wings. For your amusement and amazement, this man will defy gravity and meddle with centrifugal force. In other words, ladies and gentlemen, he'll risk his neck just to give you a thrill and something to tell your grandchildren."

Jack took Duke up for his stunting. It was always a heck of good time, and Duke never disappointed.

One day, Jack's engine started cutting out over Independence Hall, so he hightailed it back to the airfield as fast as he could. It was the first time something like that had happened to him at an air show, but he made it in fine. The airplanes were army surplus to begin with and were showing their age.

Just as Philadelphia had welcomed the circus, the circus bid Philadelphia a grand goodbye as reported by the newspaper:

A farewell tour was made over the city at 4 o'clock yesterday afternoon. Three planes flew in wedge formation to the outskirts of Sinking Springs and then in line formation to the Penn Street Bridge. Here the signal was given to separate and 'stunt.' Followed by a series of loop the loops, side turns, twists, drops and other daredeviltry. Below thousands were watching on Penn Square and in other parts of the city. From a height of 2,000 feet the planes then dropped to 500 feet for a quick spin about town. Then, they circled and hopped home, turning at Centre House and gliding along the field where they stayed last night.

Early this morning the propellers will again hum and the men will be off to Tamaqua, where they will give another exhibition.

Sometimes, Jack got keyed up from the constant flying and had to have a couple of snorts to calm his nerves before he went to bed. They'd been so busy doing exhibitions that they hadn't had much time to go into town and blow off steam. It would be that way until the end of the year, but he was having a hell of a good time. When there was a chance to party, he did, and there were always plenty of girls available.

Their last stops for exhibitions before the National Air Races were in Wilmington, Delaware, and Easton, Pennsylvania, where the fall colors blazed. Jack don't know if it was being constantly on the go and the stress of having to line up show after show or what, but Gates seemed to be drinking more and acting out. Hazel usually caught the brunt of it verbally, but he also insulted the personnel and destroyed his and circus property in his rampages. After their performance at Easton, he blew a cork.

There was a storm coming, so the pilots and crew had to take extra time and care to tie down their planes. Even as they were tying them down, it started raining. The wind was blowing a gale as they desperately pounded the stakes into the ground. Pang helped, but Gates and Daws went into town drinking. It took a while, but they finally got the airplanes secured and headed back to the hotel, exhausted and soaking wet. When they arrived, Mickey Efferson was sitting in the lobby, obviously upset. He even looked like he had been crying.

"What's the matter with you?" Pang asked.

"Gates. He fired me," Mickey said.

"Don't listen to him," Pang said. "I make the decisions about who works for the circus." Pang walked over to the counter to get his key from the little old man behind the desk.

The old fellow shuffled over to Pang and handed him the key to his room. His eyes were wet, and there was a welt on his cheek.

"What happened to you?" Pang asked.

"That man named Daws slapped me," the poor old guy said.

"Why?" Pang asked.

"He said I didn't get his key fast enough," the clerk mumbled.

"What the hell's going on? I've got to get to the bottom of this," Pang said. He marched toward the Gateses' room, motioning for Jack to follow.

Pang knocked. Gates opened the door. Jack caught a glimpse inside the room. There was money neatly laid out all over the bed, the money that the group had taken in that day. Hazel was counting it and putting it in bundles, then placing the bundles in a suitcase as she always did. It looked like thousands of dollars. Judge was lying on the floor, his eyes moving from person to person.

"Come in," Gates said, and Pang walked through the door. The instant Pang stepped through the door, Gates slammed it shut in Jack's face and he heard the door lock. Jack was certain Gates had seen him. He stood outside and listened.

"What the hell's going on?" Pang asked. "Mickey's downstairs crying and fretting, and the hotel clerk says Daws—"

That's all Pang got out before Jack heard a hard punch, followed by a groan and a something, or someone, falling against the wall.

"I've been waiting for a chance like this," Gates yelled. Through the door, Jack could hear him clawing through the room, looking for something.

"Van, no," Hazel cried.

Jack banged on the door. "Let me in!"

Gates was so enraged he didn't hear Jack—or ignored him.

Jack kept pounding on the door and rattling the doorknob. Then he heard shots—one, two, three. "Goddammit, let me in!" he yelled, then ducked and huddled beside the door. Three more shots rang out. The last one hit the opposite wall in the hallway. Then it was quiet. Jack prayed that none had hit Pang.

Again, Jack pounded on the door. This time, he heard it being unlocked. Cautiously, Jack pushed it open and peered through the gap between the door and doorjamb before he walked in. Poor Hazel was sitting on the bed, crying. Bills were scattered everywhere. Gates just stood there in a daze, holding a gun at his side. Pang was slumped over the washbasin on the opposite wall, holding his jaw, blood oozing from his mouth. There were bullet holes and splattered plaster in the wall above his head.

"What the hell happened here? Give me that!" Jack demanded, but Gates dropped the pistol on the floor. It fell with a thud. Jack picked it up and tucked it in his pants behind his back.

"My God," Gates said, coming out of his trance and looking around. "What have I done?" He looked at Pang and rushed over and threw his arms around him. "Oh my God. I'll never take another drink."

Pang tried to push him away but had no strength.

"I'm taking you to the hospital," Gates said. With that, he put Pang's arm around his shoulder and drug him out the door. "Hazel, if anyone wants to know what happened, you tell them it was an accident."

As he and Pang passed Jack, Gates said, "This is none of your damn business, Jack. Take care of Hazel."

When they had gone, Jack turned to Hazel. "What the hell went on in here?"

"Van hit him, Jack. Hard enough to knock him uncon-scious, but Clyde kept standing. I don't know how. He just fell against the wall over there and slumped down," Hazel said, shaking her head and crying.

"Then Van started shooting. He could've killed him, Jack, but he didn't. Remember that." Still crying, Hazel started picking up the money and tidying up to get her mind off the incident.

Jack checked out the room and the bathroom to make sure everything was okay. He found poor Judge wedged between the wall and the bathtub, shaking horribly.

"It's okay, boy," Jack said, kneeling to pet the dog. "You can come out now." But the dog wouldn't budge. "That's okay," Jack said. "You take care of Hazel and I'll take care of Pang, okay?" He gave Judge one last pat on the head and left the room.

"I'm going to the hospital. Lock the door and don't let anybody in," Jack told Hazel and rushed out. On the way, he stopped at his room to hide the gun. Ed looked at him quizzically, but Jack just shook his head and rushed out. Gates would never see the firearm again, but Jack knew he would just get another one.

At the hospital, the doctor examined Pang. "What happened?"

"I slugged him," Gates answered.

"Did he fall into a sand pit or something?" the doctor asked, seeing the plaster in Pang's hair.

"Nah, I shot at him. Bullets hit the wall above where he was standing," Gates replied like it was a normal thing to do. The doctor looked at Jack, and all Jack could do was shrug and shake his head.

The pain was so intense that Pang consented to a teaspoon of laudanum. The nurse pried his mouth open, dispensed the drug, then forced his mouth closed. The doctor gave it a few minutes to work, then wrapped Pang's face in gauze followed by layers of plaster of Paris. Pang was wheeled to a room several minutes later. Gates and Jack followed them to make sure he was settled in and comfortable, as much as he could be with his face in a cast.

Outside the door, Jack let Gates have it. "Why the hell did you do that?" he asked. "You could've killed your own partner and the show's lead pilot. Then where would we be?"

"This is none of your damn business, Jack," Gates said. "Your job is to fly planes and make money. This is between me and Pang, so butt out."

Gates walked over to Pang and told him that he would check in on him tomorrow, then left for the hotel. Pang nodded, then fell fast asleep.

Before he left the hospital, Jack stopped to talk to the doctor. "Excuse me, Doctor, could I please have a word with you?"

The doctor nodded, and he and Jack stepped aside where no one could hear them.

"This is kind of a touchy situation for us, if you know what I mean?" Jack said. "We're in town for just a short time, and we need this gig to make some money. If the police learn of this and the press catch wind of it, our business could be ruined. Do you understand what I'm saying?"

The doctor nodded.

"This is an internal affair, and we would appreciate it if you and your staff would keep this little incident to yourselves. Some of our fliers send home money to family, me included," Jack said.

"I understand," the doctor said. "The report will read that he got slugged hard stopping a fight and fell into sand."

"Thank you, sir," Jack said gratefully.

"I'll let it go . . . this time," the doctor said, and walked off.

"Thank you, sir. I'll stop by tomorrow to check on him," Jack said.

On the way back to the hotel, Jack decided he and the rest of the gang needed to discuss the matter. It was nearly midnight by then, so it would have to wait until the next morning when he'd had time to think things over. He tiptoed past the Gateses' room and stopped at the door to listen. To his relief, it was quiet.

The next morning, Jack, Judge at his side, got the gang together and laid out everything as plainly as possible to the guys.

"Did you all hear the ruckus last night?" he asked.

"I damn sure did," Al said. "I was reading this book and had come to a part that said, 'and George, seeing a suspicious figure outside the door, fired twice,' and I'll be damned if I didn't hear gunshots. Scared the shit out of me. I ducked under my bed and didn't come out for an hour."

The guys got a kick out of that, and Jack had to admit that he thought it was funny, but he quickly got down to business.

"Well, it was Gates who fired those shots—at Pang. He got drunk last night and came undone. Again. It was really bad this time. Gates slugged Pang in the face so hard it fractured his jaw, and then the damn fool shot at him. Gates had to take him to the hospital. It's a wonder he didn't kill Pang. According to Hazel, he could have if he'd wanted to. I don't know what to think. He was drunk as a bootlegger."

"Gates threatened to fire me," Mickey said. "He and Daws had already been drinking some and hit that poor ole feller behind the desk last night."

Daws lowered his head and stepped off to the side.

They had picked up a new pilot in Easton named Wilmer Stultz. Ive looked at him and explained. "Gates and Daws tend to go on these benders. This is the worst since I've been on board, though." Stultz just shrugged.

"Hurting Pang like he did was too much," Jack said. "I don't know about you guys, but I'm getting pretty damned tired of this."

"We don't need Gates," someone said. "Why don't we just form our own group? We have enough experience."

Some of them were of the same mind. "I don't know about that," Jack said. "We would have to get people like Jim and Al and Daws, and get our own mechanics and vehicles. Let's go see Pang to see what he wants to do."

Jack turned and started to leave, the others following him, but then he turned back. "Oh, the doc and I had a chat last night. He won't report the incident to the police, and for the record, Pang got slugged stopping a fight and fell in some sand."

Jack looked fiercely at Daws. "You snoop around the press room to make sure nobody has caught wind of this, and *you* mind your p's and q's."

Daws nodded meekly.

"When we get to the hospital," Jack continued, "Ive, you and Freddie distract whoever you need to so I can sneak Judge in. He's the best medicine for Pang right now."

At the hospital, Pang's eyes lit up at the sight of Judge. Judge jumped on his bed but was confused that he couldn't lick Pang's face, so he barked. Pang and all the guys shushed the dog, and Judge lay contentedly beside his master. The guys lined up alongside the bed. A nurse looked in, surveyed the room suspiciously, then left.

Duke took one look at Pang and said, "Damn, Pang, you look worse than Jack said." All Pang could do was roll his eyes to express the misery he was feeling.

"I took Gates's gun, and he'll never get it back as long as I'm around," Jack said. "What do you want us to do? We'll quit if you want, or we'll tell Gates to scram and buy him out."

Pang picked up a pad and pencil from the bedside stand and wrote a message.

Jack read aloud what Pang had scribbled to the group. "'Don't bust up the group. Go back to work.'"

"Okay, if that's what you want, that's what we'll do," Jack said, and Pang nodded. They left him to his pain and to his thoughts. The group had a show to do without their number one pilot. They wouldn't let him down.

CHAPTER 10
OFF TO THE RACES

Poster of the Gates Flying Circus, 1925. *Courtesy of Cindy Weigand.*

October 1925
Trenton, New Jersey

Their next stop on the way to the National Air Races was Trenton, New Jersey. Under the auspices of the *Trenton Times*, the first thing they did was drop newspapers with tickets in them. Jack had to do this ahead of schedule because of the weather. It was supposed to rain. Afterwards, they flew around for people to guess their altitude then skedaddled back to the airfield. After some typical stunting, Jack took Duke up to the delight of the spectators.

The biggest deal for Jack was that he was going to fly in an exhibition for a trophy the *Times* was giving away on October 11. Jack, Pang, Freddie, Eddie Brooks, and Eddie Bond were scheduled to enter the race. Bond was new to the circus. Pang's jaw had healed well enough, and he was determined to compete even though his face was still bandaged. The rules were simple. They would fly for fifteen minutes and perform military and stunt maneuvers of their choice. During this time, they weren't allowed drop lower than three hundred feet. The competitors kept secret the maneuvers that they would fly. A couple of army fliers and one amateur were the judges.

The newspaper announced the contest ahead of time. The article described each of them, but Jack always homed in on what was said about him.

Dare Devils Fly Today for Times' Trophy.

Pilot Ashcraft, called 'Big Jack' is six feet tall and husky. Because of his enormous strength, he usually pilots the plane on which Diavalo does his stunts. It takes muscles to keep the stick of an airplane upright when a man weighing 175 pounds is playing around on the far end of the top wing. He had over-seas flying service.

Bond dropped out at the last minute, so that left just four of them. Jack thought he could hold his own against Lund and

Brooks, but he was worried about Pang. They hadn't competed since Pang beat him in the race over New Orleans. Having worked with him and watched him fly for nearly a year, Jack knew not to underestimate the man or get too confident. Jack was the next to the last to go. Pang was last. For some reason, the time limit was changed to ten minutes.

Lund and Brooks performed stunts that were very good, but Jack noticed a few flaws and was certain the army judges would as well. Jack was confident he could outperform them. He would have to give it all that he had, because Pang would follow him. For the competition, Jack had decided not to plan the maneuvers ahead of time, but to just do what he felt like doing and pull out all the stops. He knew the routines so well that he could practically do them blindfolded. The paper described his performance:

Ashcraft uncorked an amazing series of loops, spins, and dives. He was vigorously applauded by the crowd as his mighty plane landed.

Jack delighted in that show of appreciation, for he thought it would be his only reward. Stepping out on the wing, he waved and waved to the crowd as they applauded with a standing ovation with whistles and cheers. He couldn't get enough.

Finally, the spectators settled down and it was Pang's turn to fly. Watching him made Jack nervous, because he knew what the guy could do and knew he was doing a damn good job. Pang didn't hold anything back, and his performance was flawless as far as Jack could tell. Jack's heart sank as he watched, especially when Pang flew by upside down past the bleachers. As usual, the crowd cheered raucously. Jack just knew he was beat, but he had given it his best shot. Then came the word that Pang had been eliminated because he'd flown eleven seconds over the ten-minute time limit. Jack was declared the winner. The speaker called Jack over to the stand, held up his arm, and officially announced him the winner, then handed Jack a handsome loving cup trophy. He receive it the next day for keeps after it had been engraved. On it were the words:

> "*TIMES* FLYING TROPHY
> AWARDED FOR FIRST PRIZE
> MILITARY AND FANCY FLYING
> JOHN W. ASHCRAFT
> GATES FLYING CIRCUS
> TRENTON, N.J., OCT. 11 "25"

Pang was a good sport about it. "Good flying, Jack. You deserved to win."

"I learned from the best," Jack said.

"Guess I was the one who got a little too excited. We're even now," Pang said with a crooked grin and strode off.

Jack decided then he needed to expand his horizons beyond the circus at some point, but flying with Gates, he was seeing the country. More importantly, he was making lots of contacts with pilots and businesspeople. He was also reconnecting with aviators that he hadn't seen in a while and was making darn good money. Plus, he was winning trophies. Yes, sir, his future looked bright.

While he was having fun in Trenton, the National Air Races were gearing up at Mitchel Field on Long Island. The newspaper said that planes from all over the country were gathering at the field. They expected five hundred. There were a lot of races scheduled, about ten or so, and even an "On to New

York" race just to get to there. Another article highlighted the main event, a simulated battle. There would be three groups of fifteen planes each. The attack group was from Kelly Field, San Antonio, Texas; the pursuit group was from Selfridge Field, Mt. Clemens, Michigan; and the bombardment group was from Langley Field, Hampton, Virginia.

The whole plan was based on the supposition that an enemy had blockaded the navy on the Pacific by blowing up the Panama Canal. The American fliers would search for and discover an enemy naval fleet with aircraft carriers that could launch one hundred planes. The theoretical enemy base would be at Chesapeake Bay, but the American planes wouldn't "discover" them before Saturday, which was the last day of the races. There would be dropping of bombs, pursuit planes, and laying of smoke screens.

The planes would simulate a bomb attack on the enemy fleet after the races were over on Monday. It would be great fun to watch the most advanced military planes do their work. Major Hap Arnold gave the details of the war maneuvers, but the main guy running that portion of the races was Brigadier General James E. Fechet. His chief of staff was Major Carl Spaatz, who Jack remembered from the war. He'd been decorated for bringing down five Krauts.

October 1925
National Air Races, Mitchel Field, Long Island, New York

From Trenton, they flew to Mitchel Field. The National Air Races were scheduled for the eighth through the thirteenth, but had to be postponed when a gale with winds that would have competed with a Kansas storm blew in. Winds up to seventy-two miles per hour swept through the area, blowing over planes, and knocking down tents. The place was a shambles, but everyone pitched in to get everything in order and repair damaged planes. The races would go on, but the start was delayed until Monday.

Anybody who was anybody in aviation was there. The most famous was Orville Wright himself. Jack said hello and got his autograph. Plane designers Glenn Curtiss and Tony Fokker were there. Casey Jones flew a Curtiss Oriole in a race. Walter Beech and Clarence Chamberlin were there. When Jack saw Chamberlin, he looked around for a guy he knew Chamberlin had been flying with that people called "The Black Eagle of Harlem." Sure enough, not far away was Hubert Fauntleroy Julian himself, and he was a dandy. He looked fine in his brown suit with green bowtie, flying helmet, and goggles. He saw Jack looking at him and nodded; Jack nodded back. Seemed like a nice guy. He flew a Bellanca. Seeing Julian reminded Jack of Eugene Bullard, who'd flown for France during the war and was known for killing a German flier.

While he was musing, Jack noticed a Negro woman in a long leather aviator's coat, unbuttoned. Underneath she had a hunter green military-style jacket, a silk scarf wound around her neck, tan jodhpurs, and tall laced boots. To complete her attire, she wore a fisherman-type hat with an eagle with spread wings on it. She looked around as if searching for someone, and when she spotted Julian, she walked over to him. They greeted one another warmly, chatted for a few minutes, then left together. Jack guessed that the woman was Bessie Coleman—Queen Bess, as they called her—who had set up headquarters and was flying in Houston.

Others there were Roy Ahearn and George Haldeman. Roscoe Turner flew in with his lion named Gilmore. He was quite a character. One guy Jack remembered meeting when he flew out west was Charles Lindbergh. Some people called him "Slim." He was a quiet sort and stayed to himself. He flew a

Standard in from somewhere. Jimmy Doolittle performed amazing exhibitions throughout the week.

There was quite of variety of airplanes, big and small, on display. One little plane Jack thought was just funny, and that was the Dormoy Bathtub with its 20-horsepower motorcycle engine. All it consisted of was a compartment for the pilot and a tail, with nothing much in between. Jack with his bone and sinew couldn't have fit in the silly thing. One big plane was the Huff-Daland XHB-1. It had an open cockpit for a pilot and inside seating for passengers. Jack thought that odd. Why not get the pilot out of the elements as well?

Gates and Daws had gone ahead to make some arrangements. Since they had an agreement with Texaco and this was a national event, Pang, Gates, and Daws thought it crucial that the circus be there. They were also the largest flying circus on the East Coast, and their reputation preceded them. Jack had to admit, their bright red Standards with the Texaco emblem looked impressive lined up on the airfield. Other pilots admired them, and thousands of spectators milled around them and the other pilots, asking for autographs. At the same time, they looked like the antiques they were next to the modern aircraft.

There were also a few nice-looking women pilots, whom people called aviatrixes. All the guys took notice of the gals. Some of the ladies seemed serious about flying, but Jack got the impression that others were there to get attention from the male pilots. The numbers were certainly in their favor. There was one that he was particularly impressed with.

Jack and Pang were moseying around when they heard a young girl's voice. "Hey, Mr. Pangborn. Pang. Remember me?"

The two turned around to see a young girl running their way. She didn't look more than twelve or thirteen.

"Well, I'll be darned," Pang said. "If it isn't little Elinor! You've grown some since I last saw you." He gave her a quick hug, then put his arm around her shoulders. "How the heck are you?"

"Doing swell, just swell," she said. "How about you?"

"Can't complain. You still flying?" Pang asked.

"Oh, yes, sir. Every chance I get," she said.

"Wait a minute," Jack said. "You're not saying this little thing can fly an airplane, are you? No offense, ma'am."

"That's exactly what I'm saying," Pang said. "She started when she was ten. I know because I taught her. I had to put blocks on the rudder pedals so she could reach them."

"Well, I'll be damned," Jack said. "Excuse my language."

"Oh, that's all right. You can't walk into a hangar without hearing bad words," Elinor said.

"Gentlemen," Pang said to the Gates personnel around him. "This is Miss Elinor Smith. Elinor, I want you to meet some of my flying buddies with Gates Flying Circus." He then proceeded to introduce the crew. She shook each of their hands. Hers was tiny, but she had a firm, confident grip.

"So, Pang here taught you to fly, huh?" Jack teased. "Well, I think you need to get a real pilot to teach you the right way."

"Oh, Pang did just fine," she said seriously. "So did Freddie. He taught my daddy, too, and flew him all over the place."

"Freddie Lund?" Jack asked.

"Yes, sir," Elinor said.

Jack looked on in disbelief.

"You guys remember this little lady's name. E-l-i-n-o-r Smith," Pang said. "Not only is she a pilot, but she's also a darn good one and will make her mark in history. You'll see."

"Thanks, Pang," she said. "I've got to go now. Daddy's waiting for me. We want to check out all the planes. He's thinking about buying one. Boy, is he going to be surprised that I saw you. Tell Freddie hello for me. Bye, now." She trotted off.

If Pang said that she was a good pilot, Jack believed him, but he was still amazed.

As impressive as Jack thought their troupe was, he still couldn't believe the modern military planes there. The army had Curtiss R3C-1s, P-1s, and PW-8s. The navy was showing off its Curtiss R3C-1s as well. He couldn't get enough of them. They were fast and agile. Pilots who entered flew four times in a circuit around pylons—faster than he had even dreamed about.

The fastest was four miles in a minute. Then they "demonstrated" barrel rolls, loops, and tailspins, maneuvers the circus did every show, but their pilots did them faster. First Lieutenant Cyrus Bettis won the race having reached 249 miles an hour. In addition to his exhibitions, Lieutenant Jimmy Doolittle won the Schneider trophy flying the army's seaplane.

Jack met the infamous General Billy Mitchell. To Jack, the new planes only confirmed what Mitchell was saying, and that was that the United States needed a separate air force. If the US had planes like these, other countries darn sure had them as well, or would soon, and the US needed them to defend the country. It was also obvious that aviation was progressing and leaving the circus behind in so many ways. Their ships were getting old and looked it. And with the new regulations they kept hearing about, he wondered how long an outfit like theirs could stay in business.

Jack flew with a great bunch of guys, and he thought he was the star, but they all shared the spotlight. Truth be known, people came out half hoping to see a crash. If anyone was a "star," it was Duke. It was then that he decided he would give the circus another year or so to save up some money, but his long-range plan was to strike out on his own. One of his goals was to enter a National Air Race in a couple of years. As much as he loved the guys, he knew that eventually he would have to go his own way.

After their appearance at the races, they were scheduled to fly back to eastern Pennsylvania for some exhibitions. The weather was getting too cold and unpredictable to fly much, and they planned to perform engine overhauls and other maintenance on the planes before heading south for the winter season. Heaven knew they'd had a workout the last few months. Their schedule had been grueling, and it showed on the ships.

Jack and the other pilots gathered back where the Gates planes were parked to fly back to Curtiss Field. Jack was putting on his helmet when a model plane hit him on the back of the head and fell to the ground at his feet. He picked it up and was examining it closely when a boy ran up. He looked about ten years old, with ginger hair and freckles across his nose and cheeks. He wore knicker pants, a blue shirt with suspenders, a tweed jacket, and brown shoes with argyle socks.

"I'm sorry, sir," the boy said. "I guess I threw it a little harder than I thought."

"Don't worry about it," Jack said. "I like a man with enthusiasm. What's your name?"

"Billy. Billy Racey."

"That's a fine name for a young fellow like you," Jack said.

Just then, a man ran up to them, out of breath. "Billy, I've told you not to run off like that! I didn't see where you went for a time! He's not bothering you, is he, sir?"

"Not at all," Jack said. "He was just showing me this fine model he built." Jack handed it back to the boy.

Suddenly, the boy's eyes widened, and he pointed to Jack's plane. "Are you the Cowboy Aviator?"

Jack smiled and bowed slightly. "At your service."

"Gee," Billy said, "I saw your picture in the newspaper. You're my favorite because you're from Texas! Will you sign my model?"

"Be glad to," Jack said, and Billy handed the plane back to him.

"I'm going to set the record straight, though," Jack said, searching for a pencil in the pocket of his jacket. "I was born in Oklahoma Territory and grew up in Kansas. I was transferred around Texas when I joined the army."

"But you lived in Texas. That's good enough for me," Billy said, and Jack laughed.

Jack found a pencil in his jacket pocket, signed the model, and handed it back to Billy.

"What do you say, Billy?"

"Thank you!"

"Thank you, Mr. Ashcraft. You've been very kind," Billy's father said. "Now we must get home to dinner, Billy."

As they took off, Jack noticed a woman walking around, stopping and talking to the pilots and crewmen, and scribbling on a notepad. He watched her out of the corner of his eye as she strolled from plane to plane. From the clothes she wore and the way she carried herself, Jack could tell that she was a different class of woman than usually came around the fliers. Her wavy auburn hair was cut short in a bob that was the fashion. And she wore trousers and a knee-length leather coat. Some leered at her, while others acted annoyed at her questions and gave her smart-aleck answers. Some tried to impress her.

Jack would be more than happy to talk to her if she came up to his plane. He pretended to work on it, all the while watching her out of the corner of his eye, but she surprised him by coming up on his other side and introduced herself.

"How are you today, Jack Ashcraft?" she said in a husky, melodic voice. "My name is Mavis Perkins."

Jack rose up quickly and bumped his head on the engine cover. He stepped down rubbing his head and she extended her hand.

He wasn't accustomed to shaking hands with a woman, especially two in one day. To his surprise, she had a firm handshake. "How do you know my name?"

"It's on your airplane," she said matter-of-factly.

"Of course," he said, trying to laugh it off, all the while feeling like a teenage schoolboy and a little out of his league. He'd never gotten nervous talking to a woman before.

"It's nice to meet the 'Cowboy Aviator' in person," she said, smiling.

"The Cowboy Aviator, brave and glorious, at your service, ma'am," Jack said with a bow. "How did you hear about me?"

"How could I not? You're in the *Times* and other newspapers a lot, and circus posters are everywhere. You certainly have an active front man," she said.

"Daws does his job really well."

"I do a little flying myself," she said.

"Is that right? Maybe you could take me up sometime," Jack said, trying to tease her, but she didn't take the bait.

"You seem like a nice guy, Jack. Let's just keep this pilot to pilot, shall we?" she said.

"What kind of plane do you have?" Jack asked, changing the subject.

"I fly a Waco 9 that I co-own with my father. How about I fly over Saturday morning, and I'll take you for a flight? There shouldn't be much going on then. I'll give you a tour of my city like you've never seen. If there's fog in the morning, I'll see you as soon as it lifts."

"That would be great. I'd love to see New York City from the air," Jack said.

"See you then. Bye, now," she said and walked away.

Duke walked over just as she left. "Damn, Jack. Who was that? She's a real looker."

"Name's Mavis Perkins, and you're right, she's one of the best-looking dames I've ever met. And classy. We're going flying Saturday," Jack said.

"You work fast. Think Pang will let you take a plane up?" he asked.

"She's flying me," Jack said and walked off, enjoying the surprised look on Duke's face.

CHAPTER 11
MAVIS

Clipping from and undated newspaper clipping,
circa 1925. *Courtesy of Cindy Weigand.*

October 1925
New York City from the Air

The next morning, Jack looked out the window of his room to see a thick fog and groaned. He could barely see the outline of the building across the street. Hoping it would lift soon, he got up and showered to get ready for his flight with Mavis. He scrubbed his hands and fingers and under his nails until they were raw to get the oil and dirt from underneath them, then rubbed his calluses with Vaseline.

He pulled out his best leather flight jacket, a clean white shirt, and a pair of recently cleaned and pressed breeches. He buffed his tall boots so that they shone like new. Then he got dressed.

It was still foggy and didn't show signs of lifting anytime soon, but he wanted to be ready when she came, if she came. Duke sat on his bed and just shook his head and laughed.

"You're going to a lot of trouble for nothing, you know," he said.

"Maybe, maybe not. We'll see, but I think the joke's going to be on you," Jack said. "I want to be ready."

To keep himself occupied, he checked the weather periodically. No matter how many times he checked, it was the same. Fog. He tried reading the newspaper but couldn't concentrate on the words. Contenting himself with looking at the pictures and reading the captions, he soon tossed it on the bed. Lighting his fifth cigarette of the morning, he gazed out the window again. No matter how many times he looked out the window, the heavy mist wasn't going to dissipate by him willing it to happen.

"Hell, I'm going to the hangar," he said, squashing the cigarette butt in the ashtray.

At the hangar, the mechanics had the panels of the planes opened, tinkering with the motors. Parts were everywhere, but carefully laid out so that they could be inspected before they were put back in. Jack decided to look over the struts and wires to take his mind off the weather. It didn't look like he and Mavis were going to do much flying that day. Busying himself with the planes, he didn't notice the fog lifting and the day getting brighter. Then he heard a motor overhead. His heart started to pound. Excitedly, he rushed outside.

A blue and yellow Waco swooped over the hangar and circled back to land. The pilot cut the motor, and it rolled up to the hangar door and stopped. Out jumped Mavis, wearing a long leather flight jacket, riding britches, and a white flying helmet with just the right number of auburn curls sticking out around her porcelain face. As far as he could tell, she had the right amount of everything. Mavis smiled when she saw Jack and waved. "Hey, Cowboy Jack. You ready for a tour of New York?"

"Darn tootin'," he answered.

"Darn tootin'?" she laughed. "That's so funny. What does that mean? I've never heard that expression before."

"It means you're absolutely right. You'll probably hear a lot of expressions you never heard coming from me," he said, laughing. "I've got to check out this beauty."

Jack took a few minutes to appreciate the ship and look it over from propeller to rudder. He liked the plane, but he also wanted to check out everything to make sure it was in good shape.

"Don't worry, Jack," Mavis said. "I checked everything this morning while I was fogged in. I'm not going to fly an unsafe plane, but suit yourself."

"Just admiring this fine ship," he said, not letting on that she had figured out what he was up to.

"You know what it is," she said. "Dad wanted newer technology, but didn't want to spend a lot. It handles like a dream, especially after that old Jenny that I learned to fly in. The president of the company brags that I'm flying it. You know the line, 'If a woman can fly it, anyone can.'"

"Not me. I know that not just anyone can fly," he told her. "You have to have a feel for it. You know, have a rapport with the plane. The plane sure as hell doesn't know who's at the controls. It sure is a handsome ship. Let's go. I'm anxious to see what it'll do and glad to be a passenger for a change."

They were about to climb aboard when another plane flew in. Mavis looked over at the Curtiss Hawk and waved to the pilot, who waved back.

"Come on, Jack. I want you to meet a friend of mine," Mavis said.

He could hardly believe it. Another pretty woman climbed out of the cockpit.

"Well, I'll be damned. I'm definitely not in Kansas anymore," he said.

"Jack, I want you to meet my friend Frances Harrell. She's a fellow Texan," Mavis said.

"Whereabouts in Texas are you from?" he asked, shaking her hand.

"Born in Del Rio, but was living in Houston before I moved here," Frances said. "How about you?"

"Texarkana and other parts while I was in the service," Jack replied.

"Not only is Frances a good pilot, but she's also a darned good mechanic. Works for Curtiss on the exhibition team," Mavis said. "She's my go-to person on all things mechanical, especially when I think the guys are trying to get money from me or pull my leg, as you would probably say."

"What are you two up to?" Frances asked.

"I was just about to give Jack a tour of New York from the air," Mavis said. "Come join us."

"As tempting as that is, I have business to take care of," Frances said. "You two have fun."

"Been flying long?" Jack asked as they walked back to the Waco.

"Soloed last week," she said, laughing when she saw Jack's reaction. "Relax. I've been flying a couple of years, but no stunting." She hopped into the back cockpit while Jack climbed into the front.

"Are you nervous flying with a woman?" she asked.

"Not in the least," he said. Besides, he knew that he could take over if he needed to.

"Ever been to New York?" she asked.

"A few times, when I was in the army, but I've never seen it from the air."

"You're going to love it," she said.

"Hey, I'm not flying unless I can return the favor," he said, pulling his goggles down.

"Relax. You can take me up sometime and show me some stunting," she said. "I pretty much fly straight and level in fair weather. I don't have time to fly as much I would like."

Mavis hit the ignition, revved up the engine, and made a near perfect takeoff, and they were in the air. Leveling out at about five hundred feet, she banked left and headed south over the Upper Bay and headed toward Liberty Island. When they got to Lady Liberty, she throttled back, descended to two hundred feet, and made a couple of lazy circles around the grand ole lady. The crisp fall sunshine glinted off the water.

Jack relaxed and started to enjoy himself. He looked the statue in the eye and gave her a proud salute. Then he raised his hand as if he was holding a torch and looked back to see if Mavis was watching. She laughed and pulled up into a steep climbing turn across the Lower Bay, headed for Manhattan.

Gaining altitude, she flew toward the city. Never in his life had he looked down on buildings so tall. The sight fascinated him. Then he thought of Billy Mitchell and got an idea.

As they flew over them, Mavis pointed out points of interest. A lot of them he recognized from pictures. There was the Flatiron Building and the Woolworth Building, which he remembered to be about eight hundred feet tall. With winter setting in, there was a lighted billboard that caught his eye. In giant letters it read, "It's June in Miami!" *That's good,* he thought, because they were headed to Florida after Christmas to take advantage of the land boom. *We should fly by that and get pictures,* he thought.

She banged on the plane again and pointed to the inside of the cockpit and wiggled the wings, asking Jack if he wanted to fly the plane.

He had flown lots of biplanes, but that ship wasn't like anything he had ever flown before. The stick was small and smooth, designed for its purpose, not like grasping a baseball bat. The plane responded instantly to his commands. He took the airplane up and down and turned slightly right, then left. Once he reached the north end of the island, he circled over the harbor and retraced their flight path. It was a wonderful machine, and he vowed to buy one as soon as he could.

Mavis let him fly for about fifteen minutes, then jiggled the stick to indicate that she was taking over. He wasn't ready for the flight to be over, and it wasn't. She headed up the Hudson River for a short distance before banking to head south back to Curtiss Field. Mavis tapped Jack on the back and mouthed, "Broadway," and Jack nodded that he understood.

Mavis started out at a reasonable altitude, but the closer she got to the south end of Manhattan Island, the lower she descended. Jack watched the buildings flash by and saw people hanging out the windows, watching them go by. Some smiled and waved, some had surprised expressions on their faces.

Others shook their fists. By the time she reached Battery Park, her altitude was only two hundred feet. Then she banked left and headed back to Curtiss Field at about five hundred feet.

After they landed, Mavis cut the switch and the plane rolled to a stop. Out of the airplane, Mavis pulled off her helmet and shook out her hair. "That was darn good flying," Jack said. "I can't believe you flew so low down Broadway. Can't you get in trouble for that?"

"You can, but it's worth the risk once in a while when you're trying to impress someone," she said, grinning impishly. "Besides, it's Saturday morning. People are just now getting up and thinking about what to do tonight. If anyone calls to complain, my father knows people in City Hall. He'll take care of it. Won't be the first time," she said with that same grin.

Frances walked over to them and looked at Jack. "How was the flight?"

"Good. Real good, and more than I expected," he said.

Frances looked at Mavis. "You flew low down Broadway, didn't you?"

"Maybe."

"When Jimmy Walker sends the law after you, you can hide out at my place," Frances said.

"I may have to take you up on that," Mavis laughed.

"I've got to go back to Roosevelt Field for something," Frances said, giving her friend a hug. "Nice to meet you, Jack. Bye for now."

Mavis turned to Jack. "Now, would you like for me to show you around my fair city from the ground?" she said. "Unlike Midwestern towns that roll up their streets at six in the evening, New York is just waking up."

"Sounds good to me. Just get me back by ten tomorrow morning," Jack joked.

"You're a big boy, Jack. You can take care of yourself," she said. "I'll fly back to Roosevelt Field and get my car. Meet me back here in an hour, and we'll drive into the city."

After she took off, the few guys at the field started giving Jack a hard time about flying with such a classy dame. He ran back to his room, showered quickly, and changed into regular pants, shoes, and his military-style tweed jacket. He hoped it would be okay. He didn't have a suit or anything better to wear.

A Night in the City

Mavis was waiting for Jack at her car, looking elegant as she leaned against the canary yellow convertible. The top button of her coat was open to reveal a pink silk blouse. A matching cloche hat had replaced her flying helmet. Jack still couldn't believe his luck and wondered what she saw in him.

"Climb in," she said. "We'll stop at my place, and I'll change before we go on into town."

"Nice car. I confess, I don't know what this is," Jack said. He gave it a going-over just like he'd done with her plane. His hands slid over the smooth surface of the body and across the hood and trunk. "She's a beauty."

"It's a Stutz 695 Bearcat. It was a gift from my father for my twenty-fifth birthday," she said. "It's a consolation gift. I wanted my own plane, but he said he could only keep one plane in the air. He's an investment attorney. One of his clients went bankrupt and couldn't pay in cash, so he gave Dad this car. I told him if I couldn't have a plane of my own, he had to give me the car. He's such a softy. Want to drive it?"

"You bet I do," Jack said. Mavis tossed him the key, and they were off.

With Mavis as navigator, Jack drove through the city to her apartment, where a Negro man in a maroon uniform with epaulets and gold braiding on the shoulders stepped down to open the door for her. "How are you this fine afternoon, Miss Mavis?"

"I'm well, Gerald, thank you," she said. "How are Mabel and the boys?"

Gerald smiled a big, toothy smile. "Just fine. Just fine. Thank you, ma'am."

"This is my friend Jack Ashcraft, a pilot with the Gates Flying Circus," she said, and Gerald nodded cordially.

"Nice to meet you, Gerald," Jack said, reaching out to shake his hand. Gerald hesitated, then awkwardly extended his.

"Thank you, sir. I read about you in the newspaper," he said.

"Keep watching the paper," Jack said. "You'll see more of us."

"Yes, sir. I'll be sure to do that," Gerald answered.

Mavis smiled and handed him a couple of bills. "Would you please call a taxi to be here in an hour?"

"Glad to, ma'am. Glad to," Gerald said.

Inside, they took the elevator to the third floor and walked down the hallway to her apartment. He looked around at the wallpaper, trimmings, and carpet. The girls he usually met after air shows took him to beer joints and houses on the edge of town. He certainly wasn't used to a doorman and formality in an apartment building in downtown New York City. He wondered how well-heeled her family was. And how well-heeled she was.

"Be out in a few. Why don't you pour us something to drink while I'm getting ready." She pointed to the bar and disappeared.

Never one to turn down a snort, he obliged from her supply. She had everything he could imagine—vodka, rum, whiskey, brandy, sherry—and some he had never heard of. It certainly wasn't cheap bootleg stuff like he was used to, either.

He couldn't make up his mind, so he tasted several. Finally, he found a bottle of brandy, something he recognized and hadn't had in a while, and poured two glasses.

When he heard the shower go on, he wished he could see through the wall, but got ahold of himself and roamed around the place, feeling awkward and more than a little out of his league. Mavis had fancy furniture and nice wallpaper with paintings in gold frames hung on the walls. He particularly liked one of a green meadow with mountains in the background. There was a yellow plane flying just on the edge of the ridge of the foothills and a touch of autumn color in the trees.

"Like it?" she asked.

Startled—he hadn't heard her come up behind him—he turned his head slightly to reply. "Sure do. It reminds me of the hills where we flew in Pennsylvania."

"It's upstate New York, actually. After I soloed, I wanted to fly some cross-country, so I flew up there," she said. "I painted it to remind me of the occasion. It was so beautiful."

"You can paint too?" Jack said.

"If you can call it that," she laughed, her hand on his shoulder. Her face next to his.

"You have just the right amount of color in the trees," Jack said, pointing. "We're so busy flying that we don't have a chance to appreciate such things."

"You never see things the same way once you see them framed by the wings of a biplane, do you?" she said.

"You're right about that," Jack said. He turned to look at Mavis and tried not to stare.

She had slipped into a dress the color of champagne, sequins on the skirt, and was putting on dangly pearl earrings. She looked even more gorgeous than before.

Suddenly, he felt shabby. "Do I need to be more dressed up?" he asked, handing her the drink.

"You're fine," she said, patting his shoulder and taking the glass. "Mm, mm, brandy, my favorite. Good choice."

Her voice was low, husky, and melodic. He slipped his right arm clumsily around her slim waist, then let it drop. He had always known how to act around women, but Mavis was a lady, and he felt like the country bumpkin he was.

Smoothly, she moved away from him and laughed. "A dress isn't my first choice. I can get away with wearing trousers at the airfield and out on Long Island, but people still frown on them in town, especially in the evening. Silly, isn't it? Painting is my hobby when I have time, but flying takes most of my time outside of work. And most of my extra resources." She picked up her purse and handed Jack her long fur coat. "Shall we go?"

Jack placed the coat on her shoulders. She adjusted the coat, and they were about to walk out the door when the telephone rang. "Damn!" she muttered under her breath, picking up the receiver. "Hello. Hi, Daddy. Yes, I went flying today."

"Yes, there was someone with me," she said, smiling at Jack. "I took a pilot friend from out of town for a tour of the city. He loved it.

"What? Did I fly low? Maybe a little." She paused. "No, Daddy, I don't think I was *that* low." She looked at Jack and winked.

"Mr. Walker called you himself, huh?" she said.

"Oh, Daddy, I'd really appreciate it if you'd smooth things over with Mr. Walker for me. Tell him it won't happen again." She crossed her fingers. "I'll go by and talk to him personally tomorrow if you want me to.

"Oh, thank you, Daddy. I love you too. Bye," Mavis said and hung up.

"Everything okay?" Jack asked.

"Everything will be fine," she said, grinning smugly, and they walked out of her apartment.

. . .

Just as she had requested, there was a taxi waiting for them with Gerald holding the door open. "I'm starved, so I thought we'd go to dinner and perhaps dancing afterwards, but I need to call it an early evening," Mavis said.

"Sounds good to me," Jack said, trying to sound confident. She was probably a fantastic dancer, and he just knew a few steps to country tunes.

She had the taxi stop in front of a fancy restaurant. Fancy to him, anyway. Jack was accustomed to diners and cafés where you could get a burger and a couple of near beers for a buck or two. The place they stood in front of probably served the meal in courses and had expensive wine. Trouble was that payday was Monday and he only had about fifty bucks in his wallet.

"Is this where we're going to eat?" Jack asked.

Mavis noticed his hesitancy and sensed that Jack had not come prepared for such a restaurant.

"Actually," she said, pointing to a place across the street with a sign that said *Saul's Diner*, "I was thinking about that place. I haven't been there in ages."

"Looks great to me," Jack said, and she seemed to notice the relieved expression on his face.

"But please promise me you'll order a New York deli sandwich instead of a hamburger," she said. "After all, you are in New York. I doubt if you could get one anyway."

Heads turned when they walked to a booth in the corner. As they waited for their food, Jack looked at her and thought that he had made a big mistake in agreeing to go out with her. He pulled out a cigarette to calm his nerves. Even in a diner, they seemed worlds apart. Obviously, her father didn't own a hardware store in a small town in the Midwest. She pulled out an ivory cigarette holder and inserted a cigarette.

"Here, let me butt you," he said.

"Excuse me?"

"Uh, I'll light yours with mine," he said.

"So where are you really from, Cowboy Jack?" she asked, taking a long pull on her cigarette, blowing the smoke upward between her painted red lips. "I don't detect a Texas accent like the oilmen who come to New York."

Jack laughed. "My early life was pretty simple. My Dad made the Oklahoma Land Run on an old horse named Bird, then Mother followed him there. I was born in Oklahoma Territory, and then my folks moved back to Kansas when I was about thirteen, I guess. Dad runs a hardware store in a little town called Protection."

"How interesting, and quaint. What does this town 'Protection' need protection from?" she asked.

"Something about protection from tariffs, I think. I never thought much about it."

"Do you have brothers and sisters?"

"A passel full—five brothers and five sisters," he said. "I've lost track of nieces and nephews. Haven't been back home in a couple of years."

"We've certainly lived different lives," Mavis said.

"How about you?" Jack asked. "Do you have brothers and sisters?"

"Just a brother. He's an attorney too. Like father, like son," she said.

After a few beers, Jack relaxed and told her his whole life's story about how he'd raced motorcycles before he joined the army as a mechanic, then went to France where he learned to fly. When he got back to the States, he'd bought a surplus Jenny and struck out on his own in Kansas and the West, then in Louisiana and Texas with Buck. Amazingly, she was easy to talk to. She listened intently and seemed to enjoy his stories.

"When Gates and the MacClatchies, and especially the press, heard I'd flown in Texas, I became the 'Cowboy Aviator.' Texans are big, you know. Looks good in the papers and sounds more colorful than being a pilot from Kansas."

"And flying in from Oz doesn't sound like much fun, I suppose," she said, laughing at her own joke. "I find you quite an interesting fellow. How long have you been flying for Gates?"

"Joined up with them in December of '24. But enough about me," Jack said. "Tell me about the woman whose father calls the mayor of New York to ask forgiveness for his daughter flying low down Broadway and gives her a fancy car?"

"He is known in the city, and he's always been a doting father," she said. "I pretty much get whatever I want. I haven't asked for much since I went out on my own, though. Except an airplane."

Mavis laughed that melodious laugh again and took another elegant puff of her cigarette, pursing her lips just right as she exhaled the smoke. Jack squirmed in his seat to settle down.

"I've thought about trading the car in for an airplane but can't part with it. Besides, Dad lets me fly his anytime I want. I've pretty much lived on my own since I graduated from Columbia, but I'm not beneath asking for a favor occasionally, especially when it comes to flying. I thought we had enough lawyers in the family, so I studied journalism and started a newspaper."

She paused and took a sip of beer.

"I can't remember the last time I had beer," she giggled. "Dad and Mother think I need to marry someone who works on Wall Street, but I find them stuffy and quite boring." She put her hand over Jack's. "Frankly, I find having a sandwich in a diner refreshing and more genuine. Those guys are always trying to impress and outdo one another. Believe me, I've been to all the fine restaurants in New York, but I confess that I've never been to Saul's." She looked around the place. "I think it has a certain, what shall I say, charm of its own."

Jack grasped her hand in his and stroked it as gently as he could. Her skin felt as soft as a rose petal. Then suddenly he pulled them away. "Sorry," he said. "My hands get rough. I have to be my own mechanic too."

"Don't be," she said, taking his hands again. "These are strong hands, the hands of a real man."

The waitress brought their sandwiches. He hungrily took a bite and had to admit the Rueben she'd suggested was pretty good.

Afterwards, they strolled along the avenue, her arm through his, walking close to his side. He enjoyed himself as he never had with a woman. She seemed more equal, he guessed because she was a pilot. Heaven knew she had more education. He guessed that she could be what his mother called "head-strong" as well. Maybe that was the reason he liked her car so much. She was a bit of bearcat herself.

Jack pulled the collar up on his topcoat. "Brrr."

"I'm getting cold too," Mavis said. "I know a place where we can dance to warm up. Drinks are on me. This time."

The place was out of the way, but not down some dark alley like the places where he usually went with girls. When she knocked on the door, some guy opened the little window and let them in right away—no secret code, no questions asked. The waitress showed them to a booth in the corner. Along the way, she stopped to talk to people, and she introduced him as Jack, a fellow pilot. Jack smiled and nodded and said, "Nice to meet you," trying not to embarrass either one of them.

They settled into a booth, and Mavis ordered drinks. "So, how good is Cowboy Jack at dancing?"

"I'm afraid I'm better at flying," Jack said.

"We'll see about that," she said, and pulled him out on the dance floor for a slow dance. Pulling his body in close to hers, she gracefully swayed back and forth in perfect rhythm to the music, her thin arms amazingly strong. "Relax, Jack," she said, and before he knew it, he was dancing too. With the feel of her body in his arms and the smell of her expensive perfume, he didn't need alcohol to feel intoxicated.

After two dances, they went back to their table, where they sat close, talked, and did some hangar flying. About eleven thirty, she said she needed to call it a night because she had an early appointment the next morning.

They got a taxi and headed for her apartment. Jack stepped out and opened the door for her. He was expecting it to be the last time he would see her, but to his surprise, she asked, "So, when do I get my plane ride with stunts with you as pilot?"

"How about two weeks from today? We're heading out to New Jersey and Pennsylvania for some quick shows, then coming back here. Say, ten o'clock or whenever the fog lifts? I'll drop you a note," Jack said. "I need to do some shopping, too, and would appreciate your help. I want to get some presents for the family. From New York, we're headed to Florida to take advantage of the land boom, but I hope to squeeze in a trip home if Pang will let me."

"It's a date, then. We'll fly, go shopping, and then go to dinner that night. Be prepared for a *big* time on the town. I'll have a few surprises for you." She gave Jack a kiss on the cheek. "Good night, Cowboy Jack."

CHAPTER 12
AIR DEVILS WILL THRILL OLD GOTHAM

From an undated newspaper clipping, circa 1925.
Courtesy of Cindy Weigand, personal collection.

November 19, 1925
Attack on New York, Day 1

Jack and the circus arrived back in New York late in October. He had sent Mavis a note saying when they would be in town and that he was looking forward to taking her flying and doing some stunting on November 21.

As always, Jack picked up a newspaper to get caught up on the news and thumbed through it on his way to Curtiss Field. The headline caught his eye immediately: *GENERAL MITCHELL CALLED TO WASHINGTON TO STAND TRIAL.*

Then Jack remembered the idea he'd had when flying with Mavis. He rushed to the airfield and ran to the office. Gates, Pang, and Daws were there, discussing the next series of shows.

"Pang," Jack burst out. "I've got a great idea. I got it while flying with Mavis a couple of weeks ago."

"Let's hear it," Pang said.

"You remember at the air races, they had all these simulated attacks," Jack said. He showed them the paper.

Gates leaned forward in his chair, and Daws walked to the front of the desk.

"Go on," Daws said.

"They've called Mitchell to Washington to stand trial," Jack said. "Why don't we simulate an attack on New York to prove Mitchell right? We know the maneuvers from the war."

"I've been thinking about that too," Daws said. "Is it possible to have that many planes flying downtown at the same time?"

"It's a good idea, and yes we can," Pang said.

"Daws, can you get it in the press in time for attacks November 19 and 20?" Gates asked. "That only gives us a couple of weeks to prepare. The planes need to be in tip-top shape."

"Plenty of time," Daws replied, "and I know just the guy. Emile Gauvreau at the *New York Evening Graphic*. He'll eat it up. We can hire this reporter I know, Ed Churchill, to write some great articles for us. He can make a flower show sound like fun. I'll get right on it." He rushed out the door.

"Be sure to let Jimmy Walker know," Jack yelled after him.

All the newspapers were filled with news of General Mitchell's court-martial. The official charge was "insubordination and conduct of a nature to bring discredit upon the military service." His only "crime" was that he had demonstrated that his war-surplus planes and rebuilt bombers could sink cruisers and bomb trains. Everybody Jack had talked to agreed that the charges were bogus, but the army was carrying through with their threat. It was personal for Mitchell too. The pilot of the *Shenandoah*, Zachary Lansdowne, had been a friend of his, and he thought the *Shenandoah* crash could have been avoided.

Jack assembled everybody associated with the circus to give them the news. Bill Wunderlich had recently joined. Pilots and stuntmen were always coming and going. Sometimes the new pilots had to do double duty as wing walkers. Everyone had to be a mechanic.

"The brass is still giving General Mitchell hell. They've called him to Washington for a court-martial," Jack said, holding up the paper. "All he's saying is that the US of A needs a separate air force, and we're going to prove his point."

Jack paused. "Mitchell's said that America can be attacked from the air, and what bigger target is there than New York City? So we're going to 'attack' the city."

"What do you mean 'attack'?" someone asked.

"It's a mock attack, using the same maneuvers we learned in the army. The same maneuvers that we do in every air meet," Jack said. "It'll be a little tricky around skyscrapers, especially if there's wind, but we can do it."

"When is this 'attack' going to take place?" Duke asked.

"Thursday and Friday, the nineteenth and twentieth. The *New York Evening Graphic* is going to play it up big time. A guy named Ed Churchill is going to write articles for us.

"We're still working out the details, but at noon, we'll take off from here and fly in formation over Manhattan. Me, Freddie, and Eddie will fly the planes on Thursday. Duke, you'll stunt from my plane; Bill, you'll stunt from Freddie's. Eddie, Churchill will ride with you so he can record all the action. Go easy on him until you know what he can take.

"First, we'll fly over Battery Park and do some loops, rolls, whip stalls, things like that," he told them. "Texaco has an office there, so this will be our way of saying thanks for supplying our gas. We couldn't do what we do without 'em. After that, we'll fly in tandem down Broadway, do a few loops together, and then break up and do our own thing. Remember, we'll be flying over lots of people. Keep your wits about you."

"The wind will be doing crazy things around those buildings too," Freddie said.

Jack nodded agreement. "On Friday, we'll attack again. Me, Pang, Wilmer, and Freddie will fly. Duke and Bill will stunt."

"Hot damn! A month with the circus and I get to attack New York City. What a gig!" Stultz said, and they all laughed.

"The second day, we'll stunt over Times Square, Forty-Second Street, and Central Park. Make sure the mechanics check and double-check your planes. Go into town sometime before then and check everything out from street level. Lots of people will be watching, so we don't want any foul-ups. We never have before. Gates and Daws will be watching from the street. We want to make everyone proud of us and make an impression. Any questions?"

"Can we get a ride with that girl pilot who gave you a personal tour?" Eddie teased.

Jack looked at him and grinned. "Nope."

The headline in the newspaper on Wednesday before the day of the first attack announced the event. The editor of the paper told Ed Churchill to interview Jack, which he did on Tuesday and took some photos. Jack read part of it to the guys as they gathered for their morning briefing. It always amused Jack how reporters portrayed them.

GRAPHIC'S Circus Stuntsters [sic] Plan Daring Exploits.

Ever see a real circus in the air? Tomorrow, at Battery Park, when THE GRAPHIC-Gates Flying Circus gets under way at 12:15 p.m., you'll have your chance. Keep your eye peeled as you go out to lunch and you will see daredevils walking across the wings of planes, dizzy loops, long dives, and lazy 'falling leaves' as the educational and thrilling events under the auspices of The Graphic get underway.

With everyone there, Jack spoke to the group. "The newspaper is doing its job; now we need to do ours."

"That's right," Pang said, his jaw still stiff from when Gates had punched him.

Jack laid out the plan again to make sure they understood, reading the paper as he did to make sure he got all the details. "The paper tells people to keep their eyes peeled when they head out to lunch. Mickey, Duke, here's what the crowd's expecting."

Thrills, Thrills, Thrills. Diavalo Krantz, 26 and single, will do his day's work by standing on the top wing of Clyde Pang-born's plane while it turns over three times.

"However, there's been a change in plans," Jack said. "Duke, you'll stunt from my plane. The paper goes on with the usual stuff."

. . . try and figure out what holds him on, watch him lose his balance and plunge into space without a parachute . . .

"And so on and so forth," Jack said. "We'll wear white coveralls so they can see us well. Any questions?"

The rest of the day and the next morning, Jack concentrated on his plane. He made the mechanics go over it from top to bottom. They examined every inch of the mile of wire that held the aircraft together. They scrutinized the struts, the ailerons, the rudders, and the entire surface of the plane. Mechanics checked the engine hoses and gauges. When they finished, Jack went over it one last time. While he worked, he thought of Buck back in Shreveport and thought it would sure be nice to have him around to join them. He had gotten letters from his brother Franz wanting to join up with the circus. Jack decided to call Buck, but Franz wasn't ready to fly for the circus. He thought he could possibly get Franz on as a mechanic in a year or so.

Finally, it was time to fly.

"Give them a good show, but don't take any chances," Jack told the guys. "If you have engine problems, head back immediately. If you can't make it, head for the drink."

Jack put on his white coveralls, went through everything in his head one last time, and climbed into the cockpit. Krantz climbed in front and gave Jack a thumbs-up. At exactly twelve o'clock, Pang lowered his arm, and they roared down the runway and flew north, banking left toward the southern tip of

Manhattan Island. As planned, they were over Battery Park at exactly 12:15, said their special "thank you" to the Texaco guys, and headed up Broadway at about five hundred feet.

Everything went as planned and on time. They could see people on the tops of lower buildings, and others looked down on them from the higher buildings, waving. The buildings were so huge he felt like a midge flying next to them. Traffic stopped, and people got out of their cars and craned their necks to watch their little show. He wondered if Mavis had gotten his message and if she was watching. Once they started stunting, flying took all his concentration.

After their loops, the pilots took off in different directions. Duke climbed out of the cockpit and walked on the lower wings to get a feel for things. It was a challenge to fly in those circumstances, and Jack gripped the stick more firmly with Duke walking all over the plane. It took all his concentration and skill. He didn't have time to enjoy the crowds looking up at them anymore.

Duke did his requisite stunting, including the plunge from the plane, while Jack swooped around and between buildings. The plane jolted slightly when the stuntman reached the end of the cable. Slowly, Duke pulled himself up, a procedure that seemed to take forever. Duke stood by the cockpit a few minutes to catch his breath before his final stunt.

After half an hour, on cue, they got back into formation for their flight back to Curtiss Field. To play up the "Cowboy Aviator" bit, Duke had fastened a saddle on the back of the fuselage. He rode the saddle, and Jack made his plane "buck" as they flew back down Broadway. He imagined that they had never seen a show quite like that on the Gay White Way. If Mavis had seen it, Jack wondered what she thought. Once they were headed back to Curtiss Field, Duke made his way to the front cockpit to rest.

The guys were high and feeling cocky when they landed. Jack had never seen them raise such a ruckus after a show. There was a succession of whoops as they slapped one another on the back.

"Damn, that was fun."

"Did you see all the people watching us?"

"Must've been a million—or more!"

"Can't wait until tomorrow."

There was a photographer from the *Graphic* waiting for them. Churchill was especially excited about the flight. "I can't believe Krantz rode that silly saddle, and the way Jack made the plane buck. What a show, men, what a show! It's going to make great copy in the paper this evening. Got to go meet my deadline. Bye, now. Great flying, Jack." Ed and Jack had hit it off well.

Later, Jack and his mechanic were going over his plane to make sure it was in good shape to fly the next day. Absorbed in the task at hand, Jack didn't notice a greaseball approach. There was a guy following him, and he announced that he had a special delivery letter for "Cowboy Jack." Jack knew immediately that it was from Mavis. When no one was looking, Jack sniffed the letter to see if he could detect the fragrance of her perfume. Even over the odor of the castor oil and gasoline, he detected the faint scent. It was the same one she'd been wearing that Saturday after their night on the town. He looked forward to their flight on Saturday.

Jack, the letter read, *As the British say, "jolly good show." Can't wait until Saturday for my personal flight. Mavis.*

Jack smiled and tucked the envelope into his shirt pocket. Pilots were a superstitious bunch, so he decided to carry it with him the next day for good luck.

. . .

Jack grabbed a copy of the *Evening Graphic* to read before he went to bed. Ed had delivered with an article like he said he would. There was a nice picture of Bill Wunderlich, Freddie, Wilmer, Mickey, Duke, and Jack lined up by a plane and a picture of Jack and Duke tuning up a plane.

The headlines read:

Gaping Marvel at Daring Airmen's Stunts.

AIR DAREDEVILS THRILL THOUSANDS! TODAY WAS GRAPHIC AIR CIRCUS DAY!"

Thousands of spectators at Battery Park and down through lower Manhattan went wild as four planes swooped and dived overhead, acrobats stood on their hands on wings, hung from the running gear and then slipped and 'fell' to the end of a 50-foot steel cable. There were countless 'Ahs and ohs' as four intrepid pilots of the Gates Aerial Circus did falling leaves, Immelmann turns and barrel rolls, swooping down onto the very peaks of lower Broadway's skyscrapers.

Then it got to the meat of the matter:

THE OUTSTANDING FEATURE OF THE ENTIRE ENTERTAINMENT WAS THAT OLD MAN KNICKER-BOCKER FOUND OUT JUST WHERE HE MIGHT BE IF ANY ENEMY PLANES, BOMB-LOADED, VISITED HIM ON A MISSION OF DEATH!

THE STUNT WHICH ATTRACTED THE MOST ATTENTION WAS THAT OF DIAVALO KRANTZ, GATES DAREDEVIL WING WALKER, WHO LEAPED FROM THE PLANE PILOTED BY JACK ASHCRAFT

AND AFTER FALLING THROUGH SPACE, WAS CAUGHT AND SUSPENDED IN MID-AIR BY A STEEL CABLE. HE RETURNED TO HIS TRICKERY BY SCALING THIS STEEL CABLE."

Just about every one [sic] on lower Manhattan was there. Hucksters sold colored glasses and miniature airplanes, the crowd shrieked and yelled. It was as if the GRAPHIC had brought a whole carnival to town.

Freddie[sic] Bond and Eddie [sic] Lund [sic] flew the other two red planes, sweeping overhead at 100 miles an hour, dipping and diving. Both saw military service and worked in the movies before joining the staff of the Gates Flying Circus. They never did anything like that for the movies!

Wild Bill Wunderlich carried off the second stellar honors to Diavalo in the wing walking exhibition.

The consensus was that it had been a good day flying.

November 20, 1925
Attack on Gotham, Day 2

The next morning, as promised, the newspapers were full of coverage of the first attack plus the special gimmick. Jack read with amusement while he ate breakfast:

Thrills Galore in Store for Young at Gotham at Park
TODAY IS KIDDIES' DAY AT THE GRAPHIC AIR
CIRCUS.

Four planes, humming and whirring, will give school children the treat of their lives at 12:15 o'clock over Central Park and later will dive down over Times Square.

The planes will be red.

The pilots and wing walkers strutting their various stunts above thousands of heads will be dressed in white.

Letter to Santa. One of these topsy-turvy fliers, Freddie Lund, member of the Gates Flying Circus, will leave shortly for the NORTH POLE, the first ever to REALLY DELIVER LETTERS TO SANTA CLAUSE....

...Stunts for You. You all will have a great time just after noon. At 12:25 o'clock, to be exact. Get as near Central Park as possible. Watch Diavalo Krantz walk wings, hang by his feet in the air, fall off the plane and get back on. Watch Wild Bill Wunderlich do the same stunts.

Finally, it got to what Jack was waiting for.

Catch a glimpse of Jack Ashcraft, flying cowboy from Texas; Clyde E. Pangborn, war flyer, Wilmer Stultz, and see Freddie Lund dive, dip, loop the loop, do Immelmann turns, barrel rolls and falling leaves.

All Free! It's all free. The GRAPHIC has arranged the events with the cooperation of the Gates Flying Circus, and the only thing which will keep the airman on the ground is a gale or heavy fog. Rain, snow or clouds make no difference to these men.

"The GRAPHIC'S circus received a great reception yesterday. Thousands lined Broadway and filled Battery Park, 'Oh-ing' and 'ah-ing' as the daring circus acrobats went through their program with one thrill after another. Broadway traffic was halted.

Broadway never has seen such an exhibition as shown yesterday.

The pilots did everything that a pilot has done with any airplane and a little more.

One feature which must not be overlooked is that many of

the maneuvers staged were used during the war and will be used in possible wars of the future.

The turns, the tailspins, the nose-dives and the side flying, spectators should know, are stunts which count when machine guns are sending a pattern of bullets.

Watch for Them. The events showed Manhattan just how much chance it might have if, suddenly, enemy planes swept over the city and dropped bombs.

THEY WERE BOTH INSTRUCTIVE AND ENTERTAINING IN THE HIGHEST DEGREE.. . .

. . . .AND REMEMBER, BROADWAYITES, YOU'LL GET YOUR SHARE OF THRILLS AT ABOUT 12:45 O'CLOCK.

ALL THE SHOW COSTS IS YOUR TIME!

Jack headed over to the airfield to meet with the gang before they went up. Pang was there, joshing with the guys. "I can't let you have all the fun," he mumbled. "I'm flying today. We'll head to Central Park for the kids and then on up to Times Square like nobody's seen before. Check your planes. See you at 11:45."

Promptly at noon, they took off from Curtiss Field and headed toward Central Park. That day, it was a challenge to fly in and around the skyscrapers because of the wind. It made for a bumpy ride indeed. Jack was so intent on flying that he hardly had time to check on Duke or wonder if Mavis was watching. Duke shortened his cable for the drop, and they didn't do the bucking bronco bit. After they finished one last loop, it was time to head back to the field. Jack breathed a sigh of relief.

When he banked left to return to the airfield, his engine started to cut out. He jammed the stick forward to gain speed to level out, looking for the river. Krantz looked over, and Jack motioned for him to get back into the plane. Jack looked out to see if he could tell why the engine was cutting out. The water line was loose.

Duke saw it, too, and scrambled out of the cockpit. Hooking his legs around a strut, he grasped the line and held it together while Jack focused on getting back to the field, flying down the river until the last instant in case he had to ditch in the water. Engine sputtering, they made it back to Curtiss Field. Jack thanked his lucky stars that he was carrying Duke that day. When the stuntman saw that Jack could glide in, he let go of the tube and prepared to land. The instant Jack set down, mechanics were on their way to check out what was wrong.

Pang landed just moments after Jack and ran over. "What happened?"

"Water line came loose. Mack and Jimmy are checking things out now."

"Doesn't look like anything serious," Jimmy said. "We'll have her fixed up in no time."

"Hell, you weren't flying over thousands of people in New York City," Jack said, his hands trembling as he lit a cigarette.

"It's okay now, Jack," Pang reassured him. "Go have a smoke and relax."

It was all in a day's work, and Jack did just that, plus a snort or two. But he didn't want to overdo it because he was flying Mavis the next morning.

CHAPTER 13
BIG NIGHT ON THE TOWN

November 1925

Jack woke up Saturday morning and looked out the window. His heart sank. *Damn.* There was fog all right, and frost on the ground. Then he paused. *Wait a minute.* The sun was peeking through the clouds. "Hot dog!" he said.

Ed put a pillow over his head. "Shut your mouth. I'm trying to sleep." He had gone to the airfield after the show to celebrate with the guys and hear some hangar flying. Too inebriated to go home, he'd bunked overnight with Jack.

"Can't do it," Jack said. "I'm taking a beautiful woman flying today."

Jack showered and got dressed.

At Curtiss Field, Jimmy, the new mechanic he liked, rolled out a plane and inspected it, especially the water hose. He decided to take up a two-seater so Mavis could feel the controls when he stunted. It seemed like an antique compared to Mavis's Waco, but it would have to do. Jimmy helped him fuel up, and he was ready to go when Mavis drove up. She was wearing the long, belted leather jacket, riding breeches, and boots. Her wavy auburn hair glistened in the morning sun before she put on her flight helmet and goggles. Truth of the matter was, she looked like an ad from a magazine.

A guy in another car pulled up after her and got out, camera in hand.

"Hey, Cowboy Jack. What a great show you put on this weekend," she said. "Let's go flying."

Jack bowed with a flourish. "Once again, the Cowboy Aviator, brave and glorious, at your service," he said, grinning. He picked Mavis up and swirled her around.

"Well, you're in a splendid mood today," she said, laughing. "I hope you don't mind, but I brought along my photographer, Joe Nelson. I thought a firsthand account of what it was like to fly with a pilot of the Gates Flying Circus might be of interest to my readers."

Gates never turned down a chance for publicity. "Fine by me. We love all the publicity that we can get," Jack said, shaking Joe's hand. "I'll get one of the guys to take you up for an aerial view."

"Great," Joe replied.

"Hey, Jimmy," Jack said to the mechanic, "go see if Wilmer wants to fly today." A few minutes later, Wilmer came rushing over, putting on his helmet. He was disappointed that he was taking up the photographer.

"This doesn't look like the plane you flew this week," she said, walking around the plane, looking it over. "By the way, you should have seen the show from below. It was spectacular. The people on the street were dazzled, in absolute awe."

"Glad to hear it," Jack said.

"The planes we flew yesterday were four-seaters in the front to take passengers up," he explained. "To accommodate as many as possible, we had ladders installed, too, so we could unload on the left at the same time we load people on the right. We're quite efficient."

All the while, Joe snapped pictures and Jack tried to give him good poses.

"How interesting. You must be able to take up hundreds in a day," she said.

"That's the idea. I decided to take up this one so you could feel the controls," he said. He gave her a hand to help her onto the wing, even though he knew she was quite capable on her own. It was the gentlemanly thing to do. She fastened her helmet and adjusted her goggles on top of her head, then climbed in and buckled up. "I'm ready," she said, pulling her goggles down.

Jack reached in and tugged at the seat straps to make sure they were fastened tight and felt the warmth of her body. "I always do this. I don't want to lose you on a loop," he said, and she laughed.

"Me neither. You'd really have a difficult time explaining that to Dad and Mr. Walker."

"You can put your hand on the stick, but don't try to control it unless I tell you it's okay," Jack said. "If you get sick or anything, just let me know and I'll stop. Don't be embarrassed if you do. Otherwise, I'll take you through as many maneuvers as you want and can handle."

"Let's go for it," she said.

Jack revved the motor and Jimmy pulled the chocks, and Jack taxied to the runway. "Ready?" Jack yelled. She gave him a thumbs-up, and he took off. Thinking about his flight the day before, Jack decided to stay over Long Island in case he had to land in a hurry. Once he gained altitude, he did a quick wingover. When he finished, she turned around and grinned. Gently, he eased her into stunting by doing an aileron roll, which he called a corkscrew, out toward the ocean so she could feel what it was like to be inverted for a little longer.

Jack was as easy on the controls as possible. It was important to maintain altitude and speed, then pitch the nose about thirty degrees above horizon to neutralize the controls. He could feel her light hand on the stick. Apply left aileron and hold; left rudder to counter yaw; maintain left aileron until rollout to level position. Once she was sure the maneuver was complete, she raised her hands and clapped. Jack did some slow rolls, followed by more demanding stunts like barrel rolls, an Immelmann, and a hammerhead. She raised her fist high after each maneuver, and he could faintly hear her laughter over the motor and wind. Mavis was just fine.

After about twenty minutes, Jack decided to do some loops. He tapped her on the shoulder to tell her to get ready and to make sure everything was fastened. She motioned that she was ready, so he started a dive and then looped up and over. He waited for her response. After a few seconds, she looked back at him, grinned, then indicated that she wanted to do it again, so up and over they went, two more times. Then he had an idea. Jack tapped Mavis on the shoulder and motioned for her to take the controls to do a loop, knowing he could take over if he had to.

To his surprise, she grabbed the stick, and ever so gently he guided her through the maneuver. She had a nice touch, so he didn't need to guide her much. Once they leveled out, she looked back at Jack with that same grin on her face. In fact, Jack didn't think she'd ever stopped grinning from the time they took off. Then she motioned that she wanted to do one on her own.

He thought, *what the heck,* and let her go for it. To show her that he trusted her, Jack put his hands behind his head. Her timing was a bit off, but she pulled it off. He motioned for her to fly around the harbor before heading back to the field. For a few minutes, he enjoyed the view and the cold breeze smacking him on his face. He wanted to stay up and drift all day, but he knew the flight had to end.

On the ground, she jumped out of the plane the instant it stopped, ran up to Jack, and gave him a big hug and kiss, her goggles smashing into his nose. "Jack, that was wonderful. I've never experienced anything so exhilarating. How can I ever thank you?"

Jack laughed. "You just did."

"I can't believe you make a living having so much fun. Can we do it again some time?" she asked. "I'm sure Joe got a lot of good shots."

"I'm glad you enjoyed it. It's a tough job, but somebody's got to do it. And yes, absolutely we'll do it again sometime," he said, grinning. "Let's grab some lunch and go shopping. I'm starved."

She threw Jack the keys to her car. "I kind of like having a chauffeur."

Jack snatched the keys from the air. "And I like being one."

"See you Monday, Joe. I'll be anxious to see the pictures. Thanks, Wilmer," she said.

Wilmer stared longingly as they roared off.

After lunch, they went to a nice department store in Hicksville, a place that Jack thought appropriate for a guy like him. They were from different worlds, but there was more to him than met the eye. He was making good money with the circus—darn good money. Millions of people had seen them fly, and they brought in hundreds of thousands of dollars taking up paying customers three and four at a time for two-fifty a pop.

He'd netted nearly three thousand dollars in Pennsylvania alone and had saved several thousand so far, plus he sent some home to his mother and dad. In all, he figured he would make $30,000 or more for the year. Not bad for a kid born out in the middle of nowhere in a place that wasn't even a state. He saved for special occasions because some day, he wanted to strike out on his own and make a name for himself outside of the circus. Then when he got too rickety to fly, he would go home to Protection and sell nuts and bolts.

That day, though, Jack wanted to buy gifts for his family and have a good time. He loved flying, but a man needed a break. Mavis helped him pick out handbags for his mother and sisters and a nice woolen shawl for his mother. Noticing some diaries near the checkout stand, he added them as gifts for his sisters. His dad and brothers were harder to buy for. Everything they would like, Dad could order from the hardware store. He finally decided to get them nice leather wallets, plus a belt for his dad. Since he'd missed his high school graduation, Jack got Franz a leather flight jacket. He didn't know for sure how many nieces and nephews he had, so he decided to pick up silver dollars for them on his way home. Same with brothers-in-law.

They had been so busy with the attack on New York that he hadn't had time to plan for their big night out. He was hoping to see a nice suit or something while they were shopping.

When they stepped out of one store, he noticed a sign in the window across the street that read, *Eveningwear for Rent, Men and Women*, and got an idea.

"Mavis," Jack said. "I just remembered something I need to take care of at the airfield. How about I pick you up at seven this evening? I'll expect you to show me a *real* night on the town. None of that deli stuff."

She gave him a curious look, then smiled. "You've got a deal. I want to put some of my thoughts on paper about the flight this morning anyway. I'll see you at seven. Thanks again for the airplane ride. I'll *never* forget it. I look forward to this evening. Bye for now."

He opened the car door for her to get in, and off she sped, waving. Once her car was out of sight, Jack walked over to the establishment that rented eveningwear. Evidently, they didn't have many male customers his size, but the tailor was able to make some alterations to get a suit to fit. Looking in the three-way mirror, Jack had to admit that he was impressed with what he saw. The black suit was wool with satin lapels. Under it was a white shirt with fancy tucks in it and a black bow tie. To complete the outfit, he rented black patent leather shoes and a top hat. He hardly recognized himself. "Not bad for a country hick," he muttered. Somehow, he knew Mavis would approve.

Then he did something that he would never, ever admit to anyone. He got a manicure. He sat hunched down with his jacket collar up the whole time because he didn't want to take the chance of someone coming into town and recognizing him. Once the manicure was completed, he got a real shave and haircut in a real barber shop.

At the hotel, Ed laughed and made fun of Jack the whole time he was getting ready. He called Jack a Yankee Doodle Dandy, but it didn't bother Jack. Jack told him that he might never have another chance to have a date with a classy lady like Mavis and was going to pull out all the stops.

When Ed stepped out for a short walk and a smoke, Jack pulled out a small wooden chest that he kept personal items in, like his journal, mementoes, and extra cash. He had been putting money back for a while and wanted to have plenty of cash for the night. He unlocked the padlock and counted out nine hundred-dollar bills and a hundred dollars in smaller bills and put them in the silver money clip with a big gold "JWA" on it that he'd bought for himself. With one last admiring look in the mirror, he grabbed the wool topcoat with a fur collar he had rented and walked out of the room for a night out in New York City with a gorgeous woman. Churchill wolf whistled as Jack closed the door.

Jack peeked back in. "Don't wait up for me."

The taxi stopped in front of Mavis's apartment building. He felt like hot stuff and couldn't wait to see the expression on Mavis's face when she saw him. Trying to act like he dressed in a tuxedo every day, and hoping to get in some practice, he greeted Gerald formally at the door. "Good evening, Gerald. How might you be this fine evening?"

"Why, hello, Mr. Jack," Gerald said. "Look at you. I hardly recognized you in those fancy duds. My, my, you do look fine. You and your men put on quite a show this week. Quite a show. I walked over to Broadway on my lunch break and saw most everything."

"Glad you enjoyed it," Jack said.

"Sir, I know this is a big night for you, but I would like you to meet my son, Wendell. He's a great admirer of yours," Gerald said, pointing to a boy of about ten sitting on the doorstep. He jumped up when Gerald said his name.

"Happy to," Jack said. He walked over to the boy and shook his hand. "Nice to meet you, Wendell."

Wendell looked up at Jack in awe. He handed Jack a newspaper and tried to speak, but couldn't get out the words. "Would . . . would . . ."

"What Wendell is trying to say is that he would like you to autograph the newspaper that Miss Mavis gave him."

Jack looked closer at the copy of the *Graphic* that had his picture on the front.

"I'll be glad to," he said.

While Jack signed the paper, Wendell found his voice. "Do you think I could be a great pilot like you someday?"

Jack thought for a few moments before answering. "Yes, I do, Wendell, but I'm going to be honest. It's harder for guys like you, but I believe in possibilities."

Gerald and Wendell looked at him appreciatively.

"Give me that paper back," Jack said. "I'm going to write the names of a few pilots you need to know about."

"I'm going to read them to you to make sure you can read my scribbling. The first is Eugene Bullard. He flew with the Lafayette Flying Corps in France. That group was as good as they come. I know he was good because he came out alive. He was known as the Black Swallow. Hubert Leroy Julian is called the Black Eagle of Harlem. He flies with Clarence Chamberlin. Then there's Bessie Coleman. People call her Queen Bess."

He handed the paper back to Wendell. "And you thought I was the only pilot with a neat nickname," Jack said with a wink.

"Now, if you will excuse me, gentlemen, Miss Perkins is expecting me. Would you call us a cab for half an hour, please?" Jack said, handing Gerald a five.

Gerald smiled. "Yes, sir. Thank you for your time. It's most appreciated."

Jack nodded and pulled Wendell's cap down when he walked by. "You've got a keeper there, Gerald."

Inside, Jack strutted through the lobby humming "Jenny's Song," shoulders back, topcoat over his arm so everyone could get the full effect. People stopped talking; women eyed him approvingly. When he reached Mavis's floor, he walked to the door of her apartment like he owned the place. He rang the bell and stepped back a couple of steps so Mavis could get the full effect. The look on her face when she opened the door was worth every penny of the hundred bucks it had taken to rent the tux.

"Well look at you!" she said, enunciating each word. "Don't you look handsome?" She looked Jack over from head to toe. He turned around slowly so she could get the full effect. "What do they say in the Midwest? You clean up right nice."

"You don't look so bad yourself," he said. She was wearing a black satin dress with lace on the outside and lace sleeves.

"I apologize for being a bit late," Jack said. "Gerald wanted me to meet his son and autograph the *Graphic* article with my picture on it. Wendell wants to be a pilot like me."

"That was very sweet of you, Jack," she said. "Come in. I made us dinner reservations for eight, so we have time for a quick drink. Why don't you pour us a sherry this time? I'll be right back out." When she turned, Jack discovered the dress didn't have a back. He just about fainted at how gorgeous she looked. He poured the sherry and quickly downed a couple to settle his nerves before she returned. Reentering the room, she draped her long fur coat on the chair by the door and accepted the glass he offered.

"So, what's on for tonight?" he asked.

"First dinner, then I thought we'd go out for a show or two for some entertainment. I have a couple of surprises for you. After that, we'll go dancing. How does that sound?"

"Perfect," Jack said. They clinked their glasses together, crossed wrists, and took a sip. The closeness of her lips and body stirred emotions inside Jack with an intensity he had never felt before. This time, he sensed some desire in Mavis. He felt the warmth of the alcohol move through his body.

Mavis pulled back.

"You held your own stunting today, considering it was your first time and all," Jack said.

"Thanks. You'll never know how exhilarating that experience was for me," she said. "I wish we could fly together more. I could learn so much from you."

The phone rang. It was Gerald telling Mavis their cab was ready.

They went to the place across from Saul's that she'd wanted to go to the first time. A doorman took their coats and his hat, and they were escorted to a table. Never in his life had he been in such a fancy place. There wasn't even the tiniest hint of a grease spot on the white tablecloth on the table with fancy silverware.

After they were seated, Mavis got out her cigarette holder. He pulled out a cigarette case, offered her one, and then pulled one out for himself. He was glad he remembered the brand of cigarette she liked. Mavis accepted and placed it in her ivory cigarette holder. Jack was reaching for his lighter when the waiter appeared and lit their cigarettes for them, a first for Jack. Mavis elegantly held her cigarette holder and puckered tantalizingly when she blew the smoke out, an expression that nearly drove Jack insane.

The waiter left them with menus. Jack looked it over even though he had already decided to order a steak. He just about choked when he saw the prices.

"And what would you like to drink this evening?" the waiter asked.

Jack was about ready to answer, but Mavis beat him to it. "We'd like ginger ale."

"Domestic or imported?"

"Imported, of course."

Jack looked confused.

"That means alcoholic," Mavis whispered.

The waiter brought them cocktails, then some before-dinner snacks, but Jack couldn't remember the fancy name.

"Thanks again for the plane ride, Jack," she said. "I've never enjoyed flying or any experience so much. Could I learn to do that?"

"Yes," he said. "Takes lots of practice, though. You've got to keep your wits about you. Things don't always go smooth, and you've got to learn from your mistakes."

A guy on stage started to sing, so they couldn't talk much. Jack looked around at the other people there, suddenly feeling out of place. He was glad he had sprung for the manicure, even though he was embarrassed to be seen in the place. That would have given him away, fancy suit or not. Despite his self-consciousness, he was enjoying himself and Mavis's company.

Mavis sensed that he was uneasy, so she put her hand through his arm for reassurance. Occasionally, somebody stopped to say hello. She introduced Jack as a friend and fellow pilot. The men's hands were softer than his mother's. He grasped the women's hands like he saw the men grasp Mavis's and hoped they didn't notice how rough his hands were despite the manicure. After a couple more drinks, he relaxed more and didn't care as much.

Food was served course by course with wine for nearly two hours. Jack had never taken so long to eat a meal. Growing up with so many brothers and sisters, half of them boys, it had been a free-for-all at mealtime before the food ran out. During exhibitions with the circus, they gulped down a burger or hot dog when they could, but mostly had to wait until they were finished with the engagement. The fancy meal was a treat for him, and the food was delicious. The expensive steak nearly melted in his mouth. It cost him a pretty penny, but it was worth it. You only live once, and a night on the town didn't happen every day, especially with someone like Mavis.

Finally, they finished eating and retrieved their coats. Mavis mentioned again that she had a surprise for Jack. As soon as she'd found out they were going out that night, she'd bought tickets to go to the New Amsterdam Theatre. She had hoped to see Will Rogers, but he was on his lecture tour of the country on Billy Mitchell's behalf.

At intermission, Mavis pulled out her press credentials and they went backstage to meet the performers. To their surprise, Rogers was backstage talking to them. Mavis introduced herself and Jack. Rogers was in town for Mitchell's trial and taking a break from all the drama.

"How's it going?" Jack asked.

The cowboy philosopher rolled his eyes. "It's going." Then he signed Jack's program for his mother.

Jack knew the saying that New York never sleeps, and he was now a believer. By then it was after midnight, and Mavis had more planned for their night out. They saw a bunch of people come out of a phone booth. It took a minute for the country boy to figure out what was going on. Next, they went to a place that looked like a nice café, but instead of seating them, they ushered them to a back room where a fake bookcase opened to a fancy speakeasy. The place was going wild. People were dancing and having fun, and the liquor flowed freely. A classier place than the one back in Birmingham, that was for sure. Everyone was dressed in evening clothes. Even members of the orchestra wore tuxedos.

"Wow, I can't believe this place," Jack said to Mavis. A painted lady in a gold dress and fancy cloche hat walked up to a microphone.

"Hello, suckers," she bellowed and clapped two small paddle-like things together that made a clacking sound. "And I never give a sucker an even break. You may mean all the world to your mother, but you are just a cover charge to me."

"This is the 300 Club, or should I say will be. That's Texas Guinan," Mavis said. "The 'Whoopee Girl,' 'Queen of the Nightclubs.' She puts on a pretty good show just introducing people. Patrons say that Jimmy Walker runs New York by day, and she runs it by night."

"And by the way, you can leave your wallets at the bar," Guinan said. "If anyone asks, this place doesn't exist, so you aren't here. If you get my drift?" She laughed and turned to her right.

A young woman with giant feather fans walked up beside her. "This is Nellie. She's a sweet little girl who's going to dance for us. Give the little girl a great big hand." So everybody clapped, and Nellie danced for ten minutes, placing the feathers in different positions on her body. When she turned to exit the stage, he saw that she was wearing no clothing. Jack had never seen anything like it, not even in France.

When she finished, Guinan walked up to the microphone, clackers in hand to get everyone's attention. "I just spotted someone in the audience, and I persuaded him to sing a song or two for us. This gentleman needs no introduction, so let's give a great big hand for Broadway's biggest sucker."

A guy in a white jacket and black pants walked up to the microphone.

"Hey, that guy looks like Eddie Cantor," Jack said.

Mavis laughed. "That is Eddie. You wanted a night on the town, didn't you?"

"But I didn't expect Will Rogers and Eddie Cantor in one night," Jack said. "Texas Guinan is like a cherry on the sundae. She's a character."

Mavis laughed. "The night's not over."

It was hard to talk in a place like that, but that wasn't what they were there for. They sang along with some of the songs, and they danced. After a few more drinks, Jack was no longer so self-conscious of what he looked like on the dance floor and danced his heart out.

Jack got so comfortable with the Charleston that other

women even came up and asked to dance with him, and Mavis bowed out, amused. She danced with other guys, but when slow dances played, it was only Jack and he held her body intimately close to his. It must've been about two thirty when the place started winding down and people started leaving.

Out on the street, the cold wind felt refreshing after being inside the hot, stuffy room for so long. Somehow, they wound up at Saul's for some coffee and breakfast before going back to Mavis's place.

The coffee started sobering Jack, so he could think straight and walk down the street without wobbling. All evening long, he'd wondered what he would do when that time came. While they'd had a good time, Mavis hadn't said or done anything to indicate that she wanted any more out of their relationship. He could accept that, yet he wondered if she could see something in a guy like him. His thoughts argued with each other.

She was smart and clever, a professional woman, plus she was a pilot. Although she didn't have the experience he had, he thoroughly enjoyed hangar flying with her and talking about planes with someone other than the guys. She knew all the aviators in the know. It was nice to have a woman friend who didn't have sex on her mind all the time, but if the opportunity presented, he wouldn't turn it down. In his heart, he also knew that a long-term romance between them couldn't work.

If the evening had done anything, it had showed him even more how separate their worlds were. She was classy, destined to marry one of those Wall Street types or a lawyer like her father. He was a workingman, an avowed bachelor, whose hands were rough from being outdoors and repairing planes. A man who got grease under his nails and had to scrub them till they were raw to be presentable.

To his surprise and delight, she asked him in for a nightcap when they got to her place.

"Pour us a brandy, will you Jack?" Mavis said, taking her coat off and putting her purse on the table.

Jack draped his coat on the back of a chair and did as she asked. He handed her the glass and bent down to kiss her gently, which she allowed. Mavis took a sip of her drink, then set it down and put her arms around Jack's neck and sought out his lips. They kissed intensely.

Mavis slid Jack's suitcoat off and unbuttoned his shirt.

"Are you sure?" Jack whispered. "I'm just a country boy from Kansas."

In response, Mavis grasped Jack's hands and lowered them to her waistline in the back so he could unfasten her dress. It slid from her shoulders and fell to the floor. She drew him toward her bed.

The next morning, Jack woke up on the softest sheets that he had ever slept on, and in the nicest bed. It was nothing like the rough sheets on lumpy mattresses in cheap rooms where he usually stayed. Plus, he had spent the night with a beautiful woman. He lay there drowsing. If he hadn't died and gone to heaven, he was caught in a dream and didn't want to wake up.

"Jack, Jack," he heard an angel whispering to him. Then she started shaking him, laughing softly. "Wake up, sleepy head."

Mavis was sitting on the edge of the bed. He pulled her close and gave her a long kiss. She didn't resist. "As tempting as this is, I must go. I have lunch with my parents on Sundays," she said, standing up.

"Do you have to leave? Come on back," he said, lifting the covers.

Mavis sat down on the edge of the bed. "It was nice for me,

too, Jack, but don't make too much of it, okay?" Mavis said. "You're not the first, and you won't be the last. I know I'm not."

Jack smiled up at her. "Do you blame me for trying?"

"No," she said, "but let's take things slow. And to be absolutely honest with you, I don't think a country boy is what Mother and Daddy have in mind for my future."

"Since we're being honest, I'm not society material," Jack said.

"We'll take it slow, then," she said, smiling at Jack. "Look at the time. I need to leave. We're meeting at the country club."

"I had guessed it probably wasn't Saul's," Jack laughed.

Mavis smiled. "They have probably invited some eligible bachelor that Daddy has met. That's the price I pay for him letting me fly his plane. I indulge him and Mother with these luncheons, and it satisfies them. Make yourself at home. Just make sure the door is locked when you leave."

She paused at the door. "What are you doing Thanksgiving Day?"

"Van and Hazel are throwing a big feast for us," Jack said.

"I'm glad that you won't be alone. Happy Thanksgiving, Jack. Bye," Mavis said. "Give me a call whenever you're back in town."

CHAPTER 14
CELEBRATIONS

November 1925
Thanksgiving, Long Island, New York

Gates and Hazel stayed on Long Island for Thanksgiving. Since most of the fliers couldn't go home, they arranged a Thanksgiving dinner at the hotel for them and spared no expense. The Gateses arranged for a huge turkey with dressing, plus ham, mashed potatoes and gravy, and sweet potatoes. Any dish ever served at a Thanksgiving meal, they had it. There were delicious desserts galore. Jack tried them all, but none could compare to his mother's fresh peach pie. They also had ample bottles of wine. Jack wondered how many people Gates had bribed to get those. There was plenty of liquor too. Jack made sure his flask was filled.

Judge made the rounds begging for scraps. Hazel gave him a hambone. He retreated to a corner of the room, content to gnaw on the bone, then went to sleep after the hard work.

Jack stood to speak. "I'd like to offer a toast. I'm grateful for all of you, my flying family. Gates has allowed me to make a living doing what I love doing and do best, and that is flying. May my second year with the circus be even better than my first."

"Hear, hear," the guys agreed, and some offered their own toasts.

Afterwards, Jack stood and rubbed his belly. "If you'll excuse me, I'm going to get some fresh air and walk off some of this food. See everyone at the airfield on Monday."

While he enjoyed the meal and appreciated the effort, the holiday just wasn't the same as what he remembered back home. Suddenly, he got nostalgic about seeing the family. He walked through the lobby, where other guests were listening to the Chicago Bears game against the Chicago Cardinals like Chet and the guys were probably doing at home. Red Grange was making his professional debut.

Outside, he lit a cigarette and walked across the veranda onto the lawn. Looking out on the Hempstead Plains, he was reminded of the plains of Oklahoma and Kansas where he was born and grew up. His mind went back to a Thanksgiving when he was eighteen and Franz was about nine. He had a particular fondness for that kid, because he reminded Jack of himself. Jack had gotten up early to ride motorcycles with Troy Putterbaugh before everyone gathered at the house. He and Troy had competed in a few wooden track races together at the motordrome. Some called them murderdromes [sic]. Jack could see it in his mind's eye like it happened yesterday.

They were racing across the pasture out at Troy's, making the cattle scatter and run off, tails high, kicking up their heels. The wind was cold, and Jack was laughing hysterically because he was having such a good time. He got careless. He hit a rabbit hole and flipped his motorcycle end over end. Thankfully, it didn't land on him. Troy rode up laughing, until he saw that Jack wasn't getting up and wasn't breathing very well.

"You okay, Jack?" he asked.

"Hell no!" Jack squeaked back. "Handlebars. Ribs." It was worse than the day he'd fallen from the trapeze tied to the rafters playing circus in the barn.

Troy helped Jack get up. "You need to go see the doc."

"If my rib's broke, what the hell could he do?"

"Make sure your lung's not punctured," Troy said, but Jack waved him off.

With Troy's help, Jack limped over to his motorcycle and helped lift it up. Jack stood for a couple of minutes, leaning over the handlebars until he caught his breath and the pain subsided a bit. "For heaven's sake, don't tell Mother," he said.

It was a rough ride home, and Jack had to walk through the house like nothing had happened while his side hurt like hell. His mother worried about him enough as it was.

Franz met Jack at the door, and Jack told him what had happened. "Don't let Mother know," Jack whispered.

Franz went through the house ahead of Jack and told him when it was clear for Jack to go to the bedroom. "Find me something to wrap around my ribs," he told Franz. Jack was stove up for a week but didn't let on. It wasn't long after that Jack joined the army. He was in the motor repair unit and traveled a lot by motorcycle.

The whole family would be at the house. His mother and his sisters would be busy cooking, and the guys would be shooting the bull, listening to some football game on the radio. Franz would be about eighteen now, or was it nineteen? Lillian, Audrey, and Chester were in their thirties, and Jack was going to be twenty-eight next month. His birthday had snuck up on him, he had been so busy. The last bit of sun was disappearing behind the horizon, rays streaming through holes in the clouds where he liked to fly. He was so lost in his thoughts that he didn't hear Pang and Judge come up behind him.

"Penny for your thoughts?" Pang said.

"That's about all they're worth," Jack said, petting Judge. "Glad to see you bouncing back after Gates slugged you. Did you ever ask him why he did that?"

"I asked Hazel," he said, "but she just gave me some garbage about the guys liking me better than him. Heck, I just try to keep us all safe and flying. That's history. What were you thinking?"

"Oh, not much," Jack said. "Just thinking about the folks and all my brothers and sisters. They're all at Mother and Dad's. The house is small, so they'll be packed to the gills. After dinner, Franz probably dragged the guys out to play football or baseball. The girls join in for baseball. They're pretty good, too. And I just remembered that my birthday is in a week. Damn, another year and I'm nudging thirty."

"You old man," Pang said, and they both laughed.

"Tell you what. We're going to head south pretty quick, but you take a plane and go see your folks for Christmas," Pang said. "We don't have much scheduled until mid-December, so go to Kansas to see them. How does that sound?"

"Sounds great, but are you sure? I don't want anybody to think I'm shirking my duty," Jack said.

"Don't worry about anything," Pang said. "I'll take care of the fellas and dodge the punches. You go and have a good time. Consider it my Christmas present."

"Thanks, I appreciate that," Jack said.

Pang left, but Jack lingered, looking at the stars.

"Hey Jack," Ed said, "what are you going to do between now and Florida?"

"Pang just told me to take a plane and go see the folks, so that's what I'm going to do," Jack said. "It's been too long since I saw them."

"Don't let them talk you into taking over the hardware store," Ed said, and Jack laughed.

"You know, someday that sounds nice. A quiet life on the prairie after being on the go constantly. But that's years down the line."

"You don't have to just sell hardware," Ed said. "You could have a diner next door. Call it 'Smilin' Jack's.'"

Jack laughed. "Now that's an idea."

"You could put your trophies on a shelf and frame some of those articles you've been saving." Ed smiled.

"The main item on the menu could be 'Big Jack's Giant Burger,' or I could name the burgers after airplanes like the Jenny. That'd be your basic burger," Jack said.

Ed laughed, then yawned. "Well, I'm calling it a night. See you next week."

Jack decided to give his folks a call to give them the good news and so he could be sure to see everyone. The operator took down the number, and Jack waited for the call to go through. His parents were on a party line. He hoped she or one of the kids got to the phone before nosey Agnes White did. Everyone on the party line was supposed to have a specific code, but Agnes was a busybody and always answered on the second ring no matter what.

"Hello, this is Agnes. Who's calling?"

"Hello, Mrs. White. This is Jack Ashcraft, and I'm trying to reach the folks . . ."

"Well, hello, Johnie. How are you? You still flying?" she said. "You aren't doing any heavy drinking and fast living, are you?"

"I'm fine and still flying. Will you please hang up and let me call again? I really want to talk to the folks." After a couple more tries, he got Ivan on the phone.

"Hi Ivan, Jack here."

"Mother! It's Jack!" Even with the poor connection, he just about broke Jack's eardrum.

Everybody beat Mother to the phone—Lillian and Mary Jane, his oldest and youngest sisters, Chester and Ernest, Audrey, Helen and Clarice, Martin, and Franz.

"Hey, Jack," Franz said, "I'm getting really bored here in Protection. Can I come out where you are? I've been working as a mechanic on cars. I'm getting pretty good."

"Hey there, buddy. The circus is a lot of fun, but not just anyone can work with us. I'll talk to you more later, how's that?" Jack said, and Franz seemed satisfied for the time being. Then his mother got on the phone. Jack nearly started crying at the sound of that sweet woman's voice. "Hello, Mother. How are you?"

"Hello, Johnie. I'm fine. Just fine. Are you staying safe and behaving yourself?" Everyone in his hometown called him by his childhood name of "Johnie." The army guys had laughed at that and started calling him "Jack."

"Yes, ma'am. I have to answer to you," Jack laughed. "Sounds like everyone's there."

"Everyone except you. Wish you were here too, son. When are you coming home?"

"I'm glad you asked. I'll be home early December! We can celebrate my birthday and Christmas! Pang said to just take a plane and fly home, so I'm going to take him up on it."

"Glory be," she said. Then she started to cry. "I love you, son."

"Love you too, Mother."

"Here's your father," she said.

Jack repeated the conversation he'd had with his mother, except his dad was a little more formal and got to the point. "Thank you for the letters. Your mother really appreciates them. I do too. She says you're coming home for Christmas."

"That's right, Dad," Jack said. "It will be before Christmas. I don't know exactly what day, but you be looking for me. I'll let you know as soon as I can."

"We'll do that. It'll be good to see you, son," he said.

"You too, Dad. Bye, now."

December 1, 1925
Jack's Surprise Birthday Party

Jack took the weekend off, but on Monday it was back to work. He had several things he wanted to do before his trip home. He wished that he could be there Christmas day, but at least he could go home. The guys acted kind of strange, but he didn't think much about it. There was a lot of whispering going on that stopped when he walked up.

Tuesday, his birthday, was just like any other day working with the circus, except they did very little flying, just a test flight now and then. Cold weather had set in. By midafternoon, he noticed almost everybody was gone, but again, he didn't think much about it. Pang stopped by. "Hey, Jack. Let me buy you a burger to help celebrate your birthday."

Jack wiped his hands on a grease rag. "I believe I'll take you up on your offer. Let me wash my hands and take off my coveralls."

Pang had never offered to take him out for anything, but Jack thought it was a nice gesture. They made small talk as they drove to the café a couple of miles down the road. A waitress met them at the door and led them to a room in back. All the guys from the circus and some other guys and gals that Jack knew were there and yelled "Surprise!" when they walked into the room. Then they started singing "Happy Birthday" to Jack. It sounded so bad and so good at the same time. Judge barked his own version. Jack patted him on the head.

There was even a giant cake that said, "Happy Birthday, Cowboy Jack," complete with a red-icing biplane on it. Jack couldn't believe that not only had Pang and the guys planned a party for him, they had done it so quietly and arranged it so quickly. Jack was taken aback by the gesture. Then he heard a familiar voice behind him.

"Hello, Cowboy Jack. Happy Birthday!"

He turned around, and sure enough, there was Mavis with a big grin on her face. He gave her a quick hug.

"Well, I'll be damned."

"Pang called and asked if I could come. I told him I wouldn't miss it," she said. "And I wanted to hand deliver these before you left." She held up a newspaper with Jack's picture on the front. "I thought you might like to take this to show your parents."

"The folks are really going to love these. Thanks." Before Jack teared up, Pang interrupted.

"She even brought the cake," Pang said.

"Now, it may be Jack's birthday," Pang continued, "but the party is to say thanks to *all* of you. This has been a great year for the Gates Flying Circus, and I expect that we will have an equally great one next year, if not better."

He lifted his mug of root beer. "So, I propose a toast to all of us!" Glass clinked throughout the room.

"Let the celebration begin!" Jack said.

A local band was there and started playing. They only had near beer to drink, but they made do. Mavis danced with just about everyone and seemed to enjoy herself, and the guys behaved themselves. They acted like regular gentlemen for a bunch of rowdy pilots. She chatted with the women in the room. Jack looked around and noticed that some of the guys were missing, so he decided to drive over to the hangar to see if they were there. He didn't want them to miss out on the fun. He asked Mavis if she'd like to go.

"Sure. I need to get back to the office," she said. "How about I drive you, then I'll drop you off on the way back?"

When they got to the hangar, Jack noticed that all the doors were closed, but lights were on inside, so he checked it out. Outside the door, some guys were laughing and carrying on like they'd been on an all-night drunk.

"What's going on here?" he asked.

"Why, nothin', nothin' at all," Mickey said, slurring his words, then laughed hysterically.

"Yup," the other guy agreed, and they started giggling like schoolgirls. "Just working on the planes, that's all."

"Something's not right here," Jack said as he walked into the hangar, Mavis in tow. One step inside the hangar, and he figured out the problem. He started laughing and Mavis started coughing.

"What's that smell?" she said.

"Dope. The guys stripped a plane, re-covered it with fabric, and painted it with a lacquer called dope. They must've got cold, so they closed all the windows," he said. "The fumes can make you as high as a kite in no time."

"Frances said that she wanted to have a dope party sometime. I understand why now," Mavis giggled.

"See?" Jack said. "The morons. The damn stuff's flammable too. Fortunately, nobody decided to light up. I've told them over and over to be careful about that, but apparently, they didn't listen." Jack opened the front door to let in a rush of fresh air.

"When you guys can think straight," he told them, "close the door and come on over and join the party."

Mavis drove him back to the café. "What's next for you, Jack?"

"Gates and his wife had a great Thanksgiving for us at a

nice hotel, and I told Pang I missed the folks," Jack said. "Pang told me to take a plane and go see them. After that, we head south for the winter. Come March, we'll start heading north again."

They arrived back at the café, and Jack got out. "I keep thinking about that little guy Wendell," he said, pulling a twenty-dollar bill from his wallet. "Will you do me a favor and pick up some aviation books for him? My Christmas present to him and his dad. He's going to need all the help he can get."

"You're a good man, Jack. I'll be happy to do this," Mavis said, accepting the money. "You take care of yourself and drop me a line when you can," she said. "I'd love to hear from you."

"Sure thing," Jack said, and Mavis drove off.

CHAPTER 15
HOME FOR CHRISTMAS

Jack's parents, Lenore and John Wesley Ashcraft. Family home, Protection, Kansas. *Courtesy of Cindy Weigand.*

December 1925
Home for Christmas, Protection, Kansas

The flight home was uneventful considering the time of year. Jack had to fly around some squalls here and there, but had no problem with doing so. Sometimes it was bone-chillingly cold. The wind cut through his jacket and woolen shirt like shards of glass. He tried lowering himself below the windshield, but this was terribly uncomfortable for a man his size, so he kept his altitude low and stayed south as long as he could. Like the Jenny, he had to fly the Standard all the time, but at stops for fuels and overnight stays, the trip was a good time to think. He thought a lot about Mavis and their time together. While he'd had a good time with her, he knew there was no future for them, and he was okay with that. He didn't feel as if he was falling for her, and he knew he would see her anytime he was in New York. Jack considered her a good friend and fellow pilot.

His thoughts also drifted to the shows Daws had lined up for them in the South. There would be those Southern women to get reacquainted with and new ones to meet, but after Mavis, they didn't seem nearly as interesting as before.

Jack planned his arrival Saturday afternoon and called ahead so everyone would be at his folks' for dinner. He had made good time. What better way for a pilot son to announce his arrival to his parents and the community than to buzz the town? A couple of passes down Main Street, and front doors flew open and people ran out. It was great. Jack grinned and waved to everyone, and they waved back, clutching their jackets and sweaters around them. He couldn't hear them, but he knew they were saying, "It's Johnie Ashcraft!" and "Welcome home, Johnie!"

Jack had bought a bunch of candy. When he saw kids coming out of the houses, he flew down Main Street and around town, throwing treats out. They rained down on the children, and he delighted in watching the kids scramble for the goodies. That task finished, he headed for a field on the Putterbaughs' land outside of town. He had called Troy to tell him when he would be there.

He taxied to the south side of the barn and had barely gotten the engine shut down when people started crowding around. The first one there was Troy. Jack hadn't seen his old friend since he got out of the army. Troy was now the banker in town. Almost everyone in town came out to greet Jack, who tried to say hello to everyone.

Jack knew that people were talking to him, but he could barely hear them. The long hours of wind and engine noise hadn't subsided in his ears.

"Hey, buddy," he said loudly, grinning, shaking Troy's hand. Their handshake went on forever. "You're a sight for sore eyes."

Troy gave him a slap on the shoulder. "Good to see you too, Johnie."

"Are you going to give rides, Johnie?" a kid asked.

"What?"

"Are you going to give rides?"

"Hey, give him a break, he's on vacation," Troy said.

"I just wondered," the kid said. He looked down, disappointed.

Slowly Jack's hearing came back. He remembered that day he'd met Cal Rodgers and that silly flying contraption that looked more like a giant kite. He figured he could get six kids in the plane for a quick spin around the field.

"I'll tell you what, kids. If the weather is clear, meet me here at two o'clock tomorrow afternoon, and I'll take as many as I can up for a quick flight. *But* you have to have a note from your parents giving me permission to give you a ride. Deal?"

The kids' eyes lit up, "Deal!" They all ran off screaming, "Yay!"

"Hey, Troy, let's tie her down," Jack said, then whispered, "There's a bag in the front I need you to drop off at the house."

"Sure thing," Troy replied.

Jack worked his way through the crowd, and there stood his dear Mother and Dad waiting patiently by the car, surrounded by his brothers and sisters. The sight of the woman brought tears to his eyes. Before she could say anything, he put his arms around her and whirled her around. She protested and insisted that he put her down, but Jack could tell that she liked it. His dad just stood by and smiled. When Jack and his mother were sufficiently dizzy, she protested.

"Time to put me down, Johnie," Lenore said. Jack did as she asked and steadied her when he lowered her to the ground.

"Mother, I'm now 'Big Jack' or the 'Cowboy Aviator,'" Jack said.

"Nonsense. You're Junior to me and Johnie to everyone else around here," Lenore answered flatly, and Jack laughed.

"Mother, do I see more gray hairs?" he teased.

"What do you expect after birthing this brood?" she said, motioning to all his brothers and sisters. "Then there's you off tempting fate, flying those rickety old planes, and Franz here saying that he wants to do the same thing. What's a mother to do? It's a wonder I have any hair at all!" Everyone laughed.

"Hello, Dad," Jack said, and shook his dad's hand. Jack gave his father a quick hug. The elder John didn't resist.

"Hello, son."

"Let's get on back to the house. Your mother has dinner almost ready," his dad said.

· · ·

Inside the house, to the left of the door in the living room, hung the photos of all the Ashcraft children and grandchildren. Jack paused to look at the photos while his mother and sisters hurried to the kitchen.

"The John Wesley clan of the Ashcrafts is certainly growing," Jack said to his dad.

"Yes, it is, son. Yes, it is," his dad said softly. "Except for John Jr."

The women finished supper, and they all ate hungrily. Jack got caught up on what was happening in everyone's lives. He ate till he could eat no more. After supper, he put on a red and white Santa stocking hat and said, "Ho, ho, ho! Merry Christmas! Gather 'round, everyone." He made a big production of pulling out a giant bag full of gifts.

"Mother," he said, bowing. "Just for you." He presented her his gift.

"This paper is so lovely," she said, running her hand over the wrapping. Careful not to tear it, she untied the bow that was squashed from the long trip and meticulously unwrapped the package. Slowly, she lifted the lid in anticipation. "Junior, this is lovely," she said, removing the shawl from the box and holding it next to her. "You spent too much."

"No, I didn't, and there's more," Jack said, pleased. He draped the shawl over her thin shoulders.

"Land's sake." She lifted the tissue paper to see the handbag with nice leather gloves on top. He had picked them up on impulse as he headed to checkout. With that, she started to cry. "You're too good to me."

"No, I'm not. Here's yours, Dad," Jack said, handing him a package. His dad opened the package and removed the wallet, turning it over and over, appreciating the fine leather. Then he admired the nice belt. "These are fine. Real fine. Thanks, Junior. I'll get a lot of good out of them."

Jack gave the others their presents. "Look," Clarice said, holding up her handbag. "I got a purse from New York City! Thank you, Johnie." She held it to her chest.

"Look inside," Jack said.

Clarice and his other sisters each opened their purses to find a diary inside, another impulse purchase. They all squealed and ran to give their brother a hug and kiss.

Jack thought Clarice looked a little peaked. His mother said later that she hadn't been feeling well since her little boy was born the year before but thought she was on the upswing. She picked up her son, Mason, and introduced him to Jack.

"Mason, this is your Uncle Jack," she said. "He's a pilot."

Jack took Mason from her arms. "Hi there, buddy. Do you want to be a pilot like me when you grow up?" he asked.

Mason looked at Jack, then reached for his mother.

"See, everyone? I'm not ready to be a father," he said as took her son from Jack.

"Franz," Jack said, "Here's yours. I want to tell everybody that I got Franz a little more because I missed his high school graduation."

Franz opened the package and looked at the jacket in disbelief. "I can't believe it. My very own flight jacket. Thanks, Jack." Immediately, he put it on and strutted around like a banty rooster despite it being warm in the house.

"Hey, buddy," Jack said, "you're going to sweat it out wearing it in the house."

"Then I'll go outside," Franz said, and walked out the door.

Just as he had planned, Jack gave each of the kids a shiny silver dollar. Everyone seemed pleased. Franz came back in and took off his jacket, folding it just right, and laid it across his legs.

After the gifts were handed out, Franz asked Jack about the circus. That was when Jack really got wound up. They were all impressed when he told them all the places he had flown and how the crowds loved them. Jack handed his mother the most recent newspaper clippings and proudly held up Mavis's newspaper featuring him and their flight. The more he talked, the more dramatic and daring his exploits became. Jack knew he wasn't fooling the adults, but the kids were eating it up, so he gave them big helpings. He loved the expressions of excitement and admiration on their faces. Of course, he left out all the stuff about the women and hooch, but Martin wasn't going to let him off the hook.

"And what about all the pretty women?" Martin said with a wink. He was always giving Jack a hard time, saying what a lady's man Jack was. Martin tried his best to get more information out of his brother, but Jack just let him wonder. Besides, he couldn't talk about grown-up stuff around the kids.

Franz got his baseball glove and threw one to Jack. "Let's go out and toss a few while it's still light," he said, putting on his cap. "You need to work off some dinner before you eat some of the peach pie Mother baked."

"You're on," Jack said.

"I been thinking, Jack," Franz said when they got outside. "There's really not much to keep me here in this sleepy town."

"Sleepy has its merits," Jack said.

"You know what I mean, Jack," Franz said. "I want to come join the circus and fly with you."

"Whoa, Franz," Jack said. "That's a big step."

"You joined the army when you were about my age," Franz said. "What's the difference?"

"You've got a point there," Jack admitted. "I'll tell you what. I'm thinking about striking out on my own after next year. Let me get established and save some more money. You'll be over twenty-one then. Mother and Dad won't be able to say much."

"Okay. I'm getting to be a pretty good mechanic," Franz said. "I could do that and take flying lessons in Wichita."

"Good plan," Jack said.

Back inside, Lenore Ashcraft brought her son a slice of pie she'd made from peaches picked from the tree in the backyard. No one else made it like her. He let her keep the plate, and he took the pan. Everybody had gone home around ten o'clock so they could get the young ones to bed. Jack and his parents talked well into the night while he finished off the pie. Franz listened intently. Jack was getting very sleepy. Traveling from New York had been a long trip even for him. He leaned back on the couch and fell fast asleep. His mother put a blanket over her son and went to bed.

The next day, the weather was fair at two o'clock, so Jack headed to the field as he had promised.

"You don't have to do this, son," his father said.

"I know, but I promised, and I don't want to let the kids down. I was a kid once," Jack said, winking at his father.

"Ivan, you and Mary come help me. Mary, you take up all the permission slips. Ivan, you get everybody lined up and both of you keep them orderly and out of the propeller," Jack said, and they headed for the field.

There were about thirty boys and girls waiting for them, some with parents, some alone. He and Troy rolled out the red Standard. For the next two hours, Jack gave thirty-one kids and five adults, five and six at a time depending on size, a two-minute flight around the field at an altitude of 150 feet. Finally, the last kid got out of the plane, yelled, "Thanks, Johnie," and ran off.

· · ·

Jack had only been at home a few days when he started sensing a change in the weather, an ability pilots acquire early. Doc Kimball, a well-known weather forecaster, wasn't around, but Jack didn't need Doc to tell him that a storm was moving in. Florida was a long way away, and he wanted plenty of time to get there, plus time to stop and see Buck and his Mason buddies. Reluctantly, he decided to stay only one more day. His mother and dad were disappointed he couldn't stay longer, but knew he couldn't risk getting snowed in. It was a short time at home, but he had seen and talked to everyone he had wanted to.

The kids asked him to talk at their school, and he spent time with his dad at the hardware store. The guys with the circus wouldn't have believed it, but Jack almost got talked out. He went out to Troy's one night and pulled out some hooch he had bought in New York. They went to the barn and talked about old times, passing the bottle back and forth.

"Those board track days were great, weren't they, Jack?" Troy said.

"Yeah. You still have your motorcycle?" Jack asked.

"Yep. It's right over there under the tarp." Troy walked over and pulled back the stiff canvas. "I don't ride it much, but once in a while, I get it out, tune it up, and take it for a spin. Darlene loves to ride with me."

"Still looks like it's in pretty good shape. I have one I take wherever I go," Jack said. "How's life for you here?"

"It's quiet, but good," Troy said. "Your life isn't for me. They wouldn't admit it, but John and Lenore are proud of you."

"How do you know?" Jack asked.

"Because your dad shows everyone the newspaper clippings that you send to the store. Everyone knows what you're up to," Troy said.

"Well, I'll be damned," Jack said. "They sure give me a hard time about it to my face."

"Oh, they fear for you, but they think it's pretty neat that you get your name in the papers," Troy said.

Jack thought about that for several moments.

"Well, I gotta go, buddy," Jack said, standing. "I've got some long flying days ahead of me."

Troy handed him the bottle.

"Keep it as a Christmas present," Jack said. Unlike other places in the country, good liquor was hard to come by in the land of Carrie Nation.

The next morning, Franz came in to talk while Jack was getting his things together.

"Hey, Jack," he said, "don't forget about me, okay? You promised." Franz was the only one who called him Jack, because he thought it sounded more grown up.

"The circus is no place for you right now. Things will go according to the plan we talked about, okay?" Jack said. He knew that he was being a protective older brother and imagined that this was how his parents must have felt when he left home.

Somehow, Jack felt bribery was in order. He reached into his pocket, pulled out a wad of bills, and peeled off four fifty-dollar bills.

"Here you go," he said, handing them to his brother. "See about getting some flying lessons, and work on as many planes as you can. Okay?"

"All right! Thanks," Franz said, stuffing the bills in a pocket of his new leather jacket.

"This is between you and me. Come on, let's go get some breakfast," Jack said.

John Sr. was just sitting down. Lenore turned from the stove when they walked in.

"Wish you could stay longer, Junior," she said, "but I know you need to get back before the snowstorm."

"We sure appreciate you coming home," his dad said. "It's been good to have you."

"It's been good to be home," Jack said, quickly eating his breakfast.

There was a knock on the door just then. It was Troy to take Jack to his plane. His mother handed Jack a paper sack full of sandwiches and other goodies, just like she'd done so many years ago when he and Troy went to see Cal Rodgers.

"Fly safely, now," she said, her voice catching. "You're a good son. I love you." She gave Jack a hug and kissed him on the cheek, tears running down hers.

His dad nodded and shook his hand. "Bye, son."

Jack's heart was heavy as he got into Troy's pickup. "Damn, that was hard," he said to Troy. "Harder than I thought it would be. The folks are certainly getting older."

"I hear you," Troy said, but they didn't say more during the short ride to his plane.

Jack checked the plane over carefully and shook Troy's hand before he climbed into the cockpit. "Thanks, buddy."

"Glad to help out," he said.

Snow started to fall. "I've got to go. Check on Mother and Dad occasionally for me, will you?"

"Sure thing," Troy said, and turned Jack's propeller. The ground was hard, and the snow was just beginning to collect on the dry grass. Jack's plane bounced across the field, then lifted off. He flew over the house, and there they were on the front porch, waving to him. His mother clutched her new shawl tight around her shoulders and went inside, but his dad stayed outside. Jack watched him until he was a speck, just like that day when his dad had taken him and Troy to the railroad station. Jack buzzed the house and town one last time to say goodbye and headed south to Texarkana. Buck was still flying out of there, and Jack was determined to talk him into flying with the circus.

Texarkana, Texas

Jack buzzed Buck's place and landed. Buck ran out and was so glad to see Jack he just about shook his arm off. "Jack, you son of a gun. How you been?"

"Been good, doing good," Jack said.

"Let's go to Gil's, and you can tell me all about it," Buck said.

They sat down in their favorite booth, and Tessa came up. "Well, if it isn't Jack," she said.

"In the flesh," Jack said with a laugh. "Only now it's 'Big Jack, the Cowboy Aviator'!"

"Well, whoop-de-do," Tessa replied. "You're still Jack to me and will always be. What'll it be? The usual?"

"You bet."

"So, tell me all about it. What's it like to fly for Gates?" Buck asked.

"It's great. Best thing I ever did," Jack said. "We fly all over the east. Thousands of people come to watch us and take rides. I'm making good money, but you know what the best part is?"

Buck leaned closer. "What?"

"The dames fall all over us," Jack said. "We have our pick."

Buck shook his head and laughed. "Same ole Jack."

"Like I said, the pay's good. Real good. We're always looking for good pilots and mechanics," Jack said. "Why don't you come join us? We've even got advance guys and barkers. You name it, we have it. It's a real racket, let me tell you. The people eat it up. You'd have a ball."

"You got me. Give me a couple of weeks to wind things up here," Buck said, and they celebrated into the night.

Jack Ashcraft (l) and Troy Putterbaugh (r), circa 1915.
Courtesy of Allen Keller.

CHAPTER 16
FLORIDA

Jack Ashcraft, Florida, 1926. *Courtesy of Allen Keller.*

December 1925–March 1926

Buck was to meet up with Jack in New York and head to Richmond, Virginia, then to Macon, Georgia. Jack was considering the city as a southern base of operations for when he struck out on his own. Gardner Nagle, who had given Jack some flying instruction back in Shreveport, had suggested the city and was considering partnering with Jack on the venture.

After the incident over New York City, Jack had hired his own mechanic. The other guys were good, but they had too many planes to take care of, and Jack wanted one dedicated to his plane. An amiable fellow, his name was Jimmy Scott. He and Jack were chatting away, waiting for Buck to fly in, which could be anytime.

They were putting away their tools for the morning when they heard a plane.

"That's probably Buck now," Jack said.

The aircraft circled the field, touched down, and took off again. When it did, the pilot maneuvered the plane to make it look like it was bucking.

Jack laughed. "Now I know it's Buck. See how the plane looks like it's bucking? That's how he got his nickname."

Buck eventually landed and taxied near Jack's plane and popped up out of the cockpit. "Hey, Jack, let's go to Florida!"

"Let's do it!" Jack said, greeting his friend warmly. "This is my mechanic, Jimmy Scott. We'll check out your plane and head out this afternoon. After a quick stop in Macon, we'll be off to Jacksonville."

Several years before, Henry Flagler had decided that the transportation system in Florida wasn't up to snuff, so he'd decided to do something about it and had built a railroad along the Atlantic Ocean. When it reached one destination, that area would get a freeze, so Flagler would decide it needed to go farther south. When all was said and done, he'd built his railroad all the way south of Miami and out to Key West.

More and more rich easterners were taking advantage of the railroad and building vacation homes in the state. Land was selling and reselling like hotcakes. There was speculation on both coasts of Florida. What better way to advertise to promote a business and attract attention than to have a flying circus to do the advertising? Gates intended to take full advantage of the massive gambling on land. Daws had been sent ahead of the fliers.

The year had ended much the way it started—with tough luck all the way around. In Richmond, the guys were using the infield of a racetrack as a landing field. Stultz hit some furrows the wrong way and knocked the landing gear off his plane. Jack did the same thing in Orangeburg, South Carolina. They hit some of the same cities going south as they had when working their way north earlier in the year. Along the way, they had to deal with snow, wind, fog, and rain, but they finally got far enough south that the weather was somewhat more predictable.

Jack and Buck stopped in Macon, but the others headed on to Florida. Pang, Eddie, and Freddie made it with four planes that operated reasonably well, but Wild Bill Stultz, Duke, and Mickey Efferson drifted in and out of the organization. The planes were Standard J-1s with 180-horsepower Hisso engines.

Jack caught up with them in Gainesville.

"Where's Buck," Pang said.

"He's not here?" Jack asked.

"Nope, haven't seen him."

"We caught some pretty heavy fog on the way down. Maybe he turned back," Jack said. "He'll be here, though."

Daws got them hundreds of contracts for good money. It seemed people had more money than Florida had oranges. The circus got $3,000 when they had four planes in the air. Some weeks they got $5,000–6,000 and up to $500 for stunts. Unfortunately, a lot of money was going into plane repairs.

From Gainesville, they went to Ocala for some demonstrations over Christmas. The engagements involved more gimmicks than skilled aerial maneuvers, which didn't impress Jack much. An article in the paper showed what poor shape the planes were getting to be in, and gave information about Jack that Pang and the others hadn't heard before.

> Ocalans and other Marion County people were given a chance yesterday to see their city and surrounding community from the air when one of the large red passenger planes of the Gates Flying Circus arrived in town for a three-day stay. The aviation field is located just beyond the fair grounds.
>
> Many people were on hand to witness the arrival of the plane. According to schedule four planes weer [sic] to have been sent to Ocala. Motor and other trouble kept three planes from making the trip but it is stated that one plane from Gainesville may arrive this afternoon to be on hand for tomorrow.
>
> While no definite figures could be gathered it was estimated that approximately 125 people made flights yesterday in the passenger plane. Many more than this number are expected to make the trip tomorrow as it is possible that two planes will be on hand. At times as many as ten people were waiting to be carried on flights on the long trips they were given many stunts.

Ocala Evening Star, December 26, 1925

Who made the decision to include stunts after the incident in Baton Rouge, or why, is not known, but they only included simple wingovers and Immelmann maneuvers. Later, the reporter looked up Jack to learn more about him and his experience.

The plane which arrived yesterday is piloted by the skilled hands of Jack Ashcraft, who for 18 months served with Uncle Sam overseas as the official test pilot of the 306 Flying Squadron located at Romorantine, France. When he was not busy testing out planes, Pilot Ashcraft flew over the lines and on one occasion was wounded while engaged in combat with a Bosche airman.

After the armistice Mr. Ashcraft returned to the United States and since has been engaged in commercial aviation. He has thrilled spectators with his stunts and daring. He has speeded around the rack tracks at 100 miles an hour so close to the ground that at intervals of five feet he would touch the ground with the tip of his wing. He has set up a line of pop bottles and speeding his plane to its utmost capacity has swooped down a great distance and knocked the bottles over.

While flying for the Gates circus in Wilmington, Dela., Ashcraft broke the world's record for a number of flights in one day. He flew the plane from the ground and landed that day 150 times. This is a world's record and one that any aviator would be glad to hold. The aviator is a 32nd degree Mason in the El Krubal Temple at Shreveport, La.

In an interview with a Star reporter this morning after a flight the young aviator stated that ever since 1915 he had been interested in flying. When he graduated from high school it was prophesied that he would be an aviator and that in 1925 he would fly over New York city and while flying over the city would lose one of his boots. This prophecy came true except that he didn't lose one of his boots.

The article continued to tell what spectators were to expect the next day and that George Babcock, their Diavolo for the tour, would be doing several stunts. From Ocala, the group would go to Leesburg for three days.

Two more planes did indeed arrive the next day, and Pang was flying one of them. He picked up a newspaper to catch up on the news of the last couple of days. When he read the article about Jack being a test pilot for the army, he just smiled and shook his head. He caught up with the others under the tent drinking coffee.

"Hey, Jack. Seems like I learn something new about you every day," he said.

"How's that?" Jack said, taking a sip of coffee.

"Says here that you were an official test pilot for the 306 Flying Squadron in France," Pang said.

Jack spit out his coffee. "Let me see that." He grabbed for the paper, but Pang jerked it out of his reach.

"Says here that you even crossed enemy lines and were wounded in battle," he said, handing Jack the paper.

"Why Jack, you poor thing," Eddie teased. "You sure recovered well. There must have been some pretty nurses with miraculous cures." The others laughed.

"I can't believe he wrote that about being a pilot and getting wounded," Jack said, shaking his head in disbelief. "Reporters and their readers are suckers for military rank."

Responding to the expressions of his colleagues, Jack added a caveat. "I swear I wasn't drunk. All I have to say is that I was in service to my country, so I can neither confirm nor deny that this account is true," he said, tucking the paper under his arm.

"As for knocking down the pop bottles, I will be happy to

demonstrate that exhibition of amazing skill. But for now, I'm taking a break and going fishing," he said and walked off.

From Ocala, it was south to Leesburg, Tampa, and Bradenton. A lot of women surrounded the fliers when they landed, but there was a woman in Bradenton that Jack thought particularly fine. At their next stop, he missed her so much that he wrote her a letter to tell her that they were heading for St. Petersburg and suggested that she meet him there.

They were in St. Pete and were finished for the day. While Jack worked on his ship, he kept looking for the woman, but she never showed. Then a roustabout came over and told him there was a guy looking for him. Jack wiped his hands and walked over to the man, who acted nervous and fidgety. He wore a jacket even though the day was hot and sultry. When Jack was about twenty feet away, the man confronted him.

"Your name Ashcraft?" the man said.

"Yep," Jack said.

The man pulled out a gun that Jack swore looked bigger than Gates's .45 and pointed it at Jack, then hid it back in his jacket.

Jack held up his hands. "Hey, buddy, what's this about?"

Everybody around them spooked and scattered like cattle, ducking behind vehicles.

"You know a woman named Doris?" the man asked.

"Sure do. She's one fine woman," Jack said, and immediately regretted it.

"I'll have you know that fine woman is my wife!" the man said. He was so furious that he started shaking badly and pulled the gun out again.

His hand shook so badly that Jack was afraid the man would accidently pull the trigger. By then, Jack was sweating profusely. He looked like somebody had turned a sprinkler hose on him.

"Now, calm down," Jack said, sweat trickling into his eyes. "Let's talk this over."

"What's there to talk about you, you adulterer," the man said.

Jack figured it best to keep him talking. "Well, now, you'll have to forgive me, sir. I swear I didn't know that she was married. I'm not one to go breaking up marriages."

The man relaxed a bit, and the gun barrel lowered slightly.

Jack sensed an opportunity. "Why don't you just put the gun back in your car?" Jack said. "Tell you what. I'll buy you a beer at the local joint and we'll talk this over."

The man raised the gun again and pointed it at Jack's chest. "I don't want no damn beer, and I don't want to talk this over. And I don't want to kill you," he said. "I just want you to stay away from my wife."

"You got it. I'll never see her again, I promise," Jack said, looking down the gun barrel.

"Okay. You come around Doris again, and I'll use this next time. Hear?"

"Yes, sir, I hear you loud and clear. I'll stay away from her, I promise," Jack said.

The guy got in his car and sped off.

Pang ran over. "Damn, what was that all about?"

"Evidently, I put a move on his wife, but I swear I didn't know she was married," Jack said, wiping the sweat from his brow with his shirtsleeves.

"I declare, someone's going to shoot you someday," Pang said.

"Damn. That gun was bigger than Gates's," Jack said.

Pang just shook his head and walked off.

All Jack knew was that he needed some hooch. Thinking about the incident later, he knew he would honor his word. If the man would point a gun at him, he shuddered to think what he'd do to Doris.

There was another nice-looking woman who took a liking to Jack. She told him that she would pick him up after the show the next day. Sure enough, he hadn't been on the ground more than five minutes when she drove up, a chauffeur at the wheel. It was ninety degrees out, but she was wearing a fur coat.

He walked over to Pang.

"Hey, Pang, loan me twenty bucks. I need to buy some hooch for my date with that dame," he said, pointing his head in the direction of the car.

Pang shook his head and handed Jack a twenty-dollar bill. "This will be taken out of your earnings," he said.

"No problem," Jack answered.

As they sped off, the woman revealed the reason she was wearing a fur coat. It was the only article of clothing she was wearing. That was just the beginning of a night unlike any Jack had ever experienced. He was so hungover the next morning, he barely made it back to the airfield.

Something the circus hadn't done much before was fireworks displays. Pang and Stultz scheduled a night show in Daytona and took off in separate directions. When they reversed direction, they nearly collided before they got their flares lit. One night, a bearing burned out on Pang's plane, and he had to land immediately.

One of their new stuntmen, George Babcock, was going to do a transfer from a speeding boat on the Halifax River to an airplane. Eddie Bond was at the controls in the airplane. He released the rope ladder and flew over the boat, but the boat couldn't go fast enough, and the plane couldn't slow down without stalling, so the plane flew past too fast for Babcock to catch the ladder. Eddie flew around again, flying a little slower, and Babcock was able to grab a rung. One problem solved revealed another: a bridge loomed ahead. Eddie had to pick up speed and altitude quickly, or they would slam into the bridge.

Babcock's bottom drug the water, but they made it over, and Babcock pulled himself up and got into the cockpit, relieved that he'd survived. When they landed, Gates told Babcock that he would give him extra money if he went up again and dropped into the water, so up he went with Eddie in the cockpit. Eddie lowered the rope, and Babcock dropped into the water. He bounced a few times like a stone and went underwater, emerging triumphantly ten anxious seconds later. Jack couldn't believe what he saw.

Another stunt Babcock perfected that went over well wherever they performed was his Ponce de León act. For it, he put together a costume that consisted of what Jack considered tight purple underwear, a wide-brimmed hat complete with ostrich-feather plume, and a black belt with a scabbard attached to resemble Ponce de León. In his hand, Babcock held a sword like a Templar knight. Jack couldn't believe that Babcock had the guts to stand on the wing of Pang's plane like that while he flew around. Jack thought it took balls for a man to fly around in purple tights, but the crowds loved it, and the pay was good. Jack decided that Gates couldn't have paid him enough.

Tragedy struck as well. A new young stuntman named Jack Parks wanted to make a name for himself. He had specially designed snaps that connected to rings so he could do what he called "the Breakaway." He would drop from the landing gear spreader bar, and the cable would halt his fall. Pang was skeptical that the snaps would hold, but Parks had tried it a couple of times at low altitudes. Parks begged Pang to let him stunt, and Pang relented. Jack took Parks up at Monson Field near Lake Alfred. At about three thousand feet, Parks attempted his stunt. To Jack's horror, the snaps didn't hold, and Parks plunged to his death.

The incident prostrated Jack, and he became hysterical and unable to fly for a few days.

One day, the circus had a big contract in Daytona, and Eddie's plane wouldn't start. The contract was for $3,000 for four planes in the air. Jack had resumed flying and flown a lot, so he was scheduled to sit this one out. Four planes, $3,000; three planes, nothing. And Eddie's engine wouldn't start. Everybody tried, but no one could start the plane.

"I can't get it started," Pang said, out of breath after four tries. "Someone go get Jack."

The plane had a big Hardman propeller that was difficult to pull. Jack grabbed the propeller. Eddie was in the cockpit.

"Switch off," he yelled.

"Switch off," Eddie yelled, and Jack pulled the propeller to get fuel in the line and other liquids out.

The switch wasn't off. The motor kicked back and knocked Jack to the ground. Immediately, he grabbed his arm.

Eddie jumped out of the plane, and he and the others ran over to Jack. "How could I be so stupid? You okay, Jack?"

Jack thought then that his arm was broken, but if four planes didn't fly, they wouldn't get paid. The show had to go on, so he answered with the only thing he could say. "Yeah, I'm okay. Just got the breath knocked out of me."

Eventually, someone got the plane started, but Eddie's wife was afraid for him to fly it.

"Let Jack fly it," she said. "He's single, and if he gets killed, he won't ruin a wife's life."

"Jack can't," Eddie said. "Can't you see he's hurt?"

Jack waved him off. "I'll fly."

"You sure, Jack?" Pang asked.

"Yep. Just twisted my arm a bit," Jack said, rubbing his upper limb. It hurt like hell, but he climbed into the cockpit.

Somehow, Jack did everything he was supposed to do. After he landed, he stepped out of the plane and immediately fainted. They took him to the hospital. The doctor didn't immediately know what was wrong with him. When he figured it out, he put Jack's arm in a cast and told him not to fly for a week.

The cast didn't keep Jack from flying, and it didn't keep him from meeting girls. In fact, it helped. His broken arm got him attention and sympathy, and he milked it.

The women would say, "Oh, Jack. You're so brave to fly with a broken arm. Come to my place after the show and relax. I'll take care of you."

Buck still had not shown up, and there was no news of him. Jack was getting worried.

CHAPTER 17
HANGAR FLYING

Buck Steele and Jack Ashcraft, circa 1926. *Courtesy of Cindy Weigand.*

March 1926
Heading Back North

The circus traveled to Miami, where Jack competed in the State Society Air Race and won the South Miami Kennel Club Trophy in Coral Gables before they made their way back north. The event was reported in the local paper:

> *Members of four state societies will witness the presentation of a silver loving cup to Jack Ashcraft, winner of the society's air race on Tuesday. Thursday night at the South Miami Kennel Club. Ashcraft represented Ohio state society and he will be presented with the cup by the South Miami Kennel club in recognition of his feat in winning the race.*

The article also talked about other societies represented in the air race and included a program of entertainers, as well as greyhounds running in races.

Even though he had won another trophy, overall Jack didn't feel the flying was up to par in the state, and Florida weather didn't agree with him. The ploys to draw the crowds were too gimmicky. The air was too warm and humid, and he couldn't seem fly out of it no matter how high he flew. The women were beautiful, but none more so than Mavis. They certainly weren't as classy.

He was glad that they were heading back north.

(An undated letter Jack wrote home. Edited for readability and the passenger's name is changed.)

> *We were out at the field after an air meet chewing the fat in West Palm Beach when an old ship came wobbling in. We all wondered who it was. The ship circled our field and got the lay of the field and the wind direction, did a wing over and*

commenced to slipping in to land. As per the usual custom when a strange ship comes in, we all rushed over to see who the pilot was.

I did not have to go far because the pilot was looking around to see who was there and he spotted Jack and shouted, "Well if it's not Old Big Jack. Haven't seen you since that night ride across the swamps in the fog."

Having not seen Buck for some time and being on the same trip in two different ships, and both going to different destinations, one arrived, one didn't, we had a lot to talk over.

Well Jack, how did you get down that night?" Buck asked as they walked to the hangar.

Well, I don't hardly know," Jack replied. "Just luck and a few prayers and I guess the Lord had me by the shirt tale [sic], or I surely would have cracked up that night, but was lucky and got away with it. In fact it was either land where I did or run out of gas and then sure enough crack up.

The rest of the boys gathered around and after seeing two friends meet and having those for remarks wanted to hear the rest of the story of that wild ride over the swamps that night.

We were both enroute from N.Y. to Jacksonville and after flying through fog, rains, and bucking high winds, we reached Richmond, Virginia. All the way down that fare, we encoun-tered all the disagreeable weather that a flyer can have. There was ten inches of snow on the ground and the Hudson River was frozen over when we left. This condition lasted all the way to Richmond. Leaving Richmond we had nice weather until late in the afternoon. We had been making good progress and was doing fine until we hit Goldsboro, North Carolina. There I developed a little engine and oil trouble, so was forced to land. Buck circled and landed along side [sic].

We all pitched in and made the necessary repairs because we wanted to make Wilmington that day. We got everything ready to go and had one hour and half of daylight left to make Wilmington in so we took off.

We made good progress for about fifty miles, then is where our trouble started. We ran into a storm, fog and a very high wind. I had been in Wilmington before and knew exactly where to land, but Buck had not so knowing this I took the lead and decided to go on in even though it would be almost dark upon arriving there. But I figured I would land first and light a gas flare for him to land by.

Well, the storm progressed fine, better than we did. The wind increased, and the clouds lowered, and darkness was close on. Well there was only one thing left to do there, that was to go on, so we lost altitude and got under the fog and kept going. We were over the swamps there and no place to land so on we went. Conditions were tough. It was too late to go back, so the only thing to do was to go on. In ten minutes, it was pitch dark and we were flying fifty feet over the trees.

My thoughts then were about my engine if she would quit now. Well, we would not know much about the wreck because the swamps were thick with trees and even tho [sic] we would not get hurt, we might have starved before getting out because at the particular part it was not travelable, nothing but trees, thick underbrush and water.

We were flying so low that forest fires and lights or any kind were not visible, and the sky was so black, that I lost all sense of direction so had to rely upon the compass.

I did not happen to have a flashlight so had to use matches to see where I was going. Because of flying so low and being on a sharp look out for high trees and other things, I might hit, a match did not last long. Just one peek at the compass and that was all. Well, I would peek and correct it then wait a few minutes then take another look. Well then, I started. I only had one box of those very safe matches and they were commencing to vanish rapidly.

After a few more peeks at the compass, I had three matches left, well I decide to light a cigarette and use the fire end of my cig for light, so I used up those last three matches before getting a light. Then it would not work. I could not see a thing from the flare of the cig.

Well after that failed, I had to think of some way, so happened to think I had a mechanic in the front seat, so asked him for some matches. Well, he had a few. It did not take long to use those up, but as long as they lasted, I kept my course and Buck was right on my tail. I did not know it but he was following my fire from the exhaust which was streaming out about five feet on each side of the fuselage.

Soon I struck the last match and did not know what to do, but just go on. I could not see, and I did not know where Buck was, and I did not know exactly where I was. All I knew I was up and flying supposed to be heading south, that's all.

You see the light ship I was flying, or any ship will turn by its own accord due to the torque of the motor and if you cannot keep an accurate check on your burieclam [sic] you will fly in a circle and not know it. Well, I guess that's what I did. I was worried about Buck and kept looking back and to both sides. Thinking I might see his exhaust. But I did not so I guess he must have run out of gas and went down so I says to myself, every man for his self and so I just quit worrying about him. I had enough troubles of my own.

Here was my fix. In an airplane, fifty feet high, bucking a sixty mile [sic] gale, dark, thick fog, off my course, no lights to watch instruments getting low on gasoline, worried.

The only thing I could do was fly. I could not see the land. I happened to have a radio dial watch and that's the only thing I did know and that was the time. That was some relief, I knew within fifteen minutes I was due to run out of gas, so I had a little consolement there. Well, the next 30 minutes I was (in) agony. But it passed, seemed like all night to me, but it went by. I don't remember how.

But I kept on going. You see I never saw a light or land mark [sic] of any kind since getting dark. Nothing to check on at all. Just guess work mostly and the wind was terrible and I could not see anything to check my drift so here I was up three hours and no place yet. Then I saw a light.

Boy howdy that's the best-looking thing in the world. I head right for it, but it was only a farmhouse, probably a _____ shack but I circled it, checked on the wind from it, and headed straight into the wind, which I knew was from the south. I passed over the house and looked at my watch and I was twenty minutes getting out of sight of that light and I was flying 50 feet high, so I figured I was getting over ground about 10 miles an hour. Well then, that light faded out. I had to do something else.

I commenced craning my neck for some other land mark [sic], and I was rewarded. I saw several lights seemed to be in a circle. I headed for them and after thinking a little while finally decided I was over a lake about forty miles west of Wilmington and I knew a highway was due east into working town. Then after looking around, I saw where the highway was by auto lights so headed that way. Wind on my right. That was south so I knew I was right. I also knew the lake was on the south side of the road.

Now flying was a little better, had something to follow and check on and that road which is only thirty feet wide looked like 200 to me. I was right over it, and so close that looked wide and in any emergency, I would have attempted landing on it. There were several cars on it, so I had lights the rest of the way in. I felt a little more easy, so hollered at Jimmy my mechanic again and that is the first time after asking for matches that I thought of him. I asked him how he was. He says fine. This was his first airplane experience, the trip south, the first hop was his first ride, and he was game, too. I'd say that for Jimmy.

Well, after discovering where I was and that was a valuable discovery, too. I was in the air three hours fifteen minutes on four hours gas. Then a new worry set in, that was – do I have enough gas to get in? Well, all along I throttled as much as I could, so I throttled a little more. I could not see what I was turning on my tachometer, but I was just turning enough to keep (loset) [sic] in the air and make a little more time.

I consoled myself by knowing that I landed in a field this side of Wilmington on this same highway, and I might get in there but that field was small, full of drain ditches and old tree stumps, then I thought of the river, well, I'll land there, I can do it and not hurt either of us. My mechanic or myself, but my ship will be ruined. Well, that's what I was going to do then I started worrying again. Maybe I won't get there. Then I took charge of myself and says out loud, wait, see what happens, then do something, don't cross the Bridge until I get there.

Well, I took things a little better, wait, that's all I had to do. Wait until my gas gave out, then get down, that's another thing. Well anyway, I sided [sic] go myself into waiting out. I had to do something do it. In a few minutes, I saw dim outlines of what in my worried mind was a lighted city, no I did not see it. I took my oil stained [sic]goggles off to see if I was seeing thin(g)s or imagination.

No, it was not. I just imagined, or maybe a lower cloud floated between us, or a high tree, or most anything could have obstructed the view, anyway every time when I was in doubt, I pulled up. I could not see ahead but I could see straight down by looking back and not ahead. It was like flying in a box with the lid open. You can see nothing and imagine plenty.

Then again, I caught sight of some dim lights. I pulled my helmet and goggles off and threw them on the floor. I unbuttoned my shirt collar and loosened my neck tie [sic], felt my brow and I was wet with perspiration, like a man having a fit or tremmors [sic] or illusions. I was not myself. Then sure enough I knew it was lights. Oh, what a feeling. I felt better and I was all right.

I was relieved and considerable, well the relief I got was just like a flat tire. You all have probably saw a tire go flat, well that's the way I felt and did, just sink back in my seat, and felt better. Took a good breath and then thought again. How will I see to get down? Well, I needed that stimulant it gave me a new set of hopes. I got to the river, had ten more minutes gas and I could see lights up in the fog and I knew I could not cross town and hit tall buildings so had to detour and go around, if I did that, how was I to find the field? Well, that's something else.

I started to go back to the river and land in it, well that would be a loss. Maybe drown and I didn't know if Jimmy could swim or not, and I thought of lots of excuses for not landing in it so finally made up my mind, I won't go down until I have too, unless I find some place to get down. I circled town, got on the east side where the field was, saw a streetcar and tried to locate the field by following it out, because the street car line bordered on the field on the north. I trailed that streetcar, circled, passed it again and again, but with no reward.

The ground was all so black and all I could see was the lights of houses, so finally decided that the field had been subdivided and built up and no more field existed so not where I will go, I thought. Ocean beamed into my very muddled mind, Beach [sic], surely the ocean has a beach. But I wonder how I'll know when I come to the ocean and its fifteen miles away and a very desolate swamp between me and the beach.

Boardwalk and everything, Wrightsville Beach, I read about it, but was never out there, so out there I went, due east, about fifteen minutes. I was there, there was a few houses lighted, and I knew it was the beach, could see the streetcar line, bridges that crossed the last part of the swamp.

"I was relieved again because I figured the lights would be on the edge of the beach and that would be a good light to land by, at least it would show me where the ground was. Having this all set in my mind I headed straight down the side of these lights and throttled my motor for a speedy landing.

But about that time, I saw right away that the beautiful picture I had in my mind was all wrong and I was just about to land on top of some houses, so I gives the motor the gun and with new worries was to where the Beach was and having over 10 minutes left of my gas supply.

"I was in a sweat. So I banked around to keep in sight of the lights and sputter-sputter went my motor. Oh, oh, gas is out. I leveled off and she caught, again and I saw then that my gas would not flow banking to the right on account of my gas line being on the left side so after that all turns to the left.

My circle over Wrightsville Beach caused more lights to be lighted, also I noticed on man on the Beach with a flashlight, that was good news to me. I knew where to look for the water. It was at least 300 feet from the lights, and it was where I thought was the deep blue sea. But after venturing out that far I could see the lines of the breakers, those that have seen the sea at night. I noticed the phosphorous in saltwater is illuminous and I could detect the lines of breakers so knew where the water stopped, and the beach began.

All things seemed ok now all set, now all I got to do is set her down so too another circle, and pulled throttle back for a landing and just about the time I was ready to "set her down" when I saw something black slip under my wing.

Now I thought in our uneasy state of mind, what was that, then another one went by under me. I thought holey [sic]Mackerel I thought it must be ______ers [sic] then another went, Boy howdy I murmured another prayer.

By this time, I was getting too far away from the lights to be comfortable, so took a steep band (bank) to the left over the water, I was sure of not letting anything out there and the pump on my gas tank was on the left, so that's really the only way I could have turned. I flew back until I passed the lights and came in again, this time not to land but just take a look. I knew if I run out of gas, I could put her down and almost wade to shore, or the breakers would bring me in.

The next time around, I saw the man with the flashlight waving it frantically and I devoted my time on that trip trying to interpret some kind of meaning to what he was waving for.

With my thick head, and jumbled brain I could now get what he wanted to show me. Then he was standing on a porch of a beach house. I could see that because he would shine his light on the roof and the porch poles.

"Well, that was of no interest to me, so I checked the man with the search light off my mind. I had something to do and do it quick. That was the second time around, what I was worried about was these felock [sic] thing that kept slipping under me and when I passed over the beach and how far apart they were. Well, all tolled [sic] I made twelve more trips around and each time I would count the distance between the black obstruction not knowing what they were.

I would count between each one and finally picked out one that according to my count was three hundred feet apart, I got that particular one down when I knew it, and getting all set for what I thought would be a grand and glorious flash and crash, but when the last black object was passed, that I was to set down over, I cut the gun and waited.

I dragged my skid first and waited then I counted on a small crack up. The best I could get out of it would be a nose over and that would mean breaking a propellor and maybe two lower longerons and no one knows what else.

Anyway, I cut the gun and waited. Tail skid drug then wheels touched, and I felt myself lunging forward then the tail, gave it the gun to bury the tail down. Went down but it was no use I was stopped rolling and was down. Then a breaker broke on my wings, and did I get a spray of water, so knew I must get out of there before the ship sank so I gave it the gun again to taxi out on dry beach. After getting there quite a crowd had assembled. I cut the engine and questions were being asked how, where, and why were and this, that, and the other.

What happened to Jimmy," one asked.

Then my thoughts came to wonder how Jimmy is and there is the joke. I asked him how he was and how he enjoyed the ride. Well, he handed me something and said, 'Here is the fire extinguisher. I took it out of the bracket and can't get it back. You put it in, will you?'"

I laughed out loud for several reasons, I was down, ship still works, and no one hurt, but the real laugh was when I asked Jimmy,

"Why did you take the extinguisher out?"

And he said, "Well when it got dark, I saw the fire coming out on both sides and going almost back to the tail of the ship. I thought it might catch on fire or something and I wanted to be ready to put the fire out in case anything caught."

We tied down and wondered how we get to town, and yes, some food.

We haven't eat [sic] yet, Jimmy said, and its [sic] 9 thirty. Let's get a way to town."

"Okay, suits me," so we got a lift on a fast going [sic] streetcar and unloaded in front of a hotel, went up, cleaned up and went down to a restaurant and had a very delightful and enjoyable dinner."

But the boys asked, "How about the pilot Buck and his ship? What became of him?"

I says "Boys, that's another story. We don't have time to tell that one, let's eat and we'll have that one later."

Undated letter written by Jack Ashcraft.
Courtesy of Cindy Weigand.

CHAPTER 18
THE SHORT SNORTER TRADITION BEGINS

Jack Ashcraft Jr., 1926. *Courtesy of Allen Keller.*

April–June 1926
Upstate New York

All in all, they had a good run in Florida business-wise. They covered both coasts. Jack made up to three thousand dollars a month on their tour in Florida, so he couldn't complain, broken arm and all. He saved everything he could because he figured the land boom would eventually have to bust. Such things always do. They might have one more good season down there, but that would be it.

New federal regulations were to take effect to encourage safety, and that meant no wing walking without a parachute, curtailing stunting, requiring pilots to be licensed, and certifying aircraft. The days of the flying circus were numbered. He would strike out on his own in 1927. The first big event he would enter was the National Air Race.

Come spring of 1926, they headed back north, but it was like Louisiana all over again. Back in St. Petersburg, they were hit by a tornado and lost two planes, including Stultz's because he didn't tie it down well enough. He went on a drinking spree, so Pang cut him loose. In Clearwater, a grass fire burned the wings off Jack's plane, and then he tore down some electric wires getting into a tight field in Columbus, Georgia. Jack hated to admit it, but their planes were worn out. They were ten years old and surplus to begin with. It was no wonder the federal regulations had been written.

Gates got some Standards with less wear and tear on them from somewhere, but the 180-horsepower Hissos had to be overhauled frequently, which the circus did before they hit the Mid-Atlantic states again. The route was essentially the same as in '25. Still, people came out to see them in droves. Sometimes schools were closed. Newspapers reported that thirty to forty thousand spectators came out in certain areas. Rides cost $2.50 for a minute and a half, and they got extra for stunting. They even did simple stunts with people who paid extra for them on their rides. Texaco continued to give them a blank check for fuel. Otherwise, it was pretty much the same routine as in '25.

There was an incident in New York in which Jack had to think fast to get himself out of trouble with Pang.

They had a particularly good run in Syracuse, Albany, and Schenectady, New York. The people loved them in those cities, especially Syracuse. Gates was very pleased—so pleased he said to Pang, "The boys have been good to us. Let's throw a big champagne party for them." As it turned out, he had an inside track to a winery in Hammondsport.

Pang walked over to Jack and Buck. "Van needs you to go to Hammondsport to pick up some champagne. A planeload each. No funny business. Just fly up there, get the bubbly, and fly back. Hear?"

"Yes, sir," Jack and Buck said in unison.

Buck was a straight shooter, but Jack saw an opportunity. When they landed in Hammondsport, there was a guy waiting for them just as Gates said. They loaded up the planes. Immediately, a couple of girls caught Jack's eye.

Jack said, "Hey, Buck, I'm going to have some fun tonight. How about you?"

"You heard Pang," Buck warned. "We're to get the bubbly and go right back. We've got what we came for, so let's go."

"I've never been to Hammondsport," Jack said. "I want to check out the sights, if you know what I mean. The party isn't until tomorrow night."

Buck shook his head. "Come on, Jack. We need to get on back," he said, tugging at Jack's sleeve.

"This is a beautiful part of the state," Jack said. "I deserve a couple of hours of free time for all my hard work." He grabbed a couple of bottles of champagne. "I'll see you later this evening." He followed the two girls.

"Suit yourself," Buck said, getting into his airplane. "What do I tell him?"

"Tell him my oil gauge was acting a little funny and I needed to check it out," Jack said.

"He's not going to believe that."

"Well, that's my story and I'm sticking to it," Jack laughed.

Buck shrugged and dutifully flew back to Syracuse, his plane packed with most of the champagne. Jack and one of the ladies celebrated on their own.

They were having such a good time that before Jack knew it, the sun was going down. He didn't have time to fly back to Syracuse, so they partied some more. Jack knew he would be in big trouble, though. The next morning, he snuck out of the room while his new friend was still asleep and headed to the airfield.

I've got to think of something to distract Pang when we get back, he said to himself as he checked out his plane.

Halfway back to Syracuse, he smiled and eased back in the cockpit for the rest of his hour-and-a-half flight.

The instant he landed in Syracuse, he put his plan into action. Just as he'd thought, Pang was standing by the hangar, arms crossed, waiting for him mad as a hornet. Jack sure hoped the gag he'd made up was going to work, because he could see steam coming from Pang's ears. He knew he had to get the first word in.

"I've got something to show you, Pang," Jack said before Pang could say a word.

"This better be good," Pang said.

"Give me two bucks."

"What?"

"Give me two bucks and I'll show you," Jack said.

Pang dug into his pocket and pulled out two one-dollar bills, and Jack took them from him. On one, he wrote, "To Short Snorter II," signed his name, and handed it to Pang.

"What's this?"

"Now you are a Short Snorter," Jack said. Jack wrote "Short Snorter I" on the other bill and handed it to him. "Now you sign this one." Pang did as Jack asked. When he finished, Jack took the bill back and put it in his pocket.

"Hey, that's my money!" Pang said.

"Not anymore. Ain't that a funny gag? You make a buck a throw. I thought I'd let you in on it first, so you could start making some money on your own," Jack said. With that, he grinned and walked off before Pang could say anything.

Pleased with himself, Jack hurriedly walked away and left Pang scratching his head. All Jack cared about was that he'd put out the fire.

Pang must have thought it was a pretty good gag, because he cleaned house that night at the champagne party. Buck shook his head. How Jack got himself out of predicaments never ceased to amaze him.

July 1926
National Air Races, Philadelphia, Pennsylvania

From New York, they headed to Philadelphia for the National Air Races over Labor Day. On their way down, they had air meets in Williamsport, where Gates arranged for a photographer to take panoramic photos of the group. They looked impressive with their five planes, a fuel truck, a concessions van, and three other ground vehicles all freshly painted red and lined up in the background with pilots and crew in the foreground. The gang consisted of Pang, Eddie Bond, Mack, and Cy Bittner, who they called Shorty for obvious reasons.

He'd just caught up with them. He was going to start out as a wing walker.

In addition, there was Buck, Bill Brooks, Duke, Charles "Slim" West, Mickey Efferson, Alf and Jim MacClatchie, Joe Parks, George Daws, Gates, and Judge. They did their best and put on a good show, but the modern planes again conveyed to Jack that the days of the circus were numbered and it was almost time for him to move on.

Jack sent a set of photos home to his parents.

As they had in 1925, that fall the group worked their way through the South toward Florida. Even though the circus's days were limited, there were a whole lot of shows in the meantime.

They stopped in Towanda, Pennsylvania, on their way south. A guy named Bert Crader, owner of Crader Oil & Supply Company, arranged for the circus to be there for the week. Pang and Cy Bittner put on a great show for the crowd. They did the usual stunting, and then Pang flew upside down and dropped baseballs to the players on the field. For his grand finale, Pang flew under the River Bridge nearby. He was so low that his wheels almost touched the water.

Crader introduced Jack and Buck to officials of the city. They were keen on building a new airfield to bring in more business to the town. Jack got along great with everyone, especially Crader, and told Bert that he wanted to talk to him more about bringing aviation to Towanda.

Gates Flying Circus Personnel, Williamsport, Pennsylvania,
1926. Left to right: Clyde "Pang" Pangborn, Eddie ?, Mack
?, Cy "Shorty" Bittner, Buck Steele, Bill ?, Jack Ashcraft,
Duke Krantz, Charles R. "Slim" West, Mickey Efferson, Alf ?,
Jim ?, Joe ?, Pat ?, George Daws, Ivan "Pote" Gates.
Courtesy of Allen Keller.

Planes and ground vehicles of The Gates Flying Circus,
Williamsport, Pennsylvania, 1926. *Courtesy of Allen Keller.*

CHAPTER 19
NEW HEADQUARTERS- GATES FLYING SERVICE

Jack Ashcraft in white shirt on the right, hand on propeller with female acrobats. *Bill Rhode Collection, Aviation Hall of Fame and Museum of New Jersey, Teterboro.*

May 20, 1927
Setting Up Shop

Gates and Pang decided the circus needed a base of operations and a mailing address, so they set up shop in Teterboro, New Jersey, and became the Gates Flying Service. It was great to have a home base where they could overhaul the planes and get parts to keep them in the air. It also allowed the circus to fly to various locations for a few shows and return. For now, they repaired their planes and others in addition to giving lessons and rides, but Gates also wanted to start an airplane factory. To ensure there was a supply of pilots, GFS gave flying lessons to anyone who wandered in wanting to learn to fly. Jimmy still worked as Jack's mechanic.

There was a group that showed up at Teterboro that Jack would never forget, and that was a troupe of girl acrobats. They did all sorts of stunts all over the airplanes, like splits and back bends. One could bend over completely backwards. Another, Helen Lach, wanted to be a parachutist. She made her first parachute jump that October. Others hung from the wings with their hands like he'd done on his homemade trapeze when he was a kid. About anything you could think of, they could do, and they could bend in parts that he didn't think were bendable. He took all of them up for rides. They even did some simple wing walking. Over at Roosevelt and Curtiss Fields, there were more women than ever flying. Times were changing.

One day in mid-May, Jack was flying over Roosevelt Field on his way to Teterboro when he noticed planes and a crowd gathering.

"What's going on at Roosevelt?" Jack asked Pang when he landed.

"Word has it that some guys are getting ready to fly the Atlantic," Pang said. "They want to take Raymond Ortieg up on the prize money he offered."

"Twenty-five thousand dollars is a good incentive. I'm going to go check it out," Jack said.

Mavis was at Roosevelt Field and gave him the scoop. They had reconnected and were able to meet for lunch on occasion.

"Isn't this exciting, Jack?" she said.

"Dang right. Who else is going to try?" Jack asked.

"Clarence Chamberlin is here, and I understand he's ready to take off. Just waiting for the fog to lift a bit," she said. "And Commander Byrd is going to try in a Fokker trimotor. I heard he has a crew, though."

"This weather is going to make takeoff tough for anyone," Jack said, and Mavis agreed.

Jack looked around. There were aviation buffs, press, curiosity seekers, and anything else he could name. They saw Frances checking it all out as well.

"Damn, this is exciting!" Jack said. "Looks like the ladies are in on the action as well."

"Lots of rumors floating around," Mavis said.

"Anybody else you think has a chance?" Jack asked.

"There's this guy named Charles Lindbergh," she said.

"I know Lindbergh. I met him when I was flying out west. Saw him at the National Air Races last year too," Jack said. "Nice fellow. Quiet."

"Well, I think he can do it. He's kind of a loner, not flashy. Shuns the limelight, but very capable. He's done everything—barnstormed, walked the wings, even delivered the mail for a while."

"If you've done all that, you can survive just about anything," Jack said.

"He was also in the Reserves and National Guard," she said. "He flew into Curtiss Field a week ago. He set the record for the fastest transcontinental flight, so I think that's a good sign. Haven't seen him here yet."

"What's he flying?"

"A Ryan specially built for him. Some businessmen in Saint Louis backed him, so he named it *The Spirit of St. Louis*," she said. "Come on, let's see if we can find him."

They roamed around, and Jack saw some guys from last year's National Air Races. All this activity and the trophies he had won gave Jack even more of an itch to do things on his own. There were some fine ships at Roosevelt that day. The foul weather didn't dampen anyone's spirits.

"How about we go grab some chow and come back?" he said to Mavis.

"You go get something for us and bring it back. I don't want to miss anything," she said.

Just then, they heard a motor and searched the skies. Sure enough, a silver Ryan circled the airfield and made a perfect landing. Several people rushed to the plane to check it out. A tall, slender guy got out. Jack immediately recognized him as Lindbergh.

Mavis and Jack walked over to say hello and wish him luck.

Mavis held out her hand to shake his. "I'm Mavis Perkins. I'm the owner of *News Today.*"

"Nice to meet you, ma'am."

"I'm Jack Ashcraft. Do you remember me?" Jack said.

"Sure do. Nice to see you again," Lindbergh said.

"Gates has set up shop over in Teterboro. You ready to fly this thing across the pond?" Jack asked.

Lindbergh smiled. "More than ready."

"Are you flying alone?" Mavis asked, notepad ready.

Slim smiled and nodded.

"Nice airplane. How do you see out?" she asked.

"The side windows. You don't really need to see in front of

you when you're flying straight, and I have a compass," Lindbergh said. "I also have a periscope to see in front if I need to."

"What motor you got in there?" Jack asked.

"Two hundred twenty horsepower, nine-cylinder Wright J-5C Whirlwind," Lindbergh answered.

"How much gas you going to carry?" Mavis asked.

"Just enough," Lindbergh said with a grin.

All the while, Mavis was scribbling in her notebook.

"When do you plan to take off?" she asked.

"Don't know. This fog is a bit of a problem. With a compass, I should be okay when I do," he said. The crowd started closing in, and Jack and Mavis walked away.

Jack hid his excitement as long as he could. "That's incredible. I got to talk to what will probably be the first man to fly solo across the Atlantic."

The days stayed foggy. A couple days later, Jack was just staggering out of bed when the phone rang.

"Jack," the voice on the line said.

"Mavis! Why are you calling so early?"

"Listen to me, Jack. Today's the day," she said excitedly.

"For what?" Jack said, still wiping the cobwebs from his brain.

"Word has it Lindbergh's getting ready to take off," she said. "Didn't make a big announcement, he just decided he was tired of waiting on the weather. I'm headed to Roosevelt now. Hope I make it in time."

"Well, I'll be damned. Thanks for—" But Mavis had hung up.

Jack sat there on the edge of the bed for a few minutes, collecting his thoughts. "Damn, I've got to get to Roosevelt. I don't want to miss this."

Jack drove his motorcycle as far as he could, but there were hundreds of people already there, and it wasn't even dawn. Word was definitely out. The Ryan was pulled out of the hangar to the runway with a car and truck. Jack saw Mavis with a photographer and ran over.

"What's the latest?" he asked.

"He's going to go for it. Byrd offered to let him use his runway," Mavis said as they watched. She frantically scribbled down notes. Slim posed in front of his plane for pictures and some dignitaries shook his hand, then his mother stood by him for photos. A couple of guys topped off the gasoline in the plane and checked things out one last time. Lindbergh put on his flight suit and got inside the plane. Somebody seemed to give him some last-minute instructions before he climbed aboard. He started the motor, and they pulled the chocks.

"I'll be damned," Jack said. "He's doing it."

Lindbergh revved up the motor, then took off. There were ruts in the runway, so he bounced and hopped until he finally lifted off, barely clearing the electrical wires along the highway. Then he disappeared into the fog. Jack looked at his watch—7:52 a.m.

"Wahoo!" Jack said, waving his cap in salute. "Godspeed, my friend!"

Jack thought about Lindbergh all day while he worked, wondering where he was and if he was okay.

"Hey, Jack, what's with you today?" Buck said. "You haven't said a dozen words, so I figure you must be sick or something."

"Nah, I've just been thinking of Lindbergh and wondering how he's getting along," Jack said, wiping his hands on a rag. Jack stepped down from the ladder. "I've also been doing some thinking about my future."

Jack looked around to make sure no one was listening. "I

think we both know the days of the circus are numbered," he said. "Truth of the matter is, most people come out to watch the stunting these days, not to see us fly."

"I've thought about that too," Buck said. "What are you thinking?"

"Let's strike out on our own," Jack said.

"I'm all for that," Buck said. "Where would we go?"

"Towanda," Jack said. "I liked it there and met some nice folks when we were there. Bert Crader and I had a great talk. They were welcoming and want to build an airport really bad."

"That sounds good. When do we make our move?" Buck asked.

"After the air show in August. I haven't committed to flying in it, but you should," Jack said. "I'm going to make arrangements to fly in that race from New York to Spokane."

"I think Bert would be all for that," Buck said. "Set up base there, and it would bring a lot of attention to the town."

"I think so too," Jack said. "I'll call Crader and run it by him. I'll ask him if he'll be my navigator."

Jack wondered about Lindbergh all night and thought about what he would do in his position. The next morning, he rushed out to get a paper. Sure enough, the aviator didn't drop into the drink, but hopped the pond solo. The headline read, *LINDBERGH DOES IT! TO PARIS IN 33 1/2 HOURS; FLIES 1,000 MILES THROUGH SNOW AND SLEET; CHEERING FRENCH CARRY HIM OFF FIELD.* The article went on to say that Lindbergh had landed in Le Bourget, France, at 10:42, but could have gone five hundred miles farther. There were hundreds of people at the airfield when he landed. Jack knew right where that was. "Holy smoke!"

. . .

When Lindberg returned home, Jack and Mavis went to the ticker tape parade they had for him in the city. Jack had never seen so many people and such a fuss over one person, and probably never would again. The tape twisted down to the street, and the confetti was like large snowflakes falling to the earth and covering the streets. They had parades for Chamberlin and Levine and one for Byrd and his crew a month later, but the big news was all Lindbergh. He was the first to fly solo.

Jack told Mavis about his plans to leave the circus to fly in the New York to Spokane Transcontinental Air Race. She encouraged him to do so.

On June 3, Jimmy came running to tell Jack that his dad had called and needed him to call home right away.

Jack ran into the office and placed the call. His parents rarely called him. The call seemed to take forever to go through. Finally, his dad was on the line.

"Hi, Dad. Jack here. Everything okay?"

"Your mother and I are fine," his dad said, "but we wanted to let you know that Clarice passed away today." His voice sounded so sad. Jack felt a pounding in his head. Clarice was three years younger than him. She was his favorite sister. Next to Franz, he was closer to her than any of his other siblings. He could see her vividly, holding her young son.

"What happened? I thought she was getting better," Jack said.

"We did too, but she took a sudden turn for the worse and never recovered," his dad said, barely able to get out the words. "They had problems getting the kidney stones out this time. Guess it was just her time."

"How's Mother?"

"Not so good, but we'll pull through."

Jack put his arm on the wall and leaned on it, fighting back tears.

"When's her service?" Jack asked.

"Day after tomorrow. We know it's too soon for you to come back but knew you would want to know."

"Thanks for calling, Dad. Give Mother my love," Jack said, and hung up.

Jack leaned against the wall for several minutes, stunned by the news. While he was sad, he felt worse for his mother and dad. Children shouldn't die before their parents.

PART TWO

CHAPTER 20
JACK MAKES HIS MOVE

August–September 1927

The 1927 National Air Races were to be held in Spokane, Washington. Gates and Pang didn't want to fly that far, so they decided to have their own show and called it the New York National Airplane Show. Truth of the matter was, they probably realized that their planes wouldn't have made it up there and back, at least in a timely manner.

Nine pilots took part in the three-day extravaganza in New York. The pilots were Pang, Bill Brooks, Lee Mason, and Stultz, who came back for the occasion. Others flew back in: Ive McKinney, Captain Warren B. Smith, Joe James, Harold McMahon, Roy Ahearn, and Gates, who had learned to fly. Duke, Mickey Efferson, Cy Bittner, and Johnny Runger were the stuntmen. Duke got to do a plane change from Jack's plane to Pang's over Teterboro for a Pathé newsreel. Jack didn't fly in the show, but Buck flew in the Air Races before he joined Jack in Towanda.

· · ·

A couple of days after the show, Jack found Pang and decided to break the news to him. Pang was in his small office in the hangar. Jack tapped on the door.

"Hey, Pang," Jack said. "Got a minute?"

"Sure," he said. "What can I do for you, Jack?"

"Well, just give me your blessings, I reckon," Jack said. "I've been thinking a lot about my future, and I've decided to see what I can do on my own."

Pang leaned back in his chair and thought about that for several seconds. "You've done a great job for us, Jack. Many times, you went above and beyond what was expected," he said. "You saved our ass more than once. Heck, you may have saved my life when Van slugged me. You're a damn good pilot. We wouldn't be where we are today were it not for your steadiness."

"Thanks. That means a whole lot coming from you," Jack said.

"I'm not going to try to talk you out of this, because I completely understand," Pang said. "I don't know what's next for us."

"Thanks. I really appreciate it," Jack said.

"If you change your mind, you've always got a job with us," Pang said. "Who's going with you?"

"Buck, Jimmy, and Al."

"Good luck, Jack," Pang said and shook Jack's hand.

On the way back to his plane, Jack thought about how he was going to miss the circus, but he knew he was making the right choice. Buck looked questioningly at Jack, and Jack gave him a thumbs-up.

"Where's Duke?" Jack asked.

"Outside working on that plane that just came in," Buck said.

Jack found Duke just where Buck had said he would. "Hey, buddy," Jack said.

"What's up, Jack?" Duke said, airplane parts carefully laid out on a tarp on the ground.

"I wanted to tell you my news. Buck I are striking out on our own," Jack said.

Duke paused for a moment, then continued working. "Doesn't surprise me much. Everyone here knows the circus's days are numbered with all the regulations coming down. Planes are wearing out. I'm wondering what my future is."

"You're a great stuntman," Jack said, "but you need to get a pilot's license. That's the way to go."

"I'm thinking about doing just that," Duke said. "I wish you the best. Keep in touch." They shook hands.

Next stop was to tell Mavis. They met for lunch at Saul's.

"What's happening?" she asked. "You sounded so excited on the phone."

"What's happening is that I'm leaving the circus. Buck and Al are going with me," Jack said.

"That is big news. What's first? Where are you headed? Tell me all about it," Mavis said.

"We're setting up in Towanda, Pennsylvania," Jack said. "We met a guy named Bert Crader who is going into business with us. Gardner Nagle will join us. City officials are hankering to get an airport up there."

"That's wonderful!"

"And guess what? They're going to buy a couple of airplanes for us to use," Jack said.

"Wacos, I hope. Go on."

"Of course. First thing I'm going to do is enter the New

York to Spokane air race, but I'm going to Elmira first to try out the new plane," Jack said. "We'll head south for the winter."

"I'm so happy for you, Jack," Mavis said, "but don't forget about me here in New York."

"I'll never forget about you," Jack answered, looking deeply into her eyes.

After a quick stop to tell Ed Churchill, Jack, Buck, and the others packed their bags and headed north. They met up with Bert and Gardner in Towanda. Gardner had given Jack advance flight instructions back in Shreveport.

They had less than a month to prepare for the New York to Spokane transcontinental air race scheduled for September 19 to 20, so they would have to hustle. First order of the day was to get the airplanes.

September 1927
New York to Spokane

The folks in Towanda greeted them warmly. The powers that be in the town wanted an airport and someone to teach people to fly. It seemed every town wanted an airport those days. The choice of plane was easy. Jack liked Mavis's Waco so much that he bought two Waco 9s for the town to use. Jack named his the *Spirit of Ammonia* as kind of a joke on the *Spirit of St. Louis*. Buck named his *Spirit of Camphor*.

Jack heard about the dedication of an airport in Elmira. There was also going to be the requisite stunting and a twenty-mile race. He decided it was a good opportunity to get his name out there separate from the circus and get some practice in his new ship. The newspapers announced the air meet.

Airplanes are Dropping out of Sky For Elmira's
Big Airport Carnival

Jack Ashcraft of Towanda, in His Waco, is First to Arrive This Morning — Famous Flyers Begin Appearing at Noon—Acosta Misses Train and Commandeers Plan to Fly to Elmira — Arthur Directs Committees Preparing for Visitors — Major Reed Chambers Reported Headed For Elmira From Washington—First Events on Dedication Program Held This Afternoon.

When Jack Ashcraft of Towanda brought his Waco airplane to earth at 9:30 a.m. today, the two-day festivities marking the dedication of the Elmira Airport were officially opened.

The airport was a busy place this morning as 'planes continued to 'drop in' for the carnival. By noon five ships had arrived . . .

The first 'plane to arrive was that of Jack Ashcraft of Towanda owner and pilot of a Waco 2736. He arrived at 9:30 a.m. Pilot Ashcraft is one of the country's best aerial dare-devils [sic], with more than 3,000 hours of stunt flying to his credit. He has been a member of several widely known flying circuses. His passengers were Pilot Buck Steele and Alfred MacClatchie of Towanda. . .

The best thing about the air meet was that Jimmy Doolittle was going to be there. It was always good press to fly anywhere Doolittle flew.

Jack Ashcraft put Towanda on Air Map By Stunts at Elmira

Local Pilot Among Best at Big Aviation Meet; Shows Elmirans How to Do the 'Dead Stick Landing'; Jimmy Doolittle's Flying one of Big Attractions.

Flying the Waco plane owned by the Towanda Aircraft Co., Pilot Jack Ashcraft Saturday and Sunday put Towanda on the map by carrying away major honors at the big aviation meet conducted in Elmira in connection with the dedication of that city's beautiful new airport.

Jack not only came in first in the 20-mile race yesterday and second in the race Saturday, but on both days gave remarkable exhibitions of stunt flying. Among the feats he performed was what is known as the 'dead stick landing.' At an altitude of 1500 feet he turned his motor off, let it get stone dead. The he nose-dived, looped-the-loop, and glided gracefully to the field, coming to a stop exactly on the spot where it had been announced that he would. 'That's turning around on a dime and dotting an eye,' exclaimed the announcer.'

No other light plane attempted the stunts put on by Ashcraft, but Lieut. Jimmy Doolittle in a 550-horsepower army plane, held the crowd estimated at 35,000 people breathless on Saturday. His machine developed 200 miles an hour and at the speed he went through the most hair-raising antics imaginable with a plane.

For two miles he flew upside down. He piloted his plane at lightning-like speed on its wind-ends. He zoomed, and zipped, and whipped through the air like a bullet. It was 'Here he comes—there he goes?'

Jimmy Doolittle sped over the hangar at the airport, missing the building by a scant 40 feet and headed straight into the heavens. He continued to climb until he was lost at times in the clouds. He was at least three miles in the air at one time. Then he dropped into a nose dive [sic], straight toward earth, and came down with the speed of a comet. He looped and twisted and turned in every shape, angle and direction. Once he drove his ship to within 50 feet of the ground and started a loop 'right from the heels.' He looped and righted his craft with Immelmann turns.

Cheers for his daring arose from his spectators time after time. In appreciation, it seemed, he continued his stunt flying making each more daring than before. Sideways, he flipped his machine over three times in rapid succession. The he climbed to a dizzy height, slowed his engine and dropped back into a tail spin [sic]. The little biplane with vast quantities of power, seemed like a toy in his hands. There wasn't anything he couldn't do with it. . .

Jack watched in awe at Doolittle's skill. "Would you look at that? Do you think I could do that if I had his plane?"

"Sure," Buck said, "but it would take lots of practice and the whole dang army behind you and the best planes like he has. He is amazing, though."

The article went on to say that Doolittle had to land and quickly slip off his flying coveralls and leave for his next appearance before everyone closed in to shake his hand. To do this, he was guarded by members of Company L, 108th Infantry, under the command of Captain James Riffe, who surrounded the ship and escorted him so he could leave the field.

CHAPTER 21
RUTH ELDER

Jack Ashcraft, I, and Ruth Elder on the propeller, Roosevelt Field, Long Island, New York, October 1927. *Courtesy of Allen Keller.*

September 1927

Pilots were staging at Curtiss and Roosevelt Fields on Long Island for the transcontinental race. On September 19, everyone would take off from Roosevelt Field in staggered starts. The official purpose of the contest was to demonstrate that a northwestern air route was practical to link together the two coasts. For pilots, it was an excuse to fly and a way to gain recognition. Manufacturers wanted to demonstrate what their planes could do. Jack and Bert arrived on September 17. There were a lot of people mingling around, particularly around a yellow Stinson. The press was taking pictures of a girl flier. That got Jack's attention.

"Come on, Bert, I've got to check her out," Jack said.

Bert rolled his eyes. "Okay, Jack, but don't get distracted. We need to register for the race and get ready."

They walked over to find out who was getting all the attention. The woman was wearing a dress, pumps, and a long leather coat.

"That's one fine looking woman. Who is it?" Jack asked a reporter next to him.

"Name's Ruth Elder," he said.

"What's she doing here?"

"She's a pilot. She and her copilot are waiting for the weather to clear so they can fly across the Atlantic. The publicity in the meantime doesn't hurt. She's a nice little gal."

"Well, I'll be damned," Jack said. "Another beautiful pilot— and brave, if she's planning on flying the Atlantic."

"Everybody wants to since Lindbergh. I know her. Come on, I'll introduce you," the guy said. "What's your name?"

"Jack Ashcraft."

"Ruth, this is Jack Ashcraft. Jack, this is Miss Ruth Elder."

"Nice to meet you, ma'am," Jack said.

"Nice to meet you too, Jack," she said in a sing-song kind of voice and fluttered her eyes.

"*American Girl*, huh? This your plane?" he asked.

She smiled the prettiest smile. "It's a Stinson Detroiter. Not mine personally. It's our sponsor's. I hope to fly across the Atlantic in it with my pilot, George Haldeman, though," she said. "What brings you to Roosevelt Field?"

"I'm playing it safe by flying to Spokane," Jack said.

"That's no simple thing," Ruth said.

"I guess. At least someone will be able to find me if I go down," Jack said.

Bert tugged on the sleeve of his jacket. "Come on, Jack, we've got to go."

"Hold your horses," Jack said. He pulled a small notepad and pencil he kept in his jacket to make notes to himself. Ruth smiled again. Jack had to keep in control of himself.

"This is my navigator, Bert Crader. Would you oblige me and give me your autograph?" Jack said.

"I'll be glad to," she said, and reached for the pencil and notepad, smiling that sweet smile again.

Bert tugged at his jacket. Jack shrugged him off.

Miss Elder handed the notepad back to Jack. "So, you're in the race on Monday?"

"Yes, ma'am," Jack said. All the while Bert was tugging at his sleeve, but Jack got the impression that he was listening too.

"I want to be the first woman to fly across the Atlantic," she said.

"Pretty risky," Jack said. "Like I said, I can land if I have an emergency."

"To me, it's worth the risks. People will know me, and maybe I won't have to live the rest of my life on four dollars a day. I'm a good pilot, but George is an excellent one. I have complete faith in him." She smiled.

Jack nodded that he understood, then Bert pulled him away.

"Good luck!" Jack yelled.

"Thank you! We're going out for a spin later!" she yelled back.

"Dang it, Bert, she was giving me the eye," Jack said. "Didn't you see that?"

Bert stared at Jack for a few moments. "What?" Jack said.

"Jack, in less than forty-eight hours, you're going to fly twenty-five hundred miles across the continent. And from the looks of the weather, it's going to be like flying through shit." He paused to let Jack think about that a bit.

"And let me remind you, I'm your passenger, and I prefer to live to tell about it, okay?"

"Okay, okay. Calm down," Jack said. "Let's go."

On the way to his plane, Jack glanced at the piece of paper and noticed that Ruth had written her phone number under her name. Bert looked back at Jack.

"And wipe that grin off your face. This is serious stuff."

"If you say so, Bert. If you say so."

The photographers kept taking pictures, and the reporters kept asking her questions.

"I'm going to blame you if I never get to see her again," Jack said.

"Yeah, yeah," Bert said. "With you, Jack, dames are a dime a dozen."

"Beautiful women who are pilots aren't."

Together, Jack and Bert went over maps and routes, but Jack felt like he had all of it under control. He just wanted to get on with the race. Remembering a ding on the fuselage that he had noticed earlier, Jack went to check it out. While he worked, he wondered if he would see Ruth again. Then two pretty legs in pumps appeared next to him.

"So, this is the plane you're going to fly in the race, huh, Jack?" a voice said.

Jack got so excited that he bumped his head hard. Rubbing his head, Jack looked to see who had spoken. Sure enough, there stood Ruth Elder.

"Careful, there," she laughed. "You need to be in good shape for the race." Then she walked around his ship, her hand rubbing the sides. "I haven't flown a Waco. Heard about them, though." She stopped when she saw the name of the plane painted on the side.

"Why the *Spirit of Ammonia*?" she laughed.

"I thought it was funny. Kind of poking fun at the *Spirit of St. Louis*, I guess. I didn't think Lindbergh would mind."

She laughed a laugh that was as melodious as her speaking voice.

"Some of the guys said that you used to fly for Gates," she said.

"Yes, ma'am. I'm striking out on my own to see what I can do," Jack said.

Jack looked around and noticed that the press had followed her to his plane.

"Can I get a picture of you and me with my plane?" Jack asked.

"Sure."

Before she knew it, Jack had lifted her and put her on top and in the middle of the propeller. The photographers loved it and started clicking away. Jack gave one of them his name and address and asked the reporter to send him a copy.

An older woman—she must've been about thirty-five—walked by just then. "Frances," Ruth called out to her, "I want you to meet Jack Ashcraft. Jack, Frances Grayson. She writes for the paper. We have this little rivalry over who is going to be the first woman to hop the Atlantic."

"Is that right? Nice to meet you, ma'am," Jack said. "I remember reading about you. Is Woodrow Wilson your uncle?"

"Yes, he is," she replied flatly, "but regarding the race, this little girl doesn't stand a chance. I've got the better plane and the best pilot."

"We'll see about that," Ruth replied. "Jack's flying in the New York to Spokane race on Monday."

"My best to you, Jack. The weather's not looking very good, so be careful. I've got to go," Grayson said.

"Oh, yes, ma'am. I sure will," Jack said as she walked off. "Pleasant lady."

Ruth laughed. "Mabel Boll is trying to get a pilot to fly her across the Atlantic as well. Well, Jack, I have an appointment, so I need to go. CAVU to you." She walked away, looking back and wiggling her fingers goodbye.

"Goodbye, 'American Girl.' Good luck!"

Bert thought Jack was going to follow her, so he grabbed Jack's arm. "We've got work to do," he said.

The next couple of days were hectic as they prepared for the race and sat in on briefings of all kinds, especially weather briefings. Bert kept at Jack. "Did you arrange for the plane to be fueled Monday morning?"

"Yes, Bert."

"Have you checked out your plane? Do you think somebody else should in case you missed something?"

"I checked the plane and Jimmy checked it."

"Do you have your warm flying suit? It's going to be pretty cold up there."

"Yes, Bert. Gloves too, and I have an extra pair."

"Do you have maps?"

"Yes, and we have rail lines we can follow, remember?" Jack said.

"Maps, always good to have maps. We're going to get hungry up there, did you . . . ?"

"Bert! This isn't my first damn time flying an airplane a long distance," Jack said.

"Okay. I'm just a little antsy to get started and get this over with, I guess," Bert said.

"Me too. Everything will go fine, you'll see," Jack reassured him.

"Yeah, I know," Bert said. "You're a great pilot, especially fog pilot. But we're going to need all the help we can get."

They were heading back to the hotel when Jack heard a familiar voice call out to him.

"Cowboy Jack!"

Jack turned around, and sure enough, there was Mavis. She ran up and gave him a big hug and kiss on the cheek. He was always glad to see Mavis.

"I wanted to wish you good luck in the race," she said.

"I sure appreciate that, I really do."

Mavis smiled at Jack. Who's your friend?"

"I'm Bert Crader, Jack's navigator," Bert said. It might have been his imagination, but Jack thought Bert had an *oh no, not again* look on his face.

"Nice to meet you, Bert." Mavis shook Bert's hand. "Jack and I are old friends." Then she turned back to Jack. "I haven't seen you in a while. Let me buy you a cup of coffee, and you can tell me all about it," Mavis said. "You too, Bert."

"Nah, three's a crowd. Someone around here has to keep his head on straight." Bert shrugged and walked off.

"Sweet guy," Mavis said when Bert was out of earshot.

"He's also my daddy for the race," Jack said.

"You're bad," Mavis said, punching Jack's arm.

"Guess who I just met? Ruth Elder. She's planning a flight across the Atlantic," Jack said as they walked off.

Bert had promised the folks in Towanda that he would keep them updated, so he sent a telegram about meeting Ruth Elder and Frances Grayson.

Spirit of Ammonia is Ready.

The following telegram was received late last night from Burt Crader who with Jack Ashcraft is taking Towanda's entry, the Spirit of Ammonia, across the country in the national air race to Spokane:

News Editor

The Daily Review,

"Towanda, Pa.

Roosevelt Field, L.I. Sept. 19,— [sic]

Saw Jack immediately upon arrival and ship is ready with Spirit of Ammonia and Towanda, Pa., on both sides. Doing the rounds. Was introduced to Miss Grayson and her pilot, Mr. Studly, also Miss Elder and her pilot. Came in for lunch, went over maps and route for about two hours. 31 ships starting in our class. Our No. is 65, starting position 30, next to last. Expect to arrive Bellefonte about 7:50. Weather condition looks bad tonight. Returning to field to see that Spirit of Ammonia is still under cover.

Both Miss Elder and Miss Grayson are out for a test and waiting on weather to make trans-ocean flight. Had hard time keeping Jack away from Miss Elder's ship because she sure is a beautiful person and a peach. She is good to look at. Will write more when we leave. Both of us will be on field at 4 a. m. Monday morning.

My regards, also Jack's, to our fine friends at home.

Burt [sic] Crader

CHAPTER 22
1927 NEW YORK TO SPOKANE AIR RACE

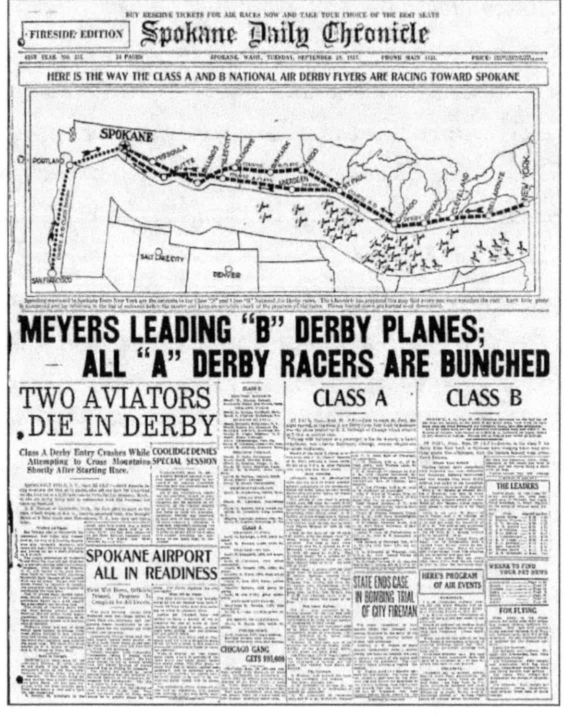

Courtesy of Cindy Weigand.

September 1927
Roosevelt Field, Long Island, New York

Great Air Race to Spokane
'Spirit of Ammonia' Towanda's Entry, Is
Tuned Ready to Go

Crader and Ashcraft Both Confident of Victory on Eve of National Air Derby; Great Assembly of Planes Waiting on Roosevelt Field, Long Island.

When the national air race from Roosevelt Field, Long Island, to Spokane, Washington, starts this morning the Spirit of Ammonia, entry of the Towanda Aircraft Corporation, will be next to the last to leave the ground, that position in starting order having been drawn. The planes are to leave one minute apart but since the machines will race against time instead of each other, this will make no difference.

Crader and Ashcraft, local pilots, have their own Waco plane tuned to its best pitch and are only awaiting the starters signal to show what they can do. Both are confident of victory and have good reason for it because of their experience in the flying game.

The plane being used is the same one that has been used around Towanda this summer, it being now just nicely "broken in". The engine, according to Crader, is in excellent condition and the new aluminum propellor that has replaced the wooden one, gives even more speed. In a test at Roosevelt Field a few days ago Ashcraft made with it 106 miles an hour. There are more than 20 planes in Class B in which the Towandians will race.

As previously announced, Crader will cover the race exclusively for The Daily Review, keeping the local readers posted on all occurrences throughout the flight."

The Daily Review, Towanda, Pa.,
Monday Morning September 14, 1927

Monday morning, Jack and Bert arose at three o'clock and headed for Roosevelt Field for final briefings before planes started taking off at five. A dense fog had rolled in, and once this happened, no one could predict when it would disperse. A light rain added to the already wet runway. They made sure the *Spirit* was still under cover, then grabbed a cup of coffee. Word made the rounds that they were going to take a vote of the pilots as to whether to start the race. Jack had flown in all kinds of weather—rain, snow, fog, high winds, heat—but never for twenty-four hundred miles over unfamiliar territory as fast as he could into more of the same.

He was deliberating how he would vote if asked, when the rain stopped and the sun peeked through the clouds for a few minutes. That was his sign. He would vote to take off. There ended up being no vote, but takeoff was postponed to five thirty.

"Damn this fog," he said to Bert.

"I have faith in you, Jack," Bert replied. "Buck told me the story about you flying down to Florida in the fog that one winter. He stopped when you kept going, and you made it. He figures you're the best fog pilot around, and I tend to agree."

"Thanks, Bert," Jack said, "but I'd flown that route before, and it was familiar to me. I'll give it my best shot. At least I have daylight in my favor, but make sure you keep your matches dry and flashlight handy just in case."

"The man to beat in the race is Charles Meyers. He designed the Waco, so that will be tough," Jack said. "Between you and me, I'll be content with any place below him."

They took the cover off the Waco, and after a last check by

flashlight and torch, Bert climbed into the front cockpit and Jack climbed into the back. "Ready, Bert?" Jack asked.

"Ready as I'll ever be. Let's get to Spokane," Bert said.

Jack taxied into place. Finally, it was time to take off. He revved up his motor, and they rolled down the runway and were off. His heart was racing about as fast as his plane engine.

Jack looked at his watch. Bert did the same.

Six thirty-one. Two and a half hours to Bellefonte, Pennsylvania, the first stop, Jack said to himself.

That first leg of the trip was the toughest Jack had ever flown. The sun had played a mean trick on him. It started to rain again, and although he had flown over these same Pennsylvania hills many times, it was colder than it had been before, and he couldn't land after a finite time of flying. The air was rough as hell, tossing the plane and them about. Sometimes the fog was so thick he couldn't see the ends of his wings. All he could do then was watch his compass and make sure he didn't drift with the torque of the propeller. It was easy to fly in circles in fog.

He tried to fly above the fog, then below it, but couldn't. The air was bumpy wherever he flew. Sweat trickled from under his flight helmet despite the cold, and his hands kept getting sweaty. After he wiped his forehead with his scarf, Jack took his right glove off to dry his hand on his pantleg while keeping his left hand on the stick. Then he switched hands.

Jack tapped Bert on the back. "I've got to check my compass. I'm going to fly low, check out the tracks," Jack yelled, pointing to his instrument panel, then pointing down.

Bert nodded that he understood. He looked at his compass as well.

Jack did this several times until he landed in Bellefonte at 10:19 for his first five-minute stopover. He'd known from the beginning his time wouldn't be good, and he was right. A trip that should have taken him two and a half hours had taken him nearly four. He had a lot of time to make up.

Jack made a quick trip around his plane to check it out, topped off the gas tank, and got back in. They were off right in the allotted five minutes. Rain and fog again, but it didn't seem as bad—or maybe it was wishful thinking. The visibility improved as he flew west, but the air was still bumpy. They rattled around in their cockpits as if in a carnival ride.

Keeping his eye on his compass, Jack lowered his altitude periodically so Bert could check the tracks. The wind had picked up, and it was getting colder. His whole body was numb by then, so it didn't matter much. They passed a couple of planes, which was a good sign.

They landed in Cleveland. Somehow, he had managed to make up some time.

The next stop was Bryan, Ohio, and the routine was repeated a few times on the way to the first overnight stop. Jack looked at his watch. Their time was better, but not enough to win. The man in charge in Cleveland told them that Meyers had a good lead on everyone. He was tempted to cut across Lake Michigan but didn't dare in the bad weather for fear of engine failure.

They landed in Chicago at 6:44 p.m. for their first overnight stop. There, they learned that they were the tenth to land.

"How far did we fly today?" Jack asked Bert.

"I figure about 840 miles or so," Bert answered.

"That's not even seventy miles per hour," Jack said. "I've got to pick up the pace tomorrow."

They rushed inside to get a weather report. "Mist and fog in the morning, then clearing," was the answer. Good news.

Jack turned to look at Bert and shook his head. "Tomorrow

will be another long day. My nerves are shot. I'm going to grab a snort and relax," he said.

"Watch it, Jack. Don't overdo it," Bert warned.

"Don't worry about that. I need it to warm up too. Damn, I'm cold," he said, rubbing his hands together and then rubbing his arms. "I'll see you at the hotel. Get some shuteye. I want to get an early start."

"How about you?" Bert asked.

"I'll get a few hours' sleep in, but I'm so hyped up, I'm on automatic now. I'll be fine until we get to Spokane. Then I can relax and get some sleep," Jack answered. "It's not that long."

"If you say so," Bert said.

The people of Towanda were extremely interested in the race and waited anxiously for every update. Bert found the telegraph office and sent a telegram.

CRADER SAYS ASHCRAFT IS GREAT FOG PILOT

The following telegram filed early Monday evening in Chicago by Burt Crader, was received at 11:20 yesterday morning by The Daily Review having been greatly delayed in transit somewhere by the Western Union:

"Jack and myself [sic] were up at 3 a.m. expecting to get away from New York at 5:30 but flight was delayed thirty minutes because of bad weather, rain and fog. We were away at 6:31 a.m. and went on the worst trip that I have ever flown. Let me say that Ashcraft is as good a pilot as ever flew in fog. The fog was so thick at times we could not see the end of the plane's wings.

"We were next to the last out of New York," he told them, "with 23 others ahead. We arrived at Bellefonte thirteenth, Cleveland twelfth, and Chicago tenth. The weather cleared at Sunbury and was good to Chicago, only awful rough.

"We hop off again tomorrow morning at 5:30 and hope to fly eleven hundred miles to Glendive, Montana, where we will spend the night Tuesday night before going on to Spokane Wednesday.

"We passed several ships between New York and Belle-fonte. The weather surely was bad on fair weather flyers. We had strong headwinds all the trip as you can see it took us twelve hours and thirteen minutes to travel 800 miles. We both are dead tired so to bed now and up at three in the morning.

'Bert and Jack'

At the airport the next morning, Jack checked out his plane and made sure it was fueled. It was a little foggy, but the kind that would burn off when the sun got higher in the sky. "We'll do the same thing as yesterday if the fog sticks around," he told Bert as they prepared to climb into the Waco. "It's a long stretch to St. Paul, but we should be okay."

Jack revved the engine and taxied. The ground was so soggy that he could barely plow his way though it with enough speed to take off. Finally, to their relief, his plane started to lift.

The first hour or so until the sun came up, he had to rely on his compass and steer slightly to the north to keep from drifting. The excitement of starting the race the day before had worn off. Now it was about slogging to the finish with the best time possible.

"You okay, Bert?" Jack yelled after they'd flown a couple of hours.

Bert gave Jack a thumbs-up and motioned for Jack to fly lower. Bert peered over the side to catch some landmark. He must have caught a glimpse of something on the ground, because Jack saw him look at the map. Then he turned to Jack.

"Doing good, Jack," he yelled.

That was a comfort to Jack, and he was glad Bert was his passenger and navigator.

After about three hours, Bert motioned for Jack to fly lower. It was late morning, and the fog had burned off. The more it cleared, the harder Jack pushed his ship. Bert looked down, then at the map again.

"I figure we're about an hour out of St. Paul," he yelled. All Jack heard over the wind noise was "hour" and "St. Paul," their first mandatory stop for the day. Thirty minutes later, he motioned for Jack to go to a lower altitude. Sure enough, there it was. Jack set down for a few minutes. They had five. They had come four hundred miles against a headwind and in bumpy air. They had maxed the range of the plane and had to fuel up. With full tanks, they should be able to make it into Glendive. There were two mandatory stops in Fargo and Bismarck, North Dakota, before they landed in Glendive for the night.

According to race officials in St. Paul, Jack was still tenth in the race and the weather was clear, so he pushed the throttle forward even more to get the maximum speed out of the *Spirit* to make up time. It was a bit risky, but he thought he could get away with it for a couple of hours. An hour or so outside of Fargo, his engine started sputtering, running roughly. *Damn it.*

Bert looked back at Jack. "What's wrong?"

"Magneto. Hang on, I'm going to check them out," he yelled.

To check them out, Jack switched to the left one and turned off the right. The engine started running smoother, but when he switched to the right one, it started backfiring again. Jack quickly switched it back to the left magneto.

"How far are we from Fargo?"

"I figure ninety miles," Bert answered.

"Hang on and say a prayer. We've got to make it on one," Jack said.

By the time they got to Fargo, the engine was backfiring again. The engine was so loud, men started running out of the hangars and buildings to watch them come in. Thankfully, Jack had made thousands of dead stick landings and sideslips. This was another day at the office for someone who'd been a barnstormer.

On the ground, a man came running up to the plane as soon as Jack got out. The guy must have been a mechanic, because he said, "Magneto problems, eh?"

"Think so. Can you fix it?"

"Have to look at it first."

"Get to it. We're going to get a cup of coffee," Jack said.

"There's coffee on the stove inside. Come back in half an hour. I'll know by then," the mechanic said.

"That's damn bad luck to have engine problems," Bert said as they walked to the hangar.

Jack shrugged. "That's part of flying. Just hope it doesn't set us back too much. I was starting to make up time."

Bert went off to talk to the race officials and tell them what had happened. The coffee was good and warmed Jack, but he needed a snort. When Bert was out of the room, he pulled out a small flask he had snuck into his coveralls and poured whiskey in his cup. Then he went to check with the mechanic. Bert came out after he finished talking to the officials.

"I checked the magnetos, and they seemed to be okay," the mechanic said. "I heard you flew through quite a bit of rain, so I dried them out in case water leaked in. Then I thought maybe you had some condensate in the gas tank, so I drained it and filled it back up."

"Thanks. Did you check the fuel line?" Jack asked.

"Yep, looked okay," the mechanic said. "I'll call ahead to make sure there are new magnetos there in case you need them."

"Thanks," Jack said, and they climbed back in the aircraft.

They took off, but the sun was low, so they could only make it to Bismarck for the night when Glendive was supposed to be their overnight stop. His plane sputtered a little, so he had it thoroughly checked out again. The next morning, they headed out early, but the magnetos went out about fifty miles out of Glendive. They had made good time. The mechanics were good and had them fixed quickly.

Because he had to stay overnight in Bismarck, race officials counted that as his second overnight. Jack then headed on to Spokane via Billings and Missoula. It was Wednesday, the last day of the race, and he had to cover more than seven hundred miles. Thankfully the weather was good.

They touched down and filled up in Billings and then again for the mandatory five minutes in Missoula. Jack didn't even get out of the plane.

"Put in just enough to get us to Spokane," he told the guy.

It was only a two-hundred-mile hop, and Jack didn't want to be on the ground a second longer than he had to be. He also didn't want the extra weight, and the plane would lighten as they traveled.

"According to the booklet they gave us, the airport is one of the best," he told Bert. "It's a mile and a half long and half a mile wide with winds primarily from the west, so finding it and landing should be no problem."

"When we cross the Spokane River, we'll know we're there, so start looking for the airfield."

They learned that Charles Meyers had landed and was the

first. A couple of guys had also been killed, but they had to put that out of our minds. Some had turned back.

The rest of the race was uneventful. Jack touched down in seventh place out of eight in his class that had completed the race. He accepted this position, considering it was his first long-distance race, plus the weather and magneto problems. He picked up several issues of the *Spokane Chronicle* and quickly found his name. They had tracked his progress since he left New York. Bert had also wired the Towanda paper.

There was another race going on up the West Coast from San Francisco at the same time they were racing from New York. Spokane had really promoted the races. They'd brought in Lindbergh a week before. Daws and the MacClatchies couldn't have done better. Festivities lasted until the twenty-fifth. Over a hundred thousand people attended. Doolittle had been there.

> . . .7*TH IN RACE*
>
> *Towanda plane, 24 Out of New York, Finishes Only Two Hours Behind Prize Winner."*
>
> *Forced Down by Magneto Trouble in Montana, Ashcraft and Crader Even Then Persist in Desperate Effort to Win.*
>
> *The 'Spirit of Ammonia,' Towanda's entry in the national air derby from Roosevelt Field, New York, to Spokane, Washington, is now in Spokane.*
>
> *Piloted by Jack Ashcraft, with Burt Crader, also of Towanda, as passenger, the Waco plane of the Towanda Aircraft Corporation reached its western destination yesterday afternoon at 4:17:52 o'clock. It was the seventh to land in the Class B race, just too late to be "in the money." Cash prizes were awarded to the first six.*
>
> *Had it not been for a little bad luck about fifty miles west of Glendive, Montana, the 'Spirit of Ammonia' which carried*

with it the hopes of Towandians but of thousands of others in this section, would have been among the winners.

The Daily Review, Thursday Morning,
September 22, 1927

Jack and Crader will remain in Spokane for the big air meet and may capture some of the prizes for stunt flying before they return.

Even last night there was already some talk of a big public reception in honor of the flyers upon their return here, to show the town's appreciation for what they have done.

Jack and Bert stayed around to take it all in. They went to the aviation ball. Jack did some stunt flying and some playing around. He met some beautiful women in the northwest, but it was time to get back. Winter would soon be setting in. He and Buck needed to set up a second from which to conduct aerial activities. They had chosen Macon, Georgia, where they would have better flying weather.

There was a letter from Mavis waiting for him in Towanda. *I followed the race on the radio and what newspapers I could find. Congratulations! Another accomplishment under your belt. Give me a call when you're back in town. Love, Mavis.*

He worked for a few weeks before heading south. One day, he picked up a paper. Ruth Elder's picture was on the front. They called her the "Miss America of the Air." She and George Haldeman had taken off on October 11 for Newfoundland for a hop across the Atlantic but had fallen short of their goal. They made an emergency landing in the ocean and luckily had been rescued by a Danish freighter. The paper went on to say that she and Haldeman had made it farther than anyone else. Frances Grayson hadn't been so lucky. Her plane had gone down, and she and her copilot were never found.

Before they headed south, Jack had one stop to make, to visit his mother and dad. Bert hitched a ride back to Towanda. He hadn't been home since Clarice's death.

CHAPTER 23
FRANZ JOINS JACK

Francis "Franz" Ashcraft, circa 1928. *Courtesy of Allen Keller.*

December 1927–February 1928
Protection, Kansas; Macon, Georgia

After Clarice died, Jack knew he had to fly home on the way to Georgia. No celebration this trip. He didn't buzz the town like he had in '25. There was no cause for celebration. Just before dusk, Jack cut his engine to avoid attracting attention and did a dead stick landing near Troy's place. Troy and Franz met him there.

Franz had been writing Jack letters since summer, begging Jack to let him come join him. He wanted to fly with Jack so badly. Jack knew that he wasn't going to be able to put him off any longer. Sure enough, the wheels of the plane had barely touched down and the propeller stopped when Franz ran over.

"Hey, Jack! Mother and Dad said I could go if you said okay. Can I?" Franz said.

"Whoa! Slow down a bit and give me a proper hello, will you?" Jack said, giving him a big pat on the back. "Don't forget the reason I came. Give me a hand with this, will you?"

Quickly, they rolled the plane near the barn, secured it, and covered it with a tarp.

"Sorry, I've just been so anxious for you to get here," Franz said while they worked.

"How are Mother and Dad doing?" Jack asked.

"Holding up okay. Clarice dying was a blow to them. They're showing their age, too," Franz replied.

"Aren't we all . . . except you, you knucklehead," Jack said. He grabbed Franz around the neck and rubbed his knuckles hard on his head.

"Owww! Stop it!" Franz yelled, wriggling out of Jack's grasp.

Franz put up his fists. "I'm not going to take anything from you, old man. I'm as big as you are now." They both burst out laughing. Jack looked at his little brother and wondered when Franz had grown so tall.

"What's this you're flying?" Franz asked.

"A Waco, and it's nothing like that Standard, I'll tell you that," Jack said.

The plane secured, Jack turned to Troy. "Hey, Troy. How's the family?" He and Troy chatted as they walked to the car, then Jack and Franz drove to the Ashcraft home.

"You sure you want to join me?" Jack asked. "I love it, but it's not an easy life. We fly in all sorts of weather and at all times of the day and night. Airplanes are improving, but flying is still a dangerous enterprise. No two ways about it. Sometimes despite your best efforts, things go wrong. I'm a good pilot and I'm careful, but I've had more than my share of close calls."

"I know all that, Jack," Franz said. Then he motioned around as they drove through town to the house. "Look around, Jack. What do you see for me here? Lillian, Audrey, Chester, and Martin have all moved on. Clarice is gone. That just leaves Ernest, Helen, Mary, and Ivan, and they'll be gone before you know it. When Dad quits the hardware business, he'll turn it over to you if you want it. I'm not sure I'm cut out for that anyway. I figure if flying doesn't work out for me, I can be a mechanic and have better options somewhere else."

"I'll talk to Mother and Dad." Jack said with resignation.

Once they got home, Jack gave his dad a hearty handshake and hug. He hugged his mother warmly. Her hair was even more gray. With his arm around her, they walked into the house. Then all his brothers and sisters started to arrive. There was a bare space on the wall where Clarice's picture had hung. His mother said that she couldn't bear to see Clarice's pretty face every day when she knew that she would never see her daughter again. His brothers and sisters came and brought enough food to feed Coxey's Army. It was a good but somber time. Jack made the rounds to meet the new additions to the family and yacked it up with his brothers. After everyone left, he and Franz sat down with their mother and dad in the living room.

"So, Franz told me that he's asked your permission to come back east to fly with me," Jack said.

"Yes, he has," his dad said without looking at either Jack or Franz. "We told him that he was twenty-one and could make his own decisions. It's not our decision to make."

"Are you sure that's what you want to do, Francis?" his mother asked. "I don't want two boys to worry about."

"Mama," Franz said, "I could get hurt or killed around here as well as anywhere else. Heck, I could have a wreck driving to work. I've got to spread my wings."

"I suppose so," she said, then turned to Jack. "You take care of him, Junior."

"I'll do the best I can, Mother," Jack reassured her. "I'll do the best I can, but you know what flying is like. He's a big boy, and I can't be with him every minute."

"How well I know," his mother said, looking away.

Jack took notice but continued talking.

"We're headquartering in Macon, Georgia, for the winter," Jack said. "We're planning the Southeastern Air Derby in February, so you can make yourself useful right away being a mechanic and general gofer."

Franz jumped up. "An air derby! Oh, boy, I can't wait. When do we go?"

"Get your stuff together," Jack laughed. "We'll leave day after tomorrow for Macon. I'm meeting Gardner Nagle, Bert Crader, and Buck Steele there. We've formed the Macon Crader-Ashcraft-Steele Flying School there."

"I can't wait!" Franz said.

"Tomorrow, I'll teach you how to fly the Waco. If you do

okay, you'll fly us to Shreveport. I want to stop in to see my Mason buddies," Jack said.

"Gee, thanks, Jack. This is just great, just great. I won't let you down, I promise," Franz said, not trying to conceal his excitement.

They hadn't been back in Georgia long when a bizarre incident happened. Jack was staying at a hotel in Terra Cotta, preparing for the air meet, when he happened upon a fellow pilot he had met in Birmingham named S. Garland Irwin. Irwin had done some stunting, including parachuting. He showed up at Miller Field one day and asked Crader to take him for a ride. Crader couldn't, so he asked Jack.

Jack took him aloft for what Jack thought was a typical flight. Irwin was a good pilot, so Jack thought it strange that Irwin wanted a ride in a plane. At about one thousand feet, the man stood up in the passenger's cockpit and stepped out on the wing.

"Hey, what are you doing? Get back in here!" Jack yelled and tugged at his coat.

Irwin got back in the cockpit but stepped out on the wing again a few minutes later. Jack coaxed him back into the plane, then he stepped out a third time.

Hanging on to the cockpit next to Jack, he leaned over so Jack could hear him. "It's all over now," he said fell from the plane. His body hurtled down to earth like a boulder—no flailing of arms and legs.

Jack landed as quickly as he could and ran to where Irwin had fallen, distraught. Jack related the story in an inquest that was reported in the local paper:

Irwin stood up in the cockpit for the passengers, and that he (Jack) told him to sit down. He testified further that he (Irwin) crawled out onto the right wing and that he leaned over to him and said something that sounded like: 'It's all over now.'"

Ashcraft Testifies

"I might say, gentlemen," said the pilot, "that it would have been an easy matter for me to have misunderstood the exact words that Irwin said to me due to the buzzing and roar of the engine at this time, and the further fact that I had to hand the control. I will say that it sounded like that is what he said to me, but I would not swear it, because I might be mistaken.

"I told him to keep his seat and to stay seated, but before I knew it he had fallen. I couldn't say that he jumped—in fact, I do not think he jumped at all, but rather I believe he accidentally lost his balance and fell."

At twenty-seven, Irwin was a seasoned aviator and had done some stunting. Crader testified that the plane had been flying smoothly and hadn't turned over in the air. The jury viewed the body. The head was fractured in almost a dozen places, and it was said that his head and shoulders were almost severed from his body and his body mangled. They questioned Irwin's brother, who didn't fault Jack. All the while, Jack's nerves got the best of him, as they had that day in Louisiana three years before. Franz fretted over his brother. In the end, Jack was exonerated of any wrongdoing. Upon hearing the ruling, Jack regained his composure in the courtroom. However, when he landed later at Miller Field, he collapsed and became hysterical and had to be put to bed at the local residence of a friend.

Buck had been out of town but arrived before sundown.

When he learned what had happened, he rushed to his friend's side. Franz met him the instant he stepped inside the door.

"Jack's in a bad way, Buck," Franz said. "He won't see me or anybody. Can you help my brother, Buck? Please?"

Buck nodded. "I'll see what I can do." He went into the room where Jack was.

Jack lay in bed, his head covered in pillows to bury his anguish.

"Jack. You awake? I heard what happened," Buck said, pulling a chair up beside the bed. "You gotta brace up. It wasn't your fault—accidents can happen any time."

"Easy for you to say," Jack said, still dazed. "For the rest of my life, I'll never forget Irwin's last words. 'It's all over now. It's all over now. It's all over now.'" Jack covered his head. His shoulders shook as he sobbed.

"Get some rest, buddy," Buck said, patting Jack on the arm. "It'll be better tomorrow." Then Buck eased back into the chair to be close to his friend where he remained until morning.

Jack collected himself for one last task to put the incident behind him. He, Bert, Gardner, and Buck flew to Birmingham to attend Irwin's funeral and pay last respects.

Airplanes Scatter Flowers At Grave of Fallen Flier

Soaring high into the late afternoon sky, three planes laden with wreaths and flowers took off from Roberts Field to pay final respects to a fallen comrade, Grantland Irwin, killed last Monday when he fell from a plane in flight.

In the flower-laden planes were Jack Ashcraft, who was piloting the plane from which Irwin fell; Buck Steel, Gardner

Nagle, H.C. Green and E.C. Woodmansee, all friends of the young aviator.

The planes circled over the Irwin home at 1607 Eleventh Avenue South, dropping wreaths and flowers. Later they flew to the grave, covering with decorations.

"They were the last respects to a flying comrade," said Jack Ashcraft upon his return to the field. "Irwin was one of the finest pilots I ever knew. I think he had more than 30 falls and I believe he hurt his leg once," Ashcraft said.

Back in Macon, Jack went to his room to pull himself together for his brother's sake and that of his friends.

CHAPTER 24
SOUTHEASTERN AIR DERBY, MACON, GEORGIA

L to r: Samuel "Buck" Steele, Gardner "Peg" Nagle, and Jack Ashcraft. *Courtesy of Allen Keller.*

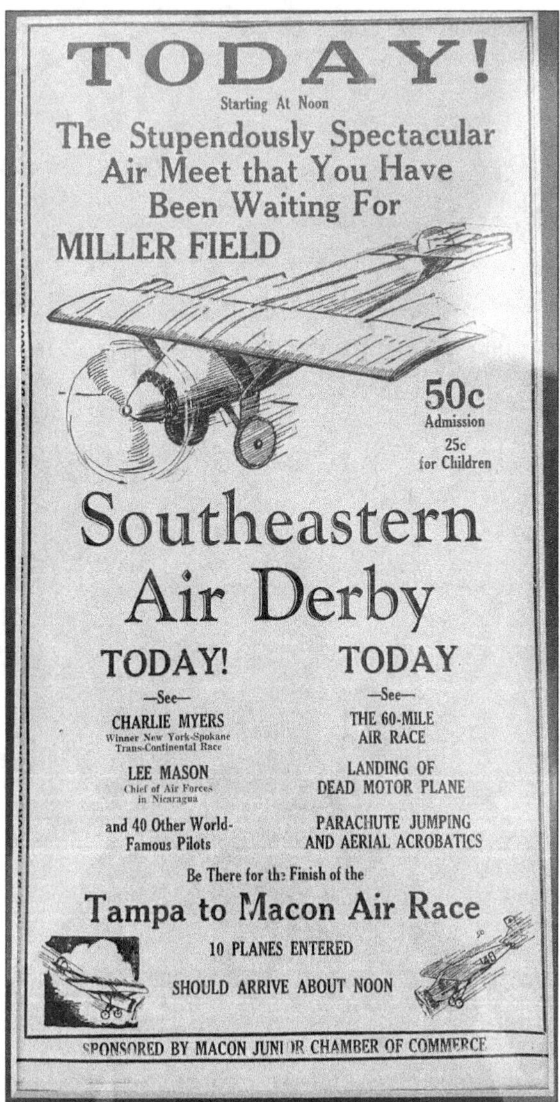

Poster for Southeastern Air Derby, February 1928. *Courtesy of Henry Lowe, Macon, Georgia.*

February 1928
Macon, Georgia

The Monday before the air derby, Franz arrived at Miller Field. He wanted to be there when Jack arrived—if he arrived. Jack didn't come back to the room last night. Franz paced back and forth as he anxiously waited for Jack.

"You're going to wear a path in the ground you won't be able to crawl out of if you keep that up," Buck said.

Franz looked at Buck, worry in on his face. "Can't help it. I'm worried about Jack."

Buck patted the young man on his shoulder. "I understand. That was a tough blow, losing Irwin like he did, but Jack will be here. You'll see. Why don't you go help Jimmy with that engine?"

"Is Franz going to be okay? It's tough to see something like that happen to your brother," Nagle said as Buck approached the office.

"I think so," Buck answered. "He's awfully young, though."

When Franz and Jack first arrived, Jack told Franz that he would learn a lot from the guys, and to listen and watch close. Buck was one of the best pilots around and could fly in any cockpit you put him. From Gardner, he learned the basics of stunt flying back in Louisiana. Bert guided Jack from New York to Spokane in the nastiest weather and thickest fog he'd ever flown in. Jack trusted them with his life. Franz knew he could learn the ropes from the guys. But he hadn't considered that he would have to learn how to lose a comrade from them as well.

"You still want to do this, little brother?" Jack said.

Franz had been so deep in thought and worry that he hadn't heard Jack walk up.

"Jack!" Franz said and on impulse, gave his brother a hug.

"Yeah. I'm not going to lie to you," Franz said. "That was a tough initiation, but yeah. I still want to do this. I still want to fly."

Jack nodded. "Come on. We've got work to do."

Watching the interaction from a distance, Bert and Nagle breathed a sigh of relief.

The poster read:

ATTEND THE
Southeastern Air Derby
MILLER FIELD, MACON, FEB. 17-18-19
'AMERICA TAKES WINGS' and MACON
—with the development and improvement of Miller Field
will soon
join the nation in this new field with
a modern and geographically impor-
tant Airport that will do much to—
Speed, Progress and Create Business
Luther Williams Bank
& Trust Co.
LUTHER WILLIAMS, President"

The local paper, the *Macon News*, had announcements about the air meet throughout the week. One day, there was a picture of Jack labeled *Experienced Flyer* above the photo. Below it read, *ASHCRAFT HAS SEVERAL YEARS' EXPE-RIENCE IN FLYING OVER COUNTRY*, and there was an accompanying article. Other announcements were:

WINNERS IN DERBY TO BE GIVEN CUPS, Telegraph *Offers Trophy to Victor in Race, MANY STUNTS ARE PLANNED.*

AVIATORS TO TRY HARD FOR PRIZES, Steele and Ashcraft Say They Will Garner Trophies, TAMPA AIRMEN TO BE HERE

AIR DERBY PLANS RAPIDLY ADVANCE, Jay-Ces' [sic] Aeroplane [sic] Carnival Is Booked for Feb. 17-18-19, EXPECT 50,000 TO ATTEND.

ONLY LICENSED PILOTS TO FLY, Men Who Have Qualified With Commerce Department Are to Enter Air Derby.

There was a picture of Charles Meyers, who had won the New York to Spokane race, announcing that he had arrived and would fly in a big race scheduled during the three-day event.

A couple of days before the air derby, Bert got an idea for a stunt to kick things off. "Here's what I think we should do to really get people excited about the show," he said. "Someone could go aloft with a passenger over Macon. At, say, three thousand feet, the passenger will light explosive noisemakers, and someone more experienced will throw them out to draw attention to the field."

Franz couldn't control his enthusiasm. "I'll do it! I'll do it!"

Bert looked at Jack.

"Okay by me, but you light the fuse. Buck will throw it out. You've got to work fast, Franz," Jack told him.

"I can do that," Franz said.

"Now go get some rocks. Bert, go get a couple of the real noisemakers," Jack said.

Bert gave Buck two real report bombs, and that was just what they looked like—small bombs. Franz walked up with the bag of rocks.

"What do you want me to do with these?" he asked.

"When Buck gets to altitude, you're going to practice

passing the rocks back to him," Jack said. "You hand them to Buck, and Buck will throw them out. Make a quick, clean handoff."

"Can't I throw some? I played baseball, remember?" Franz said.

"But Buck will be in the back cockpit, and he's more experienced," Jack answered.

Franz shrugged, disappointed.

"Now, when Buck thinks you're ready, hand him a real bomb," Jack said.

"To light it, take off the cap and strike it across the top," Bert explained. "These have a ten second fuse, so you have to work fast. Strike it and hand it to Buck immediately. Understand?"

Franz and Buck nodded.

"Be careful up there," Jack said. "When you're finished, come down and we'll talk about whether or not we actually want to do this on Saturday before the show."

Bert and Jack watched them take off and gain altitude.

"You think this is going to work, Bert?" Jack asked.

"Sure. It'll be fun," Bert answered.

Buck circled, and they saw a rock fly out of the plane. Buck must have thrown out half a dozen rocks, and then they heard a blast and saw smoke. Thirty seconds later, they heard a second one. Then the plane descended to land.

Buck had barely set down when Franz was out of the plane.

"That was fun. You should have seen them explode from up there," he said excitedly. "I can't wait until the air meet!"

"This going to work? Did you see any problems?" Jack asked his friend. "Be honest with me."

"No problems. Should be nothing to it," Buck replied. "Franz handled everything just fine."

"Are you sure?" Bert asked. "We don't want any foul-ups."

Buck and Franz looked at one another and nodded. "Seemed easy enough to do," Buck said.

"Okay. Let's go grab some grub," Jack said.

The morning of the event, the *Macon Telegraph* had a picture of Buck and his airplane. Above the photo it said, *Macon Pilot Will Compete in Air Derby Events.* The caption read:

> *Buck Steele, local pilot at Miller field, will participate in the events of the three-day derby opening today. He will do his unusual stunt of flying upside down, today and tomorrow at the field.*

Macon's First Air Derby to Get Under Way Today
Thirty Planes to Perform in Formation Flight as Opening of Program

The article that followed told what to expect during the day and included a program.

Saturday morning was cool and clear. Franz checked the plane, then paced beside it waiting for Buck, anxious to take off.

"I'm going to watch the show from the edge of town," Jack said. "You guys be careful up there. If you have any doubts, don't do it. Call it off. We'll understand."

Buck and Franz nodded, and Jack sped off on his motorcycle.

Buck and Franz got into their plane and fastened in. Bert handed Franz the fireworks. "Remember, you've got to act quick. Be careful up there," he said. He jumped down from the wing and walked to his plane. Bert and Gardner would be aloft as well, ready to do some stunting when the blasts got every-one's attention.

Buck taxied and took off, followed by Bert, Gardner, and some other pilots."

Exactly on time and as planned, the plane soared over Macon and circled a few times. Heads turned, eyes looked upward. People exited buildings. After the third time, Jack saw an object fly out of the plane, followed by a flash and an explosion. More heads turned and looked upward. *So far, so good,* he thought.

A second noisemaker flew out and exploded a minute later. More people had come out of the stores, and all heads were turned upward in anticipation. *Two down, one to go.* Jack held his breath as he waited for the third blast, but he sensed some-thing wasn't right. It was taking too long to light. The bomb exploded seconds later.

Jack watched in horror as smoke enveloped the ship and the left wing fell away from the fuselage. The plane sideslipped and went into a nosedive, gathering speed due to the revolving propeller and gravity. It crashed into the street, a mangled heap of splintered wood, torn fabric, and tangled wire, the propeller still creepily still revolving. Franz's and Buck's bodies were catapulted from the plane and landed a distance from the wreckage.

"Oh my God!" Jack said. He rode in the direction of the crash several blocks away. He dropped his motorbike and ran toward the plane.

When he arrived, so many people had rushed to the site that the sidewalk had collapsed. Bedlam ensued, and the police and fire departments struggled to keep the onlookers back. Others rubbernecked from the tops of buildings.

"Franz! Buck!" Jack screamed frantically. "Let me through!

Let me through, dammit! Where's my brother? I've got to get to Franz!" Jack shoved people aside as he struggled to get through the throng.

A policeman stopped him before he reached the plane. Jack tried to push him aside, but the officer resisted.

"Where's Franz? Where's Buck?" he asked.

"There's nothing you can do now," the policeman said.

"The pilots are my brother and best friend. Please let me through, officer," Jack said frantically, in tears.

The officer relented. "They landed over there," he said. "It's not a pretty sight."

"I don't care. I've got to be with them," Jack said. He followed the officer to where the bodies had landed. Both were covered with white sheets, blood soaking through them.

The ambulance drivers loaded Buck into their vehicle, then Franz. An arm was partially exposed and was badly burned. Sickened, Jack fell to his knees, face in his hands, and sobbed.

"Oh my God. What have I done? Franz, I'm so sorry," he cried.

The policeman was trying to console Jack when Bert arrived.

"We'll take care of him. Thank you, officer," Bert said. They tried to lead Jack away, but he continued to wander dazed around the wreckage under Bert's watchful eye.

THE MACON TELEGRAPH
MACON, GA., SUNDAY MORNING, FEBRUARY 19, 1928
TWO AVIATORS DIE AS BOMB CRASHES AIRPLANE;
FALLING SHIP FATALLY INJURES MAN ON STREET.
MANY ARE INJURED AS WRECK PLUNGES TO
CHERRY STREET

Buck Steele and Francis Ashcraft Killed when Premature Explosion of Noise-Maker Shatters Wing of Machine Soaring Above Heart of Macon's Business District, Sending It Into Meteor-Like Fall to Crowded Sidewalk.

Clyde E. Murphy, Gazing at Falling Plane, Is Struck by It and Leg and Arm Are Severed, Causing His Death; Pavement Collapses Under Weight of Frantic Crowd and Dozens More are Injured; None of them Seriously.

Premature explosion of an aerial bomb, touched off from an airplane, 2,500 feet above the heart of the business section of Macon at 12:30 o'clock yesterday afternoon sent the occupants of the plane, Samuel L. (Buck) Steele, pilot, and France [sic] Ashcraft, who was in charge of the bombs, in a skyrocket plunge to their death on the crowded sidewalk of Cherry Street.

A third person, Clyde E. Murphy, of Hollis road, a pedestrian, was struck by a wing of the plane and was fatally injured. He died at the Macon Hospital nearly two hours after the crash.

A few minutes after the plane had buried its nose into the concrete sidewalk, hundreds rushed to the scene of the crash. Then the sidewalk in front of Persons Pharmacy collapsed from the weight of scores of persons hurling them into the cellar, ten feet below. More than a dozen were injured, none seriously.

Third Bomb Wrecks Plane

Steele and Ashcraft were flying directly over the city, dropping aerial bombs to advertise the opening of Southeastern Air Derby. Ashcraft was a student flier visiting his brother, Jack Ashcraft, local aviator, during the derby.

As the plane whirred over the city, hundreds of people on the downtown streets craned their necks to watch the machine attracted to the explosion of the bomb.

Two bombs had exploded. A third was thrown from the cockpit. There was a burst of flame. Then the left wing of the plane crumpled, and the machine came hurtling to earth. It turned over once, then went into a nosedive and dropped like a meteor to Cherry Street. The nose of the ship was buried in the concrete sidewalk. The motor was still running.

Women screamed. There was a rush to the scene and in less than two minutes after the crash, Cherry Street was a mass of excited people. They jammed the entire thoroughfare. Children were trampled. Several women fainted.

Crowd in Panic

Mr. Murphy, a pedestrian, was struck by the remaining wing of the plane. His left arm was severed at the shoulder, and his right foot was cut off. He was pulled from beneath the wreckage and rushed to the Macon Hospital as soon as possible.

When the sidewalk collapsed, people screamed in terror.

Another airplane is falling," someone yelled.

A stampede followed and the huge crowd milled around the street like cattle. The show window of the Metro studio was shattered. A woman with her baby in arms was knocked down as brawny men forced their way through the pack. Policemen shouted hoarsely for order; their voices lost in the din.

All available police officers were rushed to the scene in an effort to handle the crowd. A few minutes later they succeeded in roping off the street, fight back the crowd which had now become merely curious.

When the plane fell, there was a splatter of blood all over the street. When some semblance of order had been restored, a wrecker was brought to the scene and the shattered plane was removed. The bodies of the two fliers were carried to

Burghard's. Steele's head was crushed. The top of Ashcraft's head was blown off. The impact of the crash made a deep hole in the concrete sidewalk.

When Mr. Murphy was struck, it was first believed that he had been . . .

Gardner returned to the field and rushed toward the officials in hysterics, sobbing. He told them that Buck was the best pal he'd ever had. He had taught Buck to fly years ago. "Seeing him at the crash was horrendous," he said. "The bomb got their heads . . ." He couldn't continue.

"As far as I could tell, one of the bombs went off early and was too close to the wing. I don't know," Gardner said once he regained some composure. "All I could do was watch it go down." He shook his head in horror.

"It must have been horrible for them," he said quietly. "It's a miracle that there was no explosion on the ground. The propeller was still turning."

Gardner rushed to find Bert. "How's Jack holding up?" he asked.

"The police brought him to the airfield. He's still in shock. He's going to call his folks," Bert said. "That's going to be tough."

Since so many had flown in from out of town, Bert and the other officials decided that the derby would continue, but all social events would be canceled. Later, the derby was canceled as well.

Jack stood by the phone. Picked up the receiver, then put it down again. He paced, trying to get himself together enough to call his mother and dad. He picked up the receiver and told the operator the number, trying to keep his voice from breaking.

Ivan answered. "Hello. This is Ivan speaking," he said.

"Hi, Ivan. Jack here. I need to speak to Dad."

"Mary Jane, go get Dad," Ivan said. "How are you, Jack? You and Franz having a good time?"

"I'm doing okay. How are you?" Jack avoided his question, trying to buy some time till his dad got on the phone.

"I'm doing good. I got all A's except for one B in English," Ivan said. "Now I'm playing basketball on the junior high team."

"That's good, Ivan. Is Dad there yet?" Jack asked.

"Yeah, here he is. Bye, Jack," Ivan said.

"Hi, son. Everything okay?" his dad asked.

Jack lost control at the sound of his father's voice. "No, Dad, I'm afraid not." Jack choked the words out. "It's Franz. He was killed in an accident today."

"I see," his father said. A long silence followed. Jack heard his father quietly weeping.

"You still there, Dad?"

"What happened?"

"He and Buck went up to throw out some noisemakers to get everybody to come to the air show," Jack said. "We think one of them went off early and blew off a wing of the plane. Killed Buck too."

"This will devastate your Mother," his father said. "Me too."

"I know, Dad. I'm bringing Franz home. We should be in Protection by Tuesday."

"Okay, son. We'll make the arrangements," his father said, then the phone went dead.

CHAPTER 25
TAKING FRANZ HOME

Francis "Franz" Ashcraft, 1928. *Courtesy of Allen Keller.*

February 1928
Macon, Georgia; Protection, Kansas

At the mortuary, Jack stared at the cloth-covered wooden box that contained his little brother. Two assistants stood by to make preparations for Franz's final trip home. Bert and Gardner stood by their comrade. Bert had called Pang immediately after the crash. Unable to come himself, Pang sent Ive and Al. The two men stood by Jack's side as well.

Without looking at him, Jack said to Bert, "Did you get Buck sent home okay?"

"Earlier this morning," Bert said, and Jack nodded.

Jack looked at Ive. "Did you talk to the mortician? Did they make Franz look okay in case the folks want to see him?" he asked.

Ive looked away and ran his fingers nervously through his hair. "I did, and he tried, but I ended up asking Bert for a flight helmet to put on him."

"Oh, God," Jack said. He looked away. "Can I have a few minutes alone with him?" he asked.

"Don't take long," Ive said. "We've got to get to the railroad station."

The others no longer in the room, Jack lifted the lid of the coffin to take one last look at Franz. "I'm so sorry, buddy. You were so young. Just barely getting whiskers," he whispered. Lowering the lid, Jack leaned on the box and wept.

A few minutes later, Al and Ive escorted Jack outside to the car that awaited them. Through the window, Jack watched as the mortuary workers, along with Bert, Gardner, Al, and Ive, loaded Franz's coffin into the hearse.

At the railway station, Jack stood beside the refrigerated rail car that would take his little brother home. Respectfully, Bert,

Gardner, Al, and Ive carried the coffin and set it down next to Jack. Under the conductor's watch, railyard workers wedged the box in with the dressed beef and other refrigerated items and slid the doors shut.

Jack shook his head. "What a way to take you home," he mumbled to himself.

"You're in rough shape, Jack," Ive said. "Al and I have been talking. We decided that someone should go with you. He volunteered."

The wail of the train whistle signaled that it was time to get on board.

"Come on, Jack," Al said. "There's nothing more we can do." He steered Jack to the passenger car and stepped inside.

Before Jack stepped into the car, Ive handed him an envelope. "Mavis asked me to give this to you personally," he said. On impulse, Ive hugged Jack. "I'll be thinking about you, buddy." He choked out the words, turned quickly on his heel, and walked away.

Al rapped on the window for Jack to get on board.

Jack settled in a seat and sighed heavily. Al quickly started dozing, so Jack pulled out Mavis's letter. *Jack, I'm so grieved for you over the loss of Francis and Buck. I don't know what else to say. Please let me know if there is anything I can do for you. Call when you're back in town. Love, Mavis.*

Jack picked up a newspaper that someone had left on the seat. The headline and the article recounting the accident screamed at him. Tears welled in his eyes.

Al stirred and looked at Jack. "You going to be okay?"

"I don't know. He was my little brother. Mother and Dad are devastated. Their gentle hearts are shattered," he said.

"First Clarice, now Franz. It's my fault. I shouldn't have let him come."

"I'm so sorry about what happened to Franz and Buck. Your brother and your best friend at the same time . . . golly. That's tough," Al said. "But you can't blame yourself. Franz's mind was made up. He'd been begging you for a couple of years now. As your dad said himself, he was over twenty-one and old enough to make his own decisions. Everyone in this business knows there are risks."

Jack shrugged. "Maybe. My head says one thing, but my heart says another. Doesn't make me feel any better." Jack jabbed at the newspaper. "Why did they have to go into such detail, Al? News gets around. Mother and Dad are bound to read about it."

"Because people want to read it, and it sells newspapers," Al replied.

The train engine hissed, and the wheels screeched on the rails. Jack awoke with a start.

"We're here, Jack," Al said.

Jack nodded.

The door opened and Jack stepped from the car. There stood his dad, grief and anguish etched on his face. A few family friends, including Troy, surrounded him. First Clarice, now Franz. Jack hugged his father, trying to be strong for him. "I'm so sorry, Dad."

His dad didn't relinquish a bit of the pain to Jack. "It's not your fault, Junior. Franz made up his own mind. He knew the risks."

His dad tried, but his words didn't help Jack feel any better. If anything, his heart shattered into more bits and pieces.

"How are Mother and the kids?"

"Not good. Your mother hasn't said a word since you called. She just sits in her rocker and stares ahead with his picture in her lap."

The funeral director and assistant loaded the coffin into the hearse and closed the door. Jack, the elder Ashcraft, and Al walked to the Studebaker hearse that would take Franz home.

When they arrived, Al turned to Jack. "I'll be at Troy's if you need me. I'll be at the funeral tomorrow."

Jack nodded.

There were accounts of the accident and obituaries in the Protection newspaper and in every newspaper in every town for miles around. Jack struggled to keep his composure and sanity over all that was happening. He remained silent when every inclination inside him was to scream to release the pain he suffered inside.

For all the accounts, the most thorough was in the *Towanda Daily Review*, Jack's adopted hometown. There had been time to study the accident and it's cause.

Towanda Daily Review
20 February 1928
FLYERS KILLED IN MACON
BUCK STEELE AND HIS MECHANIC
VICTIMS OF ACCIDENT WITH BOMB
Latter Francis Ashcraft, Brother of Jack
Man on Street Fatally Hurt by Falling Plane;
Sidewalk Caves in

Victims of a prematurely exploding bomb, used in stunt flying for the Southeastern Air Derby, Samuel L. (Buck) Steele and Francis Ashcraft, employees of the Towanda Aircraft Corporation, were instantly killed Saturday afternoon and a third man was fatally injured when the wreckage of their plane struck him as it plunged 7,000 feet through the air to the main street of Macon, Georgia. Three other persons were seriously injured and a dozen

slightly hurt when a sidewalk caved in under the weight of the crowd that rushed to the scene of the crash.

No responsibility for the three deaths was fixed yesterday when a coroner's jury held an inquest over the body of C.E. Murphy, 34 year old Macon blacksmith, who died in a hospital a short time after being struck by the falling

plane. He was caught by the still swiftly revolving propeller which cut off an arm and a leg and inflicted other injuries.. . .

. . .Jack Ashcraft, pilot of Towanda's plane "The Spirit of Ammonia" in the national air race from Roosevelt Field, N.Y., to Spokane Washington, last summer, was in Macon taking part in the aviation meet and saw his brother and Buck Steele, his pal, meet their tragic death. Crader said Jack was bearing up well, however, and was in perfect health. He started yesterday for the family home at Protection, Kansas, with the body of Francis. The body of Steele was sent to the home of his people in Martinville, Ind.

Buck, already had released two bombs before the accident happened. The third caught in the wings and exploded almost immediately.

Thousands Saw Tragedy

Spectators saw the plane suddenly enveloped in smoke and a moment later waver into a slide slip. In an instant it fell into a tail spin [sic], and gathered speed by the force of the still revolving propeller, it crashed close by the car tracks on Cherry Street near the second street crossing. Horror stricken cries from those who watched it fall, failed to clear the street entirely and four persons, one a Negro woman, were either pinned down by the wreckage or struck by the debris.

Thousands of noon-time shoppers seeing the plane fall rushed to the scene. In the midst of the excitement a large portion of the sidewalk collapsed and many were thrown into a scrambling heap in the basement of a drug store. Luckily none were killed.

Fire apparatus was called to clear the debris from the sidewalk and street. The wrecked plane, crushed as if it were paper, was carried away by an auto- mobile wrecker.

Wing Found Mile Away

Later the instrument board and other parts of the plane were picked up in

A coal yard, substantiating the theory of experts that the explosion occurred in the ship and that both men were killed outright or stunned. One wing as if cut off by shears, floated a mile away.

Several planes were in the air when the crash occurred, but only one was flying close enough for fellow airmen to see what happened. Gardner Ragle[sic], its pilot, said the ill-fated plane's first two bombs had exploded without mishap, but the third appeared to have exploded within a few feet of the ship.

He expressed the belief that both Steele and Ashcraft were killed instantly, the former being decapitated by the blast. Their bodies struck the street some distance from the wreckage, leading to the belief that they had been catapulted out of the craft by the explosion. Ashcraft was employed in the plane in handing the bombs back to Steele who dropped them out of the ship.

Steele Known by Many Here

The younger Ashcraft, who was about 22 years old, was

never in Towanda, having been employed since the local flyers went South for the winter. He was acting as a mechanic for the outfit.

Steele, however, was well known by thousands of Bradford County people having done much flying in this vicinity. September 6, last, he took part in an air meet ta Teterboro, NJ., where he thrilled a great crowd with a daring "dead stick landing." shutting his motor off completely at an altitude of 3,000 feet and gliding to the field.

September 13, he came to Towanda to work for the Towanda Aircraft Corporation under the direction of Bert Crader. When he arrived in town that day he and Ashcraft put on an aerial circus all their own over town. Jack had the plane later christened "The Spirit of Ammonia" and Buck had the Waco plane purchased by the corporation just before he arrived. The flyers swept over town side by side, dipped, turned, looped and did all sorts of imaginable stunts. Then just to finish off with, they both swooped under the River Bridge with their machines.

While Crader and Ashcraft were away taking part in the race to Spokane, he carried on the business here and for a time went to Albany, N.Y., with the local plane. Later both Steele and Ashcraft did considerable flying here before it was decided to go South for the winter months. Many Towandians will distinctly remember their farewell to Towanda the day they left—how they flew over town, did a few stunts, circled a couple of times, and then headed down the river expecting to return in the spring.

They did stunt and passenger flying in a number of cities in the South before finally making their headquarters at Macon. There they found much enthusiasm for aviation and did much in getting established at Miller Field, the city's airport. Then they sent for Bert Crader who made several trips

*there and finally the local men, got started the movement for
the Southeastern Air Derby, which was to have started Saturday. A number of famous flyers, among them Clearance Cham-
berlain, had agreed to take part and it had been looked forward
to as a great and happy event. What effect the tragedy will have
on the plans of the Towanda corporation is not known as yet.*

Steele Married Recently

*Buck was only 28 years old but he was considered an
expert flyer. Both*

*he and Ashcraft were with the Gates Flying Circus for
some time before coming here and Buck on many occasions
had proved his reliability and skill. About two months ago he
married a young lady of Shreveport, Louisiana, where he had
been making his home before coming to Towanda.*

Towanda Daily Review, February 20, 1928, Towanda, PA.
From a reprint September 2002. *Flyers Killed in Macon.
The Settler*, A Quarterly Magazine of History and Biography,
Volume XL, Number 3. The Bradford County Historical
Society, pp. 137-139. Used by permission.

In all, Jack spent four days at home. Those were the worst
four days of his life. His brothers and sisters were beside themselves, crying all the time. Jack caught the boys crying. They
seemed embarrassed, but Jack consoled them by telling them it
was okay; he cried too. It was a sad time, and they would all
miss Franz.

Somehow, Jack made it through the funeral. He thought
everyone in the county was there plus many from across the
state. The church was packed, and a field full of flowers
covered Franz's casket. There were so many flowers he figured
that there wasn't a petal left in any florist's shop in the state of

Kansas. Pang and Gates had an arrangement sent from the circus. It was a wreath with a propeller and the GFC logo that he'd seen on the tails of those planes that day in the skies outside of Shreveport. It seemed eons ago now.

The line afterwards was an endurance test with all the people walking by, shaking their hands, and offering their condolences. People meant well, but their words were hollow. His mother nearly fainted, and Martin and his dad took her to another room.

It might have just been his imagination, but he saw a lot of folks, two or three at a time, talking quietly and whispering to one another. He caught them looking at him and wondered if they blamed him for Franz getting killed. There were biddies and codgers alike, tongues wagging.

The whole time, Al stood quietly and respectfully to the side in case his friend needed him.

At the graveside, the finality of the moment overcame Jack and other family members. They leaned on one another for support. Jack slumped next to Al as Franz's coffin was lowered into the earth on the lonesome prairie.

Afterwards, they returned to the quiet of the house, which had once been filled with laughter and conversation but was now shrouded with gloom. There was another bare space on the wall of family photos, near the panorama photos that Jack sent them in 1926.

CHAPTER 26
NO TIME TO GRIEVE

February–May 1928

Troy was at the funeral and drove Jack and Al to the station to catch the train when it was time to go.

"Go get us a seat, will ya, Al? I'll be right there," Jack said when they reached the station.

"Don't take too long," Al said. "The train's about ready to pull out."

"Are you going to be okay?" Troy asked when Al left.

"I've got to be okay. Me, Gardner, Bert, and Jimmy are planning a big air meet in upstate New York in May. Franz was so excited about it. . ." Jack said, voice breaking. "It'll help once I get busy again and don't have time to think about it." He paused and sighed. "I'm worried about Mother and Dad. All Mother said to me the whole time I was home was, 'Don't blame yourself, Junior.' The rest of the time she just stared. Of course, that just made me blame myself more."

"But—" Troy started, but Jack interrupted.

"How the hell can I not blame myself? They trusted me. Franz trusted me."

"But you can't, Jack. Your parents are right. He was twenty-two and knew the risks," Troy said. "Heaven knows Buck did. Who knows what happened in the air over Macon that day? Who will ever know? You can't help it that the damn thing went off early."

Jack just shook his head.

"Remember the board track days and the crazy way we raced our motorcycles on those damn things?" Troy continued. "How crazy was that? It's a wonder we didn't kill ourselves. Shit happens, and you never know when it will."

"Logic says you're right, but that doesn't help much when it's your little brother and your heart is aching," Jack said.

The engineer blew the final whistle, and the engine hissed a warning for Jack to get on board. "You have to get on now, Jack," Troy said.

Al banged on the window and motioned frantically for Jack to get on. Jack waved back and nodded.

Troy hugged Jack, something he had never done before, and Jack hugged him back. "Come back to Protection and take over your dad's hardware store," Troy said. "We'll grow old together and drink hooch out in the open."

"Who knows, I just might do that." Jack stepped on the first step of the train car.

"Here's something Darlene fixed for you and Al for your trip back," Troy said, handing Jack a big paper sack. "I put a little something in there for you too."

"Thanks, buddy," Jack said.

"Take care of yourself, Jack," Troy said. "I'll check in on your folks now and then." He watched the door close.

There weren't many passengers on the train, so Jack took a window seat opposite Al, propped his feet up, eased back, and sighed, watching the brown prairie spotted with snow go by. The bleakness of the landscape mirrored his soul. Al looked at Jack, then out the window.

Jack felt like that kid he'd been a long time ago when he and Troy went to see Cal Rodgers and that silly *Vin Fiz*. Jack had gone to see Cal fly, and now people paid to see Jack fly and do all sorts of stunts for a thrill. They let Jack give them rides. Jack had wanted to be like Rodgers, and Jack's little brother had wanted to be like Jack. Now Rodgers was dead, and so was Franz. *Hell! Is it worth it?* Jack asked himself. Al continued to stare out the window. He knew Jack didn't want to talk. Besides, there was nothing more that could be said.

Jack hadn't been able to sleep since they brought Franz home, so he was dog tired, and hungry. Neighbors had brought mounds of food, but he couldn't remember when he last late. Events of the last several days blurred. All he could really remember were faces of people moving in and out of focus, looking at him—some angry, some regretful, some accusatory. The old biddies and codgers of the town whispering, then stopping when he came near. He wondered how Buck's family was doing, especially his wife.

Jack's stomach growled, and he opened the bag and pulled out a couple of ham sandwiches and some cookies and handed them to Al. "Here. Troy's wife made these for us." Al wolfed one down in about four bites, belched, and fell fast asleep.

When Jack reached in to get a sandwich for himself, he felt cold metal. Troy had put in a flask of hooch—just what Jack needed to take the edge off. And sleep. Jack took a swig, then another and another between bites of his sandwich. He felt the warmth of it flow through his body, and he relaxed. "Thank you, buddy," he whispered. After downing the contents, he fell fast asleep and slept all the way back to Macon, his slumber interrupted by nightmares of bombs exploding in Franz's and Buck's faces.

Although he wouldn't admit it to anyone, all he wanted to do was go on a drunk and be left alone for a week to forget about the last month. Every man needs to grieve in his own way. But a man honors his commitments. He had to run an air show.

Bert, Jimmy, and Gardner had headed on to Endicott, New York, to get things started for the air meet in May. From Macon, he and Al traveled to Teterboro, New Jersey, where Gates was headquartered. He would pick up George Babcock, and they would fly to Towanda, then to Endicott, with a couple of short stops in between. He couldn't wait to see his old friends and had arranged to see Mavis as well, hoping seeing everyone would lift his spirits.

Pang was the first to greet him.

"Hey, Jack. Good to see you," he said. The other guys crowded around. Not knowing what to say, they affectionately slapped him on the back. Jack was glad to see them, and it did improve his mood.

To complete the greetings, Judge ran up, jumped on Jack, and licked his face when Jack leaned down to pet him. "Hey, Judge. Good to see you too. That's the best kiss I've had in a while." Judge whined. "Thanks, I appreciate that."

"Golly, it's good to see you," Pang said. "Let's go to my office where we can talk."

Pang led Jack to a room not much bigger than a closet. "Have a seat. Let me get you a cup of coffee." Judge followed them and lay beside Jack's chair. Jack gently stroked the dog's neck while he and Pang talked.

Pang settled into his chair. "I'm sorry I couldn't make it to Macon," Pang said. "I'm so sorry that happened."

All Jack could do was nod and shrug, trying hard not to cry. "I remember you saying that you've got to be prepared to lose people if they take chances. For the life of me, I can't imagine Buck or Franz taking chances, especially not Buck. I certainly wasn't prepared to lose them. Guess that's what's bugging the hell out of me. I'll never know what happened for sure. Gardner was up at the time and thought the thing went off too soon. The only two people who know are dead."

"How are you holding up?" Pang asked.

"Doing better. Telling Mother, Dad, and the kids was awful. Taking Franz home was the worst time of my life. A nightmare. The funeral was unbearable, but I made it through. Thank goodness Al was there, and my old friend Troy."

"Must've been tough."

"Yeah," Jack said. "Poor Mother and Dad. I had a sister die last year too."

Pang shook his head, then mercifully, he changed the subject.

"So, I hear you've been managing some air meets," he said.

"Yep. There's one coming up in May in Endicott. We're headed there now," he said. "I'd be honored to have you fly in it."

"The circus is scheduled to fly in Virginia," Pang said, "but we'll see."

"It's going to be a good show," Jack said. "A damn good show."

The next stop Jack made was to meet Mavis at Saul's. He looked forward to seeing her because he could tell her things he couldn't tell the guys.

Jack walked into Saul's and spotted Mavis sitting in their favorite booth, beautiful as ever. She rushed up to him and gave him a warm hug and kissed him on the cheek—just what he sorely needed, but would never get from the fellas, that was for sure. They sat down.

She took his hands and looked straight into his eyes. "I was so sorry to hear about Francis and Buck," she said. "You must've been devastated."

"Still am," he said, his voice breaking, "but I don't have time to think about it. I've got an air meet to manage in Endicott in May."

"My god, it's only been a couple of weeks," she said. "You've lost weight and look completely worn out."

"I'll manage. A man honors his commitments. I need to stay busy, and I need the money," Jack said. "The city of Macon seized a lot of our assets. We all persuaded them let me keep my plane so I could earn a living. Nobody needs to know that except you."

"Oh, my goodness," Mavis said, shaking her head in sympathy. "If I can help, let me know."

Jack waved her off. "I'll manage. Always do."

"I read an account of the accident in the newspaper," Mavis continued. "It said they were throwing out bombs?"

"Nah, they were just noisemakers to get everyone's attention," Jack said. "Buck was throwing them out. Franz was lighting them and handing them back to Buck. Gardner was up at the same time and believes the last one exploded early. Blew a wing off. And Buck's head."

"Oh my God," Mavis said. "How horrible."

"It was bad—real bad."

She squeezed his hands.

"The plane came crashing down," Jack said. "I was watching outside of town. When I saw what was happening, I rushed to the crash site. The scene was awful. Blood every-where. Just awful . . ." he said, voice breaking.

"You poor man," Mavis said softly, then sat patiently while Jack pulled himself together.

"There's this attitude with pilots that when your time is up, it's up no matter what. I've said it myself. Now I'm not so sure. Franz was so young. . .?

Back in her office two hours later, Mavis's telephone was ringing. "Hello. Mavis Perkins speaking."

"Mavis, Clyde Pangborn here."

"Yes, Clyde. What can I do for you?"

"I just saw Jack, and he said that he was going to see you," Pang said. "How did he seem to you? I'm worried about the guy. He's been through a lot lately."

Mavis took a deep breath. "I'm worried as well. I suspect that Jack shares more with me than he does with you guys. He's lost weight and completely worn out."

"He looked that way to me too."

"I think he needs time to mourn, but maybe it's better if he keeps busy so he doesn't take to the bottle," Mavis said.

"You're probably right," Pang said.

"I really care about the guy," Mavis said. "I'm thinking about going to Endicott to watch him fly for moral support."

"Let me know if you do. I might fly up there with you," Pang said. "I'll let you know where we are."

"Sure thing."

PART THREE

CHAPTER 27
ENDICOTT AIR MEET, ENDICOTT, NEW YORK

Poster for the Endicott Air Meet, 1928. *Courtesy of Cindy Weigand.*

March–May 1928
Towanda, Pennsylvania; Endicott, New York

MARCH 5, 1928
ASHCRAFT IS BACK WITH THE "SPIRIT OF AMMONIA"
Plane Once More Is in Home Hangar and
Her Pilot is Glad to be in Towanda Again;
Says He Expects to Stay; Other Flyers Are Coming Today

That was how the local paper greeted Jack in Towanda. The article summed up Jack's activities to date.

The good ship "Spirit of Ammonia" was back in her home hanger last night for the first time since the local flyers went south last fall to spend the winter months. The Waco plane known by thousands of people in this section was flown home yesterday by its pilot Jack Ashcraft, who was accompanied by George Babcock, wing-walker for the Towanda Aircraft Corporation.

"No place ever looked better to me," said Jack on his arrival. "And I'm here to stay until I get kicked out." He has been all over the United States, but Towanda is the place he wants to call home. This is the place he is going to vote from now, he says.

Babcock was glad to get here too, but for a different reason. Even though he does hair-raising stunts on the plane, he doesn't enjoy bouncing through the air at a terrific speed when the going is as "bumpy" as it was yesterday. The plane dropped him out from under his helmet several times, due to the atmospheric conditions, but under the expert guidance of Ashcraft the "Spirit of Ammonia" weathered it all and was brought safely down on the field in East Towanda about 2:30. The flyers had left Frederick, Maryland at 1 o'clock. The exceptional speed was due to the fact that the wind was behind them most of the way.

The aviators were greeted by Bert Crader, head of the corporation, who will have them as his guests for the next two weeks. Today, Gardner Nagle, new pilot of the company, and Al McClatchey [sic], professional ticket seller, will arrive by automobile, according to a telegram received by Crader. The whole party will then go to Lake Wesauking to enjoy fishing through the ice.

Jack said when he flew over Eagles Mere Lake yesterday it looked so inviting, he almost wanted to land and enjoy the sport. There were many out sliding around and skating on the lake. The boys were cold enough by the time they arrived here, however, without any further lengthening of the trip. They had come from Roanoke, Va., since morning. The flying time in all amounted to three hours and forty-five minutes.

Between now and spring the "Spirit of Ammonia" will be given a thorough going over and it is expected another plane will be purchased. Then as soon as the weather is right, the flying business will be opened up with the possibility that an air derby attracting a number of planes may be arranged for later in the summer.

"Ashcraft is Back with 'Spirit of Ammonia.'" *The Settler,* September 2002, Volume XL, Number 3, 2002, p. 142. A Quarterly Magazine of History and Biography, The Bradford County Historical Society. Used by permission.

March 1928
Endicott, New York

By the time he got back to Towanda, Jack had pulled himself together somewhat. The paper said that he was "holding up well and in perfect health," so by all appearances, he was "holding up well and in perfect health." Three weeks wasn't much time to grieve the loss of a brother and best friend. There was no time for drinking, but he was tempted. Nightmares tormented his sleep, but not every night. Finalizing the details of the air meet in Endicott helped. He and the other organizers set up shop at 49 Washington Avenue. Faithful Jimmy Scott was his assistant.

The local paper did much to promote the air meet in Endicott. His last name was often misspelled, but otherwise he believed the article summed up the air meet well after they interviewed him.

ASHCROFT [sic]IS MANAGER

Jack Ashcroft [sic] is manager of the air meet and is in charge now of the Washington Avenue headquarters. He is an aviator of much experience, having been flying for several seasons over the country. In the Spokane Derby of last September, from the New York to Spokane, he finished seventh position. Ashcroft [sic], who is a man of engaging manner and most pleasing personality, is glad to welcome at his headquarters all interested in aviation and the Endicott Meet.

Of Ashcroft [sic] the current number of the Aero Digest says: "Jack is operating a field at Towanda, Pa., and intends to establish a line from Williamsport to any point in the world. His associates are Pilot Gardner Nagle of Shreveport, La., and Mechanic Alfred McClatchie. Jack was with the Gates Flying Circus for four seasons."

Ashcroft [sic] yesterday declined a position to do publicity work for MacFadden publications and last week he declined an offer from the Mexican government to serve as aviator with headquarters at Tampico.

Jack had become good friends with Ed Churchill of the *Graphic* since their infamous attack on New York. MacFadden Publications owned the newspaper. After Jack met with Mavis, he paid Ed a call to see how he was doing. Ed had sent Jack a letter asking him to stop by next time he was in town.

"It's great to see you Jack," Ed said. "I was so sorry to hear about Franz and Buck. Damn the luck."

Jack shrugged. He had talked about the crash all he could for the day.

"So, what's up, Ed? What angle you working now?" he asked.

"Glad you asked. It's like this, Jack. MacFadden wants to increase publicity for the paper," he said. "We think having a flier do the publicity for us is just what we need, and we want you to be that flier."

The offer sounded interesting, but Jack didn't have enough to go on. "Hmmm. Tell me what you have in mind, exactly."

Ed told Jack that they wanted him to tow banners for them at sports events, things like that. They'd gotten a hot new sportswriter in '27 named Ed Sullivan. He thought they could work together to come up with all sorts of stunts to publicize the paper. Jack told him he would think about it.

At the time, Jack and his crew were grateful for the support of the *Graphic* for the publicity stunt, and the offer was appealing in some ways. However, it wasn't a job he was interested in. Jack was all about flying and promoting aviation. That was his future. He wanted to be his own boss and not have anyone give him orders. He called Ed when he got to Towanda and thanked him for the offer but told him no. Jack didn't know how the offer to fly for Mexico came about, but that definitely wasn't for him. He loved the ole US of A too much.

Jack was getting two new Waco 10s for the Endicott meet.

The plant in Troy, Ohio, was pushing them out fast for him for the show. Jack rode the train to pick one up, and Gardner left from Towanda to get the other. While he was there, Jack talked to Charles Meyers, chief test pilot with Advance Aircraft Corporation. He had met Meyers after Meyers won the New York to Spokane race. Jack asked him to come to Endicott and participate in the race. Meyers said he would consider it.

Flying the Waco in went just fine, but flying an Air King plane from Owego was another matter. Jack had to take off in the worst storm he had ever flown in. The Air King was a big, heavy plane, and the runway was so muddy that he almost didn't get off the ground. After takeoff, he flew through wind and nasty weather to Endicott. Some guys flew with him, and Jack assured them that he had flown in that type of weather before. When he landed in Endicott, the wheels sank in the mud, but he kept the tail down. They stowed the plane in the hangar. After that tough trip, the damnedest thing happened.

It was about three o'clock in the afternoon. Jack and some other guys ran to a car to go back to town. It was raining so hard that they waited a few minutes for it to let up. They were talking about the flight when a lightning bolt ripped down a few hundred yards from the hangar. Rocks and dirt scattered everywhere.

The bolt left a hole a foot deep and three feet wide near the road to the flying field. There were holes the size of saucers where smaller bolts landed. Thankfully, they'd gotten the Air King in before the lightning struck. If they hadn't, there would have been no Air King in the meet. A lightning strike like that would have destroyed it.

Meyers called to say he would participate in the meet. Gardner was going to fly in it, as well as Cy Bittner. A friend of Jack's, J.

P. "Thrill a Minute" Jones, called to say that he would come. Jones operated a field and aviation school in Lancaster, Pennsylvania. Jack had known him for a long time and knew him as an A-1 flier who shook a wicked stick. Jack would vouch for him any day. Jones told Jack that he was bringing a parachute jumper named H. K. Knight, "The Diabolo of the Air." Jack was confident the boy knew what he was doing when he saw him hop clear of the plane with Jones in the cockpit.

Jack personally invited Thea Rasche to fly in the meet, but she was waiting for a new plane from Germany after she'd had to ditch hers in the drink.

A bunch of others signed on as well. Richard L. Bennett agreed to pilot a Cessna monoplane from the Binghamton Aero Sales Company. The company claimed it would fly 160 miles per hour. Billy Brock and Ed Schlee were coming. The two pilots had attempted to fly around the world. Nearly did it, too. Jack was scheduled to fly in the meet as well. He wasn't going to let the others have all the fun.

Things were shaping up, and they were going to have a fine air meet. Jack made sure there were no noisemakers to bring people in.

The air meet wasn't just for adults. Jack wanted to promote flying for the future of aviation. To get young people interested, he had a model plane contest for the boys and had articles in the paper encouraging entries. The boys had to make their own models, and there were some good entries, including a model of Lindbergh's plane before he flew the Atlantic.

The next day, the roads and hills were packed with spectators. Local officials estimated that twenty-five thousand people had come to see the aviators fly.

He heard a woman's voice call to him and grinned broadly.

"Cowboy Jack!"

Jack turned around to greet his friend. Mavis was still the only person who referred to him as Cowboy Jack. "It's good to see you," he said, giving her a lingering hug. She returned it, stirring Jack inside. He looked deeply into her eyes, searching. "What are you doing here?"

Mavis continued to look directly into Jack's blue eyes. She sensed a different man than the one she'd met and fallen for back in '25. His touch roused her unexpectedly. "You know, I've never seen you fly in a good plane without someone walking on or hanging from your wings or some other part of the airplane," she said. "I wanted to see what you could really do."

"I won't disappoint," Jack said, smiling.

"I know you won't," Mavis said, continuing to look into Jack's eyes.

"I, uh, I'm on a tight schedule, so I may not be here when you get back down," she said, looking away, "but I promise I will see your performance."

"I'm dedicating it to Franz and Buck," Jack said quietly.

"Now I'm really glad that I came," Mavis said, squeezing his arm. "Here's someone else you might know. He bummed a ride with me." She stepped aside.

"I'm on a tight schedule as well," Pang said, "but Gates, the guys, and I wanted you to know that we support you."

"I appreciate that. I really do," Jack said. He shook Pang's hand and smacked him on the shoulder.

"Well, I've got to go check my plane," Jack said. "I hope to see you when I get back down, but I'll understand if I don't." He leaned over to kiss Mavis on the cheek and whispered in her ear. "If you'll stay, I'll take you for a flight at twilight that you will never forget. I'll find someone to fly you home in the morning," he said.

Then he called over his shoulder. "Hey, Bert, Gardner. Look who's here. Take care of Mavis while I'm aloft, will you? Whoever that guy is that she's with can fend for himself."

Wistfully, Mavis watched Jack walk away.

When it came Jack's time to fly, he did a final check of his plane, settled into the cockpit, and buckled in. Before he took off, he pulled out two pictures from his pocket, one of Franz and one of Buck. "This is for you guys. Franz, you'll fly with me. Buck, you'll be my wingman." He tucked the pictures back into his shirt pocket with Mavis's note under his leather jacket.

Jack adjusted his goggles, nodded to his imaginary wingman, and punched his passenger in the back, who turned and gave Jack a thumbs-up. Jack taxied down the grass runway and took off. When he reached an altitude of about three thousand feet, he pulled out every trick in his arsenal. With a maximum speed of nearly 100 miles per hour, the Waco 10 was the fastest plane Jack had ever stunted in. Yet, he felt as if he was in slow motion, especially when he cut the engine during a loop. Cool air rushed past him, and he heard the *puh, puh, puh* of the wind. The rhythm changed with each maneuver. "Jenny's Song" became a rhapsody of flight.

On the ground, Mavis, Gardner, Pang, and Bert marveled at the artistry of Jack's performance. Al joined them. Under Jack's skillful hands, the maneuvers flowed beautifully from one to the next.

"Oh, Gardner, isn't that beautiful?" Mavis said, tears in her eyes.

"I've never seen Jack fly like that," Gardner said, wiping away a tear before anyone saw him.

"Me neither," Bert said. "He's truly one of the best. Of course, I knew that after we flew to Spokane. Pang?"

"No words."

"Dare I say it? It's like he's inspired," Gardner said.

"He is," Mavis said. "He told me that he was dedicating the flight to Franz and Buck."

"Dang you, woman!" Gardner said, getting out his handkerchief to blow his nose and dry his eyes.

The four of them looked at those around them. The spectators were as mesmerized at Jack's performance as they were.

Jack looked at the wingman on his left and Franz, then restarted his engine and finished his performance. The finale was his signature dead stick landing, but no bugle or fanfare that day. It was all about skill. Nimbly, he alighted from the cockpit and stood on the wing, waving to the crowd. After acknowledging their appreciation for several minutes, Jack gave a final wave and strode off to his office at the hangar to have some time to himself.

"That was amazing," a woman's voice said, and Mavis stepped from the shadows in the room and walked to him. They embraced.

"I've got a few more things I can show you, but what about your plane?"

"Pang will take good care of it."

They kissed passionately.

Jack won the stunting competition both days, plus the Moose Trophy. The local paper called him the Texas Cowboy Aviator. Their description in the newspaper commendably described his performance:

Ashcraft himself was a big feature of the two-day carnival. He won the stunting contests on both days, with one of the most masterful demonstrations at the controls ever given before a local audience. He spiraled, barrel rolled, stalled, climbed, and looped, with his new Waco Ten plane, until the thrill-seekers on the ground were literally worthless. His loop with the motor dead, performed in the 'dead stick' landing on both days of the meet, proved one of the distinctive features of the occasion.

As promised, at twilight, Jack enchanted Mavis with an even more spectacular flight.

Jack Ashcraft in back cockpit, passenger unknown, Endicott, New York, 1928. *Courtesy of Allen Keller.*

CHAPTER 28

CORTLAND AIR MEET, CORTLAND,
NEW YORK

June 1928
Cortland, New York

Jack had another air meet planned for Cortland from June 20 to 21, so they had to hustle on north after they wrapped up details in Endicott. The upcoming air show was the feature of a celebration called Cortland County Old Home Week. Jack got paid for running the Endicott show and made half the price of the ticket for people he took up. All in all, he did pretty well.

Charles Meyers, Bittner, J. P. Jones, and Gardner followed Jack to Cortland to compete, plus they brought in some new guys. The press gave them all nicknames: "Shorty" Bittner, "Thrill-a-Minute" Jones, "Safe and Sane" Gardner, and of course Jack, the daring "Cowboy Aviator." Jack guessed the reporters did this because their real names were too boring. The airport was on Groton Road. One good thing about Cortland was that there hadn't really been anyone up there to give folks a ride in an airplane, so they intended to take full advantage of the situation.

J. P. did something that no one around there had done before. The radio station wanted to try an experiment. He took up a guy named Jacob E. Mathiot, the chief engineer of radio station WGAL, with a radio to broadcast from the air. They attached two big horns to the struts near the tips of the wings on a plane. The radio and engineer weighed an extra four hundred pounds, so J. P. had to taxi and climb carefully. At about 3,100 feet, he leveled off and circled the field. Mathiot then proceeded to rain music down on the crowd.

The newspaper reported that one woman was sure that the world was coming to an end when she gazed skyward and heard the voice of a man announcing to people on the ground that he was flying at an attitude of 3,100 feet. Without exception, observers on the ground said that neither the voice nor the music could be heard when the plane was directly overhead. Only when it was at an angle of 20 degrees was it audible, and then it could be heard within half a mile.

On Tuesday, June 19, some of them were in the office drinking coffee and working out final details for the show when Cy came rushing in.

"Hey Jack, get a load of this," he said, dropping a *New York Times* in front of Jack.

The headline read:

AMELIA EARHART FLIES ATLANTIC, FIRST WOMAN TO DO IT; TELLS HER OWN STORY OF PERILOUS 21-HOUR TRIP TO WALES; RADIO QUIT AND THEY FLEW BLIND OVER INVISIBLE OCEAN.

"Well, I'll be damned," Jack said.

"Keep reading," Cy said.

The article went on to say that Wilmer Stultz and Louis Gordon had flown Earhart as a passenger across the Atlantic.

"That son of a gun," Jack said when he read Bill's name. Stultz had gone to work for Sikorsky after he left the circus. "I knew he was up to something last time I saw him, but I damn sure wasn't expecting this."

The reporters didn't seem to be interested in the guys who had manned the controls, they were more interested in Earhart. To her credit, Earhart praised Stultz and Gordon and said that she was just baggage, but the article was all about the first woman to cross the Atlantic in an airplane. It didn't matter that she was never in the pilot's seat even though she was licensed. Jack thought what Ruth Elder and George Haldeman had accomplished was more impressive. Ruth had taken the controls in rough weather to let George rest.

A lot of aviation enthusiasts and public figures showed up for the Cortland show. Their towns were eager to get airfields of their own, so Jack, Cy, and Gardner booked shows in several towns that fall, working their way south. On the flights between towns, Jack did a lot of thinking about his future in aviation. He couldn't get Franz and Buck out of his mind. While he was making good money and enjoying himself, the constant wear and tear on his body and keeping his plane in tip-top shape were wearing on him. He was tired of hustling for work. He was tired of wearing nice clothes. He just wanted to wear coveralls.

That day when he'd lost that boy back in Louisiana seemed eons ago. He thought of the near misses, like forgetting to top off his tank over Clinton Square and limping back to the airfield. Same with the attack on New York. This year alone, he'd lost another guy out of his plane. Another inquest. He had nearly gotten struck by lightning, for Pete's sake. Maybe these were omens. He didn't blame himself so much for Franz and Buck anymore, but they were gone.

Maybe it was time to take over the hardware store—his version, anyway.

June–July 1928
Towanda, Pennsylvania; Warwick, Rhode Island

On the road and in the air constantly since the first of the year, and considering the events of the year, Jack was spent when he got back to Towanda for the Bradford Air Derby on July Fourth. An article in the paper lifted his spirits and summed up his life so far. He just needed to decide what was next.

June 28, 1928

JACK ASHCRAFT HAS BOOSTED FLYING HERE

One of the leading parts in the Bradford County Air Derby to be held on the Fourth of July will be played by Jack Ashcraft, the man who has done as much as any other person in the world to inspire confidence in aviation among the people of Towanda and vicinity and bring airplanes out of the realm of fiction into the world of reality.

Jack came to Towanda about two years ago and since that time has won scores of close friends and admirers. He is a skilled pilot, as hundreds of people throughout this county will testify – they having trusted their lives to him at various times – and his daring stunt flying has revealed a courage equal to the best in the flying world. His followers here are legion, and Jack will have hundreds rooting for him in the various contests at the air meet July 4th. When he was flying the Towanda plane "Spirit of Ammonia" in the New York to Spokane air race last fall, Ashcraft carried with him the good wishes of all of Towanda. In the cockpit with him in that grueling race all Towanda flew in spirit and when the struggle was over and Jack came in seventh out of a field 27, this town and its people rejoiced in the accomplishment and were proud of the man who flew Towanda's plane. Since that flight Jack Ashcraft has been admired by all red-blooded people here while to the small boys of the town, and county as well, he is a hero whose every move is watched.

BORN IN OKLAHOMA

When the state of Oklahoma was opened after its change from the Indian territory, thousands of new settlers for the new state made the race across the border line to make their "squatter claims" for farms. Among these settlers was the father of Jack Ashcraft, who built his little log cabin on the banks of a creek near what is now the town of Aline, which is located in the very heart of blackjack timber country.

It was in this little log cabin that on December 1, 1896, Jack was born and let out his first howl, and since that memorable date Jack has done quite a lot of howling, but he refuses to say what about. In 1922 Jack flew over the site of his birthplace in a "Jenny" plane.

It was in 1917 that Ashcraft enlisted in the United States Army Aviation Corps as aviation mechanic at Shreveport, La., and was sent to Jackson Barracks, New Orleans, then was transferred to Eagle Pass and later to San Antonio, Texas, for a period of two months.

After this Ashcraft was shipped overseas and was stationed in Liverpool, and later at London, and crossed the channel from South Hampton to Le Havre, France. He then went to Romorantine [sic], France, where he was stationed at A.S.P.C No. 2, the largest aviation camp in the world, which *was 20 miles in length and was the base for all airplanes of the Allied Armies. Ashcraft was in the air service for two years, being honorably discharged from the service in July 1919, at Shelby, Mississippi.*

After leaving the Army, Ashcraft had the aviation "bug in his bonnet" and as a result he has been flying ever since. He first opened the commercial field at Shreveport, and then in succession opened similar fields in Texarkana, Texas, Kansas, and Towanda.

Ashcraft served with about four different flying organizations, the last of which was Gates' Flying Circus with whom he was connected for about 4 years. Gates is the oldest flying circus in existence. He has flown from coast to coast, and from border to border. He has been in every state in the union with the exception of four, these being, California, Utah, Nevada, and Maine.

He estimates that he has carried in the neighborhood of 150,000 passengers into the air during his service at the "controls," and has flown in that time approximately a quarter of a million miles.

He measures about 6 feet, four inches, is handsome, and declares that he is not ready to have a ball and chain attached to him yet. But sometimes they change their minds when the "right girl" comes along. You never can tell!

June 28, 1928. "Jack Ashcraft Has Boosted Flying Here."
The Settler, September 2002, Volume XL,
Number 3, 2002, pp. 143-144.
A Quarterly Magazine of History and Biography,
The Bradford County Historical Society.
Used by permission.

Ive McKinney was still in Towanda and thinking of joining

Lee Mason in forming an aircraft corporation but hadn't decided. With a specific location in mind, they were considering starting a factory in Towanda. They committed to participate in the air derby. The purpose of the meet was to help the American Legion build a landing field. Bill Brooks had found his way back from Nicaragua and would fly as well.

Jack also had something different in mind for this air derby. He took applications from women to do a parachute jump. The special girl chosen would win $100. One woman who applied was married with six children because she "sure needed the money." Another stated, "I have always wanted a thrill of this sort and I am jumping for the chance." She went on to say that she was five feet, two inches tall, weighed 120 pounds, and was eighteen years old. One applicant informed the committee making the decision that she had a good heart and was, in every way, physically fit. An employee of the American Railway Express seemed to be applying for a job. "Do you have a regular jumper?" she asked. "Could you use one?"

A man from a nearby town applied in case they couldn't find a girl to make the jump.

Jack and Bert lined up a lot of the fliers from the Endicott and Cortland air derbies to fly in Towanda.

AIR DERBY ATTRACTS THOUSANDS HERE FOR CELEBRATION OF 4TH RACING AND DEAD STICK LANDING FEATURES BINGHAMTON MAN DOES PARACHUTE JUMP GARDNER NAGLE WINS 25-MILE RACE
Local Couple Married Before Crowd

With thousands of people in attendance and the day almost perfect for such an event, Bradford County's first air derby was staged on the American Legion Field in East Towanda yester-

day. There were stunts, stunts and more stunts, everything tending to demonstrate the safety of the flying machine as it is built today.

The American Legion, which sponsored the event, made hundreds of dollars but the exact amount could not be stated last night. All of it, however, is to be put back into the field in an effort to make it one of the finest in this section of the state.

The crowd was somewhat disappointed when the parachute jump by a local girl failed to materialize but they got their money's worth when O'Neil, a professional jumper from Binghamton, did the stunt. There were seven girls who wanted to try the trick but Bert Crader, manager of the meet, decided against it at the last minute when he was advised by pilot Jack Ashcraft that it would be extremely dangerous. The day was so hot, the air so light, and the traveling consequently so "bumpy" that Jack said that it would be difficult to maneuver the plane so as to avoid an accident with an inexperienced jumper. Rather than kill or injure anyone, Crader divided the $100 in prize money between the girls who applied.

. . .The girls all were greatly disappointed and to console them each was given a free airplane ride. . . .

. . .The first thing on the program was stunt flying by Jack Ashcraft. In the 25 mile race Nagle was first, Ive McKenney of Perth Amboy, N.J. was second,

Spence Punnett of Geneva, third and "Thrill a Minute" Jones of Lancaster fourth. Nagle was so far out in front after the second lap of the course that there was nothing to it. He banked the corners in wonderful style and thrilled the crowds with his speed.

Next came the stunting contest, which McKinney won. He looped many times, nosedived, sideslipped, and tail spun, while many of the lady spectators gasped. Jack Ashcraft was second and Nagle, third.. . .

The article talked about a wedding that took place in the air, and prizes were awarded to winners of an essay contest sponsored by the American Legion.

> *Next came the dead stick landing contest which was won by Jack Ashcraft. The planes were taken high into the sky and the motors turned off completely dead. Then the planes were allowed to fall with the idea of seeing which would come closest to a white circle in the center of the field.*
>
> *After an intermission in which passengers were carried, O'Neil did his daring parachute jump, which was thrilling indeed.*
>
> *The crowd was very orderly throughout the entire day . . .*

"Air Derby Attracts Thousands Here for Celebration of 4th."
The Settler, September 2002, Volume XL,
Number 3, 2002, pp. 155-156.
A Quarterly Magazine of History and Biography,
The Bradford County Historical Society.
Used by permission.

CHAPTER 29
HEROICS

July 1928
Warwick, Rhode Island

After Towanda, the Three Musketeers—Jack, Ive, and Bill Brooks—headed out and worked air shows one after the other up and down the East Coast. Some shows paid for their oil and fuel, some didn't. Jack had to buy some on his own flying from show to show. And he had to pay Jimmy, who was much more than his mechanic; he was a darn good friend. Faithfully, Jimmy overhauled his engine, repaired wing tears, and replaced wires while Jack tended to air show business. Jimmy got him home when Jack slipped and went on an occasional bender. Jimmy earned every penny that Jack paid him. Sometimes it wasn't much, but Jack always paid him something, and Jimmy never complained.

Refueling at a stopover in Rhode Island, they happened to witness a strange accident. A small plane circled the airfield at an altitude of about two hundred feet. They were amused at the tame stunting.

There was a crowd of about a hundred people watching, one young woman with concern on her face. The plane had made several passes and turns when it suddenly plummeted to the ground and burst into flames. The crowd rushed forward, as stupid spectators will do, but airport officials held them back.

"My Tommie!" the young woman exclaimed. She started running toward the burning plane, but somebody stopped her.

"Let me go to him! My Tommie!" she screamed.

"My God, those poor boys," Jack said, running toward the plane. A policeman tried to stop him, but Jack pushed him aside.

Jack held up his arm to shield his face as he searched for the pilot and passenger.

"I'll save you, Franz!" he called out, but the fire beat him back.

He tried again. "Hold on, Buck, I'll save you!"

Jack tried several times to reach the pilots, but the flames overcame him every time. He was in shirtsleeves, which caught fire. Finally, Jack gave up. Ive and Jimmy rushed over with a blanket to put out the flames on Jack's shirt and led him away from the flaming airplane.

"That was a crazy thing to do, Jack," Jimmy said, "but I'm not surprised you tried to save those fellows." He looked at Jack's arms. "Your arms look bad. We've got to get you to the hospital."

Jimmy flagged down the driver of a car. At the hospital, orderlies laid Jack on a table. Jimmy and Ive stood nearby while the doctor cleaned and wrapped Jack's arms.

"Did you know those guys?" he asked.

"No," Jack answered. "Why?"

"Someone heard you call out to Franz and Buck, or something like that," the doctor said.

"Nah, they must have misheard me," Jack said, staring at the ceiling.

"Why would you risk your life helping two guys you didn't know?" the doctor asked.

"I'm a pilot. Airmen help airmen," Jack replied. To himself, he said, *I couldn't save Franz and Buck, so I tried to save those guys.*

"Keep your arms clean and out of the sun, and drink lots of water. They should heal okay," the doctor said. "If you get an infection, go to a doctor right away. You can leave the hospital in the morning, but no more heroics when there's fire involved."

The next morning, Ive went to get Jack while Jimmy tended to the airplanes. He took him a couple of newspapers. "You're still making the news. I thought you would be interested in reading this."

TWO FLYERS DIE AS PLANE BURNS IN 100-FOOT FALL

War Veterans Trapped in Monocoupe Dropping at Warwick, R.I.

Wife of One Tries to Save Mate—Flames Beat Back Rescuers"

Warwick, R.I. July 27 (A.P.) – Clifton H. Thompson of Foxboro Mass., and Osmond H. Mather of Hartford, Conn., were instantly killed at 7 o'clock last night when their tiny orange and black monocoupe went into a tail spin [sic] at an altitude of about 100 feet, fell like a plummet, and burst into flames 200 yards from Pothier flying field here.

"Only a few minutes before, the plane had taken off, piloted by Mr. Mather, who was demonstrating it to Mr. Thompson with a view to selling a monocoupe to the New Providence Airport at Seekonk, Mass., it said.

"Both of the victims were veterans of the wartime flying service. Mr. Thompson's wife and daughter were at the field when the crash occurred. Mrs. Thompson saw the plane fall, but was at the time unaware that her husband was in it. When she learned that he was in the cabin in the flaming ruins she screamed, "Let me go to him. My Tommie," and would have plunged into the wreckage had she not been restrained.

As the monocoupe fell, the 100 visitors at the flying field, field employees and aviator rushed to the ruins in an attempt to save the two passengers. The heat of the roaring fire drove them back, but Jack Ashcraft, member of the Gates Flying Circus, hurtled himself into the inferno in a mad attempt to open the cabin door. He was beaten back by the fire, his arms severely burned.

A newspaper man at the field on another errand saw the tragedy. He declared that he had talked with the flying field attaché regarding the safety of such stunting as vertical banks and such low altitude. The aviator said it appeared that while the plane was an exceptionally easy one to handle, it should have more altitude.

Only a short time later, as the ship went into a sharp turn, the tail swung up and the plane plunged."

Warwick, Rhode Island, July 27 (A.P.)

"They got that one about right, didn't they?" Jack said.

"Read this one," Ive said. "Not the whole thing, just these paragraphs. All pilots are important, but these guys were different."

Both of the men were skilled fliers . . .

Thompson had served with the Lafayette flying corps [sic]

in France and had revived his interest in aviation recently, making many flights from the East Boston airport . . .

Clifton D. Thompson was 34 years old and a graduate of Dartmouth in the class of 1917.

During the war, he served in France as a member of the Lafayette flying corps [sic], and he was married while he was overseas . . . Besides his widow, he leaves four small children. His parents, Mr. and Mrs. Clifton B. Thompson, live on Fairmont avenue [sic], Hyde Park, and a sister Helen, lives with them.

"Well, I'll be damned," Jack said.

"Left four kids," Ive said quietly, shaking his head.

"The hell of it is, he survived the war only to die in a crash at probably the smallest airfield in the smallest state in the US," Jack said.

"I also read that Mather served in the Air Corps," Ive said.

At breakfast, Jack picked up a newspaper that gave another account with a different spin on the crash. "Listen to this," he said, and read melodramatically:

WAR BRIDE SEES ACE DIE IN FLAMING PLANE

Providence, R.I., July 27—Death in the flaming tomb of his own plane, tragic death as the French bride war bride looked on, was the fate of Clifton H. Thompson, Massachusetts flier whom fame came and upon whom Fortune smiled when he flew unscathed numberless times over the German trenches in France.

With him to the dramatic doom, in a calamity of the air that has saddened the whole State of Rhode Island today, went Osmond H. Mather, flier, of Hartford, Conn.

While thousands looked on, among them the pretty French

girl, whom Thompson wooed and whose heart he won while in the Lafayette Escadrille in wartime, the pair died in the plane in which they had just achieved perfect stunts which hugely entertained the throng below.

DISASTER IS SUDDEN

Faces stricken colorless, aghast at the sight.

Hearts thrilled, souls chilled, minds struck with horror, with awe, with heavily weighted woe.

A black plane spearing downward falls like a plummet. Flames turning the plane into a holocaust. A new plane, plaything of experts, obedient to man's will, sensitive to man's skill, now speedily becomes man's own flaming tomb.

A shriek from the French war bride, then a brave:

My darling, let me go to him, my husband, my darling!

Crying thus, brave and eager to join the number that were battling to free him and Mather from their blazing pyre. But men about her restrained her, used force to hold her back.

And while she looked on, out darted Jack Ashcraft, a great stunt flier, to the rescue.

My God, my God, the poor boys!" he had exclaimed, as eye and brain pictured the tragedy.

BEATEN BACK BY FLAMES

Ashcraft, a member of Gates' flying circus, rushed to the plane, dashed into the flames, struggled vainly to open the cabin door—was beaten back by the flames when nearly overcome.

When rescuers reached him, they found him badly burned in his heroic efforts to get at the bodies of the two companions of the air of his, whose doom had been sealed behind that death-sealed cabin door.

There was more, but that was all that Jack could stomach, and he tossed the paper on the chair with his things. "Well, I guess each reporter has his own style." He gathered his belongings. "We need to get going."

One October evening they were sitting at an airfield warming themselves around a crackling fire. They were enjoying a bottle of hootch that Jack just happened to have, doing some hangar flying, and waxing nostalgic.

"We've sure had us a good run at this flying gig, haven't we?" Jack said.

"Yep," Ive said. "Those years with Gates were great. Wouldn't trade them for anything."

"I'll drink to that," Jack said.

"Hell, you'll drink to the campfire burning," Brooks said in that soothing voice of his. "How many people you suppose we took up? A million?"

"At least," Ive said. "Maybe more. Those were the days."

"Hell, we aren't over the hill yet," Jack said. "But I am kind of tired of this freelance stuff, always having to hustle for work."

"I've thought of that too," Ive said, and Bill nodded.

"I'm not getting any younger, either," Jack said. "Hell, I think I've broken all the bones in my arms and legs at least once. And most of my ribs. And now this." He held up his arms.

The other two shook their heads.

"How are they healing?" Ive asked.

"Pretty good. They don't look too bad, either. I thought it would be worse," Jack said. "You know, sometimes up there in the cold, I get to aching and need a quilt like an old lady, and I'm just thirty-one. Or am I thirty-two?" He laughed.

"You don't take a bottle up with you, do you?" Ive asked.

Jack shrugged. "Sometimes, but not too much so I don't overdo it."

"You watch that, buddy," Bill said.

"Don't worry. Everything's okay," Jack said. "Sometimes I think it's time to go back to Protection."

"That'll be the day," Ive said. "You're not that rickety yet."

"Then there are the guys I've lost . . ." Jack started to say, but he couldn't finish the sentence. The three just sat thoughtfully and respectfully, not saying a word for some time.

"Gates and Pang have done well setting up a fixed base in Teterboro," Jack said. "Pang said that I always had a job with them. I think I'll go back and ask for a job as an instructor and mechanic while I decide my next move."

Pang realized the barnstorming game was over and Texaco had stopped writing checks. They had their planes and were able to acquire some modern ones, so he and Gates had established the Gates Flying Service. They were training the next generation to fly, building planes, and other enterprises, including giving exhibitions and offering rides.

"Yep, that's what I'm going to do," Jack said. "I'm going to make one last swing through Georgia, then I'm going back to Teterboro."

Just as he'd said he would, Jack flew to Teterboro one day. He tied his plane to the fence and asked for a job. They welcomed him back. What possessed him to tie his plane to the fence, he didn't know, and they didn't ask. He had been called the Cowboy Aviator so much, he guessed it symbolized tying his steed to the fence. Ive and Bill flew in later that day.

L to r, Jack Ashcraft, William "Whispering Bill" Brooks, and Ive McKinney. *Photograph courtesy of Bill Rhode Collection, Aviation Hall of Fame and Museum of New Jersey, Teterboro.*

October 1928

Pang and Gates had turned the corner on the flying circus. Airmail lines and passenger services were operating throughout the country. Colonial Air Transport was landing daily in Teterboro until the Newark Metropolitan Airport opened. Fokker was rolling out tri-motored F-10A transports and selling them to Western Air Express and Universal Air Lines. The Wrights serviced all aircraft.

Jack felt the air show days were behind them as well. Still, he wasn't quite ready to give it up. They had never performed a farewell show. Bill Brooks, Ive McKinney, Homer Fackler, and Jack gathered in the back room of the new restaurant in Teterboro one evening. A debate ensued on whether to continue or not. A young boy had followed them in.

"Hey, you," Brooks roared. "You're too young to be in here. Get out of here."

"Is that you, Billy?" Jack asked.

"Yes, sir," the boy said quietly.

"He's okay. Let him stay. Bring him a root beer," Jack said, and sat down. "Never mind Bill. He's not mean, just deaf." Billy laughed.

"Let's take one more crack at it," Brooks said. "We've still got a lot to show people, and there's still lots of people who've never ridden in an airplane."

"I don't know," Ive said. "The new regulations will be in full force soon. The inspectors will be all over us."

"To hell with the inspectors," Homer said. "We keep our aircraft in top shape. We've done all we possibly can to please them."

It was hard for all of them to adjust to all the changes. Jack listened to them for a while, then spoke up. "Tell you what," he said. "The inspectors are going to be thickest here and in Florida. Why don't we head back to other parts of the South again?"

The guys liked that idea, so they made plans to go out on the road one last time in November. However, some of the new laws would put a crimp in their plans. There would be no more stunting without a parachute, and two parachutes were required. No balloon chutes allowed. No wing walking without a parachute. No commercial flying in wooden planes. Commercial flying planes had to have an Approved Type Certificate for new aircraft. In short, they'd taken the fun out of flying, although the pilots had to admit that some of the rules made sense and made flying safer.

Then they did some serious hangar flying and consoled themselves by knocking back a jug. They toasted to the past. They toasted to those they had lost. They toasted to future pilots. They toasted to just about everything that could be toasted to until the wee hours of the morning, till they could toast no more.

In November, the four pilots set out for the Southeast. Gates and Pang supplied them with airplanes, a couple of stuntmen, and some roustabouts, but it wasn't meant to be. Some places were glad to see them, and they took up lots of people in one day. Then guys would fly in showing off their modern planes, making Gates's look like the crates that the modern ones were shipped in, and took their business away. By December, they were in Richmond, and then they headed west.

Death-Defying Aerial Stunts to Be Staged at Circus Here

Exhibition stunt flying, daring wing-walking, dead-stick landings and numerous other thrilling events comprise the program of the free air show and circus which will be presented to the public of Richmond and its environs at the Comp Airport by the Gates Flying Circus, starting today and continuing until December 26, under the auspices of the American Society for the Promotion of Aviation.

The Gates aggregation, which on two other occasions has

thrilled Richmond with its unique aerial antics, has been reorganized this year and has a far more elaborate series of events to present to the South as part of the American Society for the Promotion of Aviation's campaign to make the public more air-minded, it is said.

The first evidence of the organization's arrival in town will be given at noon today when the Gates squadron of sleek planes will hurtle across the skies over the city in battle formation, giving Richmond its first glimpse of the intrepid fliers in action.

Leading the daredevil cloudsmen [sic] is Major William C. Brooks, the Nicaraguan flying ace, who holds the world's record of performing 269 loops in one flight.

Captain Ive McKinney, famous army flying instructor, will thrill those who gather at the Comp Airport with his unique stunt flying antics and dead-stick landings.

Captain Jack Ashcraft, another veteran birdman having more than 10,000 flying hours to his credit, and Lieutenant Homer Fackler will also "do their stuff."

"Diavolo" Matthews, wing-walker, will present an entirely new repertoire of stunts."

Richmond (Virginia) Times-Dispatch,
December 19, 1928, page 3

Still, they had fun as the Three Musketeers plus one, but the closer they got to the Mississippi River, the more business dried up. The area was still recovering from massive floods the year before, and the Bureau of Air dogged them at every turn, so they headed home. They wired ahead when they would be back in town because they wanted a memorable homecoming.

The four red planes roared over Teterboro late in the afternoon. Flying from the southwest in tight formation, wingtip to wingtip, they soared over Teterboro. Stuntmen and mechanics rode in their front cockpits. Three times they circled. Roustabouts, mechanics, and people in town came out of the buildings to see what was going on. The four aviators were determined to give them a good show. After five side-by-side loops at about two thousand feet, followed by fleur-de-lis, each pilot broke away and performed stunts from his bag of tricks.

That done, there was nothing to do but spin down and land, each making a perfect landing. After one final solo loop, Brooks was the last to land. They taxied to the south end of the field and cut their switches. The pilots flipped up their goggles and sat on the backs of their cockpits for several seconds, listening to the engines until they went idle. Then they removed their helmets and twirled them over their heads while letting out loud whoops. The World's Greatest Exhibition Aviators had flown their last exhibition.

Side by side, they walked to the hangar, where Gates and Pang waited for them, looking nostalgic and appreciative. If anyone looked closely, they might have seen tears in the two men's eyes. Officially, the Gates Flying Circus was no more.

June 1929
Teterboro, New Jersey

With Gates, Jack worked as a mechanic and gave flight instruction. Work was steady, and the pay was decent. One thing he liked was the young guys that came out to the airfield after school and hung out with the pilots. The pilots liked to play practical jokes on them. Ive and Bill Brooks were talking when Billy Racey showed up one day, asking for Jack.

"You can find him right over there, working on an airplane," Ive said.

"Thank you, sir," Billy said.

"While you're over there, will you do me a favor and ask Jack for a bucket of prop wash?" Brooks said, winking at Ive.

"Sure," Billy said and did as he was told.

"Hey, Mr. Jack. Do you remember me?" Billy said.

"I sure do. How are you doing, Billy? It's good to see you again," Jack said.

"I thought I'd come out and say hi. Oh, and those guys asked me to get a bucket of prop wash from you," Billy said, pointing to Ive and Bill.

"Oh, they did, huh?" Jack said, looking at Ive and Brooks, who were laughing.

"Well, you tell them that I'm all out. Grab that bucket over there, and tell them that I need two buckets," Jack said. He watched their expressions when Billy took the buckets to them.

Billy quickly caught on to the joke but played along.

All the guys, young and old, teased Jack about his coveralls.

"You ever going to wash them?" one asked.

"Nah, I'll just wear these until they're too stiff for me to walk in, then I'll get new ones," Jack laughed.

Since the boys were around, Jack was happy to show them how to repair plane engines and teach them what made planes fly. Three boys regularly took him up on his offer. The others just wanted to hang out, and that was fine too. It kept them out of trouble. Jack remembered Wendell and got an idea. He called Mavis.

"Jack, how good to hear you," she said.

"Same here," he said.

"How's domestic life for you?" she laughed.

"I'm getting used to it somewhat," he said. "Listen, the reason I'm calling is that some young guys have been hanging out at the airfield, so I offered to teach them some mechanics and stuff. Several of them took me up on it."

"That's just like you, Jack," Mavis said.

"That got to making me think about Wendell. He wouldn't have that chance. Would you have Gerald call me? I'd like for Wendell to help me clean up my shop, and I can tell him a few things when the other boys aren't here."

"That's so nice of you, Jack. I'll do that," Mavis said.

Jack and Gerald arranged for Wendell to come to the hangar from two to four o'clock on Sunday afternoons when few people would be there. Wendell tidied up his shop and cleaned Jack's tools for an hour, and then Jack talked to him for another hour about airplanes while Gerald read the paper.

Jack settled into his version of domestic life as much as he could.

Working at an airfield was better than selling nuts and bolts at a hardware store in Kansas. At least he could be around airplanes. Jack and the rest of the pilots gave Billy and the other boys small jobs at the airport and had them run errands. Billy took a liking to Jack, and Jack grew fond of the boy. He reminded him of his little brothers.

One day after Billy had worked particularly hard, Jack said, "Hey Billy, I need to make sure I got this thing working right. You want to go up with me and check it out?"

"Yes, sir!"

Jack tossed him a helmet, and they went for a fifteen-minute flight. Jack let him take the stick for a few moments. Billy looked back with excitement, grinning from ear to ear.

"Thanks, Jack! That was terrific!" Billy said when they landed. "I've got to get home now." He handed the helmet back to Jack.

"Keep it," Jack said. "You might need it again sometime."

Billy grinned and ran off, Jack smiling after him.

That Sunday, he made the same offer to Wendell and Gerald. They jumped at the chance. Wendell walked away grinning with a helmet and goggles as well.

. . .

Since he was going domestic, Jack bought a Cadillac. It wasn't Mavis's Bearcat 365, but it would do. Gates Flying Service had moved to Holmes Airport, so he leased an apartment in Jackson Heights, Queens. He couldn't complain, but the flying was tame. He missed seeing his name in the papers and missed the cheering crowds and people asking him for his autograph. He missed the ladies. Mavis had met someone that she'd fallen in love with, and her parents approved. He even had a pilot's license. Jack had met him, and he was a nice guy. They'd moved to Long Island. He and Mavis still met for lunch to do some hangar flying and talk about old times.

Jack did some flying with Eastern Air Transport, but the company was being sold, and everything had to be finalized before they could hire him.

One of the first things he did was renew his pilot's license, number 54. Orville Wright himself was still signing them. Jack also investigated other interests for when he couldn't fly as much. Taking over his dad's hardware store passed through his mind. He wished it wasn't in Kansas. All the fellas and Mavis told him that he could spin a good yarn, so he joined the News Writers Association. He was number 6382. The back of his official card said, *It's News Business I'm After*. Mavis encouraged him to write some aviation articles for her newspaper, and so did Ed Churchill.

Jack was also invited to become a card-carrying member of "Ye Anciente and Secret Order of Quiet Birdmen." His number was 1854. On the card, it read:

THE BEARER IS A CERTIFIED GOODFELLOW. HE HAD MOUNTED ALONE INTO THE REALMS BEYOND THE REACH OF KEEWEE AND MODOCK

*AND SHOULD BE ACCORDED ALL GESTURES OF
FRIENDSHIP AND AID BY FELLOW QB WHEREVER
THEY MAY MEET.*

Their meetings were like nothing he had ever been to
before. He was in good company—mighty good company—but
that was all he could say about it.

CHAPTER 31
ONE LAST CHANCE AT FAME

Undocumented newspaper clipping of Jack
Ashcraft and Viola Gentry before takeoff, June
1929. *Courtesy of the International Women's
Air & Space Museum, Cleveland, Ohio.*

June 1929
Holmes Field, Queens, New York

Still, Jack was looking for something to get his name back in the papers—nothing dangerous or risky, just something different—when a woman appeared. He had seen her around Roosevelt Field. Her name was Viola Gentry, the "Flying Cashier." She was planning an endurance flight and needed a copilot. Viola had everything arranged, but a couple of copilots she had lined up were unable to join her and went out looking for someone to accompany her. One of her friends told her to talk to Clyde Pangborn, so she tracked him down. Viola found him at Teterboro.

"Clyde Pangborn?" she asked when she saw him.

"And who do I have the pleasure of speaking with?" Pang said.

"Viola Gentry," she said.

"Say, aren't you planning an endurance flight? How are the plans going?" Pang asked.

"Everything's set up, but I need a copilot. I had a couple of guys lined up, but they got jobs, and another got sick, so I'm looking for someone. Do you know someone who might be interested?"

"Sure do," Pang answered. "You might talk to Jack Ashcraft. There's none better, and he's getting a bit antsy fixing planes and teaching people to fly."

"Great, thanks. Where can I find him?"

"Holmes," Pang said. "He flies for the L & H Aircraft Corp. Gives passenger rides in a Stearman."

Viola found Jack working on his Stearman at Holmes, just as Pang had told her.

"Are you Jack Ashcraft?" she asked.

"I am," Jack said, stepping down from a ladder. "How can I help you? Hey, I remember seeing you at Roosevelt."

"Probably so. I'm Viola Gentry. Clyde Pangborn told me I'd find you here. I've lined up everything for an endurance flight and need a copilot."

"That so? Tell me more about it," Jack said, putting down his tools.

Viola explained her situation.

"What record you trying to break?"

"One set by a couple of army guys in a plane called the *Question Mark*," she said.

"I know about that. Tooey Spaatz commanded the flight. I remember him from the war, too," Jack said. "What kind of plane you got?"

"Cabinaire. Walter Carr loaned it to me. I've named it *The Answer*," she said.

"What engine does it have in it?"

"Warner 110 horsepower."

"I've heard about it," he said. "Supposed to be a good engine and doesn't use much gas. Who's supplying the gas and oil?"

"Richfield. We've installed an extra gas tank," Viola answered.

"Where you flying out of?" Jack asked.

"Roosevelt Field."

"Sounds like you've got everything lined up," Jack said.

"Yes, sir," she said. "I can show you all the contracts."

"If I decide to join you, I want to be in charge, since I have more flying time," Jack said.

"I completely understand," Viola said. "You have the most experience."

"And I want my guys to do the refueling," Jack said.

"No problem," she said.

"I'll meet you at Roosevelt tomorrow morning at ten, and we'll go up for a test flight," Jack told her.

. . .

Jack and Viola went aloft the next day, and he found her flying good, especially for the type of flight she was planning. He learned set the first solo endurance record for a woman, so he thought, what the heck?

As they flew, Jack took closer notice of the area around Roosevelt Field that they would be flying over. There were flat fields, so there would be no problem making an emergency landing if they had to. The only tall objects were the Westbury water tower and a hickory tree close to it near Hicks Nursery. They decided to take off on June 27 if it was clear.

Jack found out some gossip on Viola. She had a love interest by the name of Bill Ulbrich who also flew out of Roosevelt Field. He and Martin Jensen would be attempting an endurance flight at the same time. Jensen's wife Marguerite was accompanying them, so it would be a friendly rivalry. That would add to the fun, and possibly break up the boredom. They called their plane *The Three Musketeers*.

Newspapers made a big deal of a woman and a man spending that much time together alone in an airplane. Jack couldn't comprehend how people thought there could be any hanky-panky when someone had to always be at the controls. Since this was of concern to some, and to quell any suspicions, they had a partition put in and a curtain installed in front of the toilet in the back of the plane. They were ready to go.

The press came around to interview them before the flight, so they got dressed up for the occasion. For pictures, the reporter insisted they put on their flight helmets with goggles propped on top of their heads. The Cabinaire had an enclosed cabin, making these items unnecessary, but the optics looked good. Jack and Viola could hardly keep from laughing when the photographer snapped the photo. Jack promised to shave his mustache before takeoff so it wouldn't get too bushy.

Undocumented newspaper clipping of Viola Gentry and Jack Ashcraft. *Courtesy of Cindy Weigand.*

June 1929
Skies over Long Island

Because not many male pilots were willing to fly with a

woman pilot, Viola was determined to do her part. She slept two hours on, two hours off to be ready to fly for however long it took to establish a good record.

They got their gasoline permit and waited for the weather to clear. In June on Long Island, the conditions could change quickly. Doctor Kimball of the Weather Bureau was hopeful, but they waited for the right time to fly. They each had a physical examination.

Jack put a couple of clean shirts in a small bag, pulled on a sweater vest, and adjusted his bow tie. At the last minute, he threw in a flask. The vessel wasn't full and he would have to be careful to only take swigs now and then when Viola was asleep. Who knew how long they would be aloft. It could be days, weeks, or hours, but he was ready to set an endurance flight record.

On June 27, they got clearance to take off. They needed only enough gas for the night, because the refueling pilot would fly down the next morning to supply them with petrol. Jack had arranged for them to be refueled twice daily, early in the morning and again just before dark.

Jack and Viola were flying for fame and fortune. Companies supplied the plane, fuel, and other items to advertise themselves and demonstrate to customers what their planes could do.

The weather was beautiful, and after a test flight, they were ready to begin.

"Wait," Jack said. "I need to call Mother to let her know that we're taking off. Throttle back, and I'll be back before you know it."

A half hour later he returned, and they took off with Viola at the controls. She flew two hours, then Jack relieved her as planned. They continued this routine until after midnight.

THE DAILY REVIEW
June 28, 1929
ASHCRAFT IN ENDURANCE FLIGHT
Local Aviator with Viola Gentry in Latest Attempt
Light Cabin Biplane Being Used in Effort to Set Endurance
Record
at Roosevelt Field.
Plane Carries 116 Gallons of Gasoline at Start:
First Refueling Some Time This Morning.

Roosevelt Field, New York, June 27 – (Special to the Daily Review) – Miss Viola Gentry took off at 3:49:26 (Eastern Daylight Time) in her second attempt to set a refueling endurance record. She was flying a light cabin biplane.

With her was Jack Ashcraft of Towanda, Pa., who placed sixth in the Spokane to New York air race last September. The plane carried 116 gallons of gasoline and plans called for the first refueling sometime tomorrow morning.

As the two took off, another plane, the Three Musketeers, also on an endurance flight, circled overhead its occupants watching the start with interest.

Jack Ashcraft is a flyer of many years' experience. For a long time, he was with the Gates Flying Circus and later conducted a flying service of his own and did barnstorming with a Waco plane, using Towanda as his headquarters. He made flying popular in that part of the country and it was largely through his activities that the American Legion post was interested in establishing an up to date flying field there.

Miss Gentry is one of the best-known woman flyers in the country.

Late tonight the plane was still circling the field and the motor seemed to be running perfectly.

Around two o'clock in the morning, fog rolled in from the ocean. Having flown on Long Island all her flying career, Viola knew this was not a good sign.

"Do you think we should land?" she asked.

"No, my partner should be able to fly up from Connecticut okay," Jack said. "I'm not worried. Are you?"

"Not yet, but I've seen these fogs stay around for days," she said.

"Look, if you're scared, we better land now and you can get another pilot," Jack said.

"Somebody asked me if I was scared of flying once, and I told them you can only die once," she said.

Jack laughed. "Good line."

"I'm not scared, or I wouldn't be flying," Viola said, "but like I said, I've been flying around here since I started. I know the weather."

"He'll make it, you'll see. Like you, I want to set a good record," Jack said. "Then I have things I want to do."

"I don't want to quit if you don't," Viola said. "You're in charge. I'll do what you say."

Three hours later, the ground was out of sight and the fog enveloped them. It was Jack's turn to take over the controls. Viola got in the back but couldn't rest. She was immediately alert when Jack called.

"I want to teach you something," he said. "In cases like this, fly in a pattern. Fly for five minutes in this direction—make a left on the compass, fly five minutes on that course, and so on, keeping a perfect square. That way, you can land quickly. Worse thing that can happen is that we make a mess of some of the nursery's shrubs."

"That's good to know," Viola said. "Thanks for telling me. You sure you don't want to land?"

"I'm sure," Jack replied.

At 5:00 a.m., there was no sight of the refueling plane and they had very little gas. With no radio contact, they had taken rocks aloft with them in case they needed to drop notes.

Jack instructed Viola to drop a note for someone to come up to refuel. Fifteen minutes later, she dropped another rock with a note urgently requesting fuel. By six o'clock, the tanks were dry.

"Okay, Viola, you were right. We're going to have to land," Jack said. "Get in the back, put on the safety harness, and hold on. It's going to be rough jumping the water tower before we settle down."

Looking down, Jack thought he recognized a road that ran from Hicksville. He knew if he followed it, the road would lead back to Roosevelt Field. Slowing down and preparing to land, Jack hopped over the water tower. The hickory tree, the only tree for miles around, was just beyond the tower. Either Jack forgot about it, or he misjudged the distance. The left wing caught some branches, and the plane crashed nose down at Hicks Nursery near Mineola. The chronometer in the plane stopped at 6:13 a.m.

At his home in Jackson Heights, Pang hung up the phone and rushed to get dressed. He called Ive McKinney. "Ive. Get Bill. Jack's crashed! Meet me at Hicks' Nursery."

"What happened?" Ive asked.

"The hickory tree. The only damned tree for acres. He nicked it and nosedived. That's all I know."

At the nursery, the ambulance, the police, and—of course—the onlookers had already arrived. The three elbowed and pushed their way to the airplane just as they were putting Viola on the stretcher. The ambulance sped off. Pang, Ive, and Bill looked on, horrified, as Jack's body was retrieved from the wreckage and placed on a stretcher. A doctor had been called in. He checked for a pulse, then shook his head. Orderlies placed a white sheet over Jack's face and body.

"Oh, my God!" Pang said.

Overcome, Pang fell to his knee, head down, hands over his face. Bill and Ive put a hand on each of his shoulders.

Pang stood, and they watched as the orderlies carried Jack's body away.

"After that kid was killed in Louisiana, I told Jack that I was prepared to lose friends if they acted foolishly," Pang said. "Jack wasn't like that. He wasn't foolish. He didn't act foolish. I wasn't prepared to lose him."

Pang blinked back tears as did Ive and Brooks. It was several moments before he could continue. "Ive, you guys look in the wreckage and get Jack's belongings if you can find anything. I've got to figure out what to tell his parents. This is going to kill them."

While officials were examining the wreckage, Billy Racey snuck in, retrieved a piece of debris, and ran off without anybody noticing. Back in his room, he sat on his bed crying, staring at the debris.

Ive and Brooks found Jack's small duffel. When Brooks lifted it, a flask fell out.

"Ive," Brooks said, and motioned for Ive to pick it up before anyone else saw it. Ive quickly slipped it into his pocket.

The three walked around the plane, examining the wreckage. Pang looked up and pointed. "Look, there!" he said, pointing. "It looks like he just barely hooked that branch, but it was enough to bring them down."

"Damn the luck. Damn, damn, damn," Brooks roared. Bystanders looked in his direction.

On the way to the car, Ive showed Pang the flask, and Pang shook his head.

"It's only about half empty, though. Jack liked his short snorts," Ive said.

The three men walked in silence, overwhelmed by the death of their dear friend and colleague.

A policeman walked up to Pang. "Are you Clyde Pangborn?"

"Yes, sir," Pang answered.

"I understand that you knew Jack Ashcraft," the officer said.

"Yes, I did. He worked for me, and we all flew together with the Gates Flying Circus for several years," Pang replied. "Do you know what happened?"

"Far as we can tell, they just stayed up too long and ran out of gas. The refueling plane couldn't fly in from Connecticut because of the fog. They ran out of luck. Too damn bad."

"Yeah, too damn bad," Pang said. "I can call his folks if you like."

"Thanks. I'd appreciate that. They would probably rather hear the news from you than me. We'll have a report later." The officer walked off.

Back at his apartment, Pang waited for his call to go through to Mr. and Mrs. Ashcraft. He could barely talk when Jack's dad answered.

"Hello."

"Uh, Mr. Ashcraft, this is Clyde Pangborn," Pang said.

"It's Jack, isn't it?"

"Yes, sir. I hate like the dickens to tell you this, but he's dead. He and Viola crashed this morning," Pang said. On the other end of the line, he could hear Mrs. Ashcraft asking who was calling.

"It's Jack, isn't it?" Mrs. Ashcraft said and started crying.

Then the line went dead. Pangborn leaned against the wall to regain his composure. Next, he had to gather Jack's belongings to send home with his body. He called Jimmy Scott and asked him to help him with that task on behalf of the organization. Placing the items that told Jack's story in boxes—his flight helmet and goggles, the trophies, the newspaper articles, and his wallet—Pang came across the short snorter bill that Jack had swindled from him and smiled, tears in his eyes. He pulled it from the rest of Jack's things and put it in his pocket. After all, it was his to begin with.

Protection, Kansas, June 1929

John W. Sr. and Lenore Ashcraft held one another in their arms and sobbed until they had no more tears. Lenore then took Jack's picture and the panorama pictures from the wall, leaving three more bare spots, and went out on the porch to her rocking chair. Clutching the photos, she rocked for hours until she fell asleep, and her rocker stilled. John Sr. sat next to her in his, staring, but seeing nothing. Their pastor came to their house the next morning to offer condolences. He found the two slumped in their rockers, asleep. Lenore's gray hair was now snow white. He helped them into the house.

News Reporting the Accident
Summer 1929

Special to The New York Times

"ROOSEVELT FIELD, L.I., June 28—Jack Ashcraft, copilot with Miss Viola Gentry, was killed and Miss Gentry injured severely at dawn today when the Cabinaire bi-plane The Answer, in which they were seeking an endurance record ran out of fuel and crashed into a tree top [sic]. The craft made a fog-obscured forced landing in a nursery on the Jericho Turnpike, in Old Westbury, about a mile from this field. The fliers had been in the air less than ten hours.

Late in the afternoon surgeons at Nassau Hospital, Mineola, who earlier had said Miss Gentry's condition was 'fair,' reported her chances of recovery as 'uncertain,' and revealed that a blood transfusion had been necessary.

Ashcraft, a barnstorming graduate of the Gates Flying Circus, and Miss Gentry, who forsook a job as a restaurant cashier to enter aviation and later hand up an endurance record for other women to shoot at, took off from this field at 8:46 last night with the intention of staying aloft 'until the engine falls apart.' They were not alone in the air. Mr. and Mrs. Martin Jensen and William Ulbrich, in whose home Miss Gentry boarded, had taken the air before them in Jensen's plane, The Three Musketeers, also in an effort to establish a record for endurance...

Piece Together Crash Story

The story of the crash had to be pieced together from evidence provided by the wrecked plane and notes that Miss Gentry and Mr. Ashcraft had dropped before dawn, only to have them land unnoticed in the scraggly land between Roosevelt Field and Roosevelt Field 2 which was formerly Curtiss Field.

The chronometer in the cabin stopped at 6:13. That was the minute the helpless craft struck earth. Nassau County police and aviation experts believed. The two twenty-one-

gallon fuel tanks on the wings were empty and the fifty-five-gallon tank, which in the impact had been torn loose from its fastenings behind the pilot's seat to crush Ashcraft against the motor contained only the fumes of gasoline.

"Miss Gentry and Ashcraft had arranged for the first refueling contact to be made at 7 o'clock this morning. Ninety-nine gallons of gasoline they had taken up with them they thought would last several hours longer than that. They either miscalculated or there was a leak in their main tank, which was smashed, experts said. It was 9 o'clock when the refueling plane, piloted by Clyde Kincaid, a friend of Ashcraft's, arrived at Roosevelt Field and heard the story of the wreck. With his head in his hands he explained that although he had been scheduled to leave the flying field at Hartford about 5 o'clock, fog had prevented his leaving until long after 7."

Offered to Refuel Plane

Even if he had been on time, Kincaid could not have helped in the opinion of other fliers. Emil Burgin and "Shorty" Wilder, who had refueled The Three Musketeers at 5 o'clock from their flying nursing bottle, fearing that gas was getting low aboard The Answer, sent word over the radio telephone to Jensen to notify Miss Gentry that they would perform a similar service for her if she wished.

But Leo Rockwell, backer of Miss Gentry's flight, received a note from her saying she had plenty of gas for another two hours of flying. By that time, he expected the refueling from Hartford, and secure in the conviction that all was well, he left the field. It was not until after the crash that workmen in the gully where Réné Fonck and more recently Francis Phillips met disaster came upon another note which told a different story. "It said, 'Need gas immediately.'

It must have been dropped between the time when the note

to Rockwell was dropped and the final downward swoop of The Answer, with empty fuel tanks, a little more than an hour.

Peter Small, night watchman at Roosevelt Field, said he saw The Answer—so called in confident challenge to the army's record-breaking plane, The Question Mark,— flying low over the field at 5:50 A.M. He was surprised at its low altitude. At 6:10 it returned, flying even lower, and this time its engine was coughing asthmatically. Small, believing Ashcraft was seeking a landing through the thick low-lying fog, switched on the beacons, but the roar of the engines died out. A few minutes later Small learned of the wreck.

. . .Physicians who examined Ashcraft a few minutes after the wreckage was found declared he was past help. His body was removed to H. J. Hutching's morgue. Miss Gentry was rushed to the hospital, where at first, surgeons were more concerned over the shock to her nervous system than about her visible injuries, which appeared to consist of a fractured arm and a deep gash in her scalp. The bleeding from the mouth continued, however, and toward the evening it was decided to resort to a blood transfusion.. .

. . .Miss Gentry, who once sat behind a cashier's cage in a restaurant on lower Fifth Avenue, made her aviation debut by flying under the East River bridges a year ago last March. Last December, by flying for eight hours six minutes and thirty-seven seconds in an open cockpit plane, she established a record for endurance among women.. .

. . .Funeral services will be held for him tomorrow afternoon at 2 o'clock at Campbell's Funeral Church, Broadway and Sixty-sixth Street. Afterwards, the body will be sent to his birthplace for burial. The following will be pallbearers: Wilmer Stultz, Ive McKinney, Major William C. Brooks, Clyde Pangborn, Warren Smith, Carl Dixon, Ivan L. Gates,

Freddie Lund, Edward Churchill, Homer Fackler, Harry Bangler, George Daws and Abraham Greenberg...

Crash of *The Answer*, Westbury, New York, June 1929.
Courtesy of the Cradle of Aviation Museum, Garden City, New York.

On Friday, June 29, 1929, his brother Martin's fiancé wrote in her diary: *John Ashcraft died in plane crash. Thelma Gasten and I went to Protection in afternoon.*

John Wesley "Big Jack" Ashcraft, Jr., circa 1929. *Courtesy of Allen Keller.*

Dressed in a black dress and a hat with a veil, Mavis stood rigidly outside the funeral chapel. Gerald and Wendell, wearing his flight helmet that Jack had given him, stood silently behind Mavis in the shadows. She stared at the plain cloth-covered coffin as it passed by. The pallbearers somberly placed it among the dozens upon dozens of floral arrangements with various aviation themes. Judge walked alongside Pang with his head down, tail straight and still, drooping to the floor. Once the casket was in place, Judge lay beside it, head on paws with his eyes rolled up, exposing the whites. He looked as mournful as his human counterparts.

Her head motionless, Mavis tracked the pilots, roustabouts, mechanics, and other Gates Flying Service personnel and people who'd known Jack as they filed into the chapel. Some tried to keep a stiff upper lip, but their stoicism served only to magnify the anguish they felt inside. Others wept openly, belying rough exteriors. Billy Racey, followed by his father, walked in, head down and sniffling, clutching the flight helmet Jack had given him. He glanced at Jack, then he and his father took a seat.

Men and women, young and old, expressed their grief in their own way as they filed past Jack's coffin. Those that had teased him about his coveralls smiled ever so slightly when they saw that he was indeed dressed in his work clothes. Pang had said that he couldn't find a suit for him, but the coveralls were the real Jack and were how he would want to be remembered. The room quickly filled. People packed in and stood on either side of the pews, knelt in the aisles, and stood in the back of the room.

Mavis was the last to enter the chapel. Slowly, she walked down the aisle, pausing midway. She closed her eyes and wavered. Pang and others ready to catch her if she fainted. While all eyes were on Mavis, Gerald and Wendell silently slipped into the chapel, hiding in the shadows in the entryway. Mavis gazed at Jack's lifeless body. Tears tracked down her cheeks, marring her once impeccable makeup. Her shoulders quivered as she composed herself. This lifeless body couldn't be the cocky pilot she'd first met four years before. Inside, she smiled at the memory of how Jack had tried to pretend he hadn't noticed her, then banged his head on his plane when she approached him. *"Darn tootin'," I remember you said.*

The pastor and attendees patiently gave Mavis her moment. That was how she wished to remember Cowboy Jack —how he'd been four years ago. A gentleman sitting at the end of a pew nearby politely offered Mavis his seat.

Gerald and Wendell had silently stood in the entryway in the shadows. The funeral director noticed them and walked toward them to ask them to leave. Mavis subtly grabbed his arm as he passed by and shook her head ever so slightly, indicating to the man to let them stay. He looked at the two sternly, warning them to stay out of sight.

A pastor who obviously didn't know Jack somberly lavished praise and platitudes on Jack. But the words didn't fit who he was. During the ceremony, a jazz band drove by blaring their horns. This would have been more to his liking.

After the ceremony, Mavis stood with everyone while the coffin was closed, and Jack's body was solemnly carried out of the chapel to the hearse. She glanced back at the door. Gerald and Wendell were gone. Everyone quietly and somberly exited.

Jack's body would travel to Towanda, Pennsylvania, his adopted hometown, for a final farewell before returning home to Protection.

On July 2, 1929, Jack's sister Helen wrote in her diary: *Jnr's body came & Jimmy Scott from Towanda, Pa. We are all grieved to death about it. Just a little tree killed him.*

TRIBUTE OF THE GATES AIRCRAFT
CORPORATION
NEW YORK CITY, NEW YORK
Letter from Ed Churchill
June 29, 1929

Dad Ashcraft,

I hope you'll forgive the informality of this letter and the opening, but Jack was always talking about "Dad" and that's the way I've known you. By the time you receive this, I guess Jimmy Scott and Jack will be with you. God knows how terribly I feel about having Jack come back to you that way.

We bunked together and ate together and flew together. I was the circus advance man. I loved Jack as a brother. Lots of times we talked about you the home you have, and how Jack hoped to come back to it some day when he got "cricks in the joints".

I just came from the funeral and wrote Jack's last story for him. It was hard to write "30" – hard to come to the final period. I wish you could have been at the services because you would have realized just what kind of man Jack was and how many people loved him.

The casket was banked with flowers. They were piled on top of each other in their profusion. There were airplanes, propellers and emblems of flowers. The Masons and Shriners of Shreveport and the lodge at Waverly responded, as you can see from the cards I'm enclosing.

The chapel was crowded with men and women who had known Jack well and for a long time and those who had not known him so long, but had fallen under the spell of his happy, carefree personality and loved and even worshipped him.

Ive McKinney, who last year lost Lee Mason, another of his dearest friends, was there overcome with grief. So were Gates and Bill Brooks. Poor Jim, who is with you now, probably went through hell.

While Jack was popular with the older folks the officials of the company and other men and women who have shared part of his eventful life, I think the greatest tribute came from the mechanics and "greaseballs" and the kids around the field, who wanted to see Jack for the last time in that old flying suit he loved to wear. They idolized him and there isn't a kid among them who doesn't want to grow up and be the kind of guy Big Jack Ashcraft was.

There isn't much more to tell.

I knew Buck Steele, too. I hope that when Jack gets where life is going, Buck and Franz and great other legions who've given their lives to conquer the air will be there to greet him to call him into Valhalla and welcome him. This is my only comforting thought that in losing him we have given them something.

With the greatest sympathy, and with deep gratitude in my heart for being able to have known such a man as Jack Ashcraft, I am [sic]

Sincerely yours,
Edward Churchill

Ever generous, Ivan Gates covered the cost of Jack's funeral.

BIG JACK, COWBOY AVIATOR John Wesley
Ashcraft, Jr. *Courtesy of Cindy Weigand.*

E d Churchill also wrote a letter to his friend Mark
Hellinger, journalist and theater critic at the *New York
Daily News*. The letter was so poignant, Hellinger replaced his
regular column with Ed's letter.

TRIBUTE FROM MARK HELLINGER
In his column in The New York Daily News.

UNSUNG BROADWAYITES:

. . .Dear Mark," he writes, "you've missed an Unsung Broadwayite [sic]. He played the highway on a bleak winter day at noon almost four years ago. He shot his airplane down into your canyon and wrestled with the stick while an acrobat danced over the wings...dived into your stone-lined valley, Mark, where a missing motor meant curtains. You must have seen him at one time or another...he loved life, Broadway, Main Street...anywhere.

He was regular. Three months after he left your big swirl he set his ship down in Daytona Beach, with the rest of the flying circus. Van Gates, his boss, signed a contract that called for four planes in the air over a certain spot at a certain time... all or nothing.

Three motors barked...and the fourth balked. Because he was six feet, two, they howled for him...

He cranked the fourth all right...but she backfired and broke his arm. He crawled into his own cockpit and shoved his throttle forward. For an hour he led the gang as he looped, rolled, and dived over the appointed place. He landed on the beach, cut his throttle...and passed out...cold as yesterday's newspaper.

He knew the gang had to eat, Mark. He was that kind of guy.

You've guessed whom I write about, Mark? That's right. Jack Ashcraft, who flew with Viola Gentry until he ran out of gas, Friday morning. Wouldn't quit and plunged through the fog. He wrote himself off...broke everything. The gas tank and the motor mount. You know what I mean.

A year and a half ago, airplanes got his best pal, Buck

Steele, and his brother, Franz. They were throwing out exhibition bombs over Macon, Ga. You read it. One went off too soon.

Jack played the sticks, Mark. He did his stuff over Jallopi and Oshkosh and Pawtuxet. They loved him out there. He drifted back here again...for greater fame.

And then, in the gray fog of a June morning, he got the works....

On Saturday, he came back to Broadway, Mark. They brought him back in his grease stained uniform. They'd never seen him in anything else. They couldn't find a blue suit in his outfit.. . .

. . .The mechanics and 'greaseballs' clicked at the funeral. The cards on the flowers smothered the coffin told the story: 'From the gang at Teterboro', 'From the boys at Holmes' ....

You see, he was so fine and so clean, so regular, Mark, that young fellows wanted to grow up and be like him...like Big Jack.

Jack talked about a home in Kansas...Protection, Kansas.

'Some day,' he said, 'I'm going back...I've got a home out there...with the flowers around it...and the folks inside....'

He was big, Mark...big as the skies he roamed. A head taller than the canyon he dived into four years ago to give you and me a thrill. His life was the sky and the sun...and the stars.

Old J.W., his dad will meet the train. Jimmy Scott, for three years Jack's mechanic, will tell the story...tell how Jack and Viola and the plane...Oh, Hell, Mark...

Jack's gone home.

And if aviators have any hereafter, his pal Buck and his brother Franz, reached down at dawn, Friday, and plucked that strong spirit from a broken body.

"The newspapers called him a 'professional aviator', Mark. Tell Rosco he was more than that. So much more than that.". . .

. . .John Ashcraft was given recognition by the aviation

*world and was universally accorded to be a pilot of exceptional
ability. He possessed the cool judgment, the steady nerve, the
ready thought that led him into the high positions of his chosen
calling in aircraft.*

*In his life, he lived the clean and wholesome, upright life
that kept him in perfect health and ready for all the exigencies
of his calling. In his character and temperament, he was
kindly, considerate, true to his friends and courteous to everyone. When he was a boy and young man at home, his consider-
ation of his parents was exceptional and his fealty to friends
remarkable.. . .*

Funeral services for Jack were held at the First Baptist
Church in Protection, Kansas. He was given full military
honors. As in New York, the church was banked with flowers
from the Gates Flying Circus, the Masons, and many other
organizations. The small church soon filled to standing room
only. John Wesley Ashcraft, Jr. aka Big Jack, Cowboy Aviator
was laid to rest in the Protection Cemetery beside his younger
brother Franz.

One year later, Clyde Pangborn honored his comrade and
Franz.

HONOR FALLEN COMRADE

*Thursday, May 29 (1930), the air squadron of 'Upside-down
Pangborn' flew from Dodge City to Protection in formation to
honor their fallen comrades, the late J.W. 'Big Jack' Ashcraft
and the late Francis Ashcraft.*

*By prearrangements with Mr. and Mrs. J.W. Ashcraft, Sr.,
and the family, they went to the Protections Cemetery at 10:00*

a.m. Thursday, and spread a sheet over John's grave and one over the lower half of Francis's grave.

At 11:00 a.m. flying in formation, Pangborn, center and leading with Pilot Herndon flying left rear and Pilot Baumgardt, right rear, the air squadron appeared, they circled the cemetery and then flew over it flying low from north to south and east to west in formation, then circling and swooping low over the grave, Pilot Pangborn dropped a mammoth wreath of carnations on the grave of "Big Jack" and one of the other pilots did the same on the grave of Francis Ashcraft.

A few minutes later, the pilots maneuvered into formation and headed north to Dodge City, after this brief pause in the busy day's work of pilots to honor their fallen comrades.

Gathered at the Protection Cemetery were Mr. and Mrs. J.W. Ashcraft and their family and a few friends.

And thus goes the world. Just a brief pause, just a tear now and then, just a fleeting moment from the busy cares of the present, just a word or two of regret for the fallen comrades so bravely sacrificed and for the friend whose untimely fate cut short such promising lives. But such is life. It is the now that calls. Sorrow must be suppressed. Regrets are laid aside as vain. It is the now, the present that calls. Action, living is kind and demands all.

But it is a fine thing to take this pause, to drop a tear, to give a thought now and then to loved ones gone on whose presence we miss and whose going has left an ever-increasing void.

Another account.

DROPS FLOWERS ON FRIEND'S GRAVE

Clyde Pangborn, whose Flying Fleet thrilled Pratt early this week flew low this over the little cemetery at Protection yesterday and dropped flowers on the graves of Francis and Jack Ashcraft who lost their lives in the service of aviation. Mr. Pangborn, whose home is in Paterson, New Jersey, was in the same aviation service with Jack Ashcraft, Wilma [sic] Stultz, William Brock and others. It was in tribute to the Ashcrafts that Mr. Pangborn led his fleet over the cemetery at Protection. Mrs. Ben H. Waltz of Pratt is a sister of Francis and Jack Ashcraft and at lunch Wednesday, she and Mr. Waltz had as their guests Mr. Pangborn; Mr. and Mrs. J. W. Ashcraft and Miss Helen Ashcraft of Protection; and Mr. and Mrs. C. P. Ashcraft and daughter Ruth of Marion, Kansas.

Grave marker for Jack Ashcraft. *Photograph by Cindy Weigand.*

JOHN W.
ASHCROFT, JR

SGT. 309 REPAIR UNIT
MTC

DECEMBER 1, 1897
JUNE 28, 1929

Brief, brave and glorious
was his young career.

Epitaph on grave marker. *Photograph by Cindy Weigand.*

From Hellinger's Column

. . .John Ashcraft had done much and gone far in his short span of 32 years of life. He was a life of vision and action, of accomplishment and its richly deserved rewards. His not to be content with the commonplace and the mere existence but buoyed and led by the visions of what future ages will see he sought and strove in his way to bring about the established facts that he so plainly saw in that vision that held his heart and hand to his tasks.

His death is a misfortune to aviation and its future....

Viola survived the crash, but her injuries were so severe that she spent more than a year in the hospital recuperating.

Viola Gentry, circa 1928. *Courtesy of Cindy Weigand.*

The End.

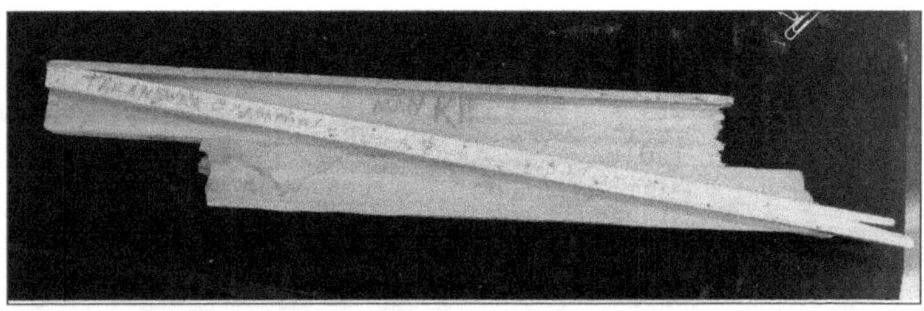

Debris from *The Answer. Courtesy of the Cradle of Aviation Museum, Garden City, New York.*

MEMBERS OF THE GATES FLYING CIRCUS
ROSTER OF PILOTS

Clyde E. "Upsidedown" Pangborn
Lowell Yerex
E.J. Eddie Brooks
A.R. Tommy Thompson*
Earl K. Parker*
William C. "Whispering Bill" Brooks*
Ed Carrington
Cloyd P. Clevenger
E.J. Eddie Bond
William Billy Brock
John F. [sic] "Big" Jack Ashcraft*
Wilmer "Wild Bill" Stultz*
Ives MacKinney (McKinney)*
Samuel Buck Steele*
Harold E. McMahon*
Errett Williams*
Joseph R. Joe James
Lee J. Mason*
Gardner Peg Nagle

Roy Ahearn*

Jess Menefee

Capt. Warren B. Smith

Henry H. "Hank" Tallman*

Freddy Lund*

Eugene Cecil*

Okey Bevins*

Chester Vogt

Homer Fackler

ROSTER OF STUNTMEN

Thornton "Jinx" Jenkins***
Wesley May***
Steve Howland
Kermit "Red" Kiehl***
Lloyd Geraldson
Paul C. Vernier*
Freddy Lund*
Milton Girten
Phil Leninger
Aaron F. "Duke" Krantz
Art Starnes
Chance Walker**
Bill Wunderlich
Jack Parks**
George Babcock***
Parker**
Johnny Runger
Cy "Shorty" Bittner

Mickey Efferson
Henry "Happy" Johnson*

*Died in plane crash
**Killed wing walking
***Parachute fatality

GENERAL STAFF

Ivan R. Gates—Promoter and General Manager
George Daws—Promoter
Charles Healy Day—Designer and Engineer
Al MacClatchie—Announcer
Red Murphy—Announcer
Charles F. "Slim" West—Chief Mechanic

Source: Rhode, Bill. *Chewing Gum, Baling Wire, and Guts.* Pp. 185-187.

STATISTICS (UNVERIFIED) FOR THE GATES FLYING CIRCUS

One ten-month period: 273 exhibitions in 75 cities
    Air meets: 2,000
    Number of states: 44
    Passengers: 750,000-1,000,000; record, 980 in one day.

Most of the events in this book regarding the life of Jack Ashcraft occurred, but dialogue and circumstances, and in a few instances chronology, are fictionalized for the sake of narrative.

Going through my mother's belongings after her death in 1992, I came across two scrapbooks of old articles, a poster for an air meet, family histories, letters, and several photographs. The articles were about Jack Ashcraft, a great uncle who was an aviator in the 1920s. I remembered Mom telling me about him growing up, but I wasn't interested at the time. I had no idea she had all this information. My adult curiosity engaged; I became engrossed in finding out all I could about this amazing man.

From these articles, descriptions of him in books, and family histories, I pieced together a narrative for his life. I knew what he did and where, but how it all came down is conjecture on my part. The result is *Big Jack, Cowboy Aviator*.

While I found several photos, I thought there must be more

family somewhere. He had five brothers and five sisters. Upon returning from vacation one summer, there was a message from a distant cousin, Allen Keller, on my answering machine. Allen is a descendent of Jack's oldest sister, Lillian. He found my name from a photo I had posted on the internet. When I excitedly returned the call, Allen told me that he had found a family photograph album in a trunk in his grandparents' basement in Greensburg, KS. This town was destroyed by an EF-5 tornado on May 4, 2007, but the album survived. Allen has graciously shared many photos to use in the book. They have enhanced the story immensely. Allen also found Jack's pilot license signed by Orville Wright and four of Jack's trophies.

As an aviator, Jack didn't reach the heights of Lindbergh or the other most famous aviators at the time. However, for a guy born in a sod hut in Oklahoma Territory who grew up in a small town on the Kansas prairie, Jack accomplished much and experienced historic events of the time firsthand. To me, he made his mark in aviation history even though he was unknown until now.

Family of
John Wesley "J. W." Ashcraft, Sr. and Lenore Crum Ashcraft

Beatrice Lillian (1891)
(Allen's Great-Grandmother)
Audrey Lenore (1893)
Chester Perry Ashcraft (1895)
John Wesley, Jr. (1897)
Clarice Ina (1900)
Martin Harold (1902)
(Author's grandfather)
Joseph Francis (1905)

Ernest Eugene (1908)
Helen Vanita (1910)
Mary Jane (1913)
Ivan Clarence (1916)

THE REAL CHARACTERS

NOTE: Information is scarce on these early airmen. The author made every effort to find the most reliable and consistent information possible.

IVAN RHUELE GATES was born in 1890 and was selling and racing cars in San Francisco by 1910. That year, he saw French aviator Louis Paulhan fly a Farman biplane for twelve minutes before a large crowd. Observing the size of the crowd, he determined that there was money to be made in aviation and purchased a flimsy biplane. He earned his license, but he didn't fly much.

From his experience racing cars, Gates proved to be a good showman when he founded the Gates Flying Circus with Clyde Pangborn. A hot-tempered individualist, he often expressed himself with his fists if anyone opposed or ignored him. Pilots, however, took a benign view of Gates slugging people. He gave them the opportunity to earn a living flying airplanes. Gates held no grudges and would sometimes apologize, then stuff some greenbacks into the pocket of the guy who had raised his ire. Easygoing, soft-spoken, and well-liked, "Pang" was a foil to the volatile Gates.

Despite his temperament, Gates proved to be a shrewd manager, and with Pang's flying skills, the circus became one of the most spectacular groups of exhibition aviators in the United States. Gates billed them as the Greatest Exhibition Aviators in the World. In its early years, the group flew in Mexico and Canada as well before moving eastward. By 1927, pilots relished an invitation from Gates to fly with the group.

Sensing the flying circus days were coming to an end, Gates teamed up with Charles Healy Day and formed the Gates-Day Aircraft Company and Gates Flying Service in 1927. The company was first based in Teterboro, New Jersey, then moved to Holmes Airport and was renamed the New Standard Aircraft Company. A windstorm destroyed his airplanes, and the Great Depression drove the company into bankruptcy. Other businesses he started foundered; Gates became despondent, and his health declined. Ever faithful, his wife Hazel loved and supported him through the most difficult of times.

His money and health gone, Ivan Gates gave up on life. On Thanksgiving Day 1932, he committed suicide by jumping from the window of his sixth-floor Manhattan apartment despite Hazel's frantic efforts to stop him. He was forty-two.

CLYDE EDWARD PANGBORN was an engineer in St. Maries, Idaho, when America entered World War I. He enlisted in the Aviation Section of the Signal Corps and trained as a pilot. Following advanced flight instruction, he was assigned to Ellington Field, Houston, Texas, as an instructor. After the Armistice, he began barnstorming. His specialty was flying upside down. While that was impressive, spectators took little notice until he got out of the cockpit and started climbing on the fuselage and hanging by his feet from the landing gear.

In 1922, he partnered with Ivan R. Gates to form the Gates

Flying Circus, with Gates as manager and Pangborn as chief pilot.

After the circus disbanded, Pangborn was the main test pilot for the New Standard Corporation, which he formed with Gates and Charles H. Day. For a brief time, he formed the Flying Fleet to barnstorm and carry passengers. The company failed to make a profit and was wiped out after the stock market crash of 1929. In July 1931, he attempted an around-the-world flight with Hugh Herndon. Their goal was to better the time set by Wiley Post and Harold Gatty, but they had to abandon the effort in Siberia.

In 1931, a Japanese newspaper offered a $25,000 prize for the first nonstop flight from Japan to the United States. Eyeing this prize, Pangborn and Herndon took from Siberia to Japan. They took off from Japan in October. Their destination was Seattle. To reduce drag and fuel consumption, and increase speed, he designed the plane so he could jettison the landing gear. Seattle fogged in, they belly landed in Wenatchee, Washington, 41 hours and 13 minutes later.

During the thirties, he was a test pilot for various aircraft corporations in the United States and England. When war broke out in Europe in 1939, Pangborn joined the Royal Air Force and assisted in organizing the RAF Ferry Command. He served through the end of the war and was discharged in 1946. Pangborn stayed connected with flying, aircraft design, and testing until his death in 1958.

ARON FABIAN "DUKE" KRANTZ was born in Sweden. He had the top-paying gig with the Gates Flying Circus. Billed as "Diavolo," his signature move was to leap from one airplane to another without a parachute. New government regulations made the stunt illegal, so he killed off his alter ego, Diavolo. Wearing a waxed mustache, he made his last performance with the circus in the summer of 1928 over Teterboro

Airport. During his time with Gates, Krantz survived roughly one thousand performances and five hundred plane changes. For his daring, he received a $5 bonus on top of his base pay. He also learned to fly.

After the circus disbanded, Krantz flew for the *New York Daily News* for almost ten years. During this time, he circled the flaming SS *Morro Castle* off Long Beach Island in 1934, and in 1937, he saw the *Hindenburg* explode above him. He captured the burning of the SS *Normandie* at Manhattan's Pier 88 in 1942. He married and had two children.

Briefly, he flew with Colonial Airlines, then went to the Willow Run manufacturing complex in Michigan, known as Air Force Plant 31. As a civilian, he flight tested B-24 bombers. Later, he test flew B-29s in Marietta, Georgia, until the end of the war. He parlayed the experience into a job as production manager for Boeing. He also served as a test pilot for Bell Aircraft in Atlanta, returning to Teterboro Airport as a pilot for Bendix Aviation.

Krantz died in 1974 after suffering a heart attack in Key Largo, Florida, his winter home. He was seventy-seven.

IVE MCKINNEY (sometimes spelled MACKINNEY) moved with Gates to Holmes Airport after the circus disbanded. He had invested in and demonstrated airplanes for Pacer Aircraft Company.

In the summer of 1929, he was scheduled to attempt an endurance test with Clyde Pangborn. A few days before the event, he made a test flight in a homemade parasol monoplane in Teterboro. A rudder cable broke, and he spun in, breaking a leg. In 1930, he purchased the New Standard Flying Service at Teterboro and took possession of the last Pacer product, known as the Pacer Racer.

That same year, he staged an air show and air races in Teterboro over Memorial Day and competed in an air race.

Only fifty feet in the air, he was rounding a pylon when the wind caught him. The aircraft cartwheeled end over end, coming to rest near the airport boundary. He died on the way to the hospital. The date was May 31, 1930.

WILLIAM C. "WHISPERING BILL" BROOKS flew with Gates out of Holmes Airport for about three years. After the business was destroyed, he gave instruction and did aerial mapping.

He returned to Central and South America and was appointed Chief of Military Aviation in Honduras. Having earned some money, he returned to Teterboro in 1936. He bought and rejuvenated some planes and took them back to Honduras in hopes of making more money to retire on. His last flight was on September 26, 1941. As he was flying a Ford Trimotor with four passengers from the mines to the lowlands, heavy clouds moved in, obscuring the tops of the Andean Mountains. Brooks crashed head on into a peak, and the plane burned.

IRA GARDNER "PEG" NAGLE towed banners from a Ford Trimotor airplane for a shoe manufacturer in the mid-1930s. At night, he towed an electric sign. He also worked as a crop duster in Florida and Central America. During World War II, he was a test pilot for Lockheed and ferried planes for them for five years. After the war, he was executive pilot for Harry Sinclair for two years, then flew for an engineering company in Texas. He retired in 1961 after forty years in aviation.

Nagle died on November 16, 1991, at the age of ninety-five following an extended illness.

BERT CRADER – No information on Crader after Jack's death could be found.

FREDERICK M. "FREDDIE" LUND (Sometimes spelled "FREDDY") worked for a while in Hollywood as a movie double, where he earned the nickname "Fearless Freddie." As a test pilot for the Waco Aircraft Company, he performed stunt exhibitions around the country. In 1930, he was World Aerobatic Champion.

Lund participated in the Los Angeles National Air Races at Mines Field in September 1928. There, he met his future wife, Bettie Elkins, who was also a stunt pilot and working in Hollywood. They married in June 1929 and worked together in a stunt flying partnership at fairs and exhibitions. Twice at the Cleveland National Air Meet, they amazed crowds with their death-defying plunges.

On October 3, 1931, Lund was killed in an air race in Lexington, Kentucky, when another plane collided with his in midair. Lund's wife Bettie witnessed the accident from the grandstand. Despite seeing her husband's fatal crash, Bettie took over his appearance contracts, then began barnstorming on her own. By the end of the 1930s she was one of the leading stunt pilots in the country.

VIOLA ESTELLE GENTRY was known as the "Flying Cashier" because of her job in a New York restaurant. Working two jobs to pay for flying lessons and commuting from the city to Long Island for the lessons, Gentry soloed in 1925. In 1926, she headed to the East River to fly under the Brooklyn and Manhattan Bridges, and in 1928, she established the first officially recorded women's solo endurance flight record.

After several months in the hospital following the 1929 crash, she was allowed to leave for a brief time. Accompanied by a nurse, Gentry attend the first meeting of the 99s International Organization for Women Pilots in Valley Stream, New York, and became a charter member.

In 1931, she gave up professional flying and worked as a cashier in a North Carolina restaurant. However, she continued to attempt to set flying endurance records and endeavored such a flight with Frances Harrell Marsalis in 1933. Gentry welcomed Amelia Earhart back to New York after her flight across the Atlantic. Throughout her life, Gentry supported women in aviation, presented lectures, and helped preserve early aviation history. She received numerous awards.

Gentry also competed in races as a passenger or copilot. She flew until grounded by cataracts in 1975. Gentry folded her wings on June 23, 1988, at the age of ninety-four.

FRANCES CARTER HARRELL MARSALIS knew she wanted to fly early on but didn't have the money for flying lessons, which required a few thousand dollars. Instead, she worked as credit manager at a Houston, Texas, department store but dreamed of flying. Then a relative died suddenly, leaving Frances enough money to learn to fly. She immediately resigned and boarded a train for New York for the Curtiss Aeroplane and Motor Company.

Wearing overalls, she worked in the shops for six months, learning all she could about motors by taking them apart and putting them together again. Dutifully, she put in her time honing the necessary skills before she strapped into the cockpit. Harrell became so skilled that she flew as a stunt flier for the Curtiss-Wright Exhibition Company. She also participated in endurance flights and set records, and was a charter member of the 99s.

Harrell was killed in an air race in Dayton, Ohio, in 1934. She was rounding a pylon when the wing of another plane bumped hers, launching it into a fiery cartwheel. Alive when pulled from the wreckage, Harrell died shortly afterward. She once said, "I have no fear of flying. I never think of it. Stunting is just my job, and I do it like everyone does his work. Of course, at first, I wasn't so 'hard-boiled.'" She thought flying "the most fascinating work in the world." She was twenty-nine when she died.

ELINOR SMITH soloed in 1927 and at the age of sixteen became the youngest licensed pilot in the world. Known as the "Flying Flapper of Freeport," she set multiple solo endurance, speed, and altitude records during her career. She was the first woman featured on a Wheaties cereal box. At age twenty-nine, Smith retired from flying to focus on her family, but resumed flying after the death of her husband in 1956. In 2000, at the age of eighty-nine, she became the oldest pilot to complete a simulated shuttle landing. She died March 19, 2010, at the age of ninety-eight in Palo Alto, California.

RUTH ELDER capitalized on her popularity after the attempted flight across the Atlantic. She embarked on lucrative speaking engagements, then was given a movie contract. In 1929, she participated in the Women's Air Derby known as the Powder Puff Derby and was a founding member of the 99s. She died on October 9, 1977, in San Francisco.

Readers are encouraged to do their own research on the above in addition to characters mentioned in the book: Calbraith Perry "Cal" Rodgers and his flight in the *Vin Fiz*, General Henry "Hap" Arnold, Jimmy Doolittle and the Doolittle Raiders, Carrie Nation, Will Rogers, Hubert Julian, and Bessie Coleman. The United States has an amazing history of aviation.

THE SHORT SNORTER TRADITION

The origins of the tradition of the short snorter is sometimes attributed to Alaskan bush pilots in the 1920s. However, most accounts and the most compelling explanations trace the origins of the short snorter to Jack Ashcraft. Ivan Gates and Clyde Pangborn wanted to treat the pilots after their successful run of performances in Syracuse, New York. In his book,

Upside-Down Pangborn: King of the Barnstormers...first to fly the Pacific nonstop, Carl Cleveland lists 1926 as the year.

At the time, a snort was slang for a swiftly swallowed alcoholic beverage. "Short" indicated a small measure. For self-preservation, pilots could only gulp small quantities of alcohol before flights and during stopovers. Soon, they jokingly referred to one another as "short snorters."

The swindle spread and even spawned a fraternal organization of flying scammers. The group established a set of rules and regulations. Membership increased during World War II and included men and women. The short snorter became synonymous with crossing a large body of water, flying across the equator, or from country to country.

According to PBS's History Detectives, the tradition entered the space age in 1965 at the opening of the Houston Astrodome, where astronauts signed dollar bills. On the Gemini III–XIII and Apollo 7–11 missions, the astronauts all carried one-dollar bills signed by fellow crew members.

FICTIONAL CHARACTERS

MONTY – The pilot who landed in the stumps near Logtown, MS. I found two different names for the pilot, so I gave him a fictional name. There were two anecdotes about the landing in Logtown. In one, the plane was totaled and beyond repair. The other was about a fuzzy-cheeked kid who landed in stumps that caught my imagination. I researched the town. When I read that it was a former logging town, I knew that I had my own version of what happened.

SAM AND MILLIE – These sweet children are fictional, but they are alive in my mind. They are a shout-out to the movie "The Great Waldo Pepper" starring Robert Redford. The film is about a barnstormer who flew a Standard J-1 as well. I like to think that Millie was so enamored by her first airplane ride that she earned her pilot's license and earned her wings in the Women's Airforce Service Pilots during World War II.

MAVIS – This lady of higher social status than Jack is fictional. I wanted Jack to have a friend and life aside from the rough and raucous world of aviation. Though Mavis didn't exist, her character is inspired by Alicia Patterson, founder and editor of a newspaper on Long Island, NY.

GERALD AND WENDELL – To me, it was reasonable that the place where Mavis lived would have a Black doorman. Researching Jack's story, I read several times what a swell guy he was and how kind he was to people, so I think that he would have shaken hands with a Gerald.

Having been stationed in France during World War I, he would have known about Eugene Bullard, a pilot with Lafayette Flying Corps. It was also well documented that Jack liked working with boys and young men, especially if they expressed interest in aviation. Airman John C. Robinson inspired Wendell's character. Robinson earned a degree from Tuskegee Institute, started a pilot school for Black pilots, and convinced Tuskegee Institute to open a school of aviation. Wendell O. Pruitt was one of the top pilots for the Tuskegee Airmen.

BILLY RACEY – In his book *Chewing Gum, Baling Wire, and Guts: The Story of the Gates Flying Circus*, Bill Rhode talks about "the kid" admiring the pilots of the Gates Flying Circus as a young boy. Billy Racey's character is a shout-out to Mr. Rhode, who has written the only biography of the aviation group.

Clyde Pangborn Collection
    Washington State University
    Pullman, Washington

Cradle of Aviation Museum
    Garden City, NY 11530

The Aviation Hall Of Fame & Museum of New Jersey
    Teterboro, New Jersey

BIBLIOGRAPHY

NEWSPAPERS IN FAMILY COLLECTION

Atlanta Constitution, Atlanta, Georgia
Baltimore American, Baltimore, Maryland
Berkshire Evening Eagle, Pittsfield, Massachusetts
Berwick Enterprise, Berwick, Pennsylvania
Birmingham News, Birmingham, Alabama
Coatesville Record, Coatesville, Pennsylvania
Elmira Star Gazette, Elmira, Pennsylvania
Harrisburg Telegraph, Harrisburg, Pennsylvania
Lebanon Daily News, Lebanon, Pennsylvania
Poughkeepsie Evening Star, Poughkeepsie, New York
Richmond News Leader, Richmond, Virginia
The Birmingham Press, Birmingham, Alabama
The Daily Review, Towanda, Pennsylvania
The Gaffney Ledger, Gaffney, South Carolina
The Graphic, New York City, New York
The Louisville Times, Louisville, Kentucky
The Macon Telegraph, Macon Georgia
The New York Times, New York City, New York
The Norwalk Hour, Norwalk, Connecticut
Somerset Messenger, Somerset, Pennsylvania
Spartanburg Herald, Spartanburg, South Carolina
Syracuse Herald, Syracuse, New York
The Tampa Telegraph, Tampa Bay, Florida
The Times Union, Albany, New York
Washington Times,
Waynesboro Press, Waynesboro, Pennsylvania
Winston-Salem Journal, Winston-Salem, North Carolina

ADDITIONAL NEWSPAPERS

Ballston Spa Daily Journal, New York
Amsterdam Recorder, Amsterdam, New York
Auburn Citizen, Auburn, New York

Binghamton Press, Binghamton, New York
Brooklyn Daily Eagle, Brooklyn, New York
Buffalo Courier Express, Buffalo, New York
Buffalo Evening News, Buffalo, New York
Corning Evening Leader, Corning, New York
Daily Star-Queens, Queens, New York
Geneva Daily Times, Geneva, New York
Gloversville Morning Herald, Gloversville, New York
Niagara Falls Gazette, Niagara Falls, New York
Oswego Palladium, Oswego, New York
Poughkeepsie Eagle News, Poughkeepsie, New York
Rhinebeck Gazette, Rhinebeck, New York
Saratogian, Saratoga, New York
Schenectady Journal, Schenectady, New York
Troy Times, Troy, New York
Yonkers Statesman, Yonkers, New York

BOOKS

Bower, Jennifer. *North Caroling Aviatrix Viola Gentry: The Flying Cashier.* Charleston: The History Press, 2015.

Brooks-Pazmany, Kathleen. *Women in Aviation.* Washington, DC: Smithsonian Institution Press, 1991.

Cleveland, Carl. *"Upside-Down" Pangborn: King of the Barnstormers.* Glendale: Aviation Book Company, 1978.

Gentry, Viola. *Hangar Flying.* Chelmsford: Privately published, 1975.

Holden, Henry M. *Images of Aviation, Teterboro Airport.* Charleston: Arcadia Publishing, 2009.

McAllister, Bruce. *Vagabonds of the Sky.* Boulder: Roundup Press, 2005.

Oakes, Claudia M. *United States Women in Aviation.* Washington, DC: Smithsonian Institution Press, 1991.

O'Neill, Paul, and the editors of Time-Life Books. *Barnstormers & Speedkings.* Alexandra: Time-Life Books, 1981.

—. *The Epic of Flight.* Alexandra: Time-Life Books, 1981.

Plehinger, Russell. *Marathon Flyers.* Detroit: Harlo Press, 1989.

Reilly, H. V. Pat. *From the Balloon to the Moon: New Jersey's Amazing Aviation History.* Palm Coast: PhotoGraphics Publishing, 2009.

Rhode, Bill. *Chewing Gum, Baling Wire and Guts: The Story of the Gates Flying Circus.* Oradel: H. V. Publishers, 1993. Originally published by Kennikat Press, Port Washington, NY. 1970..

Stoff, Josh. *Images of America, Long Island Airports.* Charleston: Arcadia Publishin, 2004.

Tessendorf, K. C. *Barnstormers and Daredevils*. New York: Antheneum MacMillan Publishing Company, 1988.

Underwood, Lamar. *The Greatest Flying Stories Ever Told: Nineteen Tales From The Sky*. Guilford: The Lyons Press, an imprint of The Globe Pequot Press, 2002.

ARTICLES

Moses, Phyllis. ""Keep Your Nose Down in the Turns"." *Aviation History* 1 September 2003: 33-36, 60.

Unknown. "AIR DERBY ATTRACTS THOUSANDS HERE FOR CELEBRATIONS OF 4TH." *The Daily Review*, 28 June 1928. Rpt. in THE SETTLER, The Bradford County Historical Society, September 2002, Vol. XL, Number 3. 154-156.

—. "ASHCRAFT IS BACK WITH "SPIRIT OF AMMONIA"." *Towanda Daily Review.* 5 March 1928.

—. *Rpt. in THE SETTLER, The Bradford County Historical Society, Towanda, PA. September 2002, Vol. XL, Number 3. 142.*

—. "FLYERS KILLED IN MACON BUCK STEELE AND HIS MECHANIC VICTIMS OF ACCIDENT WITH BOMB." *Towanda Daily Review.* 20 February 1928. *Rpt. in THE SETTLER, The Bradford County Historical Society, September 2002, Vol. XL, Number 3. 137-139.*

—. "JACK "BIG JACK" ASHCRAFT." *Towanda Daily Review.* 20 June 1928.*Rpt. in THE SETTLER, The Bradford County Historical Society, September 2002, Vol. XL, Number 3. 150-151.*

—. "JACK ASHCRAFT HAS BOOSTED FLYING HERE." *The Daily Review.* 28 June 1928. *Rpt. in THE SETTLER, The Bradford County Historical Society, September 2002, Vol. XL, Number 3. 143.*

—. "JACK ASHCRAFT KILLED IN CRASH." *The Evening Times.* 28 June 1929. *Rpt. in THE SETTLER, The Bradford County Historical Society, September 2002, Vol. XL, Number 3. 162-166.*

FILMS AND SCREENPLAY

Flyboys. By Blake T. Evans, David S. Ward Phil Sears. Dir. Tony Hill. Perf. Jean Reno, Jennifer Decker, Scott Hazell, Abdul Salis James Franco. Metro-Goldwyn-Mayer (MGM). 2006. Film.

Hell's Angels. By Joseph Moncure March, Howard Estabrook Marshall Neilan. Dir. Howard Hughes. Perf. James Hall, Jean Harlow Ben Lyon. Universal Studios, 1920. Film.

The Great Waldo Pepper. By George Roy Hill William Goldman. Dir. George Roy Hill. Perf. Bo Swenson, Bo Brundin, Susan Sarandon Robert Redford.

1975. Screenplay.

The Great Waldo Pepper. By William Goldman (based on story by) George Roy Hill. Dir. George Roy Hill. Perf. Bo Swenson, Bo Brundin, Susan Sarandon Robert Redford. Universal Studios. 1975. Film.

Upside-Down Pangborn. Dir. Jim Zimmer. KSPS PBS. 2002. Film-documentary.

Wings. By Hope Loring, Louis D. Lighton John Monk Saunders. Dir. Harry d'Abbadie d'Arrast William A. Wellman. Perf. Gary Cooper, Charles "Buddy" Rogers, Richard Allen Clara Bow. Paramount. 1927. Film.

INTERNET SOURCES

https://www.pbs.org/opb/historydetectives/feature/famous-short-snorters/

<https://www.navsource.org/>

https://www.museumofflight.org/search/?search=archives

http://www.motorsportmemorial.org/focus.php?db=a&n=12398

Rickey, Lisa. *Out of the Box, Ivan R. Gates Collection*. 15 January 2020. 2023-2024. https://blogs.libraries.wright.edu/news/outofthebox/2020/01/15/new-collection-ivan-r-gates-collection/.

Zimmer, David M. *With over 500 plane leaps, Teterboro's 'Duke' Krantz defied death with his aeronautical stunts*. 2024. 2023-2024. https://www.northjersey.com/

ACKNOWLEDGMENTS

Thank you:

Willis and Candace for your enduring love and support.

Mom for collecting some of Jack's memorabilia. You started me on quite a journey.

Karen Brinson, now deceased, daughter of Jack's younger sister Mary Jane, for being caretaker of the scrapbooks and generously making them available.

Julia Blum, gal pal and fellow aviation history enthusiast. Jules has given me personally guided tours of everything Jack on Long Island: Hicks' Nursery (the hickory tree is long gone), his apartment in Jackson Heights, Queens, the locations where Roosevelt and Curtiss Fields were, and more. We have even flown in the same airspace as Jack in a New Standard biplane at Old Rhinebeck Aerodrome. As an archivist at the Cradle of Aviation Museum, Julia was always on the lookout for photos of Jack. It was she who discovered the piece of debris from *The Answer* in a dark corner of a closet. Thanks also for always cheering me on.

Allen Keller, great-grandson of Jack's older sister Lillian, for generously sharing photographs, trophies, and more. They enhanced the story greatly.

Jennifer Bower for her wonderful biography of Viola Gentry. Also thanks to Jennifer for her enthusiasm about Jack's story, writing advice, and being an overall cheerleader.

Ron Krantz, for information about his father Duke Krantz. Meeting him and getting to know him has been a pleasure.

Pilots Don Peterson, Ron Krantz, and Mark Franz for their input.

Robert Arnold.

Uncle Jack. Thanks for saving all the articles of your exploits. By doing so, in essence, you wrote your story. I just filled in here and there.

Readers: Jennifer Bower, David Weigand, Willis Weigand, Allen Keller, Raymona Anderson, Don Peterson, Tracey Mac Gowan, and Matt Franz.

Aaron Redford and Jenny Q with Historical Editorial. They were great to work with.

Brian Coyne for the wonderful book cover design, and to Lisa Welch for the headshot.

Special thank you to the following and their staffs:

Jason Burks, Birmingham Public Library

Anna Spencer, Collections Manager, Wenatchee Valley Museum

Nathan Lott, Executive Director, Historic Macon Foundation, Macon, Georgia

Oby Brown, Director of Communications, Historic Macon Foundation, Macon, Georgia

Matthew Carl, Executive Director, Bradford County Historical Society, Pennsylvania

Fabio Pena, NavSource Naval History

Jenn Parent, Reference Archivist, The Museum of Flight, Seattle, Washington

Ralph C. Villecca, Sr., Executive Director, Aviation Hall of Fame & Museum of New Jersey

Paul Silberman, Museum Specialist (History), National Air & Space Museum Archives Department.

Elizabeth Konopka and Sara Fischer, International Women's Air and Space Museum.

I encourage everyone to visit, volunteer, and monetarily support these and other museums and collections that tell America's amazing story.

ABOUT THE AUTHOR

Cindy Weigand grew up listening to her grandmother tell stories. Now she writes her own. She is the author *Ride of Passage* and *Big Jack, Cowboy Aviator* plus an anthology and many articles in various publications. She lives in Tulsa, Oklahoma.

To Learn more, visit Cindy at: https://cindyweigand.com/

facebook.com/cindy.weigand.3

instagram.com/cindyweigand3

linkedin.com/in/cindy-weigand-2b936722

9 798987 884867